No Other Gods

No Other Gods

1.

No Other Gods

by

WILDER PENFIELD

Little, Brown and Company · Boston

Eighth Printing

*Published simultaneously
in Canada by McClelland and Stewart Limited*

PRINTED IN THE UNITED STATES OF AMERICA

Dedicated to my mother
JEAN JEFFERSON PENFIELD

Preface

❖❖

THIS IS A NOVEL, not a history nor a treatise on religion. It is the story of Abraham and Sarah during the time when they lived in Ur of the Chaldees and before their appearance in the pages of Genesis. It is a tale of adventure, love, revolt, but it is also a study of the evolution of a great leadership and the beginnings of a people unique in history.

Certain facts have been established by recent archeological excavations in the ancient cities of Iraq, facts which have to do with the customs and culture of the inhabitants of that country four thousand years ago.

Other facts are established by history: Abram, later called Abraham, was born in Ur among a people who worshiped many idols. He left the country and eventually led his people into Canaan, handing down through them his revolutionary belief in one god. Today it is his God, the God of Abraham, that is worshiped by devout Jew, Christian and Mohammedan alike.

The story is written in the light of such facts, and the plot based on the assumption that the pattern of men's behavior has not changed very much in four thousand years.

The impetus to undertake the writing of this book came to me from my mother, Jean Jefferson Penfield. She had written a novel about the life of Sarah and had finished it in 1935 in spite of failing health and advancing age. That year, when I made my annual trip to Los Angeles to see her, I found her confined to bed and it seemed likely that this might be her last illness. The manuscript and all her work notes, covering a period of fifteen years, were on the bedside table. But she was distressed and not yet satisfied with the result of her labor.

On the impulse of the moment, I offered to carry the manuscript away with me and to join her in its authorship. She accepted the offer with a sigh of relief. But alas, in the springtime three months later, news came to me in Montreal that she had died.

Following that, the manuscript lay in my desk untouched for eight years. I was a surgeon and teacher of medicine then, as now. I was involved in research and in the writing of scientific books and papers.

At last in 1943, the fortunes of the Second World War took me to Mesopotamia. At Teheran in the library of Sir Reader Bullard, British Minister to Iran, I came upon Woolley's account of the excavations of Ur, and ten days later I was on my way across the desert to see Ur, remembering the unfulfilled promise to my mother.

The ancient city had been destroyed not long after Abram left it. The green fields had disappeared and the city had vanished beneath the shifting dust of the desert. Even the Euphrates, which once washed the walls of Ur, had changed its course and so the city was eventually lost, and indeed forgotten, save for the reference to it in Genesis.

In 1854 Mr. J. E. Taylor, British Consul in Southern Mesopotamia, investigated a great mound of earth halfway between Baghdad and Basrah. This, he discovered, was ancient Ur. Subsequently, in the interval between the two world wars, the mound was carefully excavated by Sir Leonard Woolley and again abandoned to the dust of the desert.

As I approached the great tableland that hid the city, a hyena circled about to look at me before slinking away. I wandered through the deserted diggings, peering into graves and temples and houses inhabited only by foxes and blue rock pigeons.

From the top of the tableland rose a hill of bricks — Tell el Ahmar, the red hill, an Arab boy called it. Once this hill had borne on its lofty summit the shrine of Nannar the moon god. I climbed the hill and gazed out across the desert, now blazing in the summer sun, while haunting thoughts of a forgotten past came crowding about me.

It was in a state of great excitement that I returned to Baghdad and visited the Iraq Museum to study there the treasures unearthed from Ur. Finally, during the heat of that August in Baghdad, the writing of this book was begun.

Since then, whenever time could be spared from more scientific pursuits, the manuscript has been written and rewritten. It was found necessary to revisit Ur, also to become acquainted with the marsh Arabs and their life in the vicinity of Basrah and to study the archeological collections of the British Museum and the University of Pennsylvania.

In the end, nothing of my mother's text remains in the manuscript, but it is her spirit, nevertheless, that has impelled me and perhaps guided me in this effort to draw a true picture of the men and women who lived so long ago.

WILDER PENFIELD

Contents

❖❰❰❖❰

Contents

Principal Characters

Abram *   Son of Terah by his first wife
Amtelai **   Daughter of Prince Salah, Terah's second wife
Berri   Handmaid of Princess Shub-Kudur
Cush   A Habiru herdsman
Dudu   Physician-priest in the temple of the moon god
Enannatum   High priest of Nannar the moon god
Enna   Terah's concubine
Habdan   Haran's slave
Ham   Follower of Karnebo
Haran *   Son of Terah by his first wife
Igmil-Sin   Teacher of the boys' school
Jabal   Prince Salah's chief herdsman
Karnebo   Robber chief and kinsman of Prince Salah
Kerkha   A marsh native
Lot *   Son of Haran
Magog   Terah's chief camelman
Melchizedek *   Son of the king of Salem
Milcah *   Daughter of Haran and wife of Nahor II
Naamah   Governess and handmaid of Sarai
Nahor *   Hereditary chief of the Habiru in Haran and
                       father of Terah
Nahor * II   Son of Terah by his first wife

Principal Characters

Nasir-Sin	Sumerian noble and leader of Sumerian nationalists
Oni	Slave and friend of Abram
Rim-Sin	The Elamite king of Larsa and of Ur
Salah	Overseer of the sacred farms of the god Enlil at Drehem; called Karnebo in the Talmud
Sarai *	Daughter of Terah by his second wife Amtelai
Shub-Kudur	Daughter of King Rim-Sin
Terah *	Son of Nahor; idol merchant
Unzie	Kinsman of the patesi (priest-ruler) of Nippur

* Mentioned in Genesis.
** Mentioned in the Talmud.

No Other Gods

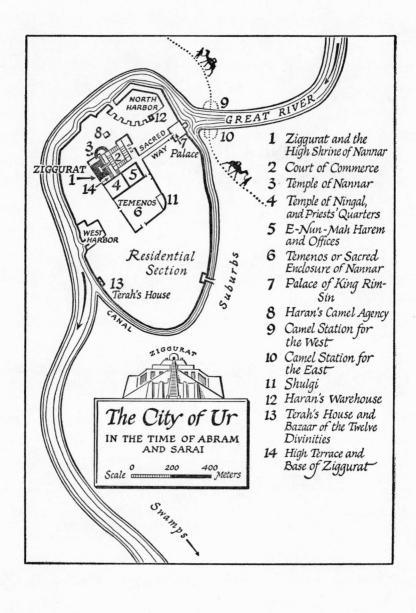

The City of Ur

IN THE TIME OF ABRAM AND SARAI

Scale 0 200 400 Meters

1 Ziggurat and the High Shrine of Nannar
2 Court of Commerce
3 Temple of Nannar
4 Temple of Ningal, and Priests' Quarters
5 E-Nun-Mah Harem and Offices
6 Temenos or Sacred Enclosure of Nannar
7 Palace of King Rim-Sin
8 Haran's Camel Agency
9 Camel Station for the West
10 Camel Station for the East
11 Shulgi
12 Haran's Warehouse
13 Terah's House and Bazaar of the Twelve Divinities
14 High Terrace and Base of Ziggurat

✦《✦

CHAPTER I

Priest of the Moon God

ONE FINE MORNING in the spring of the year, a little less than two thousand years before Christ, Abram son of Terah stood on the temple steps frowning as he stared down into the court of commerce. Many who passed him turned to look at the tall, broad-shouldered, handsome young man. His face was smooth-shaven, and his head as well, for he was a priest of Nannar the moon god. It was quite obvious that he was dissatisfied with something. Perhaps it was because he had been called from his study in the temple library to help in handling the moon god's lucrative business?

The court overflowed with merchants and farmers who had come to bring their taxes and pay their rents and also to bargain and to sell. Nannar was the principal god of the city of Ur, but he was more than that. The god was the richest landowner in the whole country of Sumer. He could demand rents from many, and tithes from all householders in the land.

This was the time of preparation for the annual spring festival, when the image of the god would be carried out into the country to bless the land. Consequently the city was crowded with pilgrims and sightseers as well as those who came to buy and sell.

Abram watched the familiar scene with distaste. In front of the stalls that lined the wall of the court, men in the long cloaks of the country milled about, shouting and gesticulating. Slaves came and went, some with trays of clay tablets which recorded the terms of earlier agreement, others with trays of wet clay ready to be made into fresh tablets for the written record of prospective financial transactions. Soldiers in short skirts, carrying broad spears above the heads of the throng, controlled the streams of traffic.

Cattle and sheep entered the court, and passed through it, bleating and bellowing, into the pens of the god, there to await slaughter. Grain and fruits, heaped up in baskets and borne on the heads of porters, flowed in one gate and out another into the god's great granary.

Standing there with the man-made mountain, the ziggurat, towering behind him, he looked down on the turmoil in the court; heard the lowing, bleating, squawking, shouting; smelled the stench of the market.

Why should he be a part of all this? Was it to serve the moon god? What was the moon god after all — an idol, nothing more. He had a feeling of helpless anger. Here he was, he thought, at the age of twenty-five years, completely dissatisfied with life. He had come to the temple as a boy filled with hope that he would discover a great truth. But the years spent inside the temple of Nannar had brought him disappointment and gradual disillusionment.

A cool wind stirred, blowing away the stench of the market. The thought occurred to him that after all it was springtime. The desert from here to the hills of Haran would be covered with wild flowers. Within him there welled up memories of boyhood like a cool spring of past experience, fresh memories of his visits to the farms of his kinsman at Drehem. He saw the green meadows, smelled the wind off the desert and felt the motion of swift camels. How wonderful it had been to be free and to live in the open, to sleep in a tent and to move at will! At last he sighed and brought himself back to his present task.

As he descended the steps he heard the sounds of a scuffle, and someone crying aloud that he could not give up his donkey. Abram approached the scene of trouble and discovered a burly soldier beating a farmer. At a little distance the donkey, the subject of the dispute, hung its head so that its drooping ears almost swept the ground. A little boy squatted beside the beast, hugging the ugly snout and crying aloud in terror.

A wave of anger swept over Abram and he seized the soldier and pulled him off. The soldier whirled about and drew the dagger from his belt; but recognizing that his opponent was a senior priest he put back his weapon, although with sullen fury. Abram turned to the scribe standing near by who seemed to be acting as judge in the little drama. "What is this?" he demanded.

The scribe was a sleek, well-fed individual. He replied with a shrug and a rising inflection: "This farmer is behind in his payments to Nannar. He says he has no barley so I sent for his livestock. He comes now with this worthless beast."

At this the farmer cried out: "For years I served as a mercenary in the king's army. I became an underofficer and then I was wounded." He cast a sidelong angry glance at his former assailant and Abram noticed that the poor fellow's left arm hung limp at his side and that the hand was clawlike and useless. "They gave me a farm," he continued, "and I have worked hard on it, but the irrigation water did not come last year and my wife and children are starving. I have only one arm with which to carry, but if you will leave me the ass, my oldest son here and I will bring in our tithe after the next harvest."

At this point the scribe broke in arrogantly: "This person belongs to the cutthroat tribe of Habiru; I wouldn't take his word for anything." Then he added with the faintest of smiles: "I hope you will forgive me. I had forgotten that you too are an Amorite."

Abram glanced at the boy, who stood listening, his little fists clenched while tears still streamed from his hollow eyes and made lines down a grimy, emaciated face. His gaunt body and his bowed legs spoke all too eloquently of want and hunger.

Abram controlled his anger with an effort. He ignored the scribe and turned to the father. "What about the other farmers, in your district where the water did not come, are they also Amorites from Haran?"

"Yes," replied the man sullenly, "almost all of them, and most of them are old soldiers too."

Abram then addressed the scribe grimly: "Let this man go. His case will come before the judge at the great gate of Dublalmakh. I will get an advocate for him. Give me his contract tablet."

The scribe sneered but he obeyed without venturing to reply. The farmer exclaimed in astonishment: "May the God of our fathers bless you!"

Abram could not trust himself to speak. So he thrust the tablet abruptly into his wallet and, turning, crossed the court and climbed the steps to the broad terrace that led to the ziggurat. Here he paced up and down for some time, muttering to himself, oblivious of the curious eyes that followed him. At last he stopped and looked down into the court again.

The scribe was rubbing his long shaven head and talking volubly to the soldier. At a little distance the farmer was in the act of placing a handful of grain in the votive box before a potbellied idol. When he saw this Abram exclaimed half aloud: "Poor fellow! You ought to know that you will never get help from Nannar either by prayers or tribute. Perhaps you would be better off in the desert with only the God of your fathers for protection."

At this point, a voice broke in on his soliloquy: "What about this god you speak of? Is he a powerful god?" Abram started and turned to find at his elbow a tall, bearded man who bowed and smiled.

"Forgive me!" the man said. "You are Abram son of Terah.

I am told that no one knows the mysteries of the gods of Sumer and the history of the kings as well as you. Your high priest, Enannatum, sent me to find you. He said you were the scholar best qualified to answer my questions. I am Melchizedek, son of the king of Salem."

Abram bowed in surprise. Then he asked the stranger what had brought him to Ur.

"My father," said Melchizedek, "sent me here to see the glory of Ur and learn wisdom from the scholars of the temple of the moon god. Our kingdom is one of many small kingdoms in the land of Canaan. As you know, Canaan is a great distance from here. In order to pass around the great desert, I had to travel northward through the seaport cities, west through Amurru and south through Akkad and Sumer. In other years I visited Egypt and the great temples by the pyramids.

"My father the king," he continued, "is priest of the most high God in Salem. I too am a priest and scholar. The Sumerian gods interest me, although we do not worship them."

Abram looked at Melchizedek keenly. It was obvious from his dress, his dignified bearing and his speech that this stranger who spoke so directly and simply was everything that he said. After a moment of silence Abram turned and pointed to the temple behind him, and spoke a little bitterly: "There sits Nannar the great moon god, the high exalted! Part of him was remade by my own father, who is an idol merchant. Yonder is the temple of the god's wife Ningal. There, you see the procession of priestesses is just now coming out of the temple. The priestesses are called the *sal-me*."

Above the hubbub of the market, there came to the ears of the two men the high-toned cadence of the chant of Ningal. "Since childhood," added Abram in a milder tone, "I have loved the beauty of their singing." The procession drew nearer, mounting the stairs that led halfway up the face of the ziggurat and then descended again obliquely to the temple of Nannar. The chanting became louder. The golden headdresses of the priestesses sparkled in the sun. The outlines of their swaying bodies could be seen through shimmering tunics.

"On entering the service of Ningal," continued Abram, "each priestess must sacrifice her virginity to Nannar the great moon god, lord of Ur and prince of gods. But strange as it may seem, Nannar takes no part in the ceremony. He remains seated on this throne, staring out at the great river."

Abram shrugged and then went on: "However, rich Sumerians pay him well in votive offerings so that each may be a god for a night. Our priestesses sometimes continue this sort of sacrifice secretly, so that the nurseries of Ningal are filled with fatherless infants, but I doubt if the goddess Ningal opens her stony ears even to the din of their wailing."

Abram's lip curled in scorn, and it was Melchizedek's turn to look at his companion with surprise. "You speak bitterly — and openly," he said, and glanced about to see if they were overheard.

Abram shrugged again. "When you spoke to me, I'm afraid I was angry over something. But no matter. I am at your service now, since it is the wish of the high priest. Would you like to ascend the holy hill of heaven?" As he spoke he pointed up to the ziggurat, which towered above them into the blue sky. "You are a priest in your own country. I can get you a robe to wear up there."

"Yes," replied Melchizedek, "but first may I ask to be shown the tablet house? The high priest has given me his permission to study your records. Scholars everywhere have heard of the archives of Ur."

It was a short walk from the terrace, where they were standing, to the tablet house. Abram guided his guest through the gate and led him past a long series of alcoves in which thousands of tablets were filed in baskets and jars, row upon row.

Abram picked up a tablet and handed it to Melchizedek. "This is very old," he said. "Baked tablets are almost indestructible. Our problem is much simpler than that of the Egyptian scholars, who deal with records written on papyrus. Even our unbaked clay tablets are indestructible unless they become wet.

"When a tablet house is destroyed and water gets in, the earthworms may pass right through an unbaked tablet as they would the earth they came from. Worms do not seem to recognize the value of the ancient wisdom recorded on these tablets!"

Melchizedek smiled. "The worm has no more respect for scholarship than he has for the scholar. We shall all of us be laid away in the earth some day. That is the kingdom of my Lord the Worm, and at last, one by one, we bow to him."

They talked and moved up and down dark corridors where tablets were stored. Finally Abram led the way to his own room. It opened on a gallery that ran along the side of the tablet-house courtyard. "Here," he said, "within these walls I am lord. You see I have clay and water and all the materials for copying from the tablets of the archives. I may bring tablets here to study when I have given the tablet keeper a receipt. Here also I sleep and keep my small store of clothing."

As they spoke, a servant in the tunic and sandals of the royal household came hurrying along the gallery and stepped into the doorway of Abram's room with elaborate bowings and greetings. "The Princess Shub-Kudur," he said, "desires to consult Abram son of Terah." The messenger withdrew to the gallery as abruptly as he had come.

Abram made a gesture of impatience. "She has consulted me before," he said. "She is collecting libation urns from the early temples, and in trying to discover the age of each she finds my king list of some use."

Footsteps sounded on the gallery and there was a faint twinkling of ankle rings and much rustling of robes. In a moment the

Princess Shub-Kudur stood in the doorway, then entered the room without ceremony. A long blue cape covered her from throat to foot and over her hair she wore a multicolored veil from beneath which heavy gold earrings showed against her warm brown throat.

She looked squarely at Melchizedek with an expression of surprise and then, ignoring him, addressed herself to Abram. Two women similarly dressed and hooded had followed her as far as the doorway. One of them, who was quite small, handed an urn which she had been carrying to the princess, who showed it to Abram.

Melchizedek noted, with practiced eye, that the princess had beauty of face, beauty of carriage and, when her shapely arm emerged from beneath her cape, he added to himself beauty of form. But he withdrew quickly to the gallery, where the smaller of the two ladies in waiting, a quick-moving, birdlike young woman with an obvious twinkle in her eye, made room for him with alacrity. She even went so far as to drop her reticule so that he could restore it to her and be rewarded by a gay laugh and conversation about the weather.

This pleasant conversation was terminated, however, by the commanding voice of the princess. "Berri, come here. Take this urn and stop your chatter."

When the court ladies had gone Melchizedek looked at Abram with a half-smile. "Remarkable interest for the daughter of King Rim-Sin to take in a priest, is it not?"

Abram shrugged. "She is interested only in her urn collection. I hope to make a copy of the king list for her so that she will no longer interrupt me in my work."

"You amaze me," Melchizedek exclaimed, and his expression of amusement was replaced by one of astonished admiration. Abram seemed quite oblivious of what was going through the mind of his companion.

"Now let us climb to the top of the ziggurat," he said, "where I can show you Ur and where no one is likely to interrupt us."

They returned to the terrace and Abram looked down again into the court of commerce. The Habiru farmer seemed to have disappeared. He beckoned to a senior scribe who was passing and gave him the farmer's tablet. He instructed the scribe to make the legal arrangements for trial for the farmer's case at the gate of Dublalmakh.

Then he turned back to Melchizedek and said: "Please pardon the interruption. There is a great deal of injustice and cruelty in the collection of rents, especially, I fear, in regard to my people. We are Amorites from Haran. Some call us Habiru."

From where they stood the main stair soared straight upward to the shrine of Nannar. Halfway to the top it was interrupted by a landing, and here it was joined by the flights of stairs from either side, one slanting obliquely upward across the face of the ziggurat from the temple of Ningal on the left, the other from the temple of Nannar on the right.

As Abram and Melchizedek climbed the central stair, the priestesses were returning from their visit to Nannar's shrine. The two men waited on the landing to let the procession pass.

"I agree with you," Melchizedek said. "Their chanting is really beautiful. But that word describes the *sal-me* also! One might suppose that Nannar had great power over beautiful women."

On reaching the top of the ziggurat they walked out on a terrace beside the shrine and looked down from that dizzy height upon a wide panorama that brought from Melchizedek an exclamation of admiration. Below them lay the island city of Ur with the mighty flood of the great river flowing around its walls. The white temples, the sparkling water and the wide expanse of green extended far beyond to the red-brown of the distant desert. It was indeed a sight never to be forgotten.

"A few miles away to the northwest," said Abram, "you see

the ziggurat of Al Ubaid, a city even older than Ur. Over there, to the south, you can see the ziggurat of the most ancient city of all Sumer, Eridu. At the foot of their ziggurat where the great river winds its way past the city, you see something white shining in the sun. That is the temple of the water god Ea. Ea or Enki is the god of the depths, the god of wisdom.

"The ancestors of the Sumerians," continued Abram, "probably lived in the mountains far to the east of us, where they worshiped in high places. But in this great plain of ours, where there is not so much as a pebble to break its flatness, the people of each city have built themselves a ziggurat so that they may continue to worship in high places. I can well understand it," he added, "for sometimes when I am up here I feel strangely exalted. I find myself no nearer to the image of Nannar, but I do feel nearer to the God of my fathers, who has no image."

Melchizedek placed his hands on the parapet and looked away to the horizon where the deep blue of the gulf seemed to meet the sky. Then he said quietly: "In my father's kingdom of Salem we worship one God only. He is the Most High. We call Him by no other name. We make no image of Him. My father the king has great wisdom, but it is wisdom without knowledge. He is not a scholar, and so he commanded me to study in Egypt and to seek the living truth. My father tells us that the Most High can be worshiped everywhere. But I too sometimes feel myself near to Him when I am in high places. Before I came on this journey I climbed alone to a mountain top in Salem. Far below me were green valleys and brooks rushing down to join the distant Jordan. I looked up. An eagle soared above me.

"What was I to do with my life? I had studied in the temples of the Nile. Men there were deafened by the din of living, blind to the present and the future. They opened their eyes only toward the past.

"Alas! the wife that I had married in Egypt had died during

our return to Salem. My father did not need me, for Canaan is at peace. I knew that in spite of all my learning of the past, I had come no nearer to what I sought. Yet I knew there were better things.

"In the silence on that lonely mountain top, I think our God spoke to me. And so — here I am in Ur and, strangely enough, I have come directly to a man who seeks the truth, as I do. You have some knowledge of the past, as I have. You are unhappy, as I was. You are driven to seek an understanding of those things that are true and that will be true always."

Abram gave an involuntary exclamation. He felt suddenly a little giddy. Had all this happened to him before? It seemed to him that it had. It seemed to him that someone had already said these things to him, in some other place, at some other time. Or were they the echo of his own inner thinking?

Melchizedek noticed that the expression in his companion's eyes had changed. He watched him and was silent. Then he said: "Tell me something more about the gods of Sumer." Abram fumbled with his robe and the pin that fastened it over his shoulder. He made a conscious effort to collect his thoughts.

"Of Sumer?" he asked. Suddenly color surged back into his face.

"Oh, yes. In Sumer, there are many, many gods, many temples." After a pause he seemed to be master of himself and he began again.

"From hundreds of altars the smoke of burnt offerings rises in a great cloud in this land. But there is no living god to smell it. No god smiles at the aroma of incense. No god speaks. I believe that none of their gods has ever spoken. Only the priests. They speak. They punish. They tax.

"In the plains and deserts out there," he said, pointing to the north, "where my people live in tents, they build no temples. They carry no god in their hands when they go to the pastures.

They have only the God of our family and no image has ever been made of Him. The god of the nomad, whatever his name may be, can have no house. But of what power is a family god if every family has a different one?"

The two men strode back and forth on the top of the ziggurat talking for a long time. A casual observer might have taken them to be men of the same race, except that they spoke with different accents. They were both tall and powerfully built. Melchizedek was bearded and of early middle age. He was obviously a man who knew the world and its ways. He had a thoughtful reserve, which gave him an air of mystery. He listened with keen interest to everything the younger man said. When he himself spoke, his words were few. He brushed aside all unimportant details and seemed to come to the heart of any matter with surprising directness.

In contrast to him, Abram talked with enthusiasm and drive, even with eloquence. He gesticulated as he developed a line of thought, and his deep voice vibrated. Sometimes his heavy features lit up as though from a fire of inner excitement. At other times his face returned to the expression of discontent which had become habitual during his recent years in the priesthood.

Their conversation was finally interrupted by the beating of a drum. A priest within the shrine drew back a great curtain, displaying a throne encrusted with jewels, the throne where the image of Nannar was to be placed at the close of day. All present on the top of the ziggurat prostrated themselves. As Abram touched his forehead to the terrace, he muttered: "Bow to the empty throne of Nannar, prince of gods — empty now and always."

They stood up, and Melchizedek said: "You have spoken the truth, for the living God does not sit here nor does He sit there. He is not walled up in a temple of stone in Sumer, in Akkad, or in

Egypt. You will find Him only when you have built your own temple out of other materials.

"I will see you again. But now, good-by."

Abram watched the shepherd-prince descend the stair and finally disappear into the throng in the great court far below. No one that he had ever known before had talked to him in this way. He would have to think over his words about temples. Was Canaan such a beautiful land? His people would be freed from the suspicion and hatred of Sumer, if Canaan could be their home.

A great desire to talk with his father came over him and he hurried down the ziggurat and out of the temenos, the sacred enclosure surrounding the temples, through a small gate. This led him directly into a narrow, foul-smelling lane. The sick and the lame who were brought to Ur for treatment preferred billets that were as close as possible to the walls of the temenos, for they hoped that by mere proximity to the moon god their ailments might receive the benefit of his healing power. Thus the houses along the lane were filled with sufferers of all types, and from the house tops they could watch the comings and goings within the temenos.

Abram picked his way through dirt and offal. He passed a slovenly stall for the sale of fruit and meat. Hornets buzzed about it in a cloud. Emaciated faces peered at him from doorways. But he walked rapidly, lost in thought, until he felt someone catch the hem of his cloak. He stopped then and saw that a little girl had grasped at it. She turned her face up to him, and as he stood and looked down at her and at the filthy lane, it occurred to him that her face was like a flower that had somehow blossomed out of the mire.

While he mused the child's grandmother hobbled up and asked him if he would carry the little girl to the gate of healing, as her own strength had failed her. Abram saw then that the child's foot

was bandaged. He took her in his arms and she smiled at him as
though to give him his reward in advance.

Abram passed down the lane, bearing his burden, while the
old woman hobbled after. On reaching their destination he
stepped carefully through the crowd of sufferers who sat or
lay upon the ground in a great square before the gate. He entered a side door and came upon a surgeon-priest who was well
known to him, a squat jovial fellow named Dudu, whose undu-
lating belly seemed momentarily in danger of bursting the soiled
tunic that was stretched over it.

Together they removed the dressing from the child's foot. It
was swollen and foul. Pus dripped from it. The surgeon washed
it and prescribed a complicated poultice. Then he dressed it
again.

But this was not all. The old woman needed further assistance.
She explained that her son, the child's father, was ill at home
and could not come to the temple. He suffered, she said, from
a swelling of the abdomen. For this condition Dudu seemed to
know exactly what to do. He instructed her that someone in
the family should bring a lamb to the temple so that it could be
sacrificed upon the altar of the god. They were then to leave the
right half of the carcass as a gift to the god and they were to
carry off the left half of the lamb to the sick man's home. There
they should lay it directly upon his swollen part.

Abram took the little girl in his arms again. Crossing the square,
he rented an ass and set the child on its back. They returned,
laughing, to the old woman, who wept and blessed him as she
climbed on the back of the ass behind the child. Abram watched
them ride off toward their lodgings, the child waving and smiling.

He turned to the surgeon, who was standing by his side. "Dudu,
the spirit of that child is fresh and sweet. The body is diseased.
Are the two not linked together?"

"Yes," Dudu replied, "they are linked more closely than most people know. A good physician must treat both. When you carried the child here and when you paid for the rent of the ass you treated the spirit. I did what I could for the foot.

"As a matter of fact, that foot should be treated with the knife, but if I were to operate and the child were to lose her foot you know what might happen — " he looked down at his own foot and shuddered — "they might cut mine off! Nevertheless," he said, brightening up, "you saw me do a good deal here in your student days and I still have my two hands and feet!"

"Yes," said Abram, "and you use your hands very effectively. You keep them busy with surgery all day and with eating and drinking all night!" Abram watched the contents of the tunic billow and shake as Dudu chuckled.

Abram clapped his friend on the back and was about to leave him when Dudu spoke. "Wait," he said. "I have something to say to you. Sometimes the spirit ails in a strong body too. I've been watching you for some months now. You are working too hard. Your lamp is lit far into the night in that cave of yours in the tablet house. When you come to the refectory you eat little and talk little. You have grown moody and even bad-tempered. Let me prescribe for you."

"Nonsense," Abram replied and started off.

But Dudu shook his head and called after him: "It is easier to cure a sick body than it is the sick at heart. A few evenings with me would be good for you."

Ur contained about a quarter of a million people and, as the houses were never more than two stories in height, they crowded the island and overflowed to suburbs across the river. Ten minutes walk through the town brought Abram to the shrine of Pa-Sag. He looked in as he passed. Some desert people were there offering sacrifices, probably his own people, he thought. Pa-Sag, though her shrine was poor and small by comparison with those of the great gods, was in special favor among nomads when they visited the city.

As Abram threaded his way through the familiar streets he realized how rarely he had seen his father during the last two years, since the high priest had set him to work in the tablet house of the temple archives. Actually, for several months he had not been home at all, for he had worked day and night on his study of the succession of the Sumerian kings. He had found contradictory evidence which he could straighten out only by consulting the tablets in the temple of Nippur. So he had only recently returned from a visit to that city. The high priest had seemed pleased with the result when he took him his own tablets with the king lists completed.

But he realized that there were other reasons for his absence from home. One was his rising resentment of his father's trade in idols. He knew he could no longer trust himself to discuss the affairs of the idol market with him. Then, too, Terah's house did not seem to be the same place that it had been in the days of his boyhood when his stepmother Amtelai had been there. After her death, Terah had taken a concubine into the house, a woman Abram disliked. His older brother Haran, whom he had once idolized, had moved from Terah's house into a house of his own and he was always busy now with the affairs of the desert trade, which had grown greatly in his hands. His younger brother Nahor bored him with his interminable discussions of buying and selling. Of course, Abram admitted to himself, Nahor would be bored, and uncomprehending as well, if he were to discuss with him his own search for the truth.

After all, he mused, what was truth? Melchizedek had said that if one listened he might hear the truth. Perhaps so, in Canaan. But here in Sumer it must be different. At all events he had tried up to the present to discover the truth by gaining greater and greater knowledge of the past, and where was it all leading him?

He stopped outside his father's house and debated whether he should enter or return to the temenos. Next door was his father's famous idol shop, the bazaar of the twelve divinities. Customers were entering it and he knew that his father's assistants were busy with them in the shop. No, the time had come, he thought, to discuss his problems with his father, particularly now that his work on the king lists had been completed. And so he knocked on the door.

CHAPTER II

Broken Idols

Wʜᴇɴ Abram stepped out of the hot street and into his father's house, he found it agreeably cool and quiet. The slave at the door told him that his father was taking his midday meal. Abram inquired hesitantly who else was present.

The servant replied: "Only your brother Nahor and your nephew Lot."

So Abram removed his turban and sandals, and, having washed his feet, put on slippers and went directly to the guest room. He entered, bowing to his father.

A little man with gray hair and beard was sitting cross-legged on the floor at the end of the room with the bread cloth spread out before him, and Nahor and Lot were seated at the side. Abram made as though to sit below Lot, but his father Terah rose and embraced him.

"Come here," he said, "and sit on my right hand. It has been much too long since we have seen you!"

As they talked of various things, Abram was struck by the fact that Terah seemed suddenly old. He also observed with interest the change in his younger brother Nahor who had matured rapidly. He was now a full-fledged merchant and man of affairs, suave, self-assured and consciously clever. It was not long since he had married his own niece Milcah. She and Lot were the children of Haran.

Presently Terah turned to Abram and said: "I regret that I have never been able to select a wife for you, my priest son. But your influence within the temple of Nannar is more important to our family than the sons and daughters you might have called yours, if you were not in the priesthood."

Abram grunted. "I have little interest in women, and the less I see of them the better I like it." He shrugged his broad shoulders as though he were a man of long experience in such matters.

His father smiled and remarked: "Nevertheless, I have a surprise for you. Today, or perhaps tomorrow, an old playmate of yours is returning from Drehem."

Abram brought his hand down on his knee with a resounding sound. "You mean Oni!" he exclaimed. "It will be good to see him."

Terah smiled again. "No, I mean your half-sister, the daughter of my second wife Amtelai. But it is true that Oni is coming with her. It is five years now since you visited Drehem. In those five years she has grown up."

"I suppose so," replied Abram. "I remember how she used to run after her mother with her auburn curls flying. Everyone at Drehem, even the shepherds, used to call her by her baby name, Little Princess. Has her grandfather Salah given her an adult name yet? What is she to be called in Ur?"

"She will continue to be called by her baby name, Sarai, Little Princess," Terah replied.

"What about Oni?" interjected Nahor. "He is your bondsman, Father Terah. I never understood why you should have given his services to Prince Salah all these years. When I lived in Drehem he was allowed much too much freedom. I used to find him arrogant. Sometimes he would allow no one to come near Sarai. Let me have him for a while here in Ur. I can use him in the idol market. Other slaves fear him because of his great strength. Let me have him. I'll bring down his pride."

"No," replied Terah. "Oni has done what I wanted him to do. He has come to be an experienced herdsman, and he has guarded Sarai. He is to be Abram's slave and he may yet prove useful to him. You have enough slaves and freemen in your market and in the idol workshop."

When the meal was ended, Abram's nephew Lot, a handsome boy of sixteen years, rose and asked his grandfather's permission to leave. "I want to be the first to greet the travelers from Dre-hem. If I know Sarai, she will arrange it so that they reach the camel station across the river before the spring festival begins. I have been watching for them in the market place and at the ferry landing. Now there are only a few hours of daylight left.

"Tonight, you remember," he added, "the great spring-festival gaiety in the market will be something worth seeing! Still more important is the fact that my school closes once and for all on the day after tomorrow! Perhaps, Grandfather Terah, you will come and introduce me to the night life of Ur, now that I am to be a man." The boy laughed aloud at the picture he had con-jured up for them, while Terah wagged a warning finger at him and Abram chuckled.

After he had gone Nahor remarked: "Tonight is the prelim-inary festival of the full moon. They carry on a whole month. It is nonsense. Lot's business probably has to do with wine and amusement. I am told that he has been seen talking with women from the temple."

Terah's face clouded and he said: "Lot is a good boy, although he has a tendency to be rather gay. He has done well in his school, I am told, although he is not the scholar that Abram was. It is only two years since he came back to Ur. Milcah says that it is time for me to choose a woman for him to marry, but I think he is too young."

Thinking now of the Amorite farmer he had seen in the court of commerce that afternoon, Abram inquired of Terah whether he knew of any recent discrimination against the Amorites in regard to the allotment of irrigation water.

His father looked grave and answered: "Yes." Then he added: "I have made official complaint, and I am told by the minister of trade in the temple of Nannar that a great deal of pressure is being brought to bear upon him by the Sumerian military party to discriminate against our people. On the other hand, the king himself has always been friendly to us. I wish you, Abram, could do something about this situation.

"You remember years ago there was bitter feeling against us that continued all during the war against Babylon. But after Hammurabi had taken the city of Isin away from Rim-Sin and after peace returned, the suspicion of us as outsiders quieted down. That was why I sent Amtelai, with Sarai in her arms, back to her father Prince Salah so that he could keep them safe at Drehem. Amtelai, my most precious possession, died on the day she was to have returned to me . . . alas.

"I warned Sarai that it was not safe for her to return now, but I had answer back that she must come now — some urgent reason, not explained." Terah smiled at his sons, and shrugged. "It seems that my only daughter has a mind of her own!

"The Sumerians," he continued, "are jealous of our prosperity and they still seem to fear us. As a people I believe that they are degenerating. They inherit the learning and culture and pride of so many years. But they have lost the vigor that they once had. Our people are more virile. Therefore they prosper. There is a feeling among the members of this nationalist military group that if we were driven out they would regain their self respect, and so they spread false stories about us.

"I had hoped, Abram, that you, as a priest in high favor, might do a great deal to stem the rising tide of antagonism. I sometimes feel that it would be better for us if we men of Haran were a little less proud of our own inheritance, if we would intermarry with the Sumerians, if we worshiped Nannar more loyally and continued to serve willingly in the army as the Habiru used to do."

At this point, Abram, who had been following his father's discussion with deference, broke in upon him: "How can anyone be loyal," he said, "to an idol? How can I recommend that to them? I must tell you, Father Terah, that a great change is coming over me. I see so many abuses, so much deceit. I see cruel, grasping men lurking behind each image to take advantage of the worshipers. You yourself do not worship the stone before your craftsman sets a chisel to it. Why should you do so afterward?"

Terah held up his hand for silence. "Let me answer your question frankly. You and Nahor are grown men now and I shall speak my mind on this subject even though I may be cursed." As he said this, Terah cast a furtive glance toward a shelf on which sat a small alabaster statue of Nannar. Then he continued:

"It is true that I do not worship the uncut stone, nor do I bow down before the graven image as it sits in my market. I have made him; I am his father. It is I who put a spirit into him, for that is my art.

"But from the time the work upon the stone is finished, he is truly the god whose name he bears. When I sell him, does he not repay me handsomely for my work? And after he leaves me, doesn't every man know that he must beware of the idol's curses?

"All Sumerians believe this and they believe, too, that the most effective charms and amulets for their protection are on sale at my shop of the twelve divinities. I, for one, would do nothing to dissuade them."

There was a smile on the old man's lips, and he shrugged his shoulders and raised his hands in the air, after the manner of merchants. But when Abram and Nahor both tried to speak, he silenced them again with an imperious gesture.

He stroked his beard for a little while, and then he said: "You see me sneer and yet you know very well that I fear these same gods. Perhaps you are wondering whether I am more sincere in my sneering or in my believing." He looked up at the ceiling and then continued. "Perhaps I do not know, myself. During many years I have watched men come to my bazaar, watched them throng the temples. What they actually believe in their hearts it is hard to tell, but each and every one of them is afraid of something. That is the common driving emotion. From birth they have been taught to fear, and when death comes they are still afraid."

Terah drew from about his neck a chain to which was attached a beautiful gold amulet inlaid with mother of pearl and gems. He let it turn slowly before them, and they saw it glow in the light like a little beacon, then go out and glow again. "This," he said, "is the *utchat* which I bought from a traveling merchant. It is the eye of the Egyptian god Horus. It protects the wearer from all evil spirits that would enter his body to give him pain. It is an amulet of such great power that behold! since I began to wear it I am free from the pain in my joints — almost. But if the devils should get into my joints again, I shall cast it aside." He paused and shrugged again. "And when I cast it aside it will bring twice the price I paid for it. I believe in the *utchat* but I remember my own advantage at the same time!

"Seriously, my sons, all peoples in all countries have worshiped their own gods, great and small, since the world began. They have done so because of fear; fear of the dark, the unseen, the unknown, the imagined. Where can they turn for protection for themselves and for the spirits of their dead if not to idols, and of whom else can they beg favors?

"Some gods seem to be weak, and some strong. Wise men learn to placate the strong gods. Every city and every country has its own special god. That god collects the taxes for the king. Can it be organized in any better way?

"What has your great learning taught you, Abram?" He finished with a gesture and turned to his elder son, who had risen and was pacing the floor with flushed face.

"My years of study," replied Abram, "have taught me only this: that idols are made by men and are generally used by clever men to get what they want out of the less clever. I have studied and catalogued five thousand god names in Sumer alone. They are all false. Of that I am certain.

"What I seek now is to discover the true God, and I am not at all certain that I can find Him. I want to find the God who made man. I hate the gods that man makes."

Terah stared at his son in shocked silence, while Nahor yawned.

Then Abram continued, addressing himself to his father: "Today a prince of Salem told me about his God, whom he called the Most High. He said his God spoke to him even without an altar when he stood upon a mountain top in the distant land of Canaan. Idols have never spoken, I know that. Perhaps the God of our fathers would speak to us if it were not for the clamor of this city. Perhaps if we could go to Canaan — "

"The land of Canaan," interrupted Nahor, who had become restive during his own enforced silence, "is said to be rich, and suitable for cattle raising. Furthermore, it is on the trade routes to Egypt and the great seaport cities." He yawned again. "But I know nothing of their gods, and surely Canaan is inhabited by rude, uncivilized people."

Abram stood for a little while lost in his own thoughts, apparently oblivious of the fact that Nahor had spoken. Then, forgetting that he was in his father's presence, he walked out of the room without a word.

Terah and Nahor looked at each other in surprise, and Terah said: "He is very much upset by his constant study. I saw the high priest, Enannatum, today and he told me that for months Abram has been working day and night in the archives, except when he went to Nippur, and that the work has been useful to him. It seems to me, however, that my son is breaking under the strain.

"The high priest also hinted that some great promotion would come to Abram in the temple of Nannar if he is willing to co-operate in the affairs of government. He said Abram could avert some danger that hangs over my people." Terah shook his head. "I fear the future very much."

As Abram was putting on his sandals, there was a loud knocking on the street door. Consequently, in order to avoid the risk of meeting strangers, he left quickly through the side entrance that led from his father's house into the shop of the twelve divinities. Passing through the bazaar, he stopped to speak to an ancient slave who was in charge of the market for the moment. The man was standing in an alcove where four idols had been placed on pedestals facing one another.

Looking at the images, Abram inquired: "When customers come to the bazaar, which of these four gods does my father Terah call the mightiest?"

"Oh," replied the slave, "Enlil here is by far the mightiest of them all, and his image is the most expensive."

As Abram stood in thought his eye lighted upon a heavy ax which some workman had left there. Suddenly he turned to the slave and said: "Go, tell your master to come to the shop at once. Tell him there is strife among the gods."

The old man looked astonished and glanced about as though he expected to see civil war break out among them. But when Abram repeated his command sternly, he hurried off. Abram then picked up the ax and laughed wildly. Turning, he approached the nearest of the lesser gods. He swung the ax above his head and smashed the idol into many pieces. He did the same with the second and third, but he left Enlil untouched. Then he tossed the ax into the corner, and breathing deeply adjusted his clothing and waited. He had not noticed that a nobleman entered the shop from the street door during the idol breaking. The newcomer had been followed by a squat, bowlegged servant, who collided with his master when the latter halted in amazement at the sight of the falling images. The two had then stepped to one side and continued to watch from behind the curtain of the doorway.

There was a sound of running feet, and Nahor appeared, followed by Terah, somewhat out of breath. There were women who followed them but Abram had eyes only for his father, who gazed in consternation at the scene of destruction. "Abram!" Terah cried, "Abram! What have you done?"

"Nothing at all," replied Abram. "See for yourself. Enlil here is mightier than the other three. He has broken them to bits."

"But that is impossible," replied Terah. "Enlil is only an image."

"Very well, Father," exclaimed Abram, "if an image cannot do that it can do nothing. And these that are destroyed here on the floor, they can do nothing. Better to destroy them all. And now let Enlil curse me if he can." With that, Abram lifted the heavy idol from the pedestal, while his audience gasped. Raising it above his head, he hurled it down upon the floor with a deafening crash. The father swayed as though he would fall, but was supported by an attendant.

Abram stood for a moment in the center of the wreckage, as though dazed. Then he held out his hand toward his father and said: "It had to come some time. I have longed to do it. I would like to smash every idol in Ur. Forgive me, Father, if you can." He passed his hand across his eyes, and turned and walked unsteadily out of the market.

As Abram passed down the street, porters were unloading asses and carrying saddlebags and camel boxes into his father's house. He realized vaguely that Oni and the travelers from

Drehem must have arrived, but his one desire was to get away as quickly as possible. The asses blocked all passage through the street and a group of idlers had gathered to watch, so he turned in the other direction.

However, he found his passage was barred in that direction also by the noble and the dwarfed servant, who had followed him out of the bazaar. They stood now shoulder to shoulder with feet planted far apart and arms folded.

The noble spoke without preliminary salutation. "Will you tell me, priest, who lives in this house?"

Abram looked at him in surprise. He saw that the man was elaborately dressed as an officer in the royal guard of some foreign city, but he replied impatiently that it was the house of Terah son of Nahor.

"Ha!" replied the officer. "The rich old idol merchant, of the Habiru. Yes, I know. But what I really want to find out is — who is the beautiful, I might say ravishing, young woman who has just entered this prison?"

"It is not a prison," replied Abram resentfully, "and I do not understand your questions."

He tried to pass by, but the officer laughed and caught hold of his mantle. "By Nannar and the lesser gods, you would understand well enough if you had seen her step from the ferry and mount her donkey. A crowd gathered there and as she passed through the market square the people stopped to watch her, a desert queen riding on an ass come to conquer our city, ha! ha! We Sumerians are blackheads; you priests have no hair; but this woman's hair is burnished copper — " he hiccoughed — "and sunshine, and her eyes they are like stars. I left my drink and my companions and followed her on foot in the dust of her pack train only to see where the lovely creature lives."

The man smote his breast. "I am Unzie, son of Gudea of Nippur. I am a close kinsman to the patesi of Nippur." He bowed, but it was done a little too elaborately and he staggered so that his diminutive servant had to come to his rescue to keep him from falling. "I shall never rest," he continued, "until I meet her." As Abram tried to push by him, he straightened up and seized his arm, shouting: "Wait, wait. That was a good show you gave us in the shop there. Good show, shood show. Enlil's a mighty god, and you a priest! Ha, ha, ha!"

In sudden anger Abram gave the man a shove that sent him spinning to the ground. At this the squat servant drew his sword and danced in a threatening manner before Abram. The noble got up on his knees, but finding it difficult to rise he drew his sword also and waved it about his head while the servant forced Abram back.

At this moment someone cried: "Stop!" and a young man leaped in front of Abram with drawn sword. He struck the weapon in the hand of the servant with such force that it fell to the ground. Abram realized that it was his nephew Lot who had come to his rescue.

Lot picked up the fallen sword and gave it back to its owner. As he did so he laughed. "A soldier and an unarmed priest. They cannot fight." He turned to Abram. "If you want to return to the temple of Nannar I will take care of this. I should be charmed to talk with Unzie son of Gudea and escort him back to his friends in the market place. I have seen him there recently." Abram nodded and passed on down the street without a word.

Lot assisted the fallen courtier to his feet and helped the servant dust off his master's clothing. As he did so someone called to him from above. He looked up and saw that a young woman was watching him from the roof top of Terah's house.

"Come back soon," she said. Lot laughed and waved. "The first time I've had the chance to draw my new sword," he called gaily.

But the noble was standing soberly now as though trying to

collect his thoughts. Then he exclaimed: "That priest spoke of Terah . . . Terah. I have it. Has Terah a son by the name of Nahor?" Lot nodded, smiling. The man turned to his servant. "The messenger, the Babylonian messenger. Where is that cursed messenger?"

The servant tried to silence him and finally reached up and put his hand over his master's mouth. Then he and Lot, each taking an arm, walked the man down the street. As Unzie went he seemed to forget the messenger, for he began to sing a bawdy song.

◄☰(

CHAPTER III

Terah

AFTER THE DEPARTURE of Abram, Terah issued orders that the door of the idol market should be closed until all evidence of the destruction was cleared away.

"What my son Abram has done," he said, "he has done." He looked at his son Nahor as he said this.

"And now," he said, "where is my daughter Sarai?" It was Sarai who had arrived in the house during the confusion in the idol market. She had watched the smashing of the idols and had then slipped quietly up to the roof, from which she witnessed Abram's encounter with the drunken noble. A servant ran to bring her to her father.

"Welcome," he cried, "thrice welcome to you, my daughter. We have long looked forward to the day of your arrival."

The old man conducted Sarai and her handmaid Naamah to their rooms and committed them to the care of his concubine Enna. Enna was prepared for them. She had fresh clothing, food and ointments in readiness, and had already ordered bath water to be carried up.

Terah kissed his daughter, and seeing that arrangements were atisfactory for her comfort, he withdrew to his couch on the oof. There the little man heaved a sigh and sat down cross-legged, alone. Now he could think. He bowed his head in his hands.

Could it be that Abram was mad? He raised his head. Would

he end by destroying the reputation of his father, the greatest idol maker of Sumer? Would the great god Enlil, whose image he had shattered, curse them all? What would Abram do next? Why should he take it into his head to behave this way just now, when he stood so high in favor with the high priest, Enannatum? These and a hundred other questions ran through his nimble mind.

Terah had long planned to use the influence of this son in the temple of Nannar for very different purposes. He thought back over his own career. Everything had gone according to plan — until now. If Abram should continue in this madness he might destroy everything that his father had built up with the help of his other sons.

Was he really mad? He recalled what Abram had said before he entered the idol market: "I want to find the God who made man. I hate the gods that man makes."

Terah listened. The night breeze was stirring the awnings above him. He breathed deeply. It was the wind from the distant desert.

Once upon a time, he thought, his own father had thought him mad when he left his flocks on the hills of Haran — to become an idol maker.

"Our people, the Habiru," his father had said, "are different from all other peoples. From time to time our young men are driven out on strange quests. You may call it madness or inspiration. There is something that comes to them, from nowhere, like the wind in the trees." It seemed to Terah that he stood again before his own father, and the wind was stirring the leaves of the oak tree above their heads — as on that afternoon so many years ago.

The next morning Sarai was awake as soon as the light began to filter through the curtains of her bedroom doorway.

She lay quite still and her mind went back over the strange events that had sent her on this hurried journey to Ur with the messages that she had yet to deliver. Her grandfather Salah had warned her to wait until she could be alone with Father Terah before she told him. He had said the news she brought might be a great shock to him. "You must be wise and discreet," he had said. "But don't be afraid. You have your mother's wit as well as her beauty."

Sarai sighed and turned over. Her mother's dressing table caught her eye. "Poor Father Terah!" she said aloud. "He has allowed no one to touch this room during all the years since Mother left him. The paints and the ointments are probably all dried up by now."

She sat up and ran both her hands through her hair. Then she rose from her pallet on the floor with effortless grace and picked up her mother's mirror. She studied her reflection for a time. Then she made a face, shrugged her shoulders and discarded the mirror.

"No," she said aloud, "I'm not beautiful nor witty, like my mother. I'm not clever like my father, nor learned like Abram. But I'm here and it's springtime." She held out both arms.

A golden pencil of sunlight slanted into the room through a hole at the top of the curtain. She opened the curtains and put her head out. The sun was peeping over the roof top opposite, while the courtyard below remained in twilight. The sky was deep, deep blue, the air cool and exhilarating.

She drew back into the room and laughed. Naamah still slept the sleep of utter weariness on her narrow pallet in the corner. "Naamah," she cried, "it's springtime." There was no response other than heavy breathing. If Namaah had been a man one would have said she was snoring.

"Naamah, I have heard from Ishtar the goddess of love that Dumuzi, way down in the underworld, has banished sleep and death and darkness." No answer. She began to dance and to sing, slowly at first.

> *"Dumuzi calls the women of the world,*
> *Dumuzi calls the women of the world.*
> *Dumuzi comes, Dumuzi comes.*
> *Nin-Anna hears — Nin-Anna hears."*

She stopped in the middle of the floor, her face glowing, and jerked her thin blue nightgown over her head and off. Then she danced round and round the room, whipping the gown above her head and in circles about her graceful body.

Suddenly, Naamah started up from her couch. "Oh!" she cried, "I must have been dreaming! But Sarai! What in the name of all the gods are you doing?"

Sarai made a flying leap, to crouch on the floor beside her like a naked little nymph.

"Naamah," she cried, "it's springtime!"

As the sun rose higher and light flooded the courtyard there were sounds of life and activity in Terah's house. Sarai and Naamah found much to do during the morning. But when noon came the sun burned down upon the city with the heat of summer, even though it was springtime. At that hour sleep descended again upon the wealthy houses of Ur, while the hubbub outside lessened until shadows began to move upward on the cream-colored walls of the hot, narrow streets. These streets were so narrow, in fact, that a tall man like Haran could touch the houses on either side with his outstretched hands.

Through those winding streets there flowed a current of life — men, women, children, donkeys — innumerable donkeys, bearing on their backs every conceivable form of burden, from bales of merchandise to laughing women and squawking geese. There were foreign-looking slaves from conquered lands and freemen of the middle class, the mush-kinu; and now that the heat of the day was past, the patricians, the amelu, would soon appear.

The great door of the house swung open and Terah stepped out, old and stooped, but as alert and quick-moving as he had been from his youth. A servant followed him closely, listening to rapid-fire instructions which Terah made more emphatic by continuous gesturing of hands and shoulders.

As he talked, the sound of laughter came from within the house; hearing it, Terah smiled a little and turned his head. But he continued his conversation with the servant. Presently, Sarai appeared in the doorway and looked quietly up and down the street. She had a graceful, girlish figure, surprisingly mature considering the fact that she was only sixteen. She drew on a blue cloak of soft wool and pinned it over her shoulder with a very long gold pin. The head of the pin was made of blue lapis lazuli, and dangling from it was a little seal, shaped like a spool. The cloak was figured with gold, which seemed to set off her eyes and hair.

She hesitated, then stepped into the street. As the two men continued deep in conference, she laughed gaily and cried: "Commerce, commerce, commerce! Surely a daughter just returned home can carry off her father for an afternoon on the river without so many arrangements. We shall not drown." Terah nodded to the servant and turned to her.

"Perhaps," she continued, "you were drawing up my wedding dowry. I warn you I shall not want it; not for a very long time yet. There are so many exciting things to do. First on the list, you are going to show me Ur from the river. Lot wanted to come with us but I put him off." She hesitated and Terah glanced at her. "You see," she continued, "I want my father all alone. I want to talk with him."

The servant smiled and bowed while father and daughter turned toward the two donkeys waiting for them in the care of a slave.

Just then the door of the house opened again and Lot came

out. "Grandfather Terah," he said, "you remember that the last day of my school comes tomorrow. Will you come to the closing exercise?"

"No, Lot," the old man replied. "I shall be busy. We expect a boatload of rare stones to be delivered to the idol workrooms tomorrow morning. However, I have word that your father is returning this afternoon and he will go, I'm sure."

"I wish you would come too," Lot replied. "My teacher is always talking about how rich you are. He says you are the richest man in Ur."

Terah swung a leg over his donkey, groaning a little as though the demon were at his back again. As soon as he was settled in the saddle, he waved at the boy, who stood now, a little wistful, in the doorway.

At that moment two men who were passing stopped and bowed. One of them said: "Can you direct us to the shop of the twelve divinities?" They were dressed in turbans and long travel-stained cloaks, and they spoke Babylonian with the accent of the north. "We understand the shop is kept by Terah son of Nahor."

Terah bowed as best he could on donkeyback. "That is my name," he said, "and yonder is the idol market, next to my own house." Through the open door it was possible to see into the bazaar of the twelve divinities with its rows of gods and goddesses.

As they spoke, Nahor emerged and addressed himself to the two strangers: "I am Nahor son of Terah, at your service in all matters." He bowed to them with his hands clasped before him. But the attention of the two strangers was now directed elsewhere. In fact, they were watching Sarai as she mounted her donkey and rode past them talking to her father.

When she had passed out of sight the younger of the two men turned back to Nahor and said: "We expected to find idols and

gods here but not a living goddess. In the name of Shamash who
is the young lady?"

"She is my half sister Sarai. She arrived in Ur only yesterday
from the farms of the god Enlil at Drehem. — But what may I
do for you?"

The stranger looked at Nahor for a moment before replying.
Then he said: "You have had dealings with Unzie, the kinsman
of the patesi of Nippur, have you not?" The three men left the
street and entered the market.

Terah and Sarai passed on down the street, a slave running on
before them. At a little distance from Terah's doorway, the street
reached the city wall and continued along its top. Here Sarai
halted her little ass and, handing the halter to the slave, dismounted
and walked to the parapet, exclaiming at the view which opened
before her. Her father joined her and they looked down over the
great brown river.

Ferries gracefully shaped at bow and stern were being rowed
rapidly back and forth, crowded with people. There were similarly shaped pleasure boats or *bellams* with gay awnings, smaller
canoe-shaped *machoufs* paddled by two or three men, and narrow
little *chinkos* paddled swiftly by a single man. There were a few
gouffas, piled high with heavy sacks of grain. These moon-shaped
boats, patiently paddled by a man perched on the load, seemed to
move scarcely at all.

Pointed barges or *mahailas* moved slowly, propelled by oar and
sail, while beautiful seagoing *dhows* came sailing gracefully up
the river, like swans from far away, their triangular sails belly-
ing forward in the evening breeze.

On the bank across the river Sarai could see lines of lofty date
palms, and, under their branching tops, cream-colored houses and
inviting gardens. The incessant sound of turtledoves, *oo oo-oo,
oo oo-oo*, made a curtain of sound along the riverfront. Peace —
peace and security — seemed to envelop Ur.

"It was long, long ago," Terah said, "that the first city was built on this island. It was destroyed and rebuilt several times, and it was covered by a great flood. Each time, the city was built up again upon the rubble of its predecessors, so, you see, the streets of the city are now high above the surface of the great river, almost as high as the top of the city wall.

"That is the way with life. We stand upon the backs of our buried fathers. We see a greater distance and we think ourselves safer. Knowledge increases with each generation. But understanding and wisdom? They lag so far behind. I thought to find them once, when I came to this great city."

As they stood together in silence, Sarai heard an eerie sound, a whistling that ended in a long, sustained tremolo. This sound had been familiar to her from childhood. She looked up. A great vulture was wheeling slowly on motionless wings over the city, and beyond him were others coming down from nowhere out of the distant blue.

"At Drehem we would say they smell death," she said.

"Yes," her father replied. "It is the same here, but here it is the men who die."

While Terah and his daughter continued on their way through the city, a pleasure boat was entering the gates of the north harbor, a *bellam* elegant in every detail from the graceful high curve of its prow to the slightly lower curve of its stern. It was propelled by swarthy oarsmen and steered by a boatman who stood on the afterdeck to guide it through the maze of shipping in the busy harbor.

Sweating sailors turned to watch the sleek craft with admiration. There was an awning forward which reflected the light of the setting sun as though threads of gold were woven into it, and under the awning, cushions and rugs.

She slipped smoothly up to a vacant berth at a wharf, where

a tall slave caught hold of her and made her fast. Idlers along the waterfront drew near and stared. One of their number, a squat, black-haired man with a misshapen nose, spoke to the tall slave.

"This looks like the *bellam* of a Sumerian patrician. What's it doing here at this landing?"

The slave did not answer. He was watching the stairway that led up the incline to a large warehouse.

The boatman, barefooted and dressed only in a kilt, jumped lightly onto the dock and was about to run up the stairs when Terah emerged from the warehouse and came down to the boat. He was followed by Sarai, who nodded and smiled at the boatman and slave. When they were comfortably seated in the *bellam*, a handsome man of early middle age came running down the steps and stood on the landing to talk.

The slave moved forward to hold the bow in to the dock, and the man with the broken nose approached him again. "That old man is no Sumerian aristocrat." He grunted. "Looks to me like a Semitic merchant, of the mush-kinu. He might be from Babylon and then again he might come from farther north."

The big slave looked down at him in surprise. "Don't you recognize him?" he said. "That is Terah, the idol merchant. He is the chief of the men of Haran. And his daughter Sarai is with him, and his oldest son Haran. You know who the Habiru are, don't you? They come from Amurru."

The man nodded and grunted again. "I certainly do. I've heard a lot about the Habiru in the city lately and I've heard still more about this son Haran. He manages the merchandise that enters this warehouse, doesn't he?"

The slave did not reply.

"I know he does," the man continued, "and most of it is either coming from Babylon or going to it." He stepped closer to the slave and lowered his voice. "Look here," he growled, "you know as well as I do that we are going to have war with Babylon. Why should Haran be allowed to help the enemy and maybe admit spies into Ur?" A wicked gleam came into the black eyes set so close on either side of the misshapen nose. "I'd like to know where Haran goes every day, just to be sure that he's really not mixed up with spies, you know. If you can help me, there might be a lot of silver in it for you, enough to buy your freedom."

The slave looked down at him strangely and turned away, thinking to himself that he had seen the face of a wild animal stalking its quarry.

"What is your name?" the man said savagely.

The slave scowled and drew himself up. "My name is Habdan. I am an Amorite, and Haran is my friend as well as my master."

The man grunted again and drew away to a little distance where he could watch and listen.

Meanwhile Terah and Haran had carried on a lively conversation regarding the goods expected in the camel station across the river. "It will come across by ferry tomorrow but our warehouse will hardly be large enough to hold it all."

As Sarai gazed idly about the harbor, she became aware of music, the music of harps. It seemed to come from a gracefully pointed barge surmounted by gay awnings, and moving with rows of oars. It was proceeding straight toward them, and now she heard women's voices and laughter. When the luxurious barge was quite close in, it veered away toward the harbor gate and the open river.

On board there were women in elaborate headdresses, cloaks and jewelry, and Sarai realized that one of them was staring at her intently. It seemed to be the gesture of this woman that caused the boat to veer away suddenly.

Terah turned to his startled daughter. "That was the royal barge. I never saw it come in close like that before. The Princess Shub-Kudur and her court ladies are out for a ride on the river."

They made ready to cast off, and Sarai called to Haran: "Remember that Lot expects you at the school of Igmil-Sin tomorrow, one hour before noon."

Haran smiled. "I shall not forget the boy. He will become a man now."

The *bellam* pulled out from the landing and made for the harbor gate. When it was a little way off, there was a commotion among the idlers. Some of them were running along the waterfront abreast of the boat and began to shout: "Habiru, Habiru, Habiru!"

Sarai started up and looked around at them. When she turned back to Terah, her face was flaming. "Why should they call out at us like that?"

"It is the fear of war that has made people suspicious of us. They are afraid that Hammurabi will strike again from Babylon and some few think that because we are not Sumerians we might play them false. It was so in the last war, the same suspicion. That was why I eventually sent you and your mother away. But it is of no importance — put it out of your mind. The suspicion will soon disappear."

An uneasy silence fell upon them. Sarai watched her father furtively. Finally she said: "Was that why you sent word that I should delay my present visit to Ur?"

"Yes," Terah replied. "That was the reason. But why did you not obey me?"

"I came in spite of your message," Sarai said, "because I had news for you. I am a woman but I am your kin, and this was not a message which a stranger should carry. I might have told you last night, but I arrived as Abram was breaking idols in the bazaar. It seemed to me you would be better prepared for the news today."

Terah looked at her as though surprised. When she was silent he turned away from her and after a little time, he said: "Well?

You are going to tell me that my father Nahor is dead?"

"Yes," Sarai replied.

Terah dropped his head in his hands and after a time he asked: "Did he send me his deathbed blessing?"

"No." Sarai was trembling now, for she did not know how her father might take this.

Terah raised his head and looked at her fiercely. "So, the leadership of the Habiru goes to one of my brothers in Haran after all?"

"No," Sarai said, "it goes to Abram."

Terah leaned back on his cushions and drew his breath in through his teeth. "Well, tell me about it."

"Your father Nahor arrived at the farms of Drehem. We had no warning of his coming. The old man had been traveling by camel train for more than a month and he thought to pass right on to Ur. He wanted to see you before he died. But he was weary and weak and so he took to bed on arrival.

"They sent for me that night. Salah was with him and I stood there before them, my two grandfathers. I wanted to run away. I wanted to cry, but I knew Salah would have been ashamed of me." A tear ran down her cheek now and splashed on her breast. But she held her head high, ignoring this sign of weakness. She cleared her throat.

"This is what Nahor said: 'Tell Terah I have waited for his return according to my promise. The Habiru, from Haran to Ur, are waiting — waiting in their tents for a leader. I do not wish my people to be led by a merchant and so my choice falls on Abram!'

"He sent his blessing to Abram. Then he drew his feet up into bed and that night he died. He was buried at Drehem. Salah will keep his camels there until he hears from Abram." Terah made no reply.

"So, my father," she continued after a long silence, "your

daughter returns to you at last. I am sorry she brings bad news."
Terah did not seem to hear.

The boat had passed out of the north harbor and turning to
the right had followed the city wall until it came to the palace
of Rim-Sin. There it turned away from the city and proceeded
upstream. A familiar odor came to them across the water.

"This must be the camel station where I arrived yesterday,"
Sarai said.

"Yes," her father replied quietly.

"I should like to make fast to the shore here," Sarai said. "We
can see Ur from here." Terah shrugged but directed the boatmen to make fast to the bank according to her request.

"Is this the only station?" she continued.

"No. Across the river there is the other camel station. Caravans
may thus approach Ur either on the west or the east side of the
great river. All merchandise is discharged and comes across by
boat. I control this traffic almost completely, with the help of my
son Haran."

Sarai knew how heavy a blow her news had been to Terah
and she was acting now according to her woman's instinct. When
they had made fast she begged to be taken through the caravan
station, and Terah accompanied her in silence. Here the smells
as well as the sights and sounds brought back vivid memories.
Men spoke and bowed to Terah with great respect. The new
caravan had just arrived and a precious cargo was being taken
from the backs of the kneeling camels — gums, spices, precious
metals, rugs and dyes.

They returned to the *bellam* and Sarai chattered about her
childhood. They sent the oarsmen off to get their supper and
made themselves comfortable in the little boat. Sarai opened a
box which Enna had prepared and found dates, cold meat, barley
cakes and wine of pomegranate.

Opposite them, across the muddy surface of the river, the city of Ur rose above its great brown ramparts in distant perspective. The curving lines of houses and the shining temples gleamed white as though made of ivory, and the ivory was washed with gold now in the light of the setting sun.

"Tell me, Father Terah," Sarai said, "about Ur when you first came here as a boy, and about the farms at Drehem. My mother told me what she could. Now I can hear it from your lips. I wish she were here too." Sarai laid her head against his shoulder.

Terah smiled. "Your grandfather Salah has probably told you how I first arrived at his farms years ago, with a little string of camels that my father had given me to take me from the hills of Haran to Drehem. Your mother was not yet born then. I returned to find her years later, after Haran and Abram and Nahor were born here in Ur and their mother had died.

"When I reached Drehem the first time, Salah had just married your grandmother. She was beautiful, like your mother and like you." Terah fell silent. Then he continued: "The journey had taken me two months, and so I sent the camels back and remained some time in Drehem. I was hardly twenty years old.

"Your grandfather was young and energetic. It was not long after the patesi of Nippur, who owned the farms, had changed his name from Karnebo to Salah and had made him a prince. He was full of new ideas and good humor. He showed me his flocks and herds. He took particular pride in the enormous bulls that have always been so popular for sacrifice in Ur and Babylon. Even at that time he was making a very good profit for the patesi.

"One evening, as we sat on the roof top looking out over the rolling meadows, I remember how he urged me to become a herdsman. 'Stay away from Ur,' he said. 'It belongs to Nannar and to the Sumerians. The flocks, the rolling meadows and tents — these are the things that are ours.' My father had talked the same way." He fell silent and heaved a sigh.

"I would listen to no one. I wanted to become an idol craftsman. I dreamt of the idols I should make and the admiration I should have in the eyes of men. Also I intended to get for myself, and for my family, wealth and ease such as my people had never known.

"So, one day, I left Drehem for Nippur. There I hired a little skiff, a *machouf*, and I took the camel boy Magog, whom my father had given me. I put into the *machouf* a little bag containing clay images which I had made in Haran and we paddled down the great river. It was an exciting experience for me.

"I saw for the first time the dikes and irrigation ditches of King Ur-Nammu and fields of wheat and barley and onions and vegetables. At last one morning, above the haze of the shimmering heat, I saw the ziggurat of Ur, and shining on its summit the shrine of Nannar! It was strange the way I saw it first. A mirage mirror hid the rest of the city, but the ziggurat I could see floating high above and I could see it also reflected in the mirror upside down. Both ziggurats seemed to wave and beckon to me.

"As we came closer, there was a fortunate occurrence. I look back on it now as an omen. A large seagoing ship barred our path. It was turning in the river to make a landing, and it had piles of cut stone amidships. As I watched, the sailors rolled the sail up on the boom and passed a rope from the top of the mast to the shore. You have seen them do it many times.

"But it was all new to me. I watched the skipper, standing high up above me on the afterdeck, guiding the boat in with the long tiller. We made our *machouf* fast, and I crawled out onto the landing to see the ship unloaded. I had actually happened upon the delivery of materials for the idol-making workrooms of the temple of Nannar.

"What a strange piece of luck that was. Or was it something else? I have often observed that those who have the will to work are guided to the way of working by some strange spirit. See if you can get a decision as to what god is responsible for that from my learned son Abram." Terah smiled, and Sarai giggled a little with relief.

"There were blocks of black diorite and white marble and sparkling alabaster. There were precious stones such as I had never seen, and lapis lazuli, mother-of-pearl, carnelians, shells. I followed the porters and they led me to the very place I hoped to find, the workshop of idol makers. From the workshop I went into the bazaar where the idols were sold.

"This was what I had come so far to see. I've no idea how long I stood there staring at the rows of gods and goddesses, carved demons, plaques and amulets, all beautifully polished and smooth to the touch. But eventually I was startled by a laugh and someone said: 'Do you like the feel of them my boy?' I turned about, and there was the chief merchant watching me.

" 'Oh,' I said, 'if you will show me how you cut and polish these stones, I will make you better images.'

"There was a shout of laughter at that, and then I realized, for the first time, that the attendants and customers had been watching me also. But I paid no attention to them. The merchant didn't seem to like what I had said, for he proceeded to tell me that there were no workmen in Sumer or Akkad or even in Egypt who could compare with the workmen he had in the workshop of Nannar. 'Do you think,' he said, 'that you can improve on their craftsmanship?'

" 'Yes,' I said, 'I can. Let me show you. Wait for me and I will return.' As I ran off, the shop seemed to echo with laughter. But I made my way down to the *machouf* and before long I came back, carrying my little bag of idols. The white-haired merchant, whom I learned to know so well in later years, was just about to leave the bazaar.

"I was out of breath but I managed to say: 'Here I am, sir.' He looked amazed and tried to push me away. But I pulled out one of my best little images and ran after him. It had very good eyes of shell and was stained with berry juice. I held it up in front of him, and he stopped. Finally, he took it in his hand, his expression changing from annoyance to surprise.

"He returned to the shop without a word, and I followed him wondering. He took an image down from a shelf and replaced it with mine. Then he walked away so as to view it from a distance. All talk had stopped in the bazaar now. There was my little clay idol with its luminous, protruding eyes, the lips about to speak and the arms folded properly over the bulging belly.

"The merchant called to me: 'Tell me, where did you get this image?' — 'I made it, Master.' — 'You made it? Who was your teacher?' — 'I had no teacher, but I watched the craftsmen in the workshop of the moon god at Haran.' The merchant stroked his beard and looked at me doubtfully. 'I wonder if you are telling the truth,' he said, and paused. 'Well, anyway, bring your little bag and follow me.' He led the way through the warerooms and into the workshop behind. Here there was a noise of many bronze hammers chinking against stone, and the grinding and swishing of plates over polished surfaces, making, I thought, a very pleasant music.

"The merchant called a man from his bench and together they examined the idols in my bag. Presently, he said: 'Young man, you said you wanted to learn this craft. Come back here tomorrow and you shall have the chance to learn. I will keep your little images here until then.'

"I drifted off through the streets of Ur with a feeling of great happiness. Soon I found myself in the market place and began to look about me at the throng of people. They pressed upon me, shouting, bargaining, laughing, cursing. They seemed unfriendly, insolent. The awful smells, and the dirt and the poverty sickened me, and so I fled back to the city gate and out on the river where I could breathe pure air again.

"It is hard for a shepherd to learn to like the city; but when I returned to the bazaar in the morning, the merchant set me to work making images. You know the rest of the story well enough. When the idol merchant died, the high priest of Nannar asked me to take charge of the idol market; and eventually, as the demand increased, I enlarged the temple workshop until there was little room left for selling. Then I opened the bazaar of the twelve divinities in the house next to our own. Of course, there were objections from some of the priests at the beginning, and so I left most of the images of the great gods in the temple bazaar.

"But there are many other things in the bazaar of the twelve divinities, and these bring buyers and pilgrims from the whole world. They leave some of their wealth with me in exchange for statuettes to be used as family gods, for amulets, finger rings and bracelets. Soldiers come who want special gods carved on the handles of their weapons. Other young men want their own seals engraved. A wealthy merchant or even a king may want a statuette done in his own likeness so he can keep it in the presence of the god from whom he hopes for favors. They all want something, and the young men buy the small voluptuous female images, thousands of them!"

Terah ceased talking, and Sarai exclaimed: "That is the most exciting story I have ever heard." Then she looked at him keenly and said: "Did this satisfy you?"

"At first, yes," he replied. "Your mother Amtelai understood and she gave meaning to it all. But she was with me so short a time! In later years the thought of my father Nahor's disapproval oppressed me more and more."

The deep-throated song of the bulbul sounded from somewhere on the riverbank, and the air from over the river was cool and fragrant. As they gazed across the water, a procession of priests and priestesses began to move up the central staircase of the ziggurat. When it reached the top, the procession disappeared under the blue dome of the shrine.

Then, in the stillness of the evening, there came to their ears the sound of distant chanting. They could almost distinguish the words of praise to Nannar, words that every Sumerian knew by heart:

> *Who on earth is high exalted?*
> *Lord of Ur, of gods the prince.*
> *Who on earth is high exalted?*

The sky beyond the ziggurat turned red and then purple. Terah stood up to put back the awning. Stars had begun to burn in the blue vault of heaven. But still, as the light faded, they could see white-robed figures passing up and down the great stair. Water slapped and gurgled against the side of the *bellam*.

"It was just here," Terah said, "that I lay in a skiff at the close of my first day in Ur." He was quiet for a time and then continued. "That night the city seemed to me to be enchanted, as it does tonight. I fell asleep watching the evening procession and then I dreamed a strange dream. It has haunted me since then, and even now I sometimes dream it again."

She slipped her hand into his. "Please tell me."

Terah grunted. "I have never told this to anyone except your mother Amtelai. In my dream I saw the steps of the ziggurat soaring upward like a ladder from earth toward heaven. There were priests and priestesses ascending and descending, and I seemed to hear a voice that came down to me from the top of the ziggurat saying: 'I am the God of your father Nahor, the God of the Habiru, and I have overthrown the moon god.' I struggled to climb the steps myself so that I could see who had spoken those words, but something held me back so that I could not lift hand or foot.

"Then I heard music behind me, and I turned and found myself in the workshop of the idol market that I had visited earlier that day, and I realized that the music was made by the ting and tong of tiny hammers that struck upon the sides of a column of humming alabaster. As I watched, the column took the form of the moon god, with bulging eyes and uplifted arms, and I heard a voice that said: 'This is Nannar; I have made him; I am his father.'

"And somehow I recognized that the voice was my own and that I had actually said the words. I tried to step back, but again I could not move. Then I saw that the idol had grown to a great height and was toppling forward onto me. I struggled, but I could not escape and in my anguish I woke up sobbing."

After a pause, Sarai said: "You were Nahor's first-born son. You left him without the blessing that should have been yours, if you were to succeed him in leadership. Do you suppose that was why you wanted to climb those steps to see the God of your fathers? It was Nannar who held you back. But the Habiru throughout the land have believed that you — "

She would have continued, but Terah interrupted her. "Of course they believe I have his blessing. I have never told them anything different, and my father said nothing. He begged me to stay with him but I would not stay. I cared little about his blessing then. Now it is different. I have wealth and position here in Ur. I have chosen to be a Sumerian. How could I go back?

"Nevertheless, I loved my father. It was in order to please him that I organized the camel traffic. Father Nahor sent me hundreds of grazing camels, and I provided armed camelmen. I made them move in caravans so large that they were safe from attack. I perfected a great system of exchange of merchandise. The high priest of Nannar has often told me that Ur has never known my equal as an organizer.

"But when I sent bags filled with shekels of good silver to my father, he returned them to me. They were his due. But he said he had no use for more silver and gold. He seemed to believe that the God of our fathers wished to have the Habiru live by themselves.

"Bah! Why do I go on talking about these things to you? My heart has turned back and forth, back and forth, for so many years. Now decisions are to be made for me. My son Abram, who destroys what I have built! It is for him to lead us. But perhaps . . . after all . . . he may climb the ladder that I could not climb."

Terah stood up suddenly and called to the boatmen who were waiting on the shore: "I want to return to Ur. Take us directly to the landing stage below my house."

They began to cross back over the river, and Sarai, getting to her feet, moved forward until she could hold on to the *bellam's* curving prow. Ferries and pleasure craft were passing swiftly back and forth on the water all about her. Some of the boats were beginning to carry lighted lamps, and on the city walls moving torches cast long lines of shimmering light across the ruffled surface of the river.

But Sarai was oblivious of the night about her. She had seen in the heart of her father so many things that no one else understood — things that even Terah himself perceived but vaguely. She saw his boyish enthusiasm, his vanity and stubbornness, his sorrows, angers, hopes, and his wistful kindness.

She turned back toward him and found that he was standing close behind her.

"I did not know," she said, "that my father was so lonely after we left, Mother and I." She extended her arms and the little man drew her close to him while his tears fell, tears that no one could see — unless, perhaps, the spirit of Amtelai was present and was aware of such things.

CHAPTER IV

Sarai

ON LEAVING his father's idol market, Abram walked as though in a daze through the city and back to his room in the tablet house. Within him the long-pent-up anger that had flared during the breaking of the images continued to burn for a time. Then it died down, to be followed by depression and a feeling of loneliness. He lay on his pallet but his eyes hardly closed that night.

He recalled how pale his father had turned when he saw the destruction of his images. After all, Abram reasoned gloomily, perhaps the only result of his act had been to hurt his father.

To whom had he proved his point, that idols were not to be feared? Not to his father, nor the attendant; surely not to his brother nor the drunken onlooker. To himself? . . . Perhaps. The others were not interested in the proof. But he himself needed that demonstration. How could he be quite certain until he had done it? And he had longed to break something, to revolt in some way.

Smashing the idols had not advanced his own search for something better. Suppose now he were able to destroy or to curse every god in Sumer, what good would it do? What good? What good?

In the morning, he went about his priestly routine with a heavy heart. The evening meal in the refectory came at last. He avoided his fellow priests and sat by himself. Then he took a lighted taper and returned to his room. He lit his oil lamp and threw off his cloak.

There was a little wooden box on his table. Someone must have placed it there during his absence. He opened the top and saw that inside there was a tablet, nothing else, as he suspected. He heaved a heavy sigh and walked back and forth.

Nothing new or interesting ever happened in the priesthood. He was tired of it all. Now that he had finished the king list and the scholarly studies that led up to it, there was nothing left, nothing but anger and disbelief and discontent.

He sniffed the air; could there be a perfume somewhere? He lifted the box and smelled it. "Fresh clay," he said out loud. "But another odor as well." The clay was still soft. That was curious. He lifted the tablet out and examined it attentively.

Cut on its upper surface were the Sumerian words: *I returned home yesterday. I have a message for you. Come.* Signed to the message was the imprint of a cylinder seal. The cylinder had been rolled carefully on the tablet, leaving a clean-cut signature. He was not familiar with the seal and he studied it carefully. On the right there was the figure of a woman in a pleated skirt. She was seated on a chair as though she were someone in authority. She held a rod in her hand, perhaps a shepherd's staff. On the left was a mountain with the sun above it. Between the woman and the mountain were a ram and an ox and another animal. It was a camel walking toward the setting sun!

This was very unusual, for he knew that no Sumerian would allow the figure of a camel to appear in his seal. The seal, therefore, must be that of a member of the Habiru, very few of whom possessed seals. He turned the tablet over and found on its under surface the word *Sarai*. Abram put back his head and laughed. This was something new in the way of tablets! His little half sister! Her grandfather must have given her a seal of her own, and it was probably made up according to her own ideas.

After all, he thought, perhaps I had better obey the summons, for I shall not be able to rest until I have seen my father again. He has a right to be angry with me.

Just then a temple servant appeared in his doorway. "The slave," the servant said, "who brought this little box is waiting for the answer."

"Slave?" said Abram. "What slave? Where does he come from?"

"I do not know where he comes from," the servant replied. "But I have rarely seen a stronger man."

"I know who it is!" Abram cried. "I'll go down with you. Come along. Lead me to him."

As Abram expected, his boyhood friend Oni was waiting for him at the door of the tablet house. They embraced. "What muscles you have developed!" Abram exclaimed, squeezing his arm. Then standing back and holding up his lamp, he added: "And what a beard you have grown!"

The two friends returned to his room, and Abram removed his priestly clothes and washed and shaved. He put on a sleeveless knee-length tunic and placed a belt over it to which he buckled a leather purse and a short sword. He then drew on a fringed mantle which came to his ankles, fastening it over his right shoulder with a long pin to which his own seal was attached.

The seal was his identification, and was regularly carried in this manner by Sumerians for the purpose of signing business or other contracts. Dressed thus, he would not be recognized as a priest, and, this being a festival night, he preferred it so. His shaven head he covered with a turban. He realized that it was somewhat irregular for him to go out in civilian costume, but it was not the first time he had done so.

As they were leaving, the servant reappeared, this time with a message that Princess Shub would like Abram to come to see her libation urns. Abram shrugged with exasperation.

"Come along," he said to Oni. "She has a collection of urns in a little temple next to the tablet house. I'll try to make the visit brief."

The servant had preceded them. When they arrived at their destination, he pulled back a curtain and Abram and Oni found themselves in a low-arched room lighted by hanging lamps. The Princess Shub was sitting on a rug with two ladies in waiting, the same who had accompanied her when she visited Abram two days earlier.

She did not rise. But as Abram approached her, she called out her greeting in a rich, low voice. She extended her hand to him, and Abram noticed a great many rings of gold on her fingers and on her arm.

"I received your summons," Abram said. "Do you need my help to solve some problem?"

"Yes," she replied. "Two problems. One has to do with a broken urn, and the other has to do with — " she hesitated — "a woman in trouble." She paused, and then exclaimed: "But you aren't dressed like a priest at all! Have you grown hair under that turban? You are very handsome when dressed like an ordinary man, even if you haven't a beard."

"I should prefer not to be recognized as a priest on the streets. This is festival night."

"You are more particular," she said, "than the women of the temple. I notice that they prefer such nights and they wear no disguise. Men seem to be in no doubt as to who they are and why they come! These women, especially the younger ones, need a strong hand over them. But after all perhaps they are not to be blamed too much. You take them in when they are young and beautiful. You delight to watch the *sal-me* in their costumes. But you forget that their nature is the same as that of young women everywhere. You are not fair to them."

"I?" Abram exclaimed in surprise.

"Well, it is you and the other priests. There has been no bride of Nannar who could take authority in the temple of Ningal for years now. The *sal-me* need to be disciplined, but they also need to be understood. Suppose I were to become a priestess, I should still be the same woman with the same impulses as now."

She leaned back on the cushions and looked up at him. "You do not follow my meaning. You, the great scholar who knows all about the past; you who think about gods. You do not see into the hearts of the men and women about you."

Abram looked at her in surprise, but he did not reply.

"What led you to become a priest in the first place? Curiosity about the mysteries of the gods? Hope for a better life?" Abram stared but found no words. "But you are still a man. Did you ever stop to wonder why young women become priestesses? Some are only escaping from a life that is worse, it is true. But many of them also seek to serve the god sincerely, at least at the outset."

She looked about her. "Berri, where are you?" Then she discovered her diminutive handmaid at a little distance, gazing up at Oni. "Oh, there you are. Be careful. Don't use those black eyes of yours too effectively. Just take him to the other side of the room there and show him the recent pottery collection." She turned back to Abram and laughed. "Your father's slave, I suppose?"

"Yes," Abram replied, "and my friend."

She motioned him to sit down beside her. As he did so he became aware of a very pleasant perfume. She picked up an urn that stood in front of her and leaned toward him.

"What is this?" Abram took it in his hands. "Graceful shape," he mused, "and the greenish-white pottery with figures painted black seems to give the period approximately."

"Yes," she interrupted, "I have had pottery from the marsh natives that is like it, black figures with crosses."

Abram shook his head. "No, it is not the same. Let us compare this with your other green urns."

They talked and argued, moving about the collection until Abram said finally, "I must go now."

"Must you?" she exclaimed.

Abram looked at her as though startled. "Why yes. I have answered your questions as well as I could."

"Oni," Abram called, "we must go now."

"I saw your father today," the princess said, "and your brother Haran. He is handsome."

"But Haran is not in Ur," Abram objected.

She laughed. "You are wrong. He returned today. I have a little Habiru maid. She was with me today when my barge passed Haran's warehouse. He was standing on the waterside. But tell me who the beautiful blonde woman was with your father in his *bellam?*"

Abram shook his head in surprise, but Oni, behind him, said: "The Lady Sarai was with your father in the boat."

"And who is Sarai?"

"Sarai is only my little sister," Abram replied. "Good night and good rest to you."

Outside the moon had risen, and the friends made their way quickly through the crowded streets to the house of Terah.

When the door opened, Abram threw off his outer garment and bounded up the two flights of stairs to the roof. Here, as he expected, he found his father sitting quietly.

The old man's hair and beard looked white in the moonlight. Abram recalled another moonlit night years ago when they had sat there together and Terah had opened his heart to him, talking about his own past and his hopes for the future. That was the night before he was to be admitted to the temple of Nannar to be trained as a priest. He remembered also, with a pang, that his stepmother Amtelai had sat silently on the rugs behind them. It must have been shortly before she left Ur, forever.

Abram knelt down now before his father and asked what he could do to lessen his anger. Terah shrugged. "There is no place for anger between you and me," he said, "even if you do destroy what I create. I understand your stormy nature, my son. Your life will never be tranquil. But the time has come when you must cast off this bitterness and resentment. You and I do not think alike. I am growing old, but you are young and strong. You must build up something for yourself. It is not enough to over-throw the work of others. When you curse the gods of Sumer, you remedy nothing, and it may bring trouble to us all. Indeed it will bring great danger.

"But tonight I do not want to discuss these matters. Do you remember what your stepmother Amtelai said to us here on this roof top? It was just before she left us and I think of her words often. 'Wisdom,' she said, 'may come to merchant and prophet, but understanding is born in a woman's heart.' When you are older, you will learn to consult some woman when you are in need of understanding.

"Sarai is waiting to see you in the room that was her mother's. No one has occupied that room since Amtelai left me. All this time I have tasted loneliness, day after day and night after night." He turned and looked behind him. "Strange as it may seem, since Sarai returned yesterday, I have felt the presence of Amtelai, as on the night when she sat behind us here listening to our talk. Do you remember? She seems to be here with me tonight. Go now."

Abram passed down the stairs and around the gallery to the doorway of the room that was once Amtelai's. How well he remembered it!

"May I come in?" he called.

Naamah came to the door and pulled back the curtain. The

room was well lighted, and as he stepped in, he said: "Well, my little playmate, I come, in answer to your summons." But he stopped short, for he saw a woman, not a child; a woman so like her mother that for a moment he felt he was seeing an apparition. The same fair hair and way of standing, the same gesture as she welcomed him.

They walked into the family room and were soon joined there by Oni and Milcah. Hearing the talk and laughter, Nahor entered after a little while. He hoped secretly to turn the conversation to the subject of the breaking of the images, for Abram's brother was a man to cherish a grudge. He tried twice to change the subject of talk to the idol market but Sarai interrupted him, and he knew from old experience that he was not quick enough to cope with her banter and talk.

Finally Abram said he must go.

"No," Sarai said, jumping up. "First you must take me for a walk through the streets of Ur."

"This is festival night," he replied, "and you are too young."

"I am no longer a child, and my maid Naamah will follow us." She ignored his refusal calmly and, putting on her cloak, prepared to go out.

"It is safer for her at night," said Oni, laughing. "In the daytime she needs me to protect her rather than Naamah. We entered the city yesterday afternoon like conquerors. In the great square there was a crowd of young men, and someone shouted in a very rude manner: 'Here comes beauty from the desert!' A procession followed us and one fellow even tried to enter the house with us."

"Yes," said Abram, "he accosted me to ask her name. But he was drunk."

At this, Sarai tossed her head and flashed out at him: "Drunk indeed! It is easy to see you have spent your time in the temple and not at court all these years, for your tongue is as blunt as a shepherd's staff. Perhaps you might get Lot to teach you flattery."

Outside in the moonlight, the walls of the houses gleamed like mother-of-pearl, and the crooked lanes turned back and forth from bright light to deep shadow. Sarai touched Abram's arm as they walked. "Ur was very beautiful as our camels approached it," she said. "From a long way off it rose up out of the plain, the red-brown ziggurat, the white temples and buildings with red and blue awnings and banners on the roof tops.

"When we left our camels and crossed the water on the ferry, I was bewildered by the boats — big and little. They crowded the river. The workmen were singing as they rowed home, men and women in the pleasure boats laughing and playing harps. We came quite close to them, and I could see the women — such curls on their wigs, so much paint on their faces, and the men's cloaks so rich! This afternoon I saw the royal barge, with the court ladies in it. Ur seems to me a much gayer city than Babylon. I am glad to be here and to see you again."

Abram was silent, so she continued: "Did you know that I saw you in the shop of the twelve divinities yesterday? I also watched you from the roof top when you met Unzie son of Gudea and his servant." She giggled a little. "I wanted to call you back then, but, as you know, that would have been very difficult. It was because I must talk to you that I sent the writing. Were you surprised that a woman should write? Tell me, why did you break Father Terah's idols? You did not seem yourself."

Abram began to talk, at first as though to a child, but soon the quick sympathy and the understanding of his companion loosed his tongue, and there came a flood of discourse about the problems that had weighed upon him. This was for him a new experience, something of which he had felt the need without understanding why, and he became a little excited.

As they passed through a square, a group of soldiers burst out of a brothel singing. He drew her out of the moonlight into the shadow of a cypress tree. Women brushed past them with bracelets and ankle rings jingling gaily. Their giggling and laughter seemed to spell invitation to the soldiers, for they turned and followed them down the street.

"Those were temple women," he said. "When I was a boy about to enter the temple school, your mother Amtelai told me about them, but I was too young to understand. Later, I remembered her warning. I used to think often of your mother while I was in the temple school; I even saw her in my dreaming. Then when I began to visit Drehem before entering the priesthood, we had many talks. But you seemed to me in those days as much like a boy as you did a girl. In any case, you were much too young for my notice. Now, you are so much like your mother that you almost seem to be the woman I remember. Tell me about your life with her. Amtelai was killed in the fields by a bull, I know that. But tell me about it, for I loved her."

Sarai nodded her head and said: "She died on the very day before we were to have returned to Ur and to Father Terah. I remember that she was very happy that day. Prince Salah had given her a beautiful cloak to match her hair. It was his parting present. She thought it would please him if she wore it when we went to meet him at the shrine of Pa-Sag. It shone red-gold in the sun as she rode across the plain, and I followed her, riding on a small ass.

"Then I remember hearing the herdsmen scream: 'Take off the cloak!' But it was too late. Suddenly right before my eyes I saw the bull charging. He came bounding so swiftly, so silently past me, horns low, eyes red, straight for her. There was a dreadful thud. The ass she was riding rose in the air with her. Then the bull wheeled and —" Sarai's voice broke and she drew near to him. "I have tried to forget, but the picture returns in my dreams and I cannot."

They were silent for a time. Then she smiled and continued:

"That evening I remember walking across the common with my grandfather Salah, and we sat together as the sun set and the stars came out. He told me old tales of the land, and about the little gods who live in the plains and in the wadis of Drehem. He said the little gods loved my mother and wanted her to stay on with them where she had been happy. He said she would always be near us there, though we could not see her. And so, when he told me that I was to live on with him, and not to go to Ur, it seemed quite right to me that he and I should remain there where we could be near my mother.

"Somehow he took away my feeling of horror about her death. After that he saw to it that I was taught many things, and that Naamah my handmaid should speak Egyptian with me. I called him Father Salah, instead of Grandfather, and sometimes I went on trips with him. Once we lived in Babylon for a time. Now I am glad to see Ur and to be in my own father's house where I was born."

Abram did not reply, so she went on: "Abram, did you know that my mother used to call you Little Enoch? She said that some day you would walk with God the way Enoch did." Sarai looked up at him. "She would have to call you Big Enoch, if she could see you now. But I believe that it will be as she said."

Abram breathed deeply and looked down at Sarai. A breeze stirred the hair about her face and whispered in the acacias overhead. A long silence fell between them as they looked out over the river below. Boats passed, and sounds drifted up to them from the sparkling smooth flood.

Then she said: "There is a mysterious feeling that comes to me in the moonlight, and I love it. I love the perfume of this flowering shrub. I love being home."

Abram seemed lost in his own thoughts. Finally he spoke: "Tonight seems to have brought me a strange peace of mind. It is not the moonlight, nor the scent of the acacia. It must be you. No one has understood me since your mother left and I entered the priesthood. Why have you stayed away so long?"

They sauntered back together through the moonlit streets toward Terah's house, Naamah following them at a respectful distance. All too soon it seemed, they stood before Terah's house and Sarai turned to him.

"I had a message to give you," she said, "a most important message. That was the reason I sent for you. That was why I asked you to walk with me. But tonight was so beautiful. It seemed to have been meant for something else." She smiled at him and touched his arm lightly. "Come to see me soon again and I will deliver the message. Now, good night."

The great door swung open, allowing the two women to disappear into the house, and then closed again, leaving Abram motionless in the street.

Why, indeed, he mused, had she remained so long away? Life might have been quite different for him these last few years if he could have talked with her. Why should Sarai affect him this way? Had she merely reminded him of her mother? Was it only that? Or was Sarai herself really different from all other women?

Curiously enough, as he made his way back to the temenos he gave no thought to the message she was bringing. Instead he wondered what could be the cause of the excitement that he felt, and the strange sensation in his chest.

❖❲❲

CHAPTER V

Death to the Camelmen

ON THE FOLLOWING DAY the sun burned down into the court-yard of a boy's school, the most select in the city of Ur. The teacher was pacing restlessly back and forth across the court and into the cool shadow of the open classroom. It was obvious to his pupils that he was expecting someone. He had not yet removed his sandals, although his cloak and turban were off.

The whole house resounded to the treble chorus of the class which sat cross-legged on the floor repeating aloud the lesson of the day. The repetition was not in unison. Each scholar was hold-ing in his hand a lump of clay which he had rolled and flattened on one surface by pressing it against the mixing board. On the flat surface he had copied with a bamboo stylus the day's lesson, and now he was committing it to memory, trusting in the vigor of his own voice to protect him from the general din.

The year's work had been exacting. There was a large body of knowledge for these boys to master. They must learn to write in ancient Sumerian, since legal documents were always written in that tongue, although the spoken language had come to be largely Babylonian. Then, too, they must study a wide variety of subjects, for the Sumerian people could boast of great intellectual achieve-ments during the twenty to thirty centuries of their cultural evolution.

Lot sat silent. He seemed to have forgotten his task, and there was a faraway expression in his prominent dark eyes. He was a little older than most of the boys, and his arms and legs were longer and thinner. But, aside from that, it was in the cut of his features and the form of his body that he differed from the thick-set, blackheaded Sumerian lads about him. He was popular with his schoolmates because of his great good humor.

The boys had various ambitions — some to be scribes, others lawyers, professional soldiers, merchants, priests. They knew that on this, the last day of school, they would be examined by a senior priest from the temple of the moon god.

At last the heavy wooden street door opened and closed, and the sound it made could be heard through the house. A hush fell upon the classroom. All eyes were turned toward the curtains of the vestibule, and Igmil-Sin, the teacher, hurried across the court and disappeared into the vestibule. The boys could hear talking and the sound of water being poured out for the wash-ing of feet.

Then the curtains parted, and the examining priest appeared. He was a rather paunchy, sleek person, his head shaven in priestly fashion so that it shone in the sunlight. For a time he laughed and talked in lowered tones with Igmil-Sin. Finally he turned to the business of the day, the examination of the pupils.

The teacher produced from his locker the tablets which had been prepared by his best pupils at different times during the year. The clay had hardened so that the writing, which at first glance might seem to resemble the tracks of tiny birds in the mud, was preserved in an indestructible form upon the surface of the tablet. These tablets were inspected and marked for legi-bility, form and content.

Each boy was then requested to carry out problems in addi-tion, subtraction, multiplication and division. They were asked to conjugate difficult Sumerian verbs. Then, while they worked on fresh clay tablets, the examining priest walked back and forth behind them, occasionally stooping to erase faulty answers with a sweep of his thumb across the surface of the clay.

Presently a fat boy who was sitting next to Lot began to weep over an apparently insoluble problem which had beset him. Tears streamed upon his tablet, muddying its surface. Lot reached over and took the tablet from the boy, blotting it on his own tunic to restore the clay to workable consistency.

Observing the difficulty, the examiner chuckled and remarked to Igmil-Sin that it looked like the flood. Then he said: "Stand up, fat boy, and tell me the story of the good man Uta-Napishtim." Stifling his sobs, the boy rose and, after he had pressed a clay-smeared fist against each eye, launched forth in a quavering treble on the well-memorized legend:

"Once upon a time the gods gathered together because they were very angry about the way men were behaving. After much talk they decided secretly to drown every one of them. But the god Enki did not keep the secret. Instead, he thought he would warn the good man Uta-Napishtim, who dwelt in the village of Shuruppak on the great river. But Enki took care not to tell the good man directly for fear of the anger of the other gods. Instead, he whispered to the good man's hut:

" '*Reed hut, reed hut, wall, O wall,*
O reed hut, hear, O wall, understand.'

"And Uta-Napishtim, hearing the message, built a boat and loaded into it all the harvest of life, the beasts and the herbs and also his own family. And when the young dawn came, a black cloud arose. Adad roared in it, and Nabu, Nergal and Inurta marched with it.

"For six days and nights it rained and stormed, until the gods themselves could not see each other for the darkness, and they fled and climbed into the high heaven of Anu.

"When the seventh day came, the hurricane abated, the sea was still, and all mankind was buried in mud. But the boat of Uta-Napishtim floated upon the surface of the water. And it came to an island and it was Mount Nitsir. So the good man sent forth a dove, but it came back. He sent forth a swallow, but it returned, for there was no place to rest. He sent forth a crow, and behold, the waters had receded and it did not return.

"And Uta-Nipishtim left his ship on the top of the mountain and made a sacrifice to the gods. Now the gods had grown hungry for the lack of sacrifice during the time that the temples were under the water, and so when they scented the sweet savor, like flies they gathered above the sacrifice.

"After that, they decided never to destroy mankind again."

The fat boy came to the end of the recitation. He had done well and his teacher nodded approvingly. He sat down, and there was silence for a time. The teacher and priest talked together in low tones.

Finally the teacher called out: "Lot son of Haran."

Lot rose to his feet and waited; his hands began to sweat and his mouth became dry.

"Lot," the teacher said, "the examining priest would like to hear you recite the full chant of Ningal."

A whispering went around the schoolroom, for this was considered difficult. But Lot's memory was very good, although his work with the tablets had not always been above reproach. He had often watched with fascination the march of the priestesses in their procession to the temple of Ningal and listened to their chanting. He probably did not know himself whether it was the beauty of the *sal-me* or their singing that interested him most. In any case he intoned the full hymn from beginning to end.

When he had finished, the priest smiled and said: "Well done, my boy. Your kinsman Abram will be pleased to hear of this."

At last the examining was over and the appointed hour arrived. The hour when each pupil had a feeling of self-importance and achievement because his work was to be reported to his parents.

Members of the pupils' families were ushered into the court. It was a fashionable company, fathers or brothers in court costume or military uniform. Some mothers were there, with sleek, well-groomed hair and luxurious cloaks; matrons of dignity who were, it was clear to be seen, quite conscious of the respect that was due them in public.

Lot was delighted when he saw his father enter. Haran was tall, handsome and extremely successful as a merchant, and the son often thought he would like to follow in his footsteps, although his great admiration for his uncle Abram made him feel at times that he too might enter the priesthood.

When the time came for father and son to take their departure, the teacher asked them to remain, as he wished to have a private conversation with them. After the others were gone Igmil-Sin introduced Haran to the examining priest.

"I have had two excellent dinners in the house of Haran," the teacher said. "I wish there had been more." He winked at the priest and smacked his lips. "A poor teacher would have a thin life indeed without such hospitality."

Haran and the priest smiled. Then the latter said: "Your son Lot has done well enough. If he would like to enter the priesthood there will be a place for him in the temple of Nannar."

Haran looked at him in surprise. "I had expected my son to be a merchant like myself."

They turned to Lot, who was listening with surprise and delight. "If I enter the priesthood," he exclaimed, "is it possible that I may become high priest and make the sacrifice on the altar when the *sal-me* climb the ziggurat?"

The priest laughed ironically. "No man of the Habiru people, and no other Amorite for that matter, has risen any higher in the priesthood than your kinsman Abram. The high priest, Enan-natum, seems to be in good health, very good health. He is vigor-ous enough to collect all the taxes for the king. This leaves him very little time to make burnt offerings on the altar of Nannar, but still, I don't think he wants a camel boy as his substitute, at least not right away."

He laughed loudly at his own witticism, and Haran, who seemed to see no humor in these remarks, said sharply: "You misinterpret the boy's enthusiasm."

The priest stopped laughing and turned to Haran. "Perhaps you are right," he said. "It is obvious that this son of yours has a good mind. I think he could become a scholar, and Enan-natum has a special need for such men. As you probably know, there is great activity in the tablet archives of the temple at the present time.

"I don't have to tell you, though, that many in Ur look with dislike on your people. However, the high priest is not of that way of thinking, although some of the rest of us are. He seems to look on your brother Abram with favor, and he tells me he would like another one of the Habiru in the priesthood. You ought to realize that this is a great honor for the son of a middle-class mer-chant." The priest turned away. Then, as Haran remained haughty and silent, he turned back and continued:

"Semites have come to high position in Babylon. Take as an example King Hammurabi himself. He is a Semite, although not of your group. Our king, Rim-Sin, is also an outsider, of course. But there are very few outsiders in the priesthood of the moon god. We are pure-blooded Sumerians."

The examining priest had made this declaration with some show of pride. Haran smiled and said: "Our people, who live in the hills of the north, are herdsmen and proud of it. I am named for the city of Haran, which is not far from the headwaters of the great river. As you know, that city takes Nannar as its principal god, just as Ur does. When my grandfather Nahor is not following his flocks, he pays tribute and makes sacrifice to the moon god in that city, just as we do here."

The priest shrugged. "We have no prejudice against the herders of sheep and cattle; provided, of course, that they live in their pastures and do not try to become merchants in a city of culture like Ur.

"But the camel is a strange and ugly beast." He spread his hands out and gave a grunt of disgust. "Camels were unknown in Sumer and Akkad until recent years when your people appeared, riding in on them out of the desert. Our farmers are afraid of them, for they bring bad luck to the land. We do not own camels; we will not ride on camels when we can avoid it, and we dislike anyone who has anything to do with camels.

"However, those in the high places of the temple may overlook the fact that this boy's people are camel drivers. I suppose you, who have come in so recently from the desert, can hardly understand why we in Ur despise the camelmen." His lip curled in contempt. "Your father Terah is an idol merchant. Some people do not like him. Perhaps they are a little jealous of his success and his great wealth. But you, Haran, were born here, as I understand it, and although you manage the camel trade with such profit, you have lost the smell of the camel — almost."

Haran had flushed with resentment during this unexpected tirade and was about to reply when he was interrupted by a soldier dressed in the kilt of the royal Sumerian guard. The man had entered unobserved and stood waiting with obvious impatience for an opportunity to speak.

He broke in now rather unceremoniously: "Greetings. I am looking for Haran son of Terah. If you are Haran, I beg to inform you that a messenger has come to you from Hammurabi king of Babylon. He is waiting for you now in your place of business near the north harbor. Please go there at once."

Haran looked at him in astonishment and was about to demand an explanation; but the soldier held up his hand in salute and, turning on his heel, left the house abruptly.

"Hammurabi!" exclaimed the priest. "Most people think he is an enemy of Ur."

Lot saw that his father was angry now. He stood straight and spoke slowly and distinctly.

"I have no dealings with Hammurabi. Perhaps at another time you and I will have the opportunity to discuss this matter further. But let me tell you now that my people, the Habiru, are very different from the Semites of Babylon. Furthermore, there is culture in the land of Amurru from which our people came, as well as in Sumer. However, we have chosen to become citizens of Ur and we are as loyal to our ruler as you are."

Father and son took their leave. In the street they paused, and Haran placed his hand on Lot's shoulder and looked at him with a smile. "You have done well, boy. You are a man now, and I am proud of you. I do not want you to become a priest. I think it would be better for you to become a merchant like your father; or, if not that, then I would have you return to the hills where Grandfather Nahor lives and lead the life of a shepherd."

Then Haran frowned and turned away. "I am puzzled that this soldier — he was a rude fellow — should bring me such a message instead of one of my own bondsmen. In any case, why should Hammurabi send me any message at all? I have had no dealings with him."

"I will follow you," said Lot, "and wait for you, so that we can go home together. But first I must get my stylus and the best tablets to show to Father Terah."

Haran hurried off, and the boy remained standing where he was for a little time, oblivious of passers-by. His eyes followed Haran as he proceeded down the narrow street until he had turned a corner and passed out of sight.

Then he realized with surprise that the soldier who had brought the message about Hammurabi had stepped out of a doorway and followed after Haran, down the street and around the same corner. For a moment Lot stood irresolute. Could the man mean some harm to his father? He ran down the street and turned the corner, hoping to catch up with Haran. But when he arrived there, neither Haran nor the soldier were anywhere to be seen. After all, he thought, why should anyone want to do his father harm?

Nevertheless, he returned to the school with an uneasy feeling. Here he was delayed for a time by Igmil-Sin, who wanted to talk. The teacher also showed him the handsome present which Haran had left as an added reward for his years of teaching. Igmil-Sin then waxed eloquent over many things, but especially about the vanity of the priests of Nannar and the courtesy and generosity of Haran.

Lot finally managed to escape and set off in haste to follow his father. The streets through which he passed were narrow and crooked. There were fewer pedestrians than usual, as it was high noon, and he threaded his way past donkeys and workmen returning home. He followed bystreets at first, but as he emerged into a main thoroughfare he heard a great shouting and clattering of hoofs. He jumped into a doorway just in time to let a chariot rush past, pulled by galloping asses. It was unusual to see chariots in the city. There was a soldier in this one fully armed, and spears ready in the chariot's quiver.

He knew that this must mean trouble somewhere. As the asses were galloping in the direction he was taking, he followed at a run in the wake of the chariot. It led him directly to a little square in front of Haran's business house. Here he found a great turmoil and many people shouting. He stood still in amazement. In the hubbub he could hear cries of: "Death to the desert people! Drive out the spies of Babylon!" Then he saw that Elamite police with spears in their hands were forcing a mob away from the space in front of Haran's agency.

He ran across the square and was approaching the door of the agency when an ugly little man with a large misshapen nose stepped in front of him barring his path. "Who are you," he said, "another of the Habiru?" Lot pushed him aside and pounded on the door but the little man seized one of his hands in a powerful grasp and began to drag him away, shouting: "Here's another one of them — Habiru! Habiru!"

But the door had opened and Haran's slave Habdan appeared. With a shout he threw himself upon the little man, bearing him to the ground. Then he picked the man up again and hurled him like a sack of grain out into the square.

"Come in, Lot, quick." Habdan slammed the door behind them and barred it.

"What has happened?" Lot cried. "What has happened?" He looked at Habdan.

The slave moved his mouth but made no sound. Lot pushed him aside and ran past him and on into the central court of the house. An awful fear seemed to clutch his throat. He called aloud: "Haran, Haran, Haran, Father Haran!" There was no answer.

He crossed the court and stood in the doorway of Haran's room. There inside the room a body lay sprawled across a low table in an ugly attitude. Blood dripped from the table into a dark red pool on the floor. From the square he could hear the distant shouting: "Kill the desert men! Drive out the spies of Babylon!"

Lot stood still, shuddering. "Haran, my father, my father!" Finally he turned around and found that Habdan was standing at his elbow. "Who has done this?" Lot asked.

The slave shook his head. "I only know," he said, "that I was here with the old scribe. We closed the curtains of the doorway

but not the door, as was our custom. We were taking a noonday
sleep and I waked to hear a voice, Haran's voice, calling for help.
I rushed to this room just in time to see a man run out. He
covered his face so I could not see it. I heard men shouting outside in the square and they would have come into the house,
but we closed the door against them and then the police arrived
and drove them off."

When Habdan had finished Lot spoke as though he had not
heard him. "Why have they killed my father — why, why?"

The old scribe raised his voice in loud lamentation, but Lot
turned and walked into the center of the court and stood there
without another word.

After a time the shouting in the square quieted down, and a
sergeant of the Elamite police entered.

Lot demanded of him: "Who killed my father?"

The officer was a burly fellow from the mountains of Elam.
Like many of the police in Ur, he had been brought there to
keep order when Rim-Sin, the king of Larsa, had conquered Ur
with his Elamite followers, twenty years earlier.

Lot repeated his question: "Who killed my father?" The sergeant, ignoring the questioner, had entered the room where Haran
lay, but he returned now.

"If you mean the man lying dead in there, I don't know who
did it. They tell me the dead man is Haran son of Terah. Too
bad! I don't know who killed him. It must have been one of those
blackheaded Sumerians out there, but we will never be able to
pick out the murderer now."

He turned his slow gaze more carefully on Lot. "Who are
you?"

"I am Haran's son and I want to go to the house of my grandfather Terah at once to tell him about this."

"You can't do that," replied the sergeant. "I can't let you out
into any of the main thoroughfares. Someone might know who

you are. I don't want any more trouble. We Elamites have a hard enough time keeping the peace for the king without making unnecessary trouble."

"No one will know that I belong to the Habiru," Lot cried, his voice breaking, "and if they do I don't care." He started for the door.

"Wait a minute, wait a minute," and the sergeant held out a large hand to bar his way. "You're half boy, half man, but I'd know you were not a Sumerian. You look different." He put his head on one side, holding Lot at arm's length and appealing to the old scribe for corroboration. "You see, he is different from one of them blackheads. His nose is curved at the bottom like a fishhook. That's the Habiru nose. The Sumerian noses, now, they are cut square. He might be taken for an upper-class Babylonian, of course, or even an Elamite, but no one would ever think he was a Sumerian."

Tears stood in Lot's eyes and his voice broke from a defiant bass bellow to a treble cry. "I'm going home to Father Terah. Get out of my way." He made a rush past the Elamite, but the street door was bolted.

They dragged him back while Habdan reasoned with him. "Wait, Lot. Be patient. Terah knows about this. The police have taken word to him. You go down to the north harbor and wait at our warehouse. The barge loaded with goods from the camel station will be arriving at the dock soon and I'll come down when I can leave here and I will take you around the city in a skiff, all the way to Terah's house."

The Elamite nodded his assent. "That's it. Wait here a little while till this crowd is gone. Then you may go down to the river."

Lot passed out a narrow alleyway into a street that led in the direction of the north harbor. There was a lump in his throat, and when anyone looked at him he held his breath for fear a cry like the one he had heard in the square would be raised. He must look different, he thought; the Elamite policeman had said so. If only he had been with Haran he could have fought for him, and together they would have killed all who stood in their path! Fancies of combat danced through his mind.

He entered a narrow street that led down to the water's edge. It was roofed over to keep off the sun, and the walls on either side were lined with booths filled to overflowing with things to be sold. Customers and merchants argued, gesticulated, laughed nd shouted. Donkeys came and went, carrying burdens so large hat only the quick-moving little feet indicated the nature of the beast beneath.

He paused before a brazier of coals and watched slabs of meat on a spit turning slowly. Each piece of meat was separated from the next by a chunk of red vegetable, and there was an appetizing spitting and chuckling sound which caused his mouth to water. A hot sensation in his stomach reminded him that it was long past mealtime. As he watched hungrily, he was startled to see a fat face rise up from the booth behind the spit.

The face leered at him and a harsh voice cried: "Sit down, boy. Don't stare and bulge your eyes as though you could eat my roast that way. You look as though you thought you were the great god Nannar and could take in a burnt offering just by looking at it and smelling it." He gave vent to a belly laugh. "Sit down, boy, sit down."

Lot recoiled and then hurried on without a word. Why should the keeper of this stall be so insulting, he wondered. Presently, as he continued on his way, a sunburned little peddler passed him, balancing on his head a tray heaped high with crisp brown cakes. Fresh baked they were, and as they came close to his nose the aroma put an end for the moment to other thoughts and emotions. He reached into his wallet and found enough barley to buy a cake.

Passers-by jostled him as he continued on his way. They seemed hostile and unfriendly. A woman of the temple brushed against him as she passed, and he was aware of a heavy perfume and the tinkling sound of ankle rings. He looked at her olive cheek, the golden circlet that crossed her forehead, and noticed that her eyebrows were plucked so as to arch strangely. Aware of his scrutiny, she turned and gazed into his eyes in a way that startled him. He broke into a run, and the woman laughed loudly.

Finally, at the harbor's edge he emerged from the covered passageway into the dazzling sunlight. Here he was forced to stand aside while a line of slaves climbed up from the edge of the water, bearing heavy loads of merchandise on their backs. Magnificent dark-colored fellows they were, slaves from some conquest. Lot watched their muscles ripple in the hot sun. Beads of sweat came from under their carrying pads and rolled across their shining backs to fall on the dusty surface of the hot roadway, making dark spots there.

These slaves, he mused, had had their sorrows too. In all probability they had been carried away from their homes. Perhaps their families were killed, stabbed to death like Haran. They must have had a very weak god to defend them. What his own people needed was a stronger god.

Perhaps he could get Abram to talk with him about that sometime. Now that Haran was gone, probably no one would listen to him except Abram. Terah was always too busy and Nahor cared about no one but himself.

He walked along the waterfront of the harbor until he reached the landing before his father's warehouse. Here he climbed the steps and tried the door. It was barred. He pounded on the door. No answer. So he dropped to his knees and put his mouth to the opening beneath the great door. He heard his voice resounding within the empty shed. "Open the door. I am Lot, Haran's son. Open the door."

But all was silence, and he lay in a disconsolate heap on the cold pavement. Loneliness enveloped him and a strange tightness seemed to grip his throat.

From where he lay he could see the harbor and above it the red hill, the ziggurat, rising out of the walls of the temenos and at its top the blue dome of the shrine of Nannar. Perhaps Abram was up there, Abram who loved his brother Haran so well.

He put his hands over his eyes and shivered with cold. He seemed to hear Haran's voice calling to him, calling for help. Habdan must have heard him call like that. He could see the body lying over the table and blood dripping on the floor.

Slow sobs shook him. He pressed his face against the door, and so he slept, slipping away into a land of strange dreams.

Some time later he awakened, slowly at first. He was being shaken and he heard a voice cry: "Get up! Get out of the way!" He scrambled to his feet in terror. The man who was standing over him laughed at his sudden panic. "You are in our way," he explained. "We have work to do here."

Then Lot realized that this workman was speaking with the accent of his own people. He rubbed his eyes and, looking about, he saw at the dockside below him a heavily loaded boat, a *mahaila*. There were men carrying up rolls of merchandise, sunburned men wearing the familiar turban and the handsome hood of the desert, his own people! Men of Haran! Camelmen!

◆《◇《

CHAPTER VI

The Hills of Haran

ABOUT NOON of the following day, Abram turned into the street that led to his father's house. The murder of Haran and the sudden outcry against the camelmen had come as a shock to him. All morning he had been lost in thought. Now he began to see the neighborhood as though for the first time. Arriving at his destination, he mounted the step and pounded on the door, then stood and looked about.

He saw the street, blazing white in the noonday sun, the awnings on the house tops, the cistern at the street corner, the shimmering of heat waves from the pavement. A young woman passed carrying a tall clay vessel of water upon her head, her body swaying gracefully. An old cripple, sitting on the bench across the way, held out a gnarled hand for alms.

His reverie was interrupted by a grating sound as a heavy bolt was drawn back and the door was opened by an aged slave. Abram remained standing in the dimly lighted vestibule, still in reflective mood. He was aware of an unwonted hush in the house. He heard the receding steps of the servant as he passed into the service rooms and then all was silent. In the half-light he looked at the panels of gods and demons on the white walls of the vestibule and stared at the small image of Nannar in the niche.

He felt an impulse to talk to Sarai so he removed his sandals and, pouring a little water into a depression in the floor, washed his feet. He dried them and pulled out the drain stopper so that the water could seep down into the earth. Then he pulled back the heavy tapestry and stepped through the arch into the large central courtyard.

The sun was pouring down on the flagged floor, except where the gallery, running around the court's well, cast its grateful shadow. He placed his hand on the cold, wet side of the great clay water jug that was suspended in the shadow. Drops were running down its sweating side and falling with a familiar musical sound from its tapered bottom into the glazed pot below — *plop, plop, plop.* How often he had heard that unending sound as a boy. He dipped a silver goblet into the pot and drank. The water was cool and good.

He walked down the court toward the flight of stairs at its end. He ran up, two steps at a time. His heels thudded along the gallery. But the family rooms were empty and no one replied to his calling.

Returning to the gallery he ran up the narrow stair to the flat roof; no one there. He walked toward the back of the house and looked down at the canal. Boats were passing. A pigeon whirred suddenly overhead and startled him. He turned then, and going to the edge of the wall looked down into the court again.

"Of course," he exclaimed aloud, "the family are already in the chapel, prepared for Haran's death ceremony. It must be later than I thought."

The chapel consisted of a walled court open to the sky on the side of the house away from the idol market. When Abram pushed the gate open he found that the members of the family and the principal servants had already assembled and were kneeling on the brick floor. Abram knelt down near the door beside Oni.

At the far end of the enclosure there was a raised terrace with an altar upon it, and above the altar a roof on a series of delicate arches. On the terrace before the altar stood Terah, dressed in the sacrificial robes of the family.

In Sumer every family of any standing had a special god of its own, and at times like this it was the head of the family who acted as priest. Thus when death came, as it had come to this family, he offered up a sacrifice in his own home to the special family god and the body was then buried, if possible, beneath the chapel floor.

Today the teraphim, the little family images, had been placed in full view upon a side table. Terah had bought these images after coming to Ur, for his father Nahor had retained the old family images.

As Abram entered, Terah was in the act of placing on the altar a lamb which he had just killed and dressed. Blood dripped down the carved face of the altar. On a shelf above was a vessel in which the sweet oil of sacrifice was burning.

A great dignity, it seemed to Abram, had descended on his gray-haired father. There was a wistful sincerity of expression in his face, a simple nobility in his bearing.

Terah was speaking now with hands raised above his head while the smoke from the burning sweet oil passed through an opening in the altar roof and rose like a pillar into the blue above. "This my son, my first-born, has died before his time. May the scent of our sacrifice be acceptable to the God of our fathers and be sweet in the nostrils of our departed."

And so Haran was buried beneath the chapel floor and there was wailing and crying. Passers-by in the street outside heard it and said: "Death has come to the house of Terah."

When Terah left the chapel he found Abram waiting for him. They looked at each other with understanding, and Terah said: "You are my eldest son now, and since my father Nahor has died we have a grave responsibility. Come to see me after the evening meal tonight."

That evening Terah sat as usual on the roof and Sarai sat with him. They heard the street door close resoundingly. Sarai laughed and said: "Your eldest son has arrived."

"Yes," Terah replied, "he always used to come into the house like that. But recently he has stayed away. My son is a man of great force of character, great knowledge, but unpredictable." After a pause he continued: "I'm afraid he is working too hard. Perhaps we do not understand each other. Have you told him about the death blessing of his grandfather yet?"

"No," she replied, "not yet. But — " she hesitated — "you are going to give him your own blessing and the inheritance that would have gone to Haran, are you not?"

"I do not know," Terah replied. "But I want you to be silent about blessings tonight."

"Very well, Father," she said.

As she spoke, Abram came bounding up the stairs to the roof.

"Greetings!" he cried, and bowed to his father and to Sarai. But before anyone could speak, he said:

"Father Terah, that brilliant star that burns with such a steady blue light over there is Nebo, is it not? — the star of the men of Haran."

"Yes," Terah replied, "it is."

Then Abram continued: "Before long it should come to the zenith. That is our star. It should bring our people good, not evil."

Terah nodded his head in assent. "Yes, yes. And yet I have lost my first-born son, the child that I named Haran."

He shook his gray head. "I knew there was danger for Haran, especially as he was in charge of the camel trade. As soon as there were rumors of war, I urged him to have an armed guard, but he laughed at the suggestion. I should have done something, something. Now it is too late. He was so fearless and — "

Terah choked and stopped talking. Abram looked at Sarai. She smiled sadly and made a silent gesture toward her father. After a pause, Abram laid his hand on his father's knee. Terah raised his head and looked up at the vault of heaven studded with so many twinkling lights.

Then he continued, his voice quavering: "We must take thought for the safety of our people."

"Father Terah," Abram said, his voice low with emotion, "you could not have prevented this. But we must ask ourselves why it has happened. Why do they treat us as enemies?"

They were silent then until Sarai said,

"Outside of the cities the Habiru people take great pride in their possessions, which are few, and in their flocks and camels. Here we are under suspicion. You told me, Father Terah, how you won your place in Ur. Do you think now that we are happier here than we would be living the life of herdsmen?"

Terah was silent, and bowed his head. Finally Abram said: "You have never talked to me of your boyhood, Father Terah. How was it that you came to leave your father to become a Sumerian?" When Terah said nothing, Abram went on:

"I for one have been proud that I was born in Ur, the greatest city in the world. I have never longed to wander across the desert in the heat and the dust, looking for grass. I do not yearn to be a camelman. I have heard too much about it. But life for us in the city sometimes seems intolerable too."

"My son," Terah replied, "you have been no more than a visitor to the plains. You should make a tent your home when the desert is in bloom. There is room to be alone out there. The silence is good and the wind across the meadows is sweet. A man is free there. And yet, I ran away from it!"

Sarai placed her hand in her father's hand. "Tell us about it."

Terah shrugged and began simply:

"Haran, as you know, is a city and a district in Amurru. The men of Haran have always been herdsmen. They are a restless people. That is why they are sometimes called *wanderers* or *habiru*.

"My father Nahor kept in touch with the men of Haran because he was their hereditary chieftain. But he would not live in the city of Haran. His house and the houses of his family were built on the hills near Haran. They built cone-shaped white towers on their roofs which could be seen from a great distance against the blue sky. There was a great well of water near my father's house. It was always full of sweet water, and below the houses were rolling pastures as far as the eye could see.

"When I was young, my father sent me to school in the temple of Nannar in the city of Haran, where I learned the Sumerian language as well as Babylonian.

"Frankly, my boyhood was not very happy. My father was stern and I never wanted to be a shepherd. When I went to school, I took very little interest in the temple, and less in my studies. In school I used to make little images with the clay on which I should have been writing, and many a time I was punished for it. In the afternoons, instead of playing with other boys, I found my way into the idol workshop that was attached to the temple of Nannar, and there I found something that interested me.

"I watched the craftsmen make small figurines which the people bought to use in their family chapels. I was fascinated when nobles and rich merchants came to have portrait statuettes made. They bought the finished portraits for large sums of silver. The craftsmen let me work in clay and sometimes even use a chisel on small pieces of stone. I loved doing these things, and the priests who came into the workshop praised my figurines and said they had life in them.

"One day a rich noble came from Martu to have his likeness carved in alabaster. He came many times to the workshop while the chief craftsman worked at his statuette. In a corner of the shop, where no one noticed me, I modeled the man in clay.

Terah seemed to have forgotten his sorrow now and was talking with excitement. Abram looked across at Sarai sitting on the other side of her father. She nodded and gave him an understanding smile as the story continued.

"At first I was not satisfied and broke the clay image when it was dry. Then the day before the chief's alabaster was to be finished, I caught the true likeness and I cut out two eyes from shell and set them in the clay with bitumen pitch. The statuette's hands were folded over his chest in the attitude of prayer. But the face was alive.

"Next day, early in the morning, I waited for the rich man outside the temple gate. It seemed hours that I waited. Finally he came, riding on an ass, with his wife and slaves following, also on asses. The noble dismounted, and as he approached the temple gate, I stepped in front of him and held up the image. I thought I wanted only to give it to him, but probably what I really wanted was to hear that the likeness was good.

"The man halted in astonishment and took the image from me. He turned and showed it to his wife, and she cried aloud: 'It is my husband. It is wonderful!'

"He gave me a bag of gold and silver and asked me my name. I realize now that it was the money he expected to pay for the alabaster image. He took my figurine with him and entered the workshop. I followed at a distance and hid where I could see the entrance to the workshop. I heard much angry shouting inside, and finally the noble left the shop door with my image in his hands. The chief workman followed him and threw his alabaster image after him, cursing him and me in a loud voice.

"Then I was frightened and, taking the money with me, ran

and hid in the rushes by the river until the heat of midday, when all seemed quiet in the town. Then I walked quickly out into the open country to the houses of my father Nahor. But he was not there. It was the time of the harvest, and all the people had taken their tents and gone down to the threshing floors in the valley of the river Belikh.

"And so early next morning I took an ass and followed their track across the plains, wondering what my father would say or do to me, for he was stern. My brothers and I feared him though we loved him too. I dared not remain in the city of Haran because of the whipping I should receive and also because I was afraid they would take the gold and silver away from me.

"As I approached the river, I could look down on the threshing floor, where oxen were drawing sledges round and round over the grain and where winnowers tossed the straw in the air so that the wind could blow it away while the wheat fell in a yellow pile. There was one large tent, and I knew that must be my father's tent; so I passed around the floor and entered. I found my mother there, and before long my father came in.

"After he had heard my story, I remember that he emptied the bag that I had received from the noble upon the rug. The gold and silver made a little pile, and he looked at me in astonishment. Then he separated out the silver pieces and gave them back to me. 'Take these,' he said, 'and go back to Haran quickly and take with you a kid and make an offering of the kid in the temple of the moon god and put the silver in Nannar's votive box. But do not return to your schoolmaster nor to the workshop. Return here and help with the harvest. After that you will tend my flocks and become a shepherd.'

"I carried out my father's commands; and on my return to the threshing floor the harvest was nearly finished and it was time for drying the wheat in the sun. My uncle was in charge of the threshing floor, and set me to work bringing clay from the riverbank and spreading it out like a flat pavement upon the ground. When this had dried in the sun, I spread wheat out upon it so that the hot sun could dry it. This is what they call a drying floor. There were other clay floors, for the harvest was large. My uncle came to inspect mine, and he scolded me because I had not made a raised margin to keep the wheat from rolling off onto the ground. He was an ugly man, fat, and he had a very large nose. I did not like him.

"But I carried more clay and made an excellent high brim all around the floor. It was good clay, so when I had finished I made little images of other workers as though they were little gods. And I made a large image of my uncle. It was even more ugly than he was in life, and I laughed as I worked. I set him in the middle with the others bowing down before him.

"That night the men gathered about to eat and drink, for it was the end of the harvest. They discovered my uncle's image and the images of my fellow workers bowing down before him, and there was great laughter and gaiety. But when my uncle came he was very angry, and he would have beaten me had not my father taken me away to his own tent.

"He told my mother about the images, and I heard him laugh. I thought he would listen to me then, and I begged to be allowed to go to Ur where I could learn to be an idol craftsman. At this he was sad and would hear none of it. And so I became a shepherd.

"After two years I had made up my mind to go, even if it must be against my father's command, even if it meant the forfeiture of his blessing and the loss of my birthright. And so I left my flock in the care of another and returned to Father Nahor without his permission."

Terah rose slowly from his couch to stretch and walk about. "My old muscles seem to be cramped," he said. "I shall return in a moment." And he disappeared down the stair.

"Has Father Terah ever told you this story before?" Sarai asked.

"No, never," Abram replied. Then after a pause he added: "Our father is a most remarkable little man. There is no one like him from here to Haran — an artisan such as this city has never known. A merchant who transforms all that he touches into gold and silver, a chief who has sent camels to the gates of every city in Akkad and Sumer!"

Terah's step sounded on the stair, a little slow, a little irregular. As he sat down again, he groaned and said: "The charm of the Egyptian god Horus which hangs about my neck seems to be losing its power. The fiends get into my joints with the night air." He pulled a fur rug up and covered himself.

"I have not told you, Abram, that my father Nahor never did give me his blessing as his successor in the leadership of our people." Abram made an involuntary exclamation, but said nothing.

"He expected my return to Haran," Terah continued, "but I did not go back. Perhaps that is why I have not talked to you nor anyone else, except Amtelai, about leaving Father Nahor. Perhaps I should not be talking now if it were not that Sarai is sitting here with us." He paused and patted her hand.

"No, I never went back. I have been trying to make a new life here in Ur for myself and for you. I suppose I have been trying to escape from the domination of my father, and my father's fathers."

Terah heaved a sigh and looked at his son and daughter. They had listened to him as though fascinated, and Sarai said: "Don't stop now. Please go on."

Her father smiled. "The rest of the story is like a picture in my mind, a story that happened long ago to someone else. It was when I was eighteen years old that the parting came. How well I can see that boy and his father!"

The old man fell silent and stroked his beard. Then he continued, as though he were really talking about someone else . . .

When he had returned home, the boy walked across the hilltop before his father's house. He was carrying a sack, half filled with irregular objects, and he set it down very carefully under a great oak tree. Then he looked about, and seeing that there was no one watching him, stooped and drew from the bag an idol no larger than a doll, but delicately made and colored. When he had placed this on the grass, he drew out others and arranged them in a half circle.

Finally, he stood up straight, for he was conscious of his short stature when in his father's presence. He was a well-built lad. By that time he must have had the beginning of a black beard on his chin, perhaps no more than a soft shadow. He stood still, wondering what would happen. He looked down at his little gods. Then he stepped toward the door of the house.

As he did so, the door swung open, and his father stepped out and stopped in astonishment. He looked at the boy, and at the little images that sat as though in mute appeal in a half circle behind him, and recognized the meaning of this unexpected visit. He turned and called to his wife, who came to the doorway. She was a lovely woman, with dark hair and eyes and heavy features. On seeing him, she ran to embrace the boy. Then she drew back and waited in surprised silence.

"I have come again," the young man said. "I want to get away from here. I am not a shepherd. Let me go to Ur. I can make images. Look at these before you give me your answer." The boy spoke rapidly now as though he feared interruption. "The priests of the moon god in Haran said they were good. They told me that if I could learn the craft in the idol markets of the city of Ur, I might become a great idol merchant. If there is no other way,

I am ready even to give up your blessing. Only let me go." He paused and then hurried on. "You have other sons. Perhaps you would like to give one of them my birthright."

He stopped now and waited with pounding heart, knowing that there was nothing further he could say. The threat of renouncing his birthright and his blessing was his last resort. His father studied him for a moment and then, stroking his black beard, he looked away across the meadows.

It was in the cool of the evening that follows the setting of the sun. Grazing cattle were etched black against the yellow glow in the western sky. The familiar sound of the cicadas, hidden among the branches of the trees, swelled and receded. In the distance, they could hear the scream of a prowling hyena, followed by a chorus of barking from the dogs.

Nahor turned and looked at his wife. She nodded and said quietly: "Yes, Nahor. This is your first-born son. He seems only a child now. But he will grow into a strong man."

Finally the father spoke: "When I die," he said, "my first-born son must become chief in my stead. If you promise that you will accept this charge, I will let you go."

Nahor paused, and his son replied: "I promise."

Then Nahor continued. "Very well. When you have given me your oath, with your hand under my thigh, you may go. I do not understand why you should want to become a city dweller. I cannot stand the stifling stench of crowding merchants." He made a gesture of disgust. "I knew that you would persist in your determination, and I foresaw this interview. Some day I expect you to return.

"But now I shall give you a new name. You want to make images of the moon god which the Sumerians call Nannar. You shall be called by the word that means moon god in the tongue of your people. I name you Terah. But remember this — that even if the God of our family should bless me with many sons and daughters, I would choose you to be my heir and my successor."

With an effort the boy controlled his impulse to shout for joy. Instead, he kissed his father's hand and replied simply: "I will bear the name of Terah, and I will do all that you have commanded."

There were tears in his mother's dark eyes as she kissed him. "Come back to us." she said and held him close.

The evening breeze had begun to whisper through the leaves of the oak tree above them. Nahor listened for a moment and then said, as though to himself: "There is a mysterious spirit that stirs in our young men. Perhaps that is what makes the men of Haran different from the other hill peoples, different from the people of the plains. We are wandering herdsmen. But our prophets find wisdom in the wind. Our merchants, though they pitch their tents in strange market places, turn back to their own people — at heart forever nomads, wanderers, *habiru*."

Nahor looked down at the images and shook his head. Then he picked up one of them, held it at arm's length and handed it to his wife.

"By the great god Anu," he said, "it does look as though it could speak! Where did a son of mine get this strange talent? When I sent him to Haran to the temple school, I meant that he should learn to read and write. I wanted him to learn the Sumerians' language so that he could trade with them. I never dreamed he would learn this too."

"Our son has changed in the last two years," replied his wife. "He had become moody and strange. You have made the wise decision, but you must protect him on his journey with enough men and camels. He seems very young to go so far."

Mother and father watched their eldest son withdraw respectfully and then run over the meadow like a wild goat, leaping for joy.

About a month later, on the first day of the new moon, the light of dawn found a group of men and women on the meadow before the houses of Nahor. At the center of the group, there were camels kneeling in a circle and riders busy with final adjustments of saddlebags, girths, water bottles, weapons. Nahor himself was there, his great height seemingly increased by a long black cape which swept the ground. A white kaffiyeh was held upon his head by a band so that it fell in folds over his neck and shoulders.

As Nahor passed from camel to camel inspecting every detail of equipment and speaking to each man, the eyes of his eldest son followed him with affection and a little remorse. The boy knew that his departure was hard for his father to bear, and yet he felt he could not escape from the urge that was carrying him away from this rural life, now grown so distasteful to him.

Finally Nahor stood before his son with Magog, the chief camel driver, at his side. "This white camel that we have given you," he said, "is swift, but sometimes headstrong."

The grinding sound which the camel had been making as he chewed his cud stopped suddenly and was followed by a gurgling sound deep down in the interior of one of his stomachs. He turned his head to look at Nahor with what would seem to be supercilious surprise.

Nahor chuckled and said to Magog: "You drivers believe they understand your speech, don't you?"

Magog showed his white teeth and nodded. "They understand all languages and they speak to those who will listen."

Nahor turned to Terah. "Magog here is an experienced camel driver and he knows the south country well even though he is only a little older than you. He came to me as a bondsman. He had been bought by traders in Babylon, and I took him in exchange for wool. I have transferred the ownership of his bond to you. If he brings you safe to Ur, make him a free man."

The swarthy face of the driver broke into a delighted smile and, raising his right hand, he cried: "By the great god Enki, I swear to serve your son faithfully."

"Now," continued Nahor, "you have provisions. You have goods which you can trade for such things as may be necessary. You have gold and silver which you may use for tribute to brigands in case of trouble. The gold which the noble gave you in exchange for his statuette you may use for your living on arrival in Ur. I would advise you not to make any more effigies like that one of your uncle." His face relaxed in a reminiscent smile, and he chuckled again.

"Give my greetings and my presents to our kinsman Salah at the Drehem farms near Nippur. Listen to what he may tell you. Once there, you are safe. But remember, in the country between here and Babylon, there are bands of thieves. Many of these thieves are our own people, alas, desperate men, outlawed from the cities but too covetous to return to the tents of their own people. Rely on the speed of your camels when you pass through that country."

Terah looked at his mother, who was standing a little way off with his brothers. He went to her and felt her arms close about him for the last time, but he did not trust himself to speak for fear his brothers might hear him cry. He returned and stood again before his father, who said:

"You have my authority over these men in your camel train. May the God of our fathers go with you." They embraced in silence.

Magog swung his leg over his saddle and seated himself. Terah and the other riders did the same. Magog then turned to look at Terah, and there was silence until Nahor said quietly to his son: "The drivers wait for your nod."

Terah bowed his head, but his eyes were brimming with unshed tears so that he could not see, and he dared not speak. He heard Magog shout the signal for the start. He pulled on the halter of his own camel and felt the rump rise suddenly, then the shoulders, and he knew the camel was up. He could hear his mother weeping and his brothers calling to him. He raised his arm to them as a signal of farewell, but he did not turn his head. There was a tight pain in his throat, and a sound in his breathing perilously like a sob.

In single file the camels of the little caravan moved off with heads held high, their bodies moving smoothly forward, their great soft feet shuffling over the ground. Their ears were back, for they knew they were leaving the green pastures, the springs and rolling hills of their homeland.

Nahor stood alone with folded arms and watched them go down the hill in single file, slipping away with the smoothness of a stream of water.

Terah turned in his saddle and looked back. He could still see his father standing motionless. Beyond, in silhouette, were the conical white towers of the houses on the hilltop and, above, flocks of pigeons wheeling and circling in the light of dawn. In the distance beyond stood a wall of mountains, where snow caught the light of the rising sun in dazzling grandeur.

Home, friends and way of life were fading into the distance, and a great sense of loneliness descended upon the boy. He raised his arm again in a final gesture of farewell. For a time the breeze brought the familiar sounds of bleating sheep and lowing cattle. But soon the sound, the sight and the smells of home were gone.

He reached into his saddlebag and drew out a tiny image of

the moon god which he held in his hands, talking to it in a low voice as though it were an understanding friend. The sun rose higher. The camel train was now leaving the red-brown earth and the rolling green pastures and entering a barren and stony country.

Terah replaced the idol in the saddlebag and looked back at his little caravan. As he did so, he became aware that in the line of silent men riding behind him many eyes were watching him. He straightened in his saddle, knowing what these men expected of the son of Nahor. He had seen some of them smile when they were told that his name was to be Terah. But many kings and civilians in Sumer had adopted the name of the moon god. Why shouldn't he?

He recalled the interview in which his father had finally given his reluctant consent for this journey. "Our people," he had said, "are different from other Amorites. Camels, cattle, sheep and goats belong to them. As herdsmen, they are free and honored in the sight of all men. But for some generations, they have been drifting into the cities of the south. They get wealth for themselves, for they are clever. But it is the wealth of others. Into the city the camel may not enter, and in the city our people are without honor."

The caravan was well out in the desert when Terah turned again to look back. He saw the heads of the camels nodding rhythmically, one beyond the other, their pouting lips seeming to smile at him with sardonic understanding.

He had often heard camel drivers, sitting about the fire of an evening near the sheepfold, sing the song of the camel. He knew they believed that camels could predict the outcome of a journey. It was only necessary, they said, to sing the song over and over, and the camels would put new words into the heart of the singer. So he sang the song, and hearing him the drivers joined in, humming the refrain. Over and over he sang it. Grad-

ually the words were altered as he sang to the rhythm of the
squeaking of his saddle:

> *"Yes, oh yes, we see the future,*
> *See the outcome of this journey.*

> *"Nomad in the gates of strangers,*
> *Pitch your tent and reap your riches,*
> *Carve your gods and see them broken.*

> *"Thus your sons will wander onward*
> *Through the rise and fall of nations,*
> *Till the dawn of understanding.*

> *"Yes, oh yes, we see the future,*
> *See the outcome of this journey."*

◆((

CHAPTER VII

Princess Shub-Kudur

Next morning Abram rose while it was still dark, for it was his duty to officiate in a special ceremony of the dawn. He left the priests' quarters and crossed the temenos. As he approached the ziggurat, its pinnacle glowed in the light of dawn; the base was still in shadow.

He began to climb the grand staircase. The hanging vines and flowering shrubs that trailed out of weep holes in this superb hill of heaven were swinging back and forth, moved by the morning breeze. Rising higher into the light of the dawn, he looked across toward the eastern horizon. It was edged with pastel colors, and as he watched, a hill of cloud began to glow on the rim of the world as though a fire had been kindled there. On approaching the top he turned again. A bar of golden light had now shot up into heaven. Then a spot of red appeared and broadened quickly, running out in both directions like molten fire escaping from the brim of a caldron.

Just above his head he heard a familiar sound — *pitche-er, pitchou, pitche-er*. He smiled and glanced up to see a flock of sand grouse winging by, their big brown breasts reflecting the morning light. "Flying north for water," he said, half aloud, "and you'll be returning when I descend." At the top of the ziggurat he often felt himself close to nature and to the wild life that he loved, the world of the out-of-doors from which he was now otherwise shut off.

He reached the top step and entered the shrine that formed the pinnacle of the ziggurat, the holy of holies. Here the god Nannar had spent the night sitting on his throne under a great dome of blue tile. A company of priests had assembled and stood ready for the ceremony. These men were naked except for loincloth, as was the custom in the presence of the god, and their faces and heads were shaven. On one side was a line of priestesses clothed in shimmering blue. They were the *sal-me*, the concubines of Nannar. Behind this line stood a woman not dressed in the costume of the *sal-me* but cloaked from head to toe in a white cape.

Abram joined the other priests, but he towered above them; for the Sumerians were a little people, whereas he was tall, muscular and handsome, now in the full vigor of his manhood.

As the sun rose like a red ball above the eastern horizon, the chanting began, and the sound of the music reverberated from the dome of the lofty sanctuary out over the silent city.

After the initial song, the *sal-me* made their bows to the god and filed down the grand staircase. Then the priests raised the idol upon their shoulders and followed them down. When the moon god was lifted, the horizontal rays of the sun caused a thousand sleeping gems in his garment to glitter in reflected glory. As the procession filed down the staircase, Abram advanced to the top of the stair and stood alone with his hands uplifted, the light shining on his naked limbs.

"*Who in heaven is high exalted?*" Abram intoned the words in a booming bass, and the priests and priestesses replied in swinging cadence:

"*Father! God enlightening earth! Lord of Ur, of gods the prince. High exalted, all producing, life unfolding from above!*"

Then Abram again: "*Who on earth is high exalted?*" and the reply:

"*Thou, thy will on earth revealest; thou subdu'st the spirits of earth!*
Thou! through heaven and earth extendest goodness, not remembering wrong."

While Abram still stood on the platform, the procession flowed smoothly down the upper stairs that faced the east, then turned to the left down the side staircase, and so out of sight to enter the great temple of Nannar, while the refrain echoed and re-echoed: "*Thou subdu'st the spirits of earth. Thou subdu'st the spirits of earth.*"

The court of Nannar far below was thronged with people who bowed and gazed at the procession and bowed again. Finally the chanting ceased and there was silence.

Abram continued to stand on the top step for a little time in exalted mood. This beauty of sight and sound always moved him. He looked up into the deep blue of heaven, thinking: "Somewhere, there must be a true God, a God who will speak to me, a God who will be with my people in their tents and on their camels."

A pair of bee catchers floated by on motionless wings. He watched their copper-gold backs and iridescent breasts. This loveliest of birds had always seemed to Abram to be something inanimate and spiritual — but now the shimmering pair seemed to him to symbolize human love. If he should leave the priesthood, perhaps after all something like that might come to him. Was there such a thing as a love that would lift two spirits high above the commonplace of life?

The bee catchers climbed with quick wingbeats and then drifted together far out over the city and the river beyond. For some reason Sarai's words about moonlight and flowering shrubs came back to him.

He turned to cross the sanctuary and discovered, to his surprise, that he was not alone. The woman in the white cape and hood still stood there under the dome. He had a sudden feeling of resentment that she should intrude upon this, his treasured moment of solitude, and, supposing her to be an audacious member of the *sal-me*, or even one of the lower grades of prostitutes, he spoke to her severely.

"Don't you know that you should not be here at this time? Who are you?"

She regarded him silently, but the hood covered her head and face, leaving only her dark eyes visible. When she did not answer, and thinking she might have missed her place in the procession from ignorance, he said more kindly: "If you are a novice to the *sal-me*, you had better leave quickly."

The woman then answered in a rich, full voice: "I am a novice, but I am more than that and I need your help, desperately. Please come with me, for I want to talk with you." She turned and walked away from him with perfect assurance that he would follow. As she did so, he caught a glimpse of a jeweled sandal, painted toenails and a shapely brown ankle.

Although his first impulse had been to consider this woman an imposter, there was something in her manner that made him decide to follow her into the recess outside the shrine where she was now waiting for him. Her voice too seemed familiar. He had thought for a moment that it was the voice of Princess Shub-Kudur. But that was of course impossible.

He stopped to put on his cloak. Then he entered the recess. As he did so she removed her hood and outer cloak with a swift movement. Abram stepped back in astonishment, for it was Shub-Kudur, the only daughter of the king of Larsa and Ur.

In his previous interviews with her, Abram had not been altogether oblivious of her charm, and he had realized that she sometimes seemed to spin out their consultations regarding the libation urns somewhat longer than was necessary. He knew also that there was gossip in Ur as to why she had remained so long unmarried, and this gossip linked her name with various suitors. However, until this moment, he had given the matter little thought because of his great preoccupation with other matters.

Now she addressed him at once. "Abram son of Terah, I know you are surprised to see me here, but I could plan no other way to talk to you alone."

He realized now that she was dressed as though for a court function. Her black hair was elaborately curled in ringlets about her face, and there were beguiling beauty spots on her cheeks, dots of black, red and delicate green which fine ladies were in the habit of applying when they wished to look their loveliest. Spiral rings of gold trembled in her hair; jeweled necklace and earrings glowed against her smooth brown skin. A clinging cloak was thrown over one shoulder, but left the other lovely shoulder bare and revealed, rather than hid, a rounded breast. Although it was quite obvious that she intended him to be conscious of her charm, she spoke seriously.

"You probably do not know that it is the decree of my father that I should sacrifice my life to Nannar. I implored him to allow me to continue to lead the life of a princess, and for several years I have managed to postpone this step. For a time I have enjoyed the gaiety of the court and the pleasures of the country. Men have even said I was beautiful." She paused and looked deep into Abram's eyes.

"Now, my father says I must take this step, says it is my duty, and that I may thus be able to bind the city of Ur more closely to his court in Larsa. He thinks it will give him a stronger hold on the Sumerians. Until recent months it was difficult for me to face the new life planned for me. But now I should be glad to escape the court, for I have learned to hate it. Also, it seems to me that life in the temple could be pleasant."

She broke off, and came closer to him. Abram was conscious of a delightful perfume. She placed one hand timidly on his shoulder and her body touched his. He felt a fire run through him and was conscious of a curious weight in his chest that made his breathing difficult. His heart pounded but he did not move.

"I have enjoyed our interviews in the archives," she continued, "although my handmaids stay so close to me!" She shrugged her shoulders. "You are a distinguished scholar. I too am interested in ancient Sumerian culture and I should gladly learn to study the records if you will teach me. You could help me with my urn collection. Perhaps I could help you. I have a great deal of influence with the king and I intend to gain more power in Sumer."

"My lady," replied Abram, "I am always at your service — in the archives. I am a Semite."

She interjected: "You will some day be chief of the Habiru and you are a giant among men." She drew back and her glance traveled over him from head to foot.

He looked down into her face. Her soft eyes seemed to melt into his, and he realized that it would be so easy, yes, so pleasant to kiss those parted lips. At the same time a voice seemed to speak at the back of his mind: "Remember your decision regarding women. She does not belong to your people. Beware especially, for she is the daughter of the king."

He bowed a little and said: "You are very kind to say such things. I am a priest of Nannar, and you are the daughter of the king and the noblest lady in Sumer. I shall always be more than glad to help you in every way."

She looked at him for a moment, and then said: "Soon I may belong to Nannar."

There was a whirring sound, and two blue-rock pigeons flew over their heads to land on the terrace rail. There they strutted, their slender bodies shining a greenish-blue. They watched the birds, and Abram, hoping to get the conversation on a less perilous plane, said: "Their color is the same as that of the new shoots of camel thorn which grow in the desert."

"Yes," she replied. "See how they preen themselves. They are temple birds, but they seem to be finding pleasure. Why should not others do so here, shut off from the rest of the world?"

At this point, they heard the heavy tread of a company entering the shrine. She took up her mantle, and, putting it over her shoulders, looked at him again, as though asking a question. Then she said: "The priests have returned, and the novice must go. I must not be seen up here now."

"But," Abram asked, "how can you get down from here without being seen?"

She smiled and said: "There is another way for the wife of the god Nannar. She can do many things. Think about this." She gave him her hand and, without quite knowing what he intended, he held it in both of his and then pressed it to his lips.

Abram descended the ziggurat in a daze; automatically he crossed the terrace at its base and entered the temple of Ningal. It was an enormous, fortresslike structure. At the far corner of the building were the priests' quarters, where he usually had his breakfast. He washed his feet, and then, instead of going directly to the refectory as he usually did, made a detour to pass the throne of the goddess. Approaching it from the rear, he watched an old priest manipulate the paraphernalia on the altar by means of strings that passed through the wall and were cunningly concealed from the eyes of the worshipers.

Then he passed around into the court before the throne of Ningal and stood among the worshipers who lay prostrate before the goddess. The throne room was completely encrusted with gold. Into it a second room opened at the side of the throne.

This second room was the bedchamber of the goddess. Through partly drawn curtains he could see the bed, the metal mirrors, the cosmetics and perfumes all in readiness. Theoretically, and perhaps actually in the minds of credulous and simple-minded worshipers, this was the nuptial chamber for the god Nannar when he should visit his goddess wife.

Actually, Abram thought to himself, if Princess Shub becomes high priestess, it may be here that she will spend many nights, if not her first night of virginal sacrifice. Again he felt as though a flush was passing through his body. Perhaps, he mused, it would be an exciting life. It would be a little like the life of the pigeons strutting and cooing on the balustrade up there.

He left the throne of Ningal and moved on through the temple. On his way he passed a bull tied down to a great ring in the floor. The bull's bellowing echoed down the corridors, as he had heard it every morning at this time. He saw an attendant swing an ax, heard a dull thud, saw the beast fall and blood run over the white marble. But this morning the routine sights and sounds of the temple seemed to him distasteful, nauseating.

Arriving at the refectory, he sat alone, wondering what would come from his strange encounter with the princess and feeling that he must have dreamed it. He remembered her eyes, the odd effect of her hand on his shoulder, and the smell of her perfume. . . . Then the face of Sarai in the moonlight came back to him. What extraordinary lashes she had, and how she had grown up!

Two priests came over to him, and one of them said: "The high priest has sent word that he wishes to see you. Come to him in his inner chamber at the end of the morning ceremonies."

The other priest was Dudu, the fat physician with whom he had talked the day before. He smiled at Abram and said: "There is to be a splendid banquet tonight; meat and wine and wonderful entertainment, new slave girls who play the harp and dance. It is all in the service of Nannar, you know," and he gave vent to a rumbling laugh.

The other priest passed on, and Dudu sat down beside Abram and clapped him on the thigh. "Come on. You think too much. Remember what I said to you. Enjoy life's pleasures before it is too late." He lowered his voice. "I know you are not satisfied with temple life. Well, I'm not either but we can't change it. Perhaps you can change things later when the high priest takes you into his inner circle. There is gossip going around about you. I'll tell you about it if you come to the banquet with me tonight. It is better to accept what you can't change and take the little pleasures life offers, before it is too late. I must go to my work in the clinic now but I'll save you a place beside me at the banquet tonight."

Abram smiled and shook his head. "Not tonight," he replied, "but perhaps some night I'll come. You would lose all your self-respect if I should keep my head while you drank yourself under the table, wouldn't you?"

"Ha," replied Dudu, "that's a challenge!"

In his private sanctum within the temple of Ningal the high priest of Nannar, Enannatum, waited for the arrival of Abram. Light entered through archways cut in the massive four-foot wall of the room. The light fell upon the points of gold, ivory and lapis lazuli that studded the dark wainscoted wall and the domed ceiling like stars in a miniature firmament.

The high priest sat on the raised ivory chair from which he and his predecessors had ruled the priesthood and controlled the whole economic structure of Sumer for generations. He was stooped by the passage of years, but his deeply lined, ascetic face was strong and his eyes alert and calculating. His fingers drummed restlessly upon the carved arm of his chair as he waited. "Come in, come in," he said abruptly, as he heard Abram approaching.

Abram entered and stood before him, wondering what was in store for him.

"I have a great deal to say to you, Abram son of Terah," the high priest said. "Your study of the ancient tablets has been well done. I have sent your summary of Sumerian laws to Hammurabi king of Babylon, and word comes from his ministers that he is very well pleased, since he desires to prepare a great code of laws for his people. The temples of Babylon have no scholars to compare with our own. Thus you have rendered real service to Nannar, for we stand in need of Hammurabi's friendship. We have had his enmity too long.

"We exceed other countries in wealth and culture, but not in military strength. Our intellectual development has been continuous from the time of the great flood till now. Other nations have always learned from us and stood in awe of us. We gave them the art of writing, codes of laws, rules of government.

"The first high priest to bear my name, the name of Enannatum, built this vast temple because the conquering king of Isin knew it would please the people. Now, it is because I wish to demonstrate the superiority of Sumerian culture to all the world that I have directed the scholar priests to compose the king lists and to record the mysteries of the gods of Sumer. It is a temple of learning that I have tried to build, and you have been one of the scholars at this time of our greatest intellectual awakening. But I have different work for you now.

"These days are perilous ones in Sumer, for the Babylonians are growing constantly in power, and the Amorites and the Elamites are casting greedy eyes upon our wealth.

"In spite of the fact that he is an Elamite, King Rim-Sin rules Sumer and also Larsa wisely. He knows that he can control the Sumerians only through the great moon god, for our people fear

Nannar and will obey his orders before they will those of a foreign king.

"Rich and civilized as Ur is, she would fall to pieces if it were not for the worship of Nannar. It is I who stand behind the god, and you have seen the power of my ministers throughout the land. With the wealth that comes into the coffers of Nannar and Ningal, I support the armies of the king."

Abram looked at the high priest in surprise. Why should he review these things so frankly, even though they were common surmise among thinking men in Sumer? Why was he now removing in Abram's presence the mask he wore before the world?

But Enannatum did not leave him long in doubt as to the purpose of this talk, for he continued: "You, Abram, are one of the men of Haran. For two hundred years your people have been drifting into Ur from the desert. They came first as mercenaries into our army. They remain here as clever merchants and good artisans. They are aggressive and sometimes unruly, whereas the Sumerians have grown soft as the result of thousands of years of wealth and luxury.

"Your people now live among us, but they walk alone. Sumer fears the Semites to the north, in Akkad, and well she might. Many Sumerians, therefore, distrust you Semites who live here among them but are not of them. It is known that you have well-trained companies of men drawn from Amorite people in the desert, but it is said that they will be used against us, not for us.

"You, Abram, will be chief of the Habiru some day. At least so it is said. I have had my eyes upon you. That is one reason that you have risen so high in the priesthood at such an early age. Your father is rich and he has been very useful to Nannar. His control of desert trade puts great power in his hands, power that will one day be yours.

"I have talked with you frankly, because I am about to offer you advancement to the post that every young priest must covet.

I am now ready to make you my minister of commerce. You may even hope to sit in this seat when I die. But in return you must teach your people the fear of Nannar. You must organize them for war, our war against anyone who may attack us. You must truly throw your lot in with us. We seem to have the friendship of Hammurabi now, but eventually war with Babylon is sure to come."

He paused, and Abram stood in silence for a moment. Then he raised his head and looked straight at Enannatum.

"You say my people walk alone. Perhaps you are right, but in time of trouble, and if they were treated fairly, they would be loyal to Sumer; and I can speak also for the armed bands in the desert. It is true that we have not intermarried with Sumerians as other Semitic tribes have done elsewhere. The Sumerians, in their pride of race, seem to shun them. They dislike camels, dislike the people who live in tents, and us who have left our tents and come to live here. But the fault may well be on our side also. Perhaps we are too conscious of our own inheritance and our direct descent from Father Noah."

At the mention of Noah the high priest snorted in disgust. "Why must you talk of Noah? The story of his ark which you tell your children is strangely like our legend of the good man of Sumer, Uta-Napishtim, who builded himself a boat and so survived the flood with all manner of beasts and herbs. But you must have learned all this when you were a child!

"You know that Nannar has been the principal god of Sumer since the memory of man, and he has been feared by Sumerian and Akkadian alike. There is no other god worth worshiping here." Enannatum made a gesture as though anxious to have done with this subject, and then continued:

"But there is more in this present matter that I must tell you. Your people are in danger now in this city. The military party, under the young noble Nasir-Sin, is urging that they be driven out of Sumer immediately, before the trouble with Babylon can begin. I fear the death of your brother is one evidence of their intention. I was sorry to hear of it.

"You may be right that the men of Haran would make our cause theirs in case of war. I should like to count on you to see that they do. By quick action, which I shall discuss with you presently, we may be able to block the plans of the military party. I will help you in this matter, if you, as my minister and as leader of your people, will undertake to make them fear Nannar and unite with us." Abram started to speak, but the high priest held up his hand for silence.

"For some years, as you know, there has been no high priestess of Nannar, no entum or first wife of the god. Now, however, following the example of King Sargon and later the great King Dungi, each of whom gave a daughter to be high priestess, King Rim-Sin desires that Princes Shub should become the entum of Nannar. It was for that that we have waited."

Abram trembled, remembering the strange advances made to him by the princess so recently and understanding now the full meaning of her invitation.

"Lord Nasir," continued Enannatum, "knows about this. He has wanted to marry her for a long time and now he has warned me that he means to send a princely gift to Nannar with the request that he may lie with her on the night that she ceases to be a virgin. But the princess is strong-minded as well as beautiful. She has other plans. Gossip at court says she is tired of Nasir." Enannatum sneered and added: "I do not inquire into such matters. However that may be, her desire falls on a certain priest who seems to be destined for greatness. You follow me? And she has great influence over her father the king. You might find her friendship useful. For my part, I dislike Nasir, and should like to block his plans. This military party is growing much too strong.

"I should prefer to have you as my own minister, increase your influence over the entum and the royal house by taking over the office of Nannar in the nuptial ceremony and perhaps afterwards. Your child, if you have one, will belong to Nannar, not to you, and will bear the name of the entum, not yours." Abram stood speechless as the whole cunning scheme was unrolled before him.

"Think this over carefully, Abram," added Enannatum. "No man could say no to this opportunity, unless he were quite mad. On the one hand you may choose power, wealth and pleasure such as have been given to few men. On the other hand you may expect persecution and death for your people and perhaps even for you.

"Now, however, prompt action may become necessary. The king is undecided in regard to the fate of your people who are called camelmen, and Nasir has recently requested an audience with him. If it is granted he will probably urge stern measures. I am told that the princess has used her influence toward leniency. I suspect you have seen to that?"

The old man shot a crafty glance of inquiry at Abram, but as Abram's expression did not alter, he went on: "I know that she has visited you in the tablet house, a rather unusual procedure!" Enannatum smiled and added: "I might even tell you that she did so first at my suggestion." He laughed, watching Abram's face. "In any case, if you want to plead the cause of your people it might be that she could have you admitted to the audience. It is better that I should seem to be impartial in all this."

"I will be ready to plead our cause at any time," said Abram.

At that the high priest clapped his hands and an attendant entered. "Beg the Princess Shub-Kudur to come here."

While they waited, Enannatum did not speak again, but drummed with his fingers upon the arm of his chair and watched Abram from time to time. Abram stood without moving, his face flushed, the arteries of his temples throbbing. Although stunned at first, certain things were now quite clear to him, and he realized that he must not betray the direction of his thinking to Enannatum until he could at least warn his father of the danger that now hung over him. He knew that upon his own action depended the lives of his family and the future of his people. He must use every advantage, not the least of which seemed to be the favor of the princess.

A curtain was pulled back and Princess Shub entered. She was dressed now in simple temple costume. After formal greeting, the high priest said:

"Is it true, my lady, that Nasir has sought an audience with the king to urge upon him strong action against the Habiru within the kingdom?"

"Yes," Shub replied, "but he cannot touch anyone within the priesthood," and she cast a furtive glance at Abram.

"If such an audience is given, could you arrange that Abram son of Terah, who stands here, should be present to plead the cause of his people?"

"I think I could," she replied.

The high priest then said: "If Abram does well and is able to bind his people to Nannar, his future will be great in Sumer. I shall leave you now, as I have other duties." Enannatum left them abruptly.

Abram and the princess looked at each other. Shub colored and her eyes faltered, for she knew that the high priest had probably placed her proposal before him frankly. "The walls may have ears," she said in a low voice, and turning she walked to the archway and looked out into the empty court. Abram felt suddenly that he must be honest with this woman, whatever the cost might be. He came and stood close behind her.

"Let me speak openly," he said, looking down at the ringlets of hair that covered her head. "You are very beautiful, very."

She remained standing with her back to him, still as a statue, waiting. He hesitated and then began to speak rapidly.

"I must make you understand. There is something within me that makes me different from other men. It is stronger than passion, stronger than ambition, stronger than fear. I am searching for a greater god, if there is one, and I can think of little else. I was young when I became a priest, and I had high hopes that I could worship Nannar sincerely. But I cannot. He is a lie."

She turned slowly toward him but kept her eyes averted. "There are too many gods already," she said. "Why not accept this life as you find it? Think of the pleasure and power that lie within your reach. Together we might find happiness and then you would forget this strange urge." She bent her head back and looked up into his eyes as she had done earlier that morning.

But Abram was now oblivious of her appeal. His eyes were shining with an excitement that came from within. "I must go on," he said. "I must seek the truth. There is no other way."

She stepped back from him and said: "I have never met anyone like you — you do not belong to Ur. You are a stranger here." Then she added a little sadly: "Perhaps that is why I hoped to find happiness and even peace of mind with you. I have never found it in the court. I too feel myself a stranger in Ur. The king and I are Elamites, and you a Semite from Haran. You seek the truth. My father seeks power. I seek something — but I cannot name it.

"My father is in the palace now. I will talk with him. If you will come to my apartment there this afternoon an hour before sundown, I will tell you what I have learned about the audience."

She cast a sidelong glance at Abram and he replied quietly: "I will be there."

She walked into the archway and putting her hands on the rail looked down into the courtyard, her eyes filled with tears.

Abram followed and stood beside her. After a little time she said in a stifled voice, but without looking up:

"The king has made all arrangements for the ceremony of my betrothal to Nannar. It will take place the day after tomorrow, but I shall still have a few days of freedom before I become the entum and must go to the couch of Nannar. I am helpless — " Her throat tightened so that she could not speak for a little time, but at last she gained control. "I am helpless to escape this thing."

She did not look up at him again, but turned and walked slowly toward the door through which she had entered the room. As she approached it the curtains were drawn aside by an unseen hand and closed mysteriously after her.

◄(

CHAPTER VIII

The Dust of His Camel's Feet

AFTER HIS INTERVIEW with Enannatum, Abram went directly to his father's house. He found the old man alone and gave him a rapid account of the happenings of the day. He outlined the offer of the high priest, the plan of Nasir to drive out all the desert people, and the opportunity that might possibly be given him to plead their cause.

When he described the advances of the Princess Shub, the old man had looked at him in amazement. "But," he cried, "she has offered you unlimited power. Think, my son, what you could do with it! You and she might some day rule Sumer like the Semitic kings of Egypt. You and Princess Shub, Habiru and Elamite! The Habiru, the wanderers who are descended from Father Noah, the tribe that brought the camel into Akkad and Sumer — we would be honored above all other Amorite tribes — honor, wealth, power!

"Abram, Abram, you cannot possibly refuse this alliance. Remember the safety of your family, of your people, of the other desert people!" Terah was gesticulating and pacing up and down. Presently he looked up at his son and saw an expression in his face which made him stop. Then he asked: "Well, what is it that you intend to do?"

Abram did not look at his father, but he replied: "I do not know. This is the great decision."

A few hours later Abram and Oni presented themselves at the palace gate. Oni entered, and soon returned in the company of the handmaid of the princess. As they came through the gate she was talking and laughing with Oni and shaking her earrings at him.

"The princess bade me meet you," she said to Abram. "Come with me, and your big servant may follow."

They passed down one corridor after another. Abram looked down at his guide. She was a pretty, black-haired little Sumerian whose golden ankle rings jingled gaily as she bustled along, trying to match the speed of his long slow stride.

Finally she smiled at him, showing her dimples coquettishly. "My name is Berri. You have very long legs. Even longer than those of your servant." She cast a glance back at Oni. "I wish you would slow down. But I like tall men. So does the princess. They say tall men have their heads in the clouds." As they passed a heavily curtained door, she put out her hand and caught his mantle to stop him.

"Not so fast, not so fast," she cried, and then giggled merrily. "This is the entrance to the apartments of the Princess Shub-Kudur."

She pulled the curtain back and knocked. While the heavy door was turning slowly on its hinges, she smiled at Oni. "Wait here," she said. "Perhaps I can return to talk with you later." Then she preceded Abram into an enclosed courtyard.

As the door opened he had heard the chattering of women's voices, but when he entered there was a sudden silence. He found himself standing in the shade of a spreading palm tree, surrounded by court ladies in elaborate costume. In the silence they eyed him with obvious curiosity. However, his diminutive guide had now assumed an air of great dignity. She ushered him across the court and up a flight of stairs leading to the gallery which ran around the court. Opposite the top of the stairs was a deep arched doorway. She pulled back the portieres and stood aside as he entered. Then she followed him in.

"This is Princess Shub's reception room," she said. "The princess is with her father the king; I hope she will soon bring you good news. Please make yourself comfortable." She flitted about the room, talking constantly.

"Here, you see, there is water for you to wash your feet and on this table I have had dates and wine set out. You may remove your cloak." Without waiting for his agreement, she climbed on a stool and reaching up with a quick movement pulled out the long pin which held the cloak over his left shoulder. The cloak dropped to the floor. She regarded him half laughing and half in obvious admiration of his physique. She picked up the cloak, folded it, patted it and returned the pin and seal to Abram.

"The princess told me to make you feel at home. If you want anything, or if you only want to talk, just pull this call rope and I will come. I love to talk. Everyone says I talk all the time. But I know when to be silent. I never talk about the princess or her affairs, and she knows that. I love her. She has been very good to me, although she can be cruel. But she is cruel only when punishment is well deserved. You understand that, don't you?

"An old Sumerian noble once said to me that he thought she was as much to be feared as the king. But he doesn't know how wise and clever she is. After all, in a cultured city like Ur we women have our rights just the same as men. Why shouldn't people be afraid of us sometimes?"

She paused to draw a long breath, and then with a droll expression said to Abram: "Did you want to say something?"

He smiled at her slowly, shook his head and said: "No, thank you."

"Perhaps your head is really in the clouds after all," she laughed. "Remember to pull the call rope if you want me." She waved and vanished through the curtains. But almost immediately she put her head back through the curtains and said: "I like your servant Oni. I hope you don't mind if I cast a spell over him, just a little spell, you know." She laughed and disappeared again.

Abram chuckled; then he heaved a deep sigh and looked about him. There were rich hangings and soft rugs, a couch, a gaming board and a large, beautifully decorated harp. He caught sight of himself in a full-length copper mirror and adjusted his turban.

Then he walked over to the single window aperture which looked out on the river. It had been cut through a great thickness of wall by King Rim-Sin, at his daughter's special request. Except for that, and the small gate below, the outer wall of the palace was unbroken to the northeast, where the great river flowed against the city embankment and turned to the north and west, to pass the north harbor on its way around the fortifications. Looking across the river he could see an open space which he knew was the camel station. In the distance a line of camels was approaching it.

From the anteroom below came soft music. Someone was playing a stringed instrument and singing softly. He walked about the room. Beautiful pieces of pottery were set along one wall. The colored decoration of these pieces proved them to be genuine examples of the work of the earliest settlers, who had probably sailed into the great river from the east.

A pleasant life for those who know how to appreciate the culture of Sumer, he mused. Then he called to mind the occasions on which Shub had visited him in the tablet library. The interest she had shown in the identification of the urns in her collection had certainly been genuine and he had enjoyed helping her to decipher the meaning of the painted figures. She was very intelligent. That had been obvious to him from the beginning, but he had been no more than vaguely aware of her physical charm until the morning at the top of the ziggurat. Yes, she might well be able to protect my people, he thought.

A wind came through the open window, blowing out the curtains at the door. He sniffed it and thought of the hills of Drehem. The odor seemed to come like a message from the camel stations across the river. The music stopped now and he heard her voice in the court below. Princess Shub seemed to be sending her women away.

Abram heard her coming up the stairs, and as she entered the room he watched her speculatively. She was a woman of medium height but her court headdress with its flowers and leaves of gold made her seem much taller, accentuating the quiet dignity of her carriage. She smiled at him faintly as she came in, and there was a quizzical expression in her black eyes, but she did not speak.

Instead, she passed him and stood before her mirror. There she removed her headdress deliberately and dropped her necklaces one after another into a jewel box. As she pulled out the pin that held her outer mantle in place, she looked at his reflection over the smooth warm curve of her shoulder. She saw that he was watching her. At last she had removed all ornaments except the boat-shaped earrings of gold that swung below her black curls. Finally she removed her sandals and turned about, standing barefooted.

"My father was occupied earlier this afternoon," she said, "and I could not see him until now. He has granted a hearing to Nasir and has set the time for the audience at sundown the day after tomorrow. Nasir and his followers will undoubtedly ask for permission to drive out the desert people. But the king will give you opportunity to speak in defense of your people. It is best that no one know this before the time comes.

"If you are ready to oppose Nasir and his followers at this audience, take a small boat and come by the river. Leave the boat at the little river gate under my window." She stepped into the deep window aperture and walked to its outer edge, motioning him to follow her. "There is the gate, you see, below us."

She looked up at him searchingly. "I suppose you are not afraid to oppose Nasir, but I am afraid for you. He is a dangerous man. If you really stand in his way, he will lay plans to kill you. I know him well, too well. He has tried to force himself on me." She made a gesture of disgust and, returning to the room, sat down suddenly on a low stool. He followed her.

"I am afraid for myself also," she continued. "You are strong. You could protect me from him, couldn't you?" She held up her hands to him and he took them in his. She continued then: "At least we have something in common, you and I, a common enemy. We could have much more in common."

Abram sat down opposite to her. "I know," he said, and fell silent for a little time. She placed a soft warm foot on each of his. He looked down at the painted toenails and the toes that seemed to clutch at him and send a soft tingling through his body.

He realized that he had become confused. Was it possible that the princess could cast a spell over him too? There were things he had meant to say. But instead he seemed to hear the words of Dudu again: *You think too much. Perhaps you can change things later as a member of the high priest's inner circle. Enjoy life's little pleasures before it is too late.*

As the princess leaned toward him her tunic relaxed a little and he could see a rounded breast. It would just fit into the hollow of a man's hand . . .

But wait! If he could only think clearly. He had a plan of action, not this. Gradually his mind cleared. He had intended to be perfectly frank with this woman. That was it. He put her hands back in her lap.

"I understand the reasons for your fear," he said quietly. "I will help you if I can, but not by lying in your bed to take the place of Nannar. That would not free you." She looked down at the floor and a blush came slowly to her cheek and neck.

"You are being forced to become the entum of the god against your will. I understand that, but when you become high priestess of Ningal, you intend to help the king by using the power of Nannar and Ningal to his purposes." He stood up suddenly.

"I hate the moon god. I hate all idols. I hate the whole system. How could I help you in your plan?

"No. There are only two courses of action for me. Either I can stay here and overthrow Nannar, break him in pieces, try to give Ur a new god — "

Shub threw her head back and laughed softly at the idea. He was striding up and down now, and she watched him fondly.

"Or I must get myself and my people out of Ur, find the true God if I can — if I can." He continued to pace back and forth in silence as though he had forgotten her.

"There is another course," she said softly.

He stopped and smiled at her. "Yes, I know. You mean that I could become minister of commerce, teach my people to be good Sumerians, and at long last I might succeed to Enannatum's position of power. That would actually please Father Terah. It is the course he would have me follow. But it would be impossible for me to do that. I should be false to everything I have come to believe right. Just what it is that is best for our people I do not know. I must think about that too."

"And what about me?" she said, clasping her hands behind her head and looking up at him with a cynical smile. "What are your instructions for the daughter of the king?"

"You must go through with the betrothal ceremony the day after tomorrow and I must plead my people's cause later in the day. After that, who knows? Perhaps something can be done to keep you out of Nannar's bedchamber. Perhaps, in the long run, after you are high priestess of Ningal you can do a great deal for the *sal-me*, who will be under your authority, and for the people who come here to worship."

"Enough!" she exclaimed. "If I hadn't lost my reason I should hate you. But somehow I cannot seem to do it. After all, who are you to tell me what to do? Only a man, a strange headstrong man — but the kind of man I could love!" She leaned forward. "And you are something else, also. Sometimes you are like the image of a god. The voice of another seems to speak through you. At such times you frighten me. . . . I wonder if I could ever understand you. I wonder if there is someone else who does understand you better than I? Do you love another woman?"

When he did not reply she rose from her stool and said with a shrug: "Well, I shall watch for you from this window. When you land at the river gate, look up to me as you step out of your boat. I shall take it as a sign if you do."

They were facing each other now and he laughed and looked into her eyes. "They say that madness may come to the man who looks too long at the moon. The bride of the moon god can also cast her spell. It would be very easy to slip into that madness, and very pleasant. You would make me forget my people, forget what it is that I am seeking." He stooped toward her as though drawn irresistibly. But suddenly he straightened up, muttering: "Madness! Madness!"

He picked up his cloak and pinned it over his shoulder. "Don't be afraid," he said. "Perhaps the God of my fathers will guide us both." He placed his hand on her head as though she were a child and strode out of the room.

Shub watched the portieres close behind him, standing as he had left her, still as a statue. She neither saw nor heard Berri as her handmaid entered the room and began to straighten up the couch behind her. But Berri could never tolerate silence for very long.

"It is a good thing that you came at last," she said. "What a man is this Abram." Then she giggled, "I could hardly keep your ladies in waiting out of this room. You know, my princess, Sumerian women reach out and take the man they want. You will have to be very watchful against them."

Shub whirled about and struck her twice across the face with the palm of her hand. "Be still, you little devil," she cried, "be still!" Berri fell to the floor, weeping, and Shub stood silent. Finally she looked down at her and kicked her gently.

"Stop your crying. I will not hurt you, Berri. Don't be afraid. I must talk to you. I must talk to someone. But, before Nannar, when I hear such nonsense from you about Abram I could kill you."

Berri got to her feet and stood with bowed head. "I know," she said between sobs, "I understand. Forgive me."

Shub walked round and round the room, talking and gesticulating. "He wants to save his people. He wants to find a new god. But what about me? Am I nothing? A little while ago I was content to become high priestess, to increase our power in Ur and to help my father. Now, something has happened, something new. I know that there is a happiness of which I had never dreamed, happiness with him, happiness with his great limbs protecting me and covering me. Bah! I suppose his strange god would come and lie between us on Nannar's bed!

"This morning he looked at me with desire and again this afternoon. But when he talks about his people and his god he treats me as though I were no more than a child. By heaven! I really believe that if I were not the Princess Shub-Kudur, I would end by joining his people. I would follow him into the desert, riding on an ass. I would follow in the dust of his camel's feet. — But I cannot change my lot. Alas! I am the daughter of Rim-Sin, and I shall become the entum of Nannar. He said I should do it. He dared to tell me what I ought to do in the temple!"

In the silence that followed, Berri took her mistress's hand and kissed it. Presently Shub spoke in an altered voice. "Berri, I am afraid. Leave me now and I shall watch the great river."

She had often been lonely in Ur, for she had few confidants and it was only at rare intervals that she could talk to her father. So it had become her habit to stand in her window and watch the great brown flood slip by, as she did now. Sometimes she found herself talking to it as though there were a spirit deep in the moving water, a spirit that could understand her and bring her comfort.

❖❖

CHAPTER IX

The Family God

ON ABRAM'S RETURN to his father's house he found that Terah had called together all of the immediate members of the family. They were waiting for him anxiously. Terah began by explaining the situation to them, except that, at the request of his son, he omitted all mention of Princess Shub. He told them also that his own agents in the city had been in close touch with Nasir and his followers and had reported a recent increase in hostility, although they could give no reason for it.

Then the keen old maker of idols turned to Nahor and questioned him closely. Finally the young merchant admitted that he had been in secret communication with Hammurabi's agents, and further, that he had dispatched a messenger to Babylon to see what guarantees of protection the Habiru might receive from the armies of Hammurabi in case war broke out a second time against Ur.

At this disclosure, both Terah and Abram looked horrified, and Terah said: "My son, that is most dangerous, and contrary to my repeated warnings. Has your messenger returned?"

Nahor changed color and replied that the messenger was actually overdue, but that he expected him any day now.

Then, trying to justify himself, he said: "There are many Babylonians in Ur who will side with an invading army. It seemed to me wise to make friends with them and with high-placed officials in Babylon so that we would have friends in case Ur should fall. Because of these friends I have been able to send idols through to Babylon without duty, and I have loaned silver there at high rates of usury."

Milcah interjected, speaking to Terah, "Since you give Nahor charge of the idol market your gains have increased greatly."

At this point Terah interrupted them. "Have done with such talk, you fools!" he said. "If this messenger has actually fallen into the hands of Nasir, which I strongly suspect, we know why Nasir has asked for an audience with the king now. That is the sort of evidence for which they have been looking, evidence that suggests that we might support Ur's enemies. Oh! stupid, stupid!" The old man stamped his foot to emphasize his words.

"You are a very clever trader, Nahor, and, I must admit, an apt pupil of mine. But you are blind, blind and foolish. Have you forgotten the murder of your brother Haran? It may well have been your action that brought about his death!"

Nahor made no further attempt to justify himself. He sat sullen and silent, but when Milcah began to sob, he exclaimed petulantly to her in an undertone: "Be still, you silly woman, how can a man think!"

Terah sat down beside Sarai and turned to Nahor so fiercely that Milcah edged nearer to her husband as though to protect him. "I am the head of this family, and it should be for me to decide whether or not we deal secretly with the Babylonians." Then he addressed his elder son:

"There are many decisions to be made for our future safety, urgent decisions for this family and for the Habiru in Ur. Sometimes I feel old and tired. If our people are to remain in Ur, it is obvious that only you, Abram, can protect them from persecution and death. It is you, therefore, who must make the present decision for me, the decision for or against exile. Nahor, Lot and I will wait for your word."

Abram was silent for a time. Finally he said: "I do not know what that decision should be. But I should like to be alone for a time."

The members of the family left the room one by one. When they were all gone Abram drew the curtains across the doorway and began to pace up and down, his head bowed and his hands behind him, as was his custom when in deep thought. Presently Sarai returned and slipped into the room. He continued his pacing as though he had not noticed her and she watched him for a time with a half-smile on her lips. At last she said:

"You are still wearing your turban and street cloak and your sandals. Give them to me."

He obeyed mechanically.

"Now sit down and wait here until I bring you food."

Again he obeyed.

She brought water and a towel and a pair of slippers. Then she washed his feet and dried them. After that she disappeared, to return in a few minutes with a large tray. She placed the tray on the floor and unrolled a cloth before him, putting bread and dates and a jug of goat's milk on the cloth. He ate and drank in silence and she continued to watch him. Finally she spoke:

"You are thinking of the future of your people. On the other hand, I am thinking of you and what the future may bring to you. If you remain here in Ur you will continue to belong to the moon god, whom you hate. You will be near his priestesses, whom I suspect you may not hate. If you return to the tents of your people, you may become a man like other men, and you will be the father of sons."

"Yes, I know," Abram replied. "It seems strange to have someone think about me and my personal problems. No one has done that since Amtelai left us. No one asks me what I am thinking in my heart, except my friend Dudu. He prescribes for me. But his prescription, when it is boiled down, is to tell me that self-indulgence would satisfy all my longings. He would make of me a priest like other priests, a man like other men, a sheep to be folded with other sheep.

"You understand me and you know what is in my heart without questioning. I have always longed to be free so that I might have sons and daughters of my own. But something within drives me on to learn a better way of life, better for me and for my people, and for all people everywhere.

"So I have sought understanding and wisdom. Understanding! It is like a rainbow, a dazzling arch from earth to heaven. I run after it but it is always beyond me — out of my grasp. Without understanding how can we be wise?"

He looked at her and his puzzled expression changed slowly into a smile. "You understand me, Sarai. But you too will have sons of your own, some day."

"Yes," she replied. "I hope so. But I have other things to discuss with you now. I told you that I was bringing a message of great importance. Your grandfather Nahor came to Drehem and he died there. You know that. It was fifteen days ago. He was on his way from Haran to Ur because he felt that death was not far off, and he wanted to give his blessing to the man he should select as the future leader of his people.

"On reaching Drehem, Nahor knew the end was near and so he sent his death blessing; he sent it to you, Abram. He believed you would return to lead our people."

"To me?" Abram cried in astonishment. After a silence he asked: "What was his blessing?"

"He used the old words," she replied, "the words handed down from father to son from early times. Nahor spoke to Prince Salah and to his servants and to me thus:

> " '*I bless Abram with the blessings of Heaven above,
> Blessings of the deep that lieth under,
> Blessings of the breasts and of the womb.*' "

Abram stared at her without speaking until at last she blushed and turned away.

"The Habiru leaders," Abram said, "have not led their people. They have given them no god of their own, no land of their own. Who am I to do this? Who will guide me?

"You, Sarai, seem to sense all that is in my heart although you cannot understand the turmoil of my thinking. As I was returning to the temenos after our walk in the moonlight the other night, an old saying came to me — *As in water, face answers to face, so the heart of man to man;* and I altered the proverb — *so the heart of woman to man.*"

The curtains opened again and Terah entered. He smiled at his son and daughter and sat down upon the rug.

"Come here, Abram," he said, "you shall have my blessing as well as that of Father Nahor. Kneel down." Abram obeyed. "I give you my blessing. When I die you will be the chief of this family. You will inherit the major share in all my goods and possessions, the share that goes to the eldest son. I have written this in a tablet according to the law of Ur."

Then Terah spoke in formal language, according to the old formula:

"*Now, therefore, may the God of our fathers give thee the dew of heaven and the fatness of the earth. Be lord over thy brother and thy sister. Cursed be everyone that curseth thee, and blessed be he that blesseth thee.*"

Father and son rose and embraced. Then Abram said: "I hope I may be worthy of your blessing and of the blessing of Nahor. A decision must be made and time is short, very short. The answer is not clear. I ask permission to sacrifice to the God of our fathers in the family chapel."

Terah looked at his son in surprise. "This is a strange request," he said. "But I grant it. We cannot hope for adequate protection from this god. He is only a family god."

Terah clapped his hands, and when a servant appeared he said: "Prepare the altar for sacrifice. Send to the market for a kid and two turtledoves, and have fire ready when my son calls for it."

He turned back to Abram. "I shall summon the heads of the principal families of our people in Ur to meet here in this house tonight, the ones that can be trusted. They must learn the danger that threatens them and must hear our own decision."

Terah went out and again Abram was alone. After a time Sarai came back to tell him that the chapel had been prepared for him. As she entered she heard him muttering, and she caught the name "Shub-Kudur." She watched him with a puzzled expression as he passed out of the room toward the chapel, still muttering and without looking or speaking to her.

In the chapel court he stood and stared at the stone slab beneath which his brother Haran had been buried. Then he turned to the altar and laid wood in order upon it. He took the kid and dressed it, and the turtledoves, and he laid the kid and the turtledoves on the altar. When that was finished, he took the fire which his father's young men had left for him, and thus he made a burnt offering upon the altar to the God of his fathers.

Smoke from the sacrifice rose into the blue sky that arched above the little chapel. And Abram stood for a long time, asking questions, thinking, waiting, listening. Eventually, peace seemed to come to him in a strange way. His decision was made. He had heard no voice, and yet it seemed to him that a voice must have spoken.

After that, he talked for a long time with his father.

That night a considerable company gathered in the house of Terah. Milcah, who had become a careful housewife, had spread rugs for them in the central court. Under her direction, the potted flowers and furnishings had been removed, and fruit, nuts, and wine had been placed on a cloth for the guests.

As the men began to arrive, Sarai and Milcah seated themselves on the gallery where they could watch what was going on without being seen themselves.

Terah seated himself on the floor at the end of the court. He looked small and venerable as he sat there. His gray hair and beard, resting on his black tunic, shone in the lamplight. Each newcomer paid his respects to the patriarch on entering. Some of the more senior citizens were bidden to sit down near him, and others walked about or sat in groups talking energetically.

They were merchants for the most part, with a sprinkling of artisans and soldiers. Some were in desert costume, but all appeared prosperous. There was an air of general anxiety, and the conversations which Sarai could overhear had to do with unfair treatment, injustice, and rumors of this and of that.

Terah rose and left the court. He was gone for what seemed a very long time to the assembled company, who had surmised that what he was going to say to them might decide their future. But when he reappeared he was followed by Abram. Silence fell.

Sarai, watching from above, observed that Abram was strangely altered. His youthful face was flushed, his eyes were wide with excitement and he held his head high. Although he was the youngest man present with the exception of Nahor, Lot and Oni, he bore himself with an air of complete assurance. Terah, standing beside his towering son with bearded dignity, turned to him and motioned him to speak.

"My children," Abram began, and Milcah exclaimed in Sarai's ear: "He is speaking to them like a high priest!" — "I have serious news for you. The Sumerian noble Nasir-Sin and his followers have laid a plan to drive you out of Ur and out of Sumer. Two days from now he will submit this plan to the king. But Rim-Sin has also granted the request that I be present at the audience. I will plead your cause there, as well as I can. If my plea should fail, you and your kinsmen will be subjected to persecution such as you have never known.

"You might well ask: Why does this military group propose such unjust treatment of the Habiru? Why this persecution? I shall try to give you the answer.

"You realize all too well that in Ur and throughout Sumer you form a race apart; feared because you are not understood, disliked because you are conscious of your own superiority, envied because you prosper, suspected because you have given only half-hearted allegiance to Sumer's gods in this time of national danger. It is because of these things that they are discriminating against you.

"Let us examine the situation clearly. The clouds of war are gathering fast over this land. Sumer, though more cultured than other nations, is decadent and it may well come to pass that Ur will fall and be completely destroyed in the not too distant future. If that should come about, you who remain here will perish in the ruins of this city. Do not hope that you will be spared when that time comes.

"This problem has long been before me. We have two choices. Either we must remain here and become Sumerians, worshiping their gods, or we must preserve our identity as sons of Noah and leave this land.

"The death blessing of my grandfather Nahor has come to me. It was his wish that I should leave the city and return to lead our people."

At this, there were exclamations of astonishment, and someone called: "What about Terah?"

But Terah held up his hand, and when they were silent he said: "It is as Abram has said. Listen to him." Then Abram continued:

"The decision that lies before us is difficult. I know it all too well. Today I made a burnt offering to the God of my grandfather Nahor, the God of Noah. And while I stood and waited for help, it was as though a voice had spoken to me. All at once I knew what we must do."

Abram hesitated, but no one in the little company stirred. Then his deep bass voice again resounded in the court, and he seemed to be addressing a larger audience.

"I tell you that the time has come for the Habiru, the wanderers from the hills of Haran, to leave Ur, leave Sumer and Akkad. I say to you — rejoin your people. Return to Haran when you can. The time is coming when the Habiru must have a land of their own. The time is coming when we must have our own God and must worship Him only."

Abram stopped again. There was silence, followed by a hum of conversation which grew louder and louder, until one of the company stepped forward and cried: "What country? What god? Who will tell us these things?"

Abram shook his head. "I cannot answer these questions, not now. I will urge your cause before the king, will ask him for fair treatment. After that I shall escape from Ur if I can. Then I shall continue to seek the answer to these questions as I have in the past. I believe the true God will lead our people — perhaps into the land of Canaan. But I must first find Him. If I succeed, I shall go to Haran to lead my people. If not, you must find a better leader." With that, he made a gesture to his father, who said:

"We have agreed that all who wish to escape at this time must leave Ur while the audience is in progress, and no one must start before that time. If the king is kindly disposed, all may be well with you for as long a time as his favor continues. However, there are special difficulties involving my family. A messenger sent by my son Nahor to Babylon has possibly fallen into the hands of Nasir's men, my eldest son Haran has been murdered, and Abram is determined to withdraw from the priesthood of Nannar. Therefore I must leave at sundown on the day after tomorrow with my whole household. Abram, we hope, will be able to follow us."

Terah looked at Abram and shook his head. Then he continued:

"I am leaving my agent here, and he will help you as best he can to make contact with caravans when the time comes for you to escape.

"We are quitting Ur forever. As soon as it is safe for us, we will make our way back to Haran. Until we see you there, may the God of our fathers bless you — and us."

CHAPTER X

Fools! Fools!

ON THE FOLLOWING DAY, Terah was at home making preparations for the flight from Ur. Servants came and went with goods of all sorts while he and Nahor and Oni made decisions as to their disposal; some to go to the warehouse; some to be abandoned where they were; a few precious belongings to go with them in great luggage bags on carrying camels.

During a lull in their own talk, Terah raised his head to listen. From an upper room came the sound of laughter. He could recognize the voices of Abram and Lot and shrieks of laughter from Sarai and Milcah. He looked at the other two in surprise. But Oni smiled and said:

"It may be, Master Terah, that I know your daughter better than you do. Wherever Sarai goes, laughter goes with her, and you will remember that even when Abram and I played together as boys his mood was apt to change suddenly. Yesterday, he was like a high priest and I hardly knew him. Today he is my friend of years ago."

"Very thoughtless, I call it," said Nahor. "Here at a time when we are about to lose everything we have in the world, he leaves the work and worry to us while he chatters with the women. If he has so much influence why doesn't he do something about our situation. Perhaps he is glad to get rid of us."

Terah shook his gray head and said a little sharply: "Nahor, re-member the old saying:

> *"Keep your tongue from guile,*
> *Let not laughter which comforteth the spirit*
> *Be discord to your ears and smoke to your eyes.*
> *Each heart must know its own bitterness."*

At this point they were interrupted by the entrance of a servant who admitted a messenger in elaborate livery. The messenger bowed to Terah and announced in an unnecessarily loud voice: "The chamberlain of the king bids me invite you, your son Nahor and your grandson Lot to the betrothal of the entum in the temple of Nannar. The ceremony is to take place tomorrow. He bids me also to convey a special invitation to the granddaughter of the prince of Drehem who has lately come to Ur."

The messenger disappeared without further ceremony and Terah rubbed his hands with satisfaction. "Important people have been gathering in Ur from many kingdoms to be present at this function. I thought the chamberlain had overlooked me. Ha, per-haps he has discovered that I am the father of Abram, priest of the moon god!"

"But surely," said Nahor, "we have done enough for Rim-Sin to deserve this honor ourselves."

"Just so," replied his father, "and it is remarkable that the invi-tation comes so late. But perhaps we are to be popular in the royal court now, when it is too late. I wonder if we are fools to run away."

"I for one wouldn't want to leave," said Nahor, "if that mes-senger of mine had returned."

"Then you do believe the messenger has been taken?" ex-claimed Terah.

Nahor nodded and turned away scowling. Terah climbed the stair and passed along the gallery to the room from which the talk and laughter were coming. He paused in the doorway unobserved.

Sarai was saying: "And now that we are to leave Ur so soon, I shall not be able to see the life at the court and the sights of the city. I've dreamed about that."

Lot spoke up. "Don't worry. Today and tomorrow I can show you a great many things in Ur, things you never did dream of, in the parade grounds, the markets, dining places, palaces and temples. I'll be your guide and your defender!"

"Splendid," replied Sarai, laughing. "But then," she added, "perhaps I should stay home so I can keep my half brother out of the idol market. Someone has to protect the idols." She laughed again, and when Abram tried to catch her in mock anger came flying out of the door and ran straight into the arms of her father. She clung to him and looked back at Abram.

"What is all this?" cried Terah, laughing a little himself. "I'll protect you from him. I have not heard sounds like these in my house . . . not since your mother left us with you in her arms. But quiet down now and come back into the room. I have something to tell you. Perhaps you will get a glimpse of the king's court after all. I am bidden to the betrothal of the entum, and so are Nahor, Lot, and Sarai. It is many years since Ur has seen this ceremony and I believe it would be wise for us to appear."

"I'll be able to wear my court costume after all," Sarai exclaimed. "Is the king's only daughter really going to marry a god?"

"Well," replied Terah, "in a sort of a way. The wife of Nannar is supposed to be the goddess Ningal, but he also has living concubines and a legitimate living first wife, who is called the entum. She is the head of all his women, who are called *sal-me*. The temple of E-Nun-Makh was rebuilt by King Bur-Sin for Nannar and Ningal both. He divided it inside into two duplicate sets of rooms. One set is for the priests of Nannar to live in and one set for the *sal-me* of Ningal. Princess Shub will live there after she becomes the entum. I do not know much about the life there, for only priests and priestesses may enter. Perhaps Abram can tell you more. But I do know this: The priestesses of the *sal-me* are very good business women. They sign financial contracts and manage the affairs of the god's household with great skill. Have you anything to add to that, Abram?"

Abram smiled and shook his head. But Lot had many questions to ask. "How is it that Sarai has managed to receive an invitation? Surely no one at court knows she is here yet."

Terah replied that no one of her rank could enter Ur without the chamberlain's knowledge. But Abram objected. "I don't believe her invitation is due to her rank at all. It must have been the influence of her drunken admirer who followed her through the city yesterday like this." And to his father's astonishment he imitated the staggering gait of Unzie son of Gudea.

Then Milcah, when she could control her laughter, exclaimed: "Abram, what under heaven has happened to you? Yesterday you were so serious you frightened me and today, today you seem to be mad! Now I am frightened more than ever." Her laughter was succeeded by weeping. "I don't know what will happen to us. Nahor is worried sick and will say nothing to me. We all rely on you and you have gone silly."

Abram answered her, with a half-smile. "You can't realize how great a weight has slipped off my shoulders, the weight of indecision. For years you have seen me silent and morose, a priest of Nannar who was gradually learning to hate the god he served. At last the great decision has been made. I know it is only a first step but just consider what this decision has done for me." He held his arms out above their heads. "I shall be a man, not a priest; a free man, and I may yet be the father of sons like the sons you expect to bear to my brother Nahor."

Then he turned to Terah. "I know that my leaving the temple

means the failure of your plans for me and your plans for many others. But I am sure this step is right — for me and for our people. I'm like a man let out of prison. I face danger. I face a multitude of problems but I rejoice for the moment. I breathe the air of freedom. I seem to smell the sweet smells of meadows and cattle and camels!

"In exile there will be many hardships. You and the others who may lead your people will have new decisions to make."

As he spoke his gay manner vanished and his whole bearing changed. They stood in silence for a moment, each occupied with his own thoughts of the future. Terah shook his head dolefully.

Then Sarai, who had been watching Abram, said: "You have many things to plan and you may be missed in the temple unless you return there soon."

Abram turned to look at her and replied: "Yes, you are right. *As in water, face answers to face, so the heart of woman to man.* Since you understand so easily what a man thinks in his heart, can you also look into the future? Can you tell me other things that I must know? For instance, can you be certain that Nahor's messenger has fallen into the hands of Nasir?"

Sarai did not reply, but Milcah said: "Don't talk any more nonsense, Abram. I'm sure the messenger will come through to us. And you must follow us into the desert, for we shall need you there."

After Abram had gone, Sarai said to Lot: "Will you help me get the information Abram needs?"

"Of course I'll help you if I can," Lot said. "I'd do anything for Abram."

"I think," she replied, "that Unzie is the man who knows about the messenger. Let us see how Nahor reacts to the mention of Unzie first."

Together they went down to the court, where Nahor was still

busy with the servants. They drew him aside, and Sarai said to him, "Nahor, you have been looking for Unzie son of Gudea, I believe."

Nahor flushed and said: "What do you know about him?" Then, after some hesitation: "Yes, at least I have been expecting him in my office. He promised to come directly there on his arrival in Ur. Surely he is not here yet."

At this Lot laughed. "Nahor," he said, "You do not spend enough time in the public drinking places. If you did you would have seen him as I have, usually drunk. You say I play too much. I say you work too much."

Sarai smiled and said to Lot: "It may be that Unzie has a reason for avoiding Nahor now, especially if he has lost the messenger. But perhaps you, Lot, could find him and bring him here. If necessary you may tell him that I have seen him following me and wish to make his acquaintance. After that if he seems afraid to meet Nahor, you will have to say that Nahor has gone on a journey. When you get him here I will see him first and Nahor afterward. It might be just as well for Oni to be near by to protect me."

"If Unzie is really in Ur," Nahor said irritably, "I'll go out and find him myself."

"If you do," answered Sarai, "you may frighten him away." She spoke now with icy emphasis. "Nahor, I wish to have it this way. You have made enough trouble already."

Lot laughed. "I'll bring him back to you. I'll catch him with the honeyed bait of flattery. I'll dangle the prospect of beauty before his dazzled eyes. But if that's not enough I'll tie him hand and foot and carry him on my shoulder, and bring his bowlegged servant under my arm."

Some hours later Lot returned from his errand. He was accompanied by an obviously willing Unzie and the servant as well.

They entered the idol market and waited there in a back room. It was true that Unzie's eyes were a little bloodshot and his face puffy, but he cut a very presentable figure nevertheless. Before long Sarai appeared, followed at a little distance by Oni. She was dressed simply. She smiled at Unzie.

He drew himself up, folding his arms reverently as though he were in the presence of a goddess. Then he bowed almost to the ground. The stocky little servant bowed deeply also, and Lot, not to be outdone, did likewise with a great flourish.

"I am the happiest man in Sumer today," Unzie said. "Since I saw you entering the city I have been as one who walks about in a dream." (Lot, who was standing behind him, staggered a little in pantomime.) "Today I gave up the company of my noble friends in the pleasant places of Ur, so that I could think of you and at the same time attend to another small matter that had to do with your kinsman Nahor. Then, what was my joy to receive a visit from this young man Lot!"

Sarai smiled at him. He swaggered a little nearer to her and continued: "I rejoice that you have looked on me with favor. In the city of Nippur where I am close kinsman to the great patesi who rules the city, I am considered — what shall I say?" He turned and bowed to his servant, who returned the bow. "I am considered to be rich, influential and not altogether lacking in those qualities which find favor in the eyes of women." He reached for her hand, but she drew back. "I have lands, houses, slaves. This evening I propose that you come with me in a cano-pied barge for a little pleasure on the great river."

At this Sarai shook her head at Lot and said: "I do not know what my kinsman Lot could have said to you. It is kind of you to have come. But my reason for wishing to see you was to ask you one or two questions. Will you answer me?"

"Of course," he replied. "Anything."

Then Sarai said: "You have been entertained in a manner that

befits your rank by Lord Nasir and his friends, here in Ur, I suppose?"

"Yes, of course," he replied.

"And in Babylon, are you equally well known in the court of
Hammurabi?"

"Oh, yes! I dined with the minister of commerce in that court
only recently."

"You do lead a pleasant life!" She continued, "And you are also
a man of affairs. No doubt you have been of assistance to Nahor
in his communications with Babylon?"

He bowed. "Then the message tablets," she said still smiling,
"that you were bringing from Babylon to my brother Nahor —
will you tell me where they are?"

Unzie seemed startled. "My Lady Sarai, I see that you are a
clever woman as well as a beautiful one. You could manage the
household of a rich noble with success as well as enjoyment."

"You flatter me," replied Sarai. "But I suppose it is true that
since the Babylonian messenger and his tablet have fallen into the
hands of the police, your life, shall I say, is in danger now in this
city. I am sorry for you. This means danger to my half brother
Nahor as well, does it not?"

Unzie and his servant looked at each other and the servant replied: "We had thought of that, my lady."

Sarai turned and nodded to Oni, who disappeared. Then she
held out her hand to Unzie, who bowed and kissed it but remained speechless.

"Thank you for answering my questions," she said. "Your silence is even more eloquent than your words."

As Sarai turned to leave the room, Nahor entered and she said
to him: "Unzie son of Gudea has kept himself away from you,
Nahor, because he was a little reluctant to admit that while he
was enjoying the hospitality of Lord Nasir, his messenger disappeared mysteriously with the message tablet."

Next morning early Terah sent for Sarai to come to him. His face was gray and haggard and he was stooped with fatigue. "I have had word from the camel station that Nahor left last night with the best camels. He did not say good-by, nor did he ask my permission to carry off the large amount of silver and gold and the goods that went with him. He told Magog at the camel station that this was according to my command. Milcah has gone with him and also Unzie of Nippur with his servant. They left on the road for the north heading for Nippur or for Babylon beyond."

Sarai put her arms about him to comfort him and said: "Wait until I can bring you food." The old man sat down on the floor heavily. "Have you told your concubine and the others yet?" Terah shook his head in the negative.

Sarai returned shortly with Terah's concubine Enna and they gave him food and drink.

Enna was a middle-aged Sumerian woman who had entered the household as the slave of Abram's mother. After the death of Amtelai, Terah had taken her for his concubine and she had managed the household for him, but she had borne him no children. Although she had grown heavy with the passage of years, her hair was black and she could still be called comely.

Sarai left them now and returning to her own room she mixed a little clay with water and rolled it into a tablet. Then she took her reed stylus and printed on it a message for Abram. When it was finished, she rolled out a thin layer of clay and wrapped it about the tablet to form an envelope and prevent its being read until the rapidly drying envelope should be broken off. She placed her seal on the blank envelope, put the tablet in a box and sent it by the hand of a slave to Abram in the temple. The message read:

The police have the message tablets in their possession. Nahor and Milcah fled secretly last night in company with Unzie. Our own future seems very dark. You alone have the strength to save your people and your family.

When Terah had eaten, he hurried off into the city on various urgent errands. He had to make new plans for the exodus of his family as well as to talk with his agents and the leading members of the Habiru colony in Ur. All this had to be done before the betrothal ceremony, for his plan was to leave Ur shortly afterward.

Meanwhile something like a state of panic broke out in his household. The concubine Enna became hysterical and had a violent altercation with Naamah, Sarai's handmaid. Their screaming filled the house, and Oni, the privileged slave, had to step between them.

Sarai scolded the concubine until the latter fell into sullen silence. Sarai herself then fled to her own room, where she wept disconsolately until Lot came to her to learn what was happening. The noise had only just wakened him.

When Terah returned for the midday meal, order had been restored. He reassured his ordinarily placid concubine that she would not be left behind and further that she should have a good camel and could take with her certain things dear to her heart. When Enna had been thus mollified he looked for Sarai and found her smiling and seemingly as gay as ever. This was a great relief to him, for the old man was himself in need of reassurance, as Sarai well knew.

"Our plans are in order again," he said, "and I hope nothing more will go wrong. We must go to the ceremony in the temple today as though nothing had happened. Please see to it, my daughter, that you dress yourself in a manner befitting the only daughter of Ur's leading idol merchant. Today the career of that merchant comes to an end!"

Sarai proceeded to carry out her father's instructions, with the aid of Naamah and her mirror. When the time came, Oni was waiting for her in the central court and his heart quickened as he watched her pass around the gallery and down the staircase.

She wore a broad ribbon of gold that passed like a coronet around her fair hair and held a golden medallion in place on her forehead. A priceless carnelian necklace encircled her curving throat, emphasizing the delicacy of her girlish features and high color. Her cloak, shimmering with silver thread, fell from shoulder and breast to little red sandals. No detail had been overlooked, from curling hair to painted nails.

In the street before the house, white asses were waiting for them. Terah, Lot, Sarai and Oni mounted the little animals and trotted off in single file down the narrow street, while slaves ran before and behind. The weather was cool, the air exhilarating, the sky deep blue. Sarai was excited now and pleased by the admiring glances that followed her.

She turned and said to Oni: "Aren't you excited?"

Oni, whose habit it was to speak little, only smiled.

As they approached the temple the crowds increased and lined the streets so completely that only a narrow passage was left for the donkeys of the invited guests — Ur's patricians of the amelu class, high-ranking army officers, wealthy merchants.

A second double line of spectators looked down from the house tops on either side. Lot, glancing up, spied a group of pretty girls and waved gaily. One of the young women took a flower from her hair and tossed it down to him. When he caught it there was a wave of laughter and applause.

When they arrived at the palace of the king they left their asses in the care of Oni and gave their names to an Elamite officer. He admitted them to the sacred way, a wide avenue about four hundred yards in length which led from the palace to the great gate of the sacred enclosure and straight on through the gate to the temple of Ningal. A thousand soldiers were drawn up in two lines that faced each other on either side of the sacred way. Behind the soldiers, on either side, the citizens of Ur stood in a dense crowd. Many of them had been waiting since dawn to see the Princess Shub ride to her betrothal.

Sarai gave an exclamation of wonder as she looked down this aisle. The kilts and shields of the soldiers seemed to make a solid wall; the sun glinted on their copper helmets and the spear blades above their heads, forming palisades of burnished metal.

Terah walked on ahead, followed by Lot and Sarai in a state of suppressed excitement. As they passed the temple of E-Nun-Makh on the left, they were halted by a line of priestesses, who filed out and preceded them down the aisle of soldiers. At the temple of Ningal they turned to the right and climbed a flight of steps to the terrace of the ziggurat. A newly made inclined roadway led up to the terrace at one side of the stair; Terah explained that this had been built to make it possible for the king and princess to ride from the palace down the aisle and up to the terrace in the king's royal cart.

Their names were taken again and they were admitted to the terrace that led along the base of the ziggurat to the lower shrine of Nannar, now facing them at the far end of the terrace. Proceeding along the terrace, they passed the staircase on their left that led to the upper shrine of Nannar at the top of the ziggurat. When Sarai looked up she gasped:

"It makes me dizzy just to look up to the top."

At the entrance to the lower shrine they were forced to wait for a little time. They found themselves standing before an alcove in which Sarai spied a table supported at either end by a statuette.

"See," she exclaimed, "the little ram caught in a thicket."

The statuette that faced them was indeed the figure of a ram caught in a thicket. The beast, which was made of gold, lapis lazuli and white shell, stood on his hind legs, his forelegs being tied by silver chains to a tree or bush of gold, into which his head of gold and horns of lapis lazuli were thrust.

"The statue," Terah said, "is very old. It represents a legend that comes down to us from the earliest days of Sumer when it was the custom to sacrifice human beings to please the gods. Once, it is said, at the time of sacrifice a ram appeared miraculously caught in a thicket. The priest took the ram and offered it up in place of a child, and ever after that animals were used."

They passed from the terrace through an arch into the lofty temple shrine. At the far end of the shrine the idol Nannar was set high above the heads of the company. He seemed to Sarai to be looking out through the archway by which she had just entered, as though he saw some amusing sight far away, a sight that no one else could appreciate. She was quite oblivious of the untold wealth of gems that glittered in his mantle but was fascinated by his curiously contemptuous expression.

She whispered to her father: "I think Nannar is laughing. He looks as though he might speak!"

Terah nodded with pleased pride and said: "Yes, I gave him that expression. Years ago I was given the task of repairing Nannar. His face was badly cracked, and I changed it ever so little, but just enough. After that, I had the feeling that he might say something, even to me while I worked on him. When I was a boy my father Nahor once said that he expected my little images to speak." Terah smiled again. "I have never confessed that to Abram."

Sarai continued to look at the idol. Finally, she squeezed her father's arm. "I know," she said, "I know what he is saying. It is: 'Fools, fools, fools!' He has been saying that all these years, and no one has understood him. He says it here, and he must be saying it when he is at the top of ziggurat and while they carry him back and forth."

They were ushered over to a position on the idol's right. The priests and *sal-me* were standing on his left. Sarai looked about her and found that she was in the company of nobles in long capes, soldiers in kilts and court ladies whose costumes were most elaborate. More elaborate than her own, for they wore enormous curled wigs covered with gold ornaments and heavy boat-shaped earrings, as well as bracelets and anklets of all kinds. Several guests spoke to Terah and many eyes followed Sarai.

Upon the steps of the altar lay the dowry of the princess, the gift of the king to the god, precious jewels, onyx, coral, pearls, sapphires and rubies, and also gold, and silver, and beautiful cloth and perfumes. A burnt offering smoked upon the altar, and an aged priest clad only in a loincloth served the god.

An expectant silence fell on the assembly as the sound of shouting reached them from the direction of the palace. This continued for a considerable time until the thud of tramping feet announced the arrival of the procession on the terrace. At last a team of two pure white oxen entered the shrine, drawing behind them a low, richly ornamented cart which rolled along silently on its leather-covered wheels. King Rim-Sin, standing in the cart, acknowledged the applause that greeted him. Seated in front of him was the Princess Shub in shimmering white. The cart was followed by the royal guard at the head of which marched a young giant bearing the mace of Ur-Namu, the mace that was the symbol of kingship in Ur.

The king stepped down from the cart and took his seat on a low throne that faced the image. The princess followed and stood at one side of his throne, while the officers of the royal guard filed in and took their places behind the throne. The mace was then presented to the king.

The company stood silent while the high priest, Enannatum, approached the throne. Taking the hand of the Princess Shub, he led her to a position in front of the god, on the altar steps beside her dowry. He then removed his cape and gave it to the master of the harem, who had followed them.

Enannatum stood naked now except for loincloth, and he cried out in a loud voice: "O Nannar! Lord of Ur, prince of gods! The mighty King Rim-Sin gives his daughter to you and with her he has presented a dowry which only the king of Ur and of Larsa could have provided."

He stooped and took a jeweled dagger from the top of the heap of presents and, advancing, laid it upon the altar. Then he withdrew, leaving Shub standing alone before the idol. She looked up and then dropped her gaze quickly to the floor. Above her towered Nannar, his great round eyes reflecting the flickering of a hundred lamps. There was no other movement. A voice spoke. It seemed to issue from the idol, but his expression of contempt did not change.

When the voice stopped speaking Sarai murmured: "Fools, fools, fools!"

The priests and the *sal-me* began to chant:

> *"Who in heaven is high exalted?*
> *Father, god enlightening earth,*
> *Lord of Ur, of gods the prince. . . ."*

Abram was playing no active part in the ceremony, but he stood in his robes with the other priests quite close to the idol, watching it all and trying to control his feeling of anger and resentment. Finally he made a conscious effort to turn his thoughts to something else, and looked over the company until he caught sight of his father. He saw suddenly how much older and how frail he appeared. He realized also how deep was his own love for this gallant, stubborn little man, now facing so perilous a future.

As his eyes traveled on to Sarai he was startled and exclaimed under his breath: "What's happened to her?" He had never before seen her in court costume. This was not the girl he had known, but a beautiful woman, and he had the feeling that perhaps he did not know her after all.

Sarai was conscious of his glance and caught the expression of amazement. She noticed too that his eyes drifted back to the princess and then returned to her as though he were making a comparison.

The chanting ceased and the sound of harps was heard. A woman entered and danced before the steps of the throne, a beautiful dark creature, scantily clad. Her movements were crude, suggestive, and Sarai blushed and looked away.

Princess Shub now knelt down before the idol and as she did so she turned to look at Abram with a faint smile on her lips. Sarai, watching all this, heard behind her a tinkling of earrings as two court ladies began to whisper. "Who is the tall, handsome priest?" — "I don't know," came the reply, "but I think she was smiling at him."

Abram looked angry, Sarai thought to herself. There was certainly some understanding between him and the princess! . . .

The dancing stopped and the concubines of Nannar entered; filing around the idol each made her bow to the god and left the shrine. Last of all, Princess Shub bowed very slightly. Then she turned and seemed to look at the audience for the first time, before she followed the concubines. The betrothal ceremony was over.

Outside the temple Lot took his leave "to say good-by to a friend."

Sarai looked after him, saying: "He will miss the city and his many friends." She turned to Terah. "And you, Father, you will miss Ur, won't you? But in a very different way."

Before Terah could answer they were joined by Abram and the three walked together down the sacred way in silence. They were conscious of the fact this was good-by to Ur forever, the end of a chapter.

Even to a casual observer this trio might have appeared unusual, and many of the passers-by stared at them — the gray-bearded little man in company with the tall shaven-headed priest, each with the heavy, sharply cut features that characterized the Amorites, and between them the delicately beautiful young woman.

Sarai overheard two courtiers jesting as they passed. One said: "Beauty and the Habiru." The other replied: "The old man is Terah. Wealth, holiness and loveliness, I should call it. What more could you ask for in life?"

Sarai glanced at her two companions. Each, she thought, has been successful in his chosen field of endeavor, successful beyond any reasonable expectation. Now they were about to sacrifice it all. Would they find something better?

She glanced up at Abram and said: "The Princess Shub is a friend of yours, I see." Abram looked down at her but did not reply. So she continued: "You do not want to talk about it? Very well!" She tossed her head. "Of course I would not inquire into your personal secrets. But there are evidently other things besides your studies of the ancient tablets that have kept you so constantly within the temple."

They came to their retinue. Oni was waiting for them in a secluded corner.

Terah spoke quietly to Abram: "Our plans are completed. We leave the house this afternoon. The carrying camels left this morning with the heavy baggage. No one should be able to distinguish them from any other caravan. I shall start from the camel station at dusk with all members of the household, except Sarai and her handmaid. They will follow last in the care of Magog."

Terah threw out his hands in a gesture of despair.

"Magog was my camel driver when I left the hills of Haran

so many years ago. He was a young man then. I had high hopes of what life in Ur would bring. Well! Now it seems that we could not become Sumerians. It is as my father Nahor said it would be, and I am to journey back to the hills of Haran, to the beehive houses, the tents, the meadows, the flocks, the wheat harvest.

"After your audience with Rim-Sin, you and Oni are to cross the river at once and join Sarai and Magog in the camel station and follow me as fast as possible. Once in the open desert, Magog will take her back to Drehem and leave her with her grandfather until it is safe for us to come for her on our way to Haran.

"I would have given you the fastest camels but Nahor took them for himself and his friend Unzie." His voice trembled. "Alas! my son Nahor!"

The others listened intently to Terah's final statement of plans, as the old man continued: "Magog will have the best remaining animals with him at the camel station. He and Sarai will wait there for you, Abram, until midnight. If you do not arrive then, they must follow me and leave camels behind for you and Oni.

"Whatever happens," Terah went on, "my plan is to postpone the journey northward for the present. We shall move out on the highroad to the east and leave it as soon as possible to continue eastward across the open desert that skirts the great swamp. We shall cross the river Idiigna in barges that are waiting for us, and proceed into the highlands of Elam. There we shall wait. If you are delayed you can learn of our whereabouts from my agent in the city of Susa."

"I will join you tonight," Abram said, "if I can. If not I will try to send you a message, but in any case I may not go with you into Elam."

Abram turned and saw that Melchizedek was waiting to speak to them. He gave an exclamation of pleasure and went to greet him. Then taking his arm he presented him to his father.

"You remember that I told you about my conversation with the shepherd-prince from the Land of Canaan. His father is king of Salem."

Melchizedek bowed to Terah and said: "I would not interrupt you now except that I must speak to you on a matter of my father's business. I know very well that these are precarious days for the Habiru in Ur, and from what I have learned today nothing should delay any action that you have planned." Terah looked at him with surprise and a little suspicion, but Melchizedek continued: "I see you need no warning from me.

"My father's business has to do with the transportation of goods from these eastern countries to Salem in the west. Camels are unknown in the west and he will pay you well to use your camel trains for this purpose. Perhaps details can be discussed later."

"Yes," replied Terah slowly and thoughtfully, "later, later. Yes, I will send a messenger to your father to draw up such a contract as he may desire — in a few months' time, perhaps."

Abram turned to Sarai, who was already seated on her donkey. "This is my half sister Sarai."

Melchizedek bowed to her and said: "I am sure you find Ur gay, a romantic setting for young life." Then he turned back to Terah. "Your daughter has great beauty. I saw quite well that at the ceremony today she stole the eyes of the audience away from the god himself! And even from the betrothed bride of the god." He laughed and looked back at Sarai. She tossed her head but gave him a brilliant smile at the same time. Then he added: "I shall look forward with impatience to our next meeting."

Again he addressed Terah: "I am a comparatively young man but I speak many languages and I have wandered through the world. I have journeyed from the land of the pharaohs to Akkad and Sumer and I have talked with many men in courts and temples, and in the tents of the wilderness. I have met men with great knowledge. But in your son I have found more. To knowledge he has added understanding." He turned to Abram. "We are both looking for the place where wisdom may be found — you and I. Surely we will find that place. Surely our paths will cross again.

"But I must leave you. May the most high God guide you all and bring you to your destination."

As he left them, Sarai exclaimed: "What a remarkable man, charming! He understands your innermost thoughts."

"Yes," said Terah. "It seemed to me he knew too much. But he made a very good suggestion. I might do business with his father. Camel traffic to Ur will soon be closed unless Nahor starts it up. I could quite well send my camels from Haran to Canaan. There is a ford across the great river there." Terah rubbed his hands together in a characteristic gesture. "It would bring us a good profit."

Abram spoke, half to himself, as though he had not heard the others. "Understanding? Wisdom? These things have no special dwelling place, unless it is in the hearts of men . . . men who seek new knowledge, men who have the courage to make their spirits free, men who can hear, who are not deafened by the world's uproar."

Sarai had turned the head of her donkey away and now looking back over her shoulder, she said to Abram: "Why don't you discuss these matters with the Princess Shub? I'm sure she would listen to you with the greatest sympathy."

◆◀(

CHAPTER XI

King Rim-Sin

LATER IN THE DAY, as the sun was setting, Sarai watched her father and the members of his numerous household ride away on their camels toward the east. As they disappeared, tears came to her eyes, but she controlled herself with an effort and turned to Magog, who stood at her side.

"How long before they will reach the open desert?"

"Three to four hours at the longest," said Magog, "and after that, no one will be able to find them unless it is when they are ferried across the river Idiigna."

Sarai and her handmaid Naamah crossed the open square of the camel station to an unoccupied plot where Magog had left his camels in the care of three Habiru drivers. One of the drivers spread out a rug for them and the two women sat down to wait, drawing their woolen cloaks about them, for with the setting of the sun, there was a sudden chill in the air.

Sarai felt lonely. The future was insecure to say the least. She began to sob quietly, and when Naamah tried to comfort her she said: "I am frightened. We are all separated now and dreadful things may happen to us. Suppose Abram and Oni do not come. Suppose we should never find Father Terah! I wish we were back in Drehem with my grandfather."

Naamah held her close to her ample bosom, as she had done so often all through Sarai's childhood. "Don't worry," Naamah said. "Your father told me we would be safer in Magog's care than with him. Soon we will be back in Drehem with Prince Salah."

Sarai was after all only a girl of sixteen years, although certainly more mature in mind and in body than most women of her age in other times and in other lands. Her upbringing had served to give her poise and self-assurance, but tonight she felt herself deserted and defenseless.

Naamah had been more a foster mother to her than she had been slave. Her hair, once black, was growing gray, but the beauty that had been hers when she was young still lingered in the sweetness of her expression like a reflection from the setting sun.

She held Sarai in her arms now, and a look of wistful sadness came into her face, as her mind slipped back over her own girlhood. Naamah had been born of well-to-do parents in the city of Isin. But when Rim-Sin had conquered that city, her father had been killed and she sold into slavery.

After the death of Sarai's mother, Prince Salah had found her in the slave market. He purchased her and made her the child's governess. As time passed she had often played the role of mother. Now she hummed an old tune until Sarai dropped off to sleep in her arms.

Midnight came, but Abram and Oni did not appear. Magog paced back and forth anxiously and waited past the hour set for their departure. Finally he directed his men to make the animals ready and called to the two women.

"We must not wait any longer. I will leave two men behind. They will hold the camels ready for Abram and Oni. But we must leave according to the command of Terah."

Sarai objected at first, but they prevailed upon her to come and tried to reassure her as to the safety of Abram.

And so, four camels moved swiftly down the broad track that

led away from Ur toward the east. They passed sleeping vil-
lages whose walls of mud seemed turned to silver in the light of
the moon. They went through long dark avenues of palms, peri-
odically emerging into the open where the moonlight fell on wide
fields of grain. Sometimes the night breeze seemed to send waves
of rolling shadow across the fields.

After a time the highway ran parallel to one of the major
irrigating canals. The walled side of the canal rose high above
their heads, for the water, like that in the great river itself, was
on a level considerably above the surrounding country. The desert had been converted into fertile fields after the great King
Ur-Nammu had established the system of irrigation.

As the camels padded swiftly forward, they overtook a man
who was running along on the wall above them. He was heading
out of Ur just as they were, and when the caravan had passed
well ahead of him, Sarai urged her camel forward and spoke to
Magog.

"That was a royal courier," she said. "He might be carrying
a message to the military stations at each crossroad to search
everyone leaving Ur."

"Yes," replied Magog, "but no one can catch us from behind
and we are ahead of him now. There are few swifter beasts than
these camels, and we carry no extra burden except a little food
and the skins of water. When we reach the desert, we are free."
He slapped the swaying back beneath him. Then he added: "We
are coming to our last crossroad before the desert right now."

They could see another road that joined their highway at
right angles and passed up over the irrigation canal in an arching bridge. At the side of the bridge was a small guardhouse, but
it was dark and the camel train slipped silently past and onward.

A little way beyond the crossroad, Sarai stopped her camel
abruptly. She had heard a shout behind them at the crossroad.
She made her camel kneel and stepped off. Magog, discovering

that she had dropped behind, returned to remonstrate, but before he could begin, she said: "The messenger is waking the guard now. I must hear what he says." With that she was off on foot, running back along the highway.

Magog's camel rocked slowly to its knees. The other driver and Naamah returned, and they waited in silence. From time to time they heard the sound of men's voices. Nothing else except the barking of dogs in a neighboring village and the crowing of a cock that heralded the approach of dawn. Presently a little figure came down the highway toward them. It was Sarai.

"I listened behind the guardhouse," she said, "and I heard everything without being discovered. The messenger repeated his instructions over and over. Lord Nasir has been put in command of the highway police and his orders are that no Habiru and no other persons riding on camels are permitted to pass out of Ur along any highway. Those trying to escape will be killed if they resist, or they will be returned to Ur under guard. Incoming travelers on camels are not to be molested."

"That must be the king's ruling after the audience," Magog said. "We have slipped through just in time, and we had better hurry on now to reach the desert before anyone can overtake us."

"But," objected Sarai, "what will happen to Abram and Oni? They may not know about the edict and they will be killed when they are caught, or they will be returned to prison."

Magog did not reply, but Naamah said: "Perhaps they could escape by water, but I suppose the river will be guarded too. They could never reach camels that way."

Finally Sarai said to Magog: "The desert runs along the border of the great swamp between here and the river Idiigna, does it not?"

"Yes," replied Magog, "and beyond the Idiigna as far as the mouth of the river Karun that runs down from the highlands of Elam."

"Then," Sarai said, "there is no one who knows the desert as well as you, Magog. Could you take camels into the desert to the border of the swamp so that Abram and Oni could come through the swamp by boat to meet you?"

"Yes," Magog replied, "I could. There is a village of the marsh natives called Suga. To the west of Suga is a little highland. During the winter months this is converted into an island by the rising water, and the natives keep sheep and goats there and visit them by boat. At this time of year, however, it should be possible for camels to reach this highland to the west. But the natives do not welcome strangers in their village even if we could get there. There are no roads, for this whole section of the desert is flooded each year. Sumerians cannot get there at all, but I know the region. Oni would have to get a marsh native to guide him by boat to the highland west of Suga."

"Good," said Sarai. "Then I shall return to Ur as fast as I can and let them know our plan, if I can only find them."

"No," Magog protested. "I cannot let you, a woman, return alone. I will send a camel boy back to Ur with the message. We must continue on into the desert and look for an encampment where we can get extra camels to send to Suga."

"Magog," Sarai said quietly. "Am I the daughter of Terah, or am I not? Am I the granddaughter of Prince Salah and of Nahor, or am I not? You were once Nahor's slave. Now you are a freed man in the employ of Terah. You shall follow my command. You know very well that the camel boy would not know what to do in Ur. I may be able to reach Abram through Oni. I may have to reach him through Princess Shub. You yourself must meet us at Suga. Send me word if you can what success you have and what news from Father Terah.

"But it would be a good idea for me not to look like a woman. I will take the cloak and the desert headdress of the camel boy." She already had her cloak off, and now she removed her headdress.

"Here," she said to the driver, "will you exchange, please?

Give me your sandals also. Oh dear, they are so big. Tie them
on my feet, Naamah."

Naamah did as she was bid, but all the time she kept protest-
ing that she would return with Sarai and that Prince Salah would
never forgive her if she let her go alone.

"No, Naamah," Sarai said, "you cannot come. Make sure that
the kaffiyeh covers my hair well and that the headband is secure.
Now give me water so that I can make my hands and face and
arms dirty."

She stepped onto the saddle, and at a word her camel rose
slowly to his feet, grunting dolefully. As the beast padded away
down the highroad, Magog stood shaking his head and Naamah
wept aloud.

When Sarai reached the guardhouse, she raised her hand in
salute to the guard, who was still standing with the messenger
drinking from a water jug.

But as she would have passed, the messenger called: "Wait,
did you see camels pass you just now?"

Sarai did her best to speak like a man. "Yes."

"How many?"

"Four, traveling fast."

"Who were the riders?"

"I don't know."

She moved on, and the guard said to the messenger: "They're
gone by now. You can't expect me to run after those cursed
beasts. They sail like a ship along the road and right out across
the desert. I remember the first one I ever saw . . ." The men's
voices trailed off into a murmur as Sarai urged her camel on
down the road to Ur.

The flight of Terah had passed unobserved. This might well
have been due to the fact the city was filled to overflowing
with holiday makers.

After taking leave of his father and half sister following the betrothal ceremony, Abram returned to his room in the tablet archives. Shortly before sunset, he dressed in his temple robe and made his way to the north harbor. Here he found Oni waiting on the landing stage with a *machouf*. Seated in the stern of the boat, with spoon-shaped paddle in hand, was a dark, well-muscled little man.

"This is Kerkha," Oni said. "There is no better boatman to be found anywhere. He is a marsh native." Kerkha flashed his teeth in a grin, while Abram settled himself in the middle of the skiff and Oni took up the oar in the bow.

The little craft passed swiftly out of the harbor and into the open river. Abram remained silent, but Oni, pleased with the opportunity of using his powerful muscles, looked back exultantly and said: "There are very few boats that could overtake us in this skiff, and none that go more silently and in shallower waters. If we were to escape into the great swamp instead of mounting our camels on the opposite shore, no one could ever find us."

It was the time of day when workmen were returning from their labor in the city to their homes across the river. These men rowed in *bellams*, with six to ten oars on a side, singing in unison as they swayed back and forth, until the whole river seemed to echo to their voices. Such a *bellam* passed close to the little *machouf*, and Abram heard the steersman chant: "*Nin-Anna wailed the cold night through*," and the oarsmen's chorus:

> "*Dumuzi comes, Dumuzi comes,*
> *Nin-Anna naked, undefiled.*
> *Dumuzi comes, Dumuzi comes.*"

"Spring will come just the same," Abram thought to himself, "regardless of whether Dumuzi finds Nin-Anna. Wheat will ripen along the river regardless of whether Nannar makes his annual journey into the fields. And yet, there must be a great spirit that moves in all the earth. . . .

"How am I to face this interview? What is there that I can say to the king that will make him forgive Nahor's treachery? He sees a second war with Babylon in the near future. Perhaps I can make him know that he needs the Habiru. He is well aware that the Sumerians are soft of fiber, self-indulgent, over-cultured."

Abram's mind was tired. He could not seem to control his thinking. The Princess Shub's apartment rose into his memory. He saw the cushions, graceful urns, fruits, he heard the harp (soft things but agreeable all the same); and he saw Shub looking at him through the warm haze of her copper mirror.

The little *machouf* passed close to the lines of anchored sailing ships from the lower sea, their lofty prows and sterns painted gaily, the holds doubtless filled with merchandise from all the world. Abram could hear the sailors shouting back and forth in the language of the far east.

Leaving the harbor, they turned into the river and neared the palace of Rim-Sin. Its cream-colored walls and gay banners contrasted with the muddy brown flood that slipped so slowly past it. Beyond the palace the ziggurat towered, and they could see men climbing the stairs that soared upward to the blue dome of Nannar's shrine.

The boatman guided his little craft in toward the palace landing stage below the small gate. Abram noted the position of the single window cut in the wall high above the water. There was movement at the window now and a curtain was drawn. He knew that Shub was looking down on them. But he gave no sign that he had seen her, nor did he look up again on landing.

He stepped out quickly and approached a sentry who stood before the gate. The sentry saluted. After a short conversation,

Abram returned to the water's edge and said: "Oni, you must know that anything may happen to me tonight. Nahor's lack of wisdom makes it unlikely that I shall return. This may be good-by. Remember, you are to return here in a short time and watch from a distance for a signal from this gate. The sentry is one of our people."

"I understand," said Oni.

Then Abram said: "Wait until midnight. If there is no signal before that time, do not wait any longer but go along after the others."

"The God of our fathers be with you," said Oni. "If you do not come by midnight, I shall send a messenger after your father to say that we have been detained, you and I." His jaw was set now and his lips quivered as he spoke. "I cannot desert you. When you are in trouble I shall always be near. Your dangers are my dangers; your enemies are mine. Your projects are my projects, and your God is mine."

Abram stood for a moment trying to reply, but his throat was tight and something seemed to blur his vision. At last he turned, without a word, and hurried through the open gate and into the palace. Oni watched the gate close behind him. In his heart there was a fierce love for this man who was his master, friend and idol. Words never came easily to him, but he had said the thing which he had long rehearsed within himself: "Your dangers are my dangers — and your God is mine."

King Rim-Sin sat in splendor high at the end of his audience chamber. His hair was white, his beard long, and before he spoke he rumbled like a bull at the beginning of its bellow. This was the rugged old warrior who, after a series of campaigns against the Babylonians, had overthrown Isin, completely destroying that city and almost completely exterminating its citizens with merciless ferocity. Now after many years he had made himself the supreme ruler of the south country, but in Ur, its cultural capital, he played the role of restorer of the city's ancient glory and champion of the moon god.

Abram was shown into the audience chamber and stood at the back of the room without being observed. His height made it possible for him to see over the heads of the assembled company.

Princess Shub, with several women in waiting, entered and sat near the king. The high priest, Enannatum, bald and hawk-like, walked about and talked in a staccato manner with one man and then another. A group of soldiers stood somewhat defiantly in the center of the hall. They were dressed in short, flounced kilts with dagger and short sword at belt, and a few wore helmets of burnished copper.

The king struck upon the floor with the enormous stone mace of Ur-Namu, founder of the third dynasty. Silence fell, and the chamberlain, a towering hulk of a man, mounted a step and cried in a high voice: "O King, you have seen fit to grant audience to Lord Nasir son of Puzer-Sin and captain in the royal Sumerian guard."

"Let him speak," rumbled the king.

Nasir, a stocky man in his thirties with short black beard, heavy features and thick lips, stepped forward from the group of soldiers. He was dressed in a short skirt of leopard skin and wore a copper helmet. He bowed and the small arms at his belt clanked. Then he began abruptly:

"I speak for the royal guard of Ur, whose duty it is to defend this land against the enemies of the king. We ask permission to deal with the enemy that is within our gates so that we may be ready to defend ourselves against whatever enemies there may be without. A desert people who from the earliest times have been shepherds and camel drivers are now increasing in number in Sumer and especially within the walls of Ur. I speak of the

Habiru, the camelmen who came here from Haran. They have become more and more powerful, amassing great wealth and taking high positions in all walks of life. These Habiru people control the trade of the desert. They own countless camels and they are organized into warlike bands. They are strong enough to protect this trade against the desert robbers. That was not difficult," he added with a sneer, "for until the Habiru came into the pay of the idol merchant Terah, these same nomads were themselves the robbers. Their trade extends north to Babylon and the Semitic tribes of Akkad.

"My Lord the King, if I may speak bluntly, these Habiru are in league with the ancient enemies of Ur. We have learned lately that they are ready to betray us into the hands of the armies of Babylon. The Habiru are the spies of Hammurabi.

"Sumer must be strong, must keep her blood pure, as it was in the time of our glory when the kings of Ur were the rulers of all Sumer, and of Akkad too.

"We ask your permission now to drive this tribe out from Ur, and the other desert people as well, even as you, King Rim-Sin, destroyed the people of Isin after your glorious victory. In this way, the wealth which they have amassed will be ours. It will be kept here. At present, they send our wealth out to other lands. We have seized a messenger coming from Babylon to Nahor son of Terah. We have found upon him a clay tablet bearing the seal of a minister of Hammurabi." He held a tablet aloft. "This tablet promises that in case of war Nahor will be considered as a friend of Babylon." There was a stir throughout the room. "We believe that others among the Habiru are also traitors and spies and ready to betray us.

"Give me the power, and my followers will strike quickly. We will root out the enemy within this city." Nasir ended his speech as abruptly as he had begun. The tablet was handed to the king, who passed it on to the high priest.

The king's chamberlain then said: "O King, one is here to speak on behalf of this people."

"Who is he?" asked the king.

"A priest of the moon god, Abram son of Terah, chief of the Habiru." There was a movement of surprise and a hum of talk.

"Silence," said the king, and his mace came down with a resounding crash. "Come forward and speak, Abram son of Terah."

Abram made his way through the throng and stood before Rim-Sin. He was silent for a time, realizing suddenly his own youth, his inexperience and the dreadful consequences to his people if he should fail them now. He saw Princess Shub whispering in the monarch's ear. He swallowed, but no words came. Nasir, watching him, gave a laugh of scorn and slapped his thigh. The laugh stung Abram like a blow in the face. He drew himself up to his towering height, and turned about to look at Nasir with an expression of contempt. Then he addressed the king:

"Let Nasir not flatter himself that his words bring fear to me. I was dumb with amazement that a noble lord of Sumer could seek to serve the king so unwisely. Every schoolboy knows that goods are carried between Babylon and Ur. This is done in two ways, by boat and by camel. It is true that the camels are owned by our people and that this traffic is directed by my father. It is obvious that camels are swift and that they could be useful to an invading army, if one should come from the north.

"Nasir has suggested that King Hammurabi is aware of these facts (remarkable discovery!). Further, we have had evidence that Hammurabi now is making an effort to take away from us an advantage that would otherwise be all ours. Has Nasir forgotten that your armies could make use of my people and their control of desert travel? Or has he promised some would-be invader that he will close the camel stations of Ur?"

At this, Nasir drew his dagger and held it above his head, and the soldiers behind him shouted and crowded toward Abram.

The king, however, made a gesture to the Elamite guards who stood about him, and they moved forward quickly so that they made a fence with their spears between Nasir and Abram.

Abram raised his voice and continued: "Nasir has intercepted a message to one member of my family. My father had no knowledge of this and has never authorized any communications other than those that deal with trade.

"The Habiru are fighting men. Many of my people came here as soldiers. They fought desperately for Sumer when Ibi-Sin was overthrown and Ur destroyed. They have served you, King Rim-Sin, in many a hard-fought battle. They will do so again unless Nasir has his way. It is true that we are not Sumerians by descent. No more are the Elamites, and no one here will question their valor or their loyalty.

"Lord Nasir says that my people are in league with the enemies of Ur because the enemy has made advances to one man. He says that they seek wealth and high position. Has anyone ever heard of those living in a city benefiting from its destruction? The overthrow of Ur would mean the end of the trade that comes in from the desert. It would bring death to Sumerian and Semite alike, and at one and the same time. The interest of the two races is the same. There is no treachery among us. But there are many false rumors about us.

"Let them have their way, O King, and you will lose the trade that comes in from the desert, and lose wealth that comes into the coffers of Nannar and the treasury of the king. Let them have their way, and you will lose the loyalty of the nomads who can be useful to your kingdom of Larsa as well as Ur. Perhaps Nasir and his followers will give up the luxury of Ur to live in tents and keep safe the caravan routes for you. Perhaps they will breed camels for you." The king chuckled at this prospect and looked through his shaggy eyebrows at the group of soldiers.

Rim-Sin then talked quietly with one or two councilors and

with Enannatum. At last the sound of his mace was heard again and he said: "The young priest has done well to remind us of the valor of the Habiru and of the prosperity that comes to Ur and to Larsa through the desert trade. But we are also aware of the valor of Lord Nasir, and we count on the loyalty of his noble friends.

"The Habiru people in Ur shall not be persecuted. They shall be protected if need be. But I forbid any of them to leave this city under penalty of death. My guards will close all highroads to them that lead from Ur until further investigations are carried out. Lord Nasir will himself assume control of the highroads outside the city. The audience is over."

The king left his throne and withdrew. A slave approached Abram and asked him to follow him, as the king wished to speak to him in private. He found Rim-Sin closeted with Enannatum. As he came into the chamber, the princess entered through another door. She looked at Abram with shining eyes, but took her place on a stool at her father's side without a word.

"Well spoken, young man. You made a fool of Nasir," the king said, and he laughed loudly, putting his hand on Shub's shoulder as he did so. She smiled and nodded. Then he looked at Abram critically. "You know that the Sumerian nobles have a powerful organization in Ur. Nasir has influence in their organization. He does not like your people, and I judge that he is not exactly in love with you at the moment! But he is a good soldier and I need him. You are not a coward, but be careful for a little while. I need you both.

"My daughter has spoken favorably of you and so has the high priest." The king turned toward Enannatum. "He believes that as minister of commerce in the temple of Nannar you could serve the god well. You would also serve me well if you could ensure the loyalty of your people to Nannar. I am told that your kinsmen worship Nannar in the city of Haran. My daughter is to become entum of the god and you know what that means."

The king rose to his feet and made a gesture to indicate that the interview was over. Then as Abram still stood silent and immobile, he paused and added: "Have you anything to say?"

Abram looked at him steadily, and replied: "Do you worship Nannar as the supreme god?"

The king looked startled. "Why, yes. I suppose I do."

Then Abram added: "You did not worship him as a young man, and when you conquered Ur you could have destroyed Nannar and his temple. There is more reason for Nannar to worship you than you Nannar."

The king looked a little disconcerted and glanced at Enannatum before replying: "Yes, yes, you might say that. Some kings have made themselves into gods, but the tithes are not paid so well. It works better this way. Taxes come in through the temple of Nannar. I rebuild the temple and defend the country with my armies. The priests conduct courts of justice and I enforce the laws. I have restored the temple of Nannar and of his wife Ningal, and also Enki, Enlil and Ishtar. I could have torn them down instead if I had been foolish enough.

"Before my daughter Shub was born, I rebuilt the temple of Nin-Khursag to make sure of a perfect pregnancy. Behold the fruit," and he laughed again. "I'm ready to worship any good god. It keeps us out of trouble."

Abram broke in on him. "Why not worship one god? The only God. The God who created the moon, the sun, the stars and man himself?"

The king regarded him with interest and said: "That seems to be a god I had not heard of. But the world is too full of gods. Every priest says his god is most to be feared, and every priest wants gifts for him. I suppose you will ask me for gifts to this one god. . . .

"Good deeds, good deeds, too many good deeds. Everyone wants charity, and before you know it some cursed demon slips in and ruins everything! But Ur belongs to Nannar and the Sumerians fear him. They can be controlled only through him. What do you say, Enannatum?"

"Yes," replied the high priest, "Nannar has always ruled Sumer. There is no other way. But I am afraid that this young priest has been studying the ancient records too late into the night. Leave him to me. He will come to his senses."

The king turned toward the door, saying: "Enough talk! I'm glad you know how to make your priests obey. But women, ah! there's the problem!" He shook his finger at his daughter.

"There are three things beyond my ken —
Women and donkeys and drunken men."

In the door, the king turned again and looked keenly at Abram. "I should like to hear more about this god of yours. When you have had time to think, we must talk further."

Abram replied, raising his voice: "If you want to save yourself and Ur, do not put your faith in the idol of the moon god. The day is not far off when Nannar will be broken in pieces. The banks of the great river will be destroyed. Vultures will darken the sky above Ur and the jackal find food in its temples."

The king growled: "Enough, enough, enough." But he stood for a moment longer, looking at Abram. Then he glanced at Enannatum and said: "Come, I want to talk with you," and left the room.

When they had gone, Shub came close to Abram and said: "You must not talk that way. You cannot leave Ur now, but you could defend yourself here with my help and the aid of the high priest."

Abram spoke as though he had not heard her. "I must get away where I can think. What was it I said to the king?"

Guards entered. One of them addressed Abram respectfully. "I am sorry. I have orders to shut you in a cell."

Abram looked at Shub as though bewildered.

She shook her head and gave him a forlorn smile, saying: "Abram, you did speak strangely. Perhaps you will change your mind when you are rested. Men do change their minds, sometimes, don't they? As well as women?"

✦❮❮❮

CHAPTER XII

Nannar

THE NEXT FOUR DAYS AND NIGHTS Abram spent in a prison cell in the temple. He slept little. Much of the time he paced up and down restlessly, sometimes muttering to himself. Once he was visited by civil guards from the city. For hours they questioned him in regard to the whereabouts of his father and brother. This visit encouraged him, for it seemed to indicate that the fugitives had not been captured. But he refused to tell his interrogators anything. They threatened torture, but the threat was not carried out.

Finally, one afternoon he was visited by the high priest himself. Abram did not rise as Enannatum entered. He only nodded and remained seated on the floor.

"Tonight," the priest began, "is the night when the lovely Princess Shub will climb the stairs of the ziggurat to lie in the bed of Nannar. The people of Sumer are delighted, and as a result King Rim-Sin has never been so popular here as now. For years I urged him to give his daughter to Nannar, but she herself was very stubborn.

"Eventually, however, she agreed," he said, rubbing his hands together in satisfaction. "Now she has balked, except on one condition. I've had a score of offers from the wealthiest men in the land, young men and old men too, men who would take the place of the god tonight. Look at this." He reached into his wal-let and drew out something which he placed upon the palm of his hand. "This is a ruby beyond price." He held it up in the narrow beam of sunlight that entered the otherwise dark little cell.

The ruby glowed red as though it had within it a hidden source of light.

"This is a little present to me from your enemy, Lord Nasir. A high price for a night's entertainment which he will never have!"

Enannatum laughed unpleasantly and sitting down on the floor beside Abram, he continued: "People who stand high in the king's court and in the affairs of the city speak very well of your defense of the Habiru. They talked about the stupidity of the nobles who would have us forfeit control of the desert traffic.

"Now that you cannot leave Ur anyway, I could still arrange for you to manage the affairs of your people as Nannar's min-ister of commerce. It might be just as well for your brother Nahor to continue his flight. We have a proverb: *He that troubles his own house shall inherit the wind.* But you may send word to your father that he is quite safe to return. The shop of the twelve divinities will flourish as it never did before."

He paused, but as Abram did not speak, he continued: "I learned to know your father Terah well when he was a young man. What a craftsman he was! He made a statue of me, chiseled out of finest limestone, eyes of shell and lapis. You've seen it. It stands before Nannar now in the shrine up there." He motioned toward the ziggurat. "When I am busy with other matters, my statue reminds the god of my needs and of my virtues, no doubt." He laughed and looked inquiringly at Abram.

At last Abram broke his silence. "Enannatum, you know and I know that Nannar cannot speak. He can neither bless nor curse nor interfere in the affairs of men. You speak for him. You bless. You curse. But what effect does it have? There are hundreds of idols in this city. All of them dumb and deaf and blind. Let us assume that they could speak. If all of the five thousand gods that Sumer has known spoke at once, what a chorus of contradictions that would be!

"You are a man of great affairs. You carry heavy responsibilities of government. You see the clouds of a terrible war gathering. You must feel the need of guidance. But where is wisdom to be found? Not from the lips of Nannar and not even in the shrine of Enki, the god of wisdom."

Enannatum, who had watched Abram at the beginning with amusement, now looked at him thoughtfully as he continued:

"There is — there must be, the great God who created heaven and earth and man and beast, one God who has all the powers of all the gods. When the moon appears at night, it is He, not Nannar, who rides across the sky in Nannar's *gouffa*. He makes the sun to rise and set, not Utu. He is in the earth and in the seed and the rain and the ripening head of wheat. Wisdom, His wisdom — we should be able to find it in our own hearts, if we could learn to listen to Him."

Enannatum nodded and made a gesture that was something like a gesture of despair.

"But first," continued Abram, "Nannar must be broken into a thousand pieces. All idols everywhere must be destroyed. You must — "

Enannatum had scrambled to his feet, and he interrupted Abram now with a shout. "Have done, have done with this rubbish! You talk like a fool. This is impossible, absurd! Someone must teach you sense. Perhaps Princess Shub can do it. She is as stubborn and as unreasonable as you are, but at least she knows she must take the gods as they are."

He opened the door to go, but then turned back and spoke

in a more conciliatory tone. "I found it necessary to tell the princess that you would be waiting for her in the bedchamber of Nannar. That is the condition she makes. Otherwise she refuses to play her part. Not even King Rim-Sin can drive her. The marriage ceremony takes place tonight. If I send one of my priests to conduct you to the proper place, will you go?"

"Yes," said Abram, "I will, if I must."

Enannatum shook his head. "You remember the king's proverb?

> *"There are three things beyond my ken,*
> *Women and donkeys and drunken men.*

But that does not complete the list. There is a fourth thing beyond my understanding. I mean the Habiru people."

He smiled a little. "You are different, you Habiru. Your father came here, a good idol craftsman. But that was not enough. He had a strange spirit in him, a demon hungry for greater power and more goods. He made other people work for him here in this city and far out across the desert. Silver and gold flowed into his coffers and he became fabulously wealthy. He curried favor and found it. But all that was not enough. He, or his son Nahor, had to curry favor in Babylon too. Now they are fugitives.

"You entered the priesthood. You became a scholar. You worked harder and longer hours than other priests. Your studies were useful to me. Now you too have succeeded beyond all expectation. You have the love of the king's daughter. But that is not enough. You would break Nannar into a thousand pieces! You would destroy all idols everywhere! You would find a new god, and I suppose you would yourself ride across the sky with him in Nannar's *gouffa*.

"Your father sought riches," he continued. "You seek wisdom, you say. And yet you throw away all the things that other men hold dear. You and your people are different. You should not try to live with others."

Enannatum disappeared, and the door of Abram's cell squeaked in wailing discord as it turned on its hinge to close loudly. Footsteps echoed away.

"Yes," Abram said aloud. "We are different. If we could only live in a land of our own, a land of our own."

A little later the same afternoon, Abram was again aroused from reverie by the squeaking of the door, and a soldier entered followed by his friend Dudu, the jovial priest-physician.

"Come along, Abram," he said. "I'm sent to escort you to your room in the tablet house."

Abram obeyed without a word. He realized that Dudu must have been selected as the high priest's messenger. The three men set off to the accompaniment of Dudu's running observations:

"I had a message from no less a person than the old hawk Enannatum himself. There I was, as busy as possible in the sacred clinic, cutting boils and dispensing medicine, as well as giving advice to women who had nothing wrong with them. Sometimes they are ill because of a beautiful young concubine who has come to live in the house. Sometimes it is one of those temple prostitutes who is making trouble from outside. Most often, however, the whole trouble is just wrong thinking."

They had reached Abram's room now. Dudu stopped here and made an effort to remove a pebble from his sandal, but, in spite of puffing and heaving, he was unable to reach around his ponderous abdomen to his sandal. Finally he held up the foot to the soldier, who carried out the operation and presented the pebble to him with a bow.

Abram smiled, and Dudu continued: "Perhaps you think fat is a worse disease. No, my boy. There is nothing wrong with this." He patted his belly proudly. "It is no more than the accumulating record of a well-spent past." He drew himself up with absurd dignity and said: "No, the most serious of all ills is wrong thinking. *As a man thinketh in his heart, so is he.*

"But although wrong thinking is so common an ailment, it is not incurable. We physicians possess a sovereign remedy. And I use the remedy with great effect." He was gesturing now. "I talk. I question. I listen. To this formula I add a little kindness and a large quantity of common sense. There, I've given away to you the secret of a physician's success.

"Now let me consider your own case, Abram. Why did they shut you up?"

Abram only shrugged.

"Never mind. You don't need to answer that. You're pretty silent. It could be a woman and, in spite of your reputation as a scholar, I am convinced that you know nothing about women. You'd better stay far away from them, if you will accept the advice of a friend.

"Your discontent could be due to a sense of failure. Failure to solve a problem that will not leave you. And the cause of failure could be no more than confused thinking. On the other hand, it could be fear. Finally, it could be due to the fact that the problem is really insoluble. You may be trying to solve the insoluble riddle, the riddle of the gods. You would not be the first man to go mad in an attempt to solve that riddle."

He slapped Abram on the shoulder. "Enough!" he exclaimed. "I have made a diagnosis, but I shall not put it to the test. Better to proceed with my treatment for the condition.

"Here is a little prescription that will banish care and sadness."

He clapped his hands and a temple servant appeared, a buxom woman of many smiles. She pulled back the curtains of Abram's study. There, on the floor of that ordinarily austere room, a thick bread cloth had been spread, and on a stool at one side was a plat-

ter bearing a roasted lamb, all set about with great browned
onions. A hissing sound issued from under the gravy, testifying
to the fact that it had just come from the oven. There were also
little cakes and bread, cheese, honey and fruit. Low stools had
been placed beside the rug and on them, conveniently to hand,
were decanters of wine and goblets.

"What ho!" cried Dudu. "This will cast a mystic spell to cure
your madness — and mine." Then he capered about the collation
chanting:

> *"The mystic spell, you know quite well.*
> *The mystic spell, you know quite well."*

Abram burst into a laugh. "Dudu! There never was anyone
like you, physician, philosopher, fun maker, friend!"

Dudu slipped an unopened flask of wine into the hands of the
soldier. The latter hid it under his cape and disappeared down
the hallway with a few dance steps meant to imitate Dudu.

The two men sat down cross-legged on the floor, the repast
between them, and began to eat and drink. Abram realized suddenly that he was very hungry.

After a period devoted entirely to the food and the drink, the
irrepressible Dudu drew a long breath and remarked: "I was
really sorry to leave the clinic. There were many there who
needed me, and there was a most charming matron waiting to
talk to me. You know the kind: curls, tinkling hair ornaments,
ear rings, bracelets, colored nails and perfume . . . and her mantle slipping off her shoulders."

He put a piece of lamb in his mouth and used both hands
to elaborate the description.

"Duty! Sometimes it is beautiful. It was my duty to stay with
her. But in spite of duty a man must eat, to say nothing of drink,
and he must obey the commands of the high priest.

"I was told to let you shave and bathe. Then I was to inquire into the state of your health and to determine the cause of your madness. By the way, you're not crazy, are you?"

Abram smiled slowly at his friend. "Yes, I suppose I am insane. It all depends on your definition of insanity. If everyone else in the world thinks one way and one man thinks another, you would call him insane. Yes, by definition, I may be crazy."

"That's not a bad definition," laughed Dudu. "I had a patient yesterday who told me he was the great god Nannar. He didn't look unlike him. He had a goiter and his eyes were bulging, you know; very interesting! He kept hearing voices that had told him he was to marry the Princess Shub. There you are: He thinks he is Nannar; I think he is a sick man who has taken an overdose of the medicine that a quack physician has been giving him. Who is going to decide which of us is crazy? But he had one good idea, and that was about Shub. What a woman she is!" Dudu whistled his admiration, and at the same time shot a searching glance at Abram.

"I was at the wrestling matches yesterday. They were on the other bank of the river and Shub came by in the king's barge, her handmaids about her. They were close to the bank, and all the people cheered. There is a great deal of public excitement about her becoming the entum of Nannar tonight."

"How long is it before the marriage ceremony?" asked Abram.

"About three hours," Dudu replied. "The great court of Nannar is already filled with people. Every house top that has a view of the ziggurat will be crowded, and thousands will collect in the river, where they can see the ziggurat lighted up and perhaps hear the chanting. They say that tomorrow when the priests carry Nannar out into the country to bless the crops, the parades that follow him will exceed anything in our lifetime."

Dudu belched with obvious satisfaction. Then, patting the smooth surface of his enormous belly, he drank a flask of wine.

He wiped his mouth on the back of his hand and looked speculatively at Abram.

"I know something has gone wrong for you. You don't have to tell me what it is if you don't want to, of course. But those of us who have known you in the priesthood thought you were chosen for high places. Now I hear rumors, and I find you locked up. At the moment the high priest seems to want to groom you and fatten you like a bull for sacrifice."

"Yes," said Abram, "it is very much like that. You are the wisest fool I know, Dudu. No one needs to tell you anything."

After a pause, Dudu passed the basket of fruit. "Eat some dates. I have to drink for both of us. You might at least do your share with the food." He poured out another flask of wine, but he set it down again and spoke more seriously.

"Look here, old friend, you know me pretty well, perhaps too well." He chuckled and hesitated before proceeding. "You seem — what shall I say — a little depressed, and I'm trying to cheer you up, but I'm not making very much progress. If there is anything I can do for you, just name it. You know you can trust me."

Abram stood up and looked down at his friend, passing his hand affectionately over the bald pate below him. "You save the barbers of Nannar a great deal of trouble, don't you, by not growing any hair on the top of your head. . . ."

Then he continued: "Yes, you can help me. It may be that I shall do something tonight that the world will call mad. I am not quite sure. I hear a voice sometimes, myself. Then again, it seems to be my own voice and my thinking becomes confused. You are right. That brings depression.

"If I should die before morning, find my slave. He is a man of mighty muscle called Oni. I don't know where you will find him — perhaps waiting with a boatman, a marsh native, in a little *machouf* near the river gate of the palace.

"Tell him that Abram was no more than a breaker of idols, that he will never light a fire before the true God.

"Give him a purse which I shall fill for you. In it will be silver and gold for him, and also a tablet bearing my seal which will make him a free man. There will also be a tablet written to my father Terah, and I may include my shoulder pin and seal.

"I have rediscovered my half sister. She is like her mother whom I loved so well in my boyhood, but she is even more beautiful." He was silent and presently Dudu asked:

"Have you a message for her?"

"No," replied Abram, "I don't think so, and I don't quite know why I spoke about her except that during these last days in prison I slept little, but when I did sleep, she appeared to me in my dreams — always laughing and gay. She must be far from Ur now. I should be sorry never to see her again. . . . You may tell her that, if you should ever see her. Also, give her my seal."

Later that night, Dudu returned to Abram's room with a little group of priests. Abram handed him a purse. Dudu took it without a word and hung it on his belt. Then they put a long black cloak on Abram's shoulders and gave him a hood for his head to prevent anyone from recognizing him. The little company walked toward the ziggurat, along the terrace above the courtyard of Nannar. An enormous throng had gathered in the court of commerce, which was lighted by lamps hung on its walls. The ziggurat was in shadow, except for the pale light of the moon.

They climbed the central ziggurat staircase to the landing where it met the two lateral flights of stairs. Here the little company of priests halted, and Dudu said to Abram: "From here you climb to Nannar's throne alone. Remember! Some problems cannot be solved by men. Don't break your heart on the insoluble riddle."

Abram had climbed these stairs many times during the last few years, in varying mood. Now his heart was pounding with excitement.

What is the way of wisdom? he thought. Was the course he was planning right? Did his decision come to him from God? Or was it the figment of disordered thinking, as in the case of Dudu's patient?

He reached the top platform and recognized the short figure of Enannatum. The moon shone on the priest's bald head as he came forward. "I hope you dined well," he said. Abram bowed without a word. "The Princess Shub-Kudur has been told that you have come here of your own will. I hope this is true?"

"Yes," replied Abram, "it is true."

"Good," said Enannatum, rubbing his hands together with obvious relief.

As the two men talked, priests were passing up and down the face of the ziggurat with torches to light enormous earthenware lamps that lined the staircase on either side. The apertures of these lamps were cut in the shapes of demoniacal faces. Thus, when the lights were lit, the stair looked, to the multitude watching below, like a ladder lined with luminous demons expressing the full range of human vice and passion.

"I might tell you," said Enannatum, "that the princess does not seem to feel very well. Even this afternoon she informed the king that she would not climb the staircase. It was then that he summoned me. There were tears, but I talked to her, and she changed her mind. I told her you would be bitterly disappointed."

"You seem to have a way with women, Enannatum. Most remarkable!" Abram said with intended sarcasm.

"I don't want to boast here in the darkness before the great god Nannar," the high priest replied, pleased by what he thought was admiration. "But in my day I have done very well."

The lamplighters, having finished their task of lighting the demons, now set a fire in two caldrons of incense so that the heavy vapor could drift down the face of the ziggurat and bring an odor of sanctity to the thousands who waited and watched down below. Finally, the priests who had done the lighting gathered before Enannatum, each with a flaming torch in his hand.

He sent them marching down the staircase holding their torches aloft. As they went, they chanted the old familiar hymn of Nannar, and the chorus echoed out over the city as Abram had heard it so often.

"Who in heaven is high exalted?
Father! God enlightening earth! Lord of Ur, of gods the prince.
High exalted, all producing, life unfolding from above!"

When the chanting had come to an end, Enannatum said: "The priests have all left us and only you and I remain. The Princess Shub will climb up here alone, but you are to keep out of sight until after she stands before Nannar. She will walk from there across into the bedchamber over there, so the people below can see her go. You will then follow her when I call to you, and the people will see, in you, the spirit of Nannar, a black form, following her. I have planned this all very well." Enannatum chuckled with satisfaction.

Then, taking Abram's silence for approval, he said: "This will be the greatest spectacle in the memory of Sumer. Here we are at the spring equinox, when people are rejoicing in their belief that Dumuzi is returning from death in the underworld, from winter sleep in the north, to Nin-Anna, who waits in the good earth of our southland. At this time, we will let them see Nannar, father of the goddess of love, going into the bedchamber of the daughter of the king."

The high priest had grown excited. "They will think god and king united! Death changed into life, love, passion, birth, marriage, mystery — these are the things men turn to in the spring. You must understand such matters if you would keep them in your power.

"It is time, now, for me to start the sacrifice."

He took off his cloak and kilt, and Abram watched as the naked little man picked up a flaming torch and approached the altar on which lay the carcass of an enormous white bull. Below the bull was a heap of wood and chunks of highly inflammable bitumen from the oil holes of the desert. As he made his preparations, the little man continued to talk to Abram, who stood in the shadow out of sight of the people below. "This is a very fine bull that I am about to burn to delight the nostrils of the god. He was bred by one of your people, Salah of Drehem, probably a kinsman of yours."

Now he held a torch on high and approached the sacrifice. He applied the torch, and the altar burst into sudden flame.

A deep-toned roar rose from the throats of men and women in the darkened court far below. It rose from the city and the river beyond, where boats of every size and shape were crowded with spectators. Abram walked off into the shadow, behind the idol, to the other side of the ziggurat and looked down from the parapet. Little lights moved along the streets and roadways of the city below, passing around the faintly checkered patterns of the lighted courtyards.

He returned to the front of the ziggurat beside the idol and looked down into the court of commerce. The lamps in the court had been extinguished now, but the light from the altar fire showed him thousands of upturned faces, like the clustering faces of flowers, he thought, on the meadows of Drehem in springtime.

He looked up at the glittering god that towered above the flame — fat, immobile, with painted face, the face with its cynical smile, the bulging eyes. What did Nannar represent in the hearts of the people down below? A menacing tyrant who took their tribute? A hope of deliverance from the fiends and demons of life that were symbolized by the grinning faces on the staircase?

After all, Abram thought, he had himself served this god. He had felt the impossibility of escaping from his tyranny. This colossal spectacle planned so convincingly by the cunning Enannatum would reinforce the belief of the gullible mightily. The old anger returned to him, the suppressed urge for revolt that had long been growing within him. A tentative plan hardened into a fixed purpose. He would destroy Nannar. Then if the God of his grandfather Nahor could not save him, very well, this would be the end.

He looked up at the sparkling dome of the heavens above him. Directly overhead, a brilliant planet burned. "God of my fathers!" he exclaimed. "It is Nebo, the star of my people." A feeling of exultation spread through him that made him tremble.

The sharp smell of burning flesh came to his nostrils. He moved around into the shadow behind Nannar. He must bide his time. He came forward to the side of the altar and looked down. The priests of Nannar and the priestesses of Ningal had begun to march in procession across the court of commerce, following an aisle that cut through the throng. On they came to the central staircase and climbed upward until they reached the landing. Then they turned to the right and the left and passed down the staircases on either side. Their chanting rose in a glorious climax of harmony.

But now the figure of a woman dressed in white was climbing on up the final flight toward him. She was quite alone. As she neared the top, she paused and looked up, then swayed forward putting both hands on a step above her. It seemed that she would fall.

Abram spoke to her then. "Come on, Princess Shub. It's only a little farther."

"Oh, Abram, it's your voice," she cried. Then she straightened up and came the rest of the way. "Oh," she said again, as she reached the platform out of breath, "I thought it might be someone else. Oh, you're really here!"

Abram said: "Yes," and drew farther back into the shadows where he could watch and not be seen.

She stepped in front of the altar and stood quite still. Again a deep-throated roar came up from the throng below and echoed across the great river. As Abram watched her, he was filled with compassion for this woman, caught as she was in the inexorable clutches of the great god.

He walked around so he could see Nannar's back. There were the poles projecting backward, the poles that were used to carry the god down the ziggurat.

He searched the platform hurriedly. No, there was no one there. He was alone with the high priest and Shub. Was it possible that he alone could carry out his plan? But before he did anything, he thought, he must continue to play his part in Enannatum's little game so that Shub would be hurt as little as possible.

He heard Enannatum telling her that the time had come for her to leave the altar and walk slowly across the platform to her bedchamber. Abram moved out from behind the idol where he could watch. The naked high priest was bowing and gyrating before the altar as Shub turned and walked across the platform. Her gown gleamed pure white in the fire's light, and she seemed to be looking for someone in the shadows as she walked. She caught sight of him and stopped. Then she moved out of the light, and he saw her pass through a doorway that was outlined by the faint glow of a lamp inside the room.

Finally Enannatum called Abram to appear and to follow where the princess had gone. Abram did as he was bid.

The people saw a tall black figure that seemed to issue from the body of the god. It paused beside Enannatum and then followed on toward the chamber. Another roar of sound rose from the onlookers far below.

But at the top of the ziggurat, Enannatum saw in Abram not a disembodied spirit, but a man with a strange expression, a man who faced him defiantly across the altar fire. He saw Abram point above his head and heard him cry:

"Look upward, high priest, look up. There shines Nebo, the star of the men of Haran, the star of the Habiru. It stands at the zenith above us tonight. It is an omen. I tell you that you will soon see Nannar bow to the God of the Habiru — the one god."

Abram turned away. Enannatum looked up, and, as he did so, involuntarily sank to his knees. Then as Abram disappeared into the bridal chamber, he scrambled to his feet exclaiming: "Fool, mad fool!"

Inside the chamber, Abram saw that Shub had removed her bejeweled overwig and stood in the soft light of a translucent shell lamp. Simple white cloak, black hair — without ornament, except for a necklace of delicate golden leaves that curved across her breast. She was breathing deeply.

"Princess Shub, you laughed when I told you that I might destroy the moon god. Now I am going to do it. I believe that somehow a new day will dawn for my people and for all people.

"For you, I cannot do very much." He smiled down at her. "But I have kept Nasir out of your bed tonight at least. They will no doubt kill me for what I am about to do. This must be good-by." He turned back toward the door, but she clung to him crying.

"What are you thinking of? Stay with me."

But he only slipped off his cloak, leaving it in her hands, and was gone. She followed him out on the platform. She cried out to him, but he did not hear.

He passed into the shadow behind the towering idol and climbed upon the supporting scaffold. Then, making sure of his footing, he stooped and took the ends of the carrying poles in his hands. "Give me strength," he muttered.

Little by little the great idol wavered and tipped forward as he straightened up. Then he struggled to change his hold, almost lost his advantage, but finally, having secured a new grip, and grunting and panting in his effort, he gave a mighty heave.

Enannatum still stood before the sacrifice, making his pantomime. Suddenly he stopped and watched as though spellbound. Nannar began to topple toward him and then came crashing headfirst onto the flaming altar.

With a scream the priest leaped aside, just in time to see the mighty idol turn over and over and over, breaking into pieces as it rolled down the ziggurat, followed by a landslide of burning embers and jewels.

Abram, standing on the god's throne, held up his arms in exultation and stood watching. A yell of consternation came up from below. At last men began to run upward.

Shub, coming from behind, shrieked at him, but he did not hear. Climbing up, she pounded on his feet. He looked down.

"Come!" she cried. "Quick, come with me, hurry!" Abram jumped to the floor and followed her into the chamber. "Here," she said, "my secret passage. Take your cloak."

She pushed aside a heavy tapestry and opened a wooden door. A black tunnel yawned before them. She lighted a torch and thrust it into his hand. She caught up a cape of her own.

"Go down there, quick. They must not kill you."

He started down the steps. She followed him and then turned to close the door behind her. She bolted it with trembling hands.

"Where does this come out?" asked Abram.

"It comes out at the foot of the ziggurat," she said, "in a little room just off the terrace. In the excitement we may not be recognized there."

The stairs were narrow, but they were well made and provided with a rope railing. The descent was interrupted by a series of landings at each of which there was a ventilating shaft to the surface.

"This is how I came up here to talk with you at dawn."

They hurried down, down, down. "Very few people know of the existence of this passage," she panted. "Enannatum knows. He may think to send someone to the lower exit. But when I saw him last, he seemed to be falling down the ziggurat with Nannar." She paused to rest on a landing.

The light of the torch framed them in the circle of the tunnel; he, stooping against the ceiling, and she, erect.

"This passage was built for the entum of the god," she said, "not for men like you." Then, after a little pause: "Abram, Abram, what a strange man you are! Why have you done this? What do you want to accomplish with your life? Do you want to die in Ur, or do you want to escape and probably be killed in the country? There will be such an uproar through the land! Every Sumerian farmer will be looking for you."

"I want to escape if I can," Abram said. "I want to get away from everyone."

"You want to make for yourself a new god, I know," she said. "Don't worry, I'm not going with you." Then she laughed out loud. "What a man you are! I'm not going with you. But if you escape, perhaps some day . . ." She put out her hand and touched his arm. "But now it is enough if I can save your life. We must make our way to my apartments before Enannatum recovers his senses. Perhaps from there you can reach the river. Your slave Oni is there."

When they emerged from the passage, they found themselves in a small room. From there they stepped out into utter confusion on the terrace; citizens, farmers, priests, soldiers, priestesses and servants were gesticulating, shouting, crowding up the stairs. No one paid the slightest attention to them.

Abram stopped to look up at the ziggurat for the last time. The fire of sacrifice was dead. The only lights remaining were in the faces of the demon lamps that lined the main staircase from top to bottom. They seemed to grin and dance with devilish glee in this pandemonium.

From somewhere up on the ziggurat, a rhythmic chorus began and gradually grew in volume. *"Nannar is dead. Nannar is dead."* Shub pulled at Abram's sleeve and they turned away. As they went on, the chorus became a dirge: *"Nannar is dead, Nannar is dead, Nannar is dead."*

❖❖❖❖❖❖❖❖❖❖❖❖❖❖❖❖❖❖❖❖❖❖❖❖❖❖❖❖❖❖❖

CHAPTER XIII

The Great River

FROM THE TERRACE of the ziggurat Abram and Shub passed unrecognized through the great gate of the temenos and along the sacred way to the palace of Rim-Sin. They even entered the palace without challenge and hurried down the deserted corridor to the courtyard within the princess's own apartments. It was well lighted but was likewise deserted. Abram closed and barred the corridor door. They stood still for a moment in the court and listened to the roar of distant shouting.

Shub gathered the skirt of her mantle in her hands and ran up the stairs to the gallery. She pulled back the portieres to her room and entered. Abram followed without a word. The room was dark except for the feeble light of a taper. She applied the taper to a lamp and the chamber was flooded with light. Then she turned to face him. He stood silent, as though he were confused.

"What are we to do now?" she said. "They may come here to search for you, you know."

He did not reply at first. Then he seemed to make an effort to collect his thoughts. "If only I knew how to find Oni," he said.

"Oh, yes," she replied, "your big slave. I sent Berri to find him this afternoon. She has probably been making love to him ever since. I thought that if you decided . . . to remain with me, you would want him, and if you decided to escape you would need him. They may be on the roof. It has a view of the ziggurat."

She returned to the gallery and clapped her hands. Someone called in reply. Shub came back into the room and they heard the sound of hurrying footsteps on the stair that led down from the roof. The curtains were parted and Berri entered. When she saw her mistress her face blanched as though she thought she was seeing a ghost. She stood trembling and speechless.

"Where is Oni?" Shub said.

"Mistress, Mistress! It is you! I could see you from the roof, climbing, climbing, and I thought . . ."

"Never mind what you thought," Shub interrupted. "Where is Oni? I sent you to fetch him."

"He is here. He has been with me." She called: "Oni!" In a moment the curtains parted and Oni appeared. He too looked incredulous and could not speak.

Then he exclaimed: "Abram! I thought it must have been you who tipped the god over. No one else could have done it. How did you come here?" He did not wait for a reply but continued: "We must get away, and quick. I have laid the plans. Kerkha is in his boat on the river. I will get him. But the river gate has been locked." He crossed to the window, pushing Shub aside, and looked out. Then he turned to her and said: "I must have a rope."

He looked about the room. Shub pointed to a tapestry on the wall. Oni understood her meaning. He pulled it down and cut it into strips with his dagger, knotting them quickly together. Then he tossed one end of the new-made rope out the window and made the other end fast to the leg of Shub's heavy couch. In a moment he was through the window and had slid to the landing stage.

Abram, leaning out, looked down and Oni called back softly: "When you hear a nighthawk crying outside here, come down."

As Abram turned back from the window, Berri, who was still standing in the middle of the room, exclaimed: "But Oni, he is gone! Such arms, such . . ."

Shub interrupted her. "Go down into the court and wait there. Let no one in. You can tell me all about Oni later. There will be plenty of time, plenty of time." Berri disappeared and they heard her sobbing as she descended the stair.

Shub laughed bitterly. "And what about me? Behold the bride of Nannar, the god you broke in pieces. Here I stand, the jilted bride in my wedding gown. I fancied you would like simple white." She looked down. "You had no eyes for the golden beech leaves on this breast." She seized the necklace and with a quick movement broke it and held it aloft. "When winter comes the leaves fall." She opened her hand and the necklace tinkled to the floor in a yellow heap. She kicked it, scattering the leaves across the floor.

"You prophesied to my father the king that Nannar would be broken in pieces, that vultures would darken the sky above Ur and the jackal find food in its temples. — You spoke the truth! We shall see the end of the glory of Ur."

Then Shub turned and looked at her reflection in the mirror. "What about me?" she said softly. "I shall have time to listen and to think, time to dream." She looked at Abram, who stood unmoving before her. "Strange that I should have loved you so. And now perhaps they will kill you. You have no weapon and I have none to give you." Then after a little thought she said: "Wait a moment." She left the room and ran along the gallery. In a little time she returned dragging something heavy along the floor and dropped it at his feet.

Abram stooped and picked up the object. It was an enormous mace. The stone head was studded with copper knobs. He laughed. "This looks like the weapon of the father of the gods." He turned it over in his hands and read the inscription. *To Nan-*

nar his King, from Ur-Nammu, the mighty man, King of Sumer and of Akkad.

He looked at Shub in amazement. She nodded her head. "Yes, it is my father's mace, the mace of the ruler of Ur. If a member of the royal guard questions you, show him this and he will do your bidding. You have broken the idol of the god of Ur, like a conqueror. You might as well be king for tonight. Few men could wield it as a weapon. My father could when he was young, and you can."

Abram pulled up the knotted rope and tied its end to the weapon. Then he lowered it to the landing stage, and, turning toward Shub, said slowly: "You are magnificent, generous, understanding, and very beautiful. I owe you my life and yet I can make you no return — none."

She came close to him and drew his arms about her, then clasped her own about him. They stood silent in this embrace, her face buried against his shoulder. At last from outside the window there came the cry of a nighthawk. She looked up at him.

"It is the end for me. For you — it is a beginning."

He bent and kissed her. Then he climbed into the window, but turned for a moment and looked back at her. "The God of my fathers. He will be with you. He will bless you and protect you. Good-by."

Holding onto the rope, he slipped down into the darkness. But when she peered down after him to the landing she could see only dark shadows. She looked out at the great river. . . . Boats were moving here and there, the larger ones carrying torches.

As she watched, a little *machouf* moved out from the shadow of the palace wall. She could make out three men in it. Their paddles flashed in the moonlight for a brief minute and then the little craft was gone.

She pressed her cheek against the cool stone of the window aperture. A breeze stirred and she could hear little waves *slap*

. . . *slap* . . . *slap* . . . on the wall below her window. The moon made a wide path of light across the great dark river. Finally she spoke to it as though it were a friend.

"Take care of him. There is a force within that man as mighty as your own." And after a little while she spoke again: "Good-by, Abram. Find your one God. Lead your own people. I know I shall not see you again — except in my dreaming."

She turned back from the window and continued aloud: "It is better so. He could not live here and I — it is strange, but I feel content. This may be the blessing of his God. I shall not be wife or concubine to any man. Perhaps I have known something better. . . ."

Outside, Abram, Oni and Kerkha unnoticed propelled the little *machouf* across the great river. There were many boats there, filled with those who had come to watch the ziggurat ceremony. Crowded ferry barges were crossing to and fro, and there was still excitement and shouting everywhere.

They turned out of the river and into the canal that followed the old city ramparts around to the south. Here there was comparative quiet. Oni and Abram laid their oars down, while Kerkha continued to paddle silently onward.

"Where are you taking me?" Abram asked.

"To the house of Terah, to get Sarai," Oni replied.

"Sarai! Is she here?"

"Yes, she returned alone after she discovered that our escape by camel was cut off. And she has arranged with Magog to bring camels across the desert near to a village of the marsh natives called Suga. We can paddle directly to Suga in this *machouf*. It was clever planning on her part. She has been living these last three days in your father's house with the caretaker."

"That is the first place they will go to hunt for me," Abram said. "We will have to get her away as fast as possible. You understand, Oni, that I do not intend to go on with you to Father Terah. Perhaps I could stay with the swamp natives. I understand their language a little."

Two *bellams* passed near to them, rowing swiftly down the canal. The occupants were calling back and forth. One voice could be heard clearly: "Oh yes, I saw it. Nannar rolled all the way down the steps of the ziggurat." Then, after a pause. "No one seems to know. Oh yes, it's dreadful! It must have been the work of some demon. It will go hard with us now if we have to fight Babylon. Their god Shamash is very powerful in war."

A patrol boat nosed along the embankment with a large torch at the prow, obviously inspecting the waterfront. The little *machouf* gave it a wide berth, passing around it in the deep shadow of the opposite shore, and a little farther on it glided up to a narrow landing stage. Above them on the embankment stood the house of Terah.

Abram picked up the mace that Shub had given him, and, leaving Kerkha in the boat, followed Oni up the steps that hung on the side of the embankment. They jumped over the wall into a lane and followed it to the street before the house. The street seemed to be deserted. The two men walked past the house, and then, finding no one about, returned and pounded on the door. There was no answer.

Oni shook his head. "I don't understand it," he said. "She and the caretaker must have gone to watch the ceremony with all the rest of the city."

Oni pushed on the door and to his surprise it creaked open. They entered cautiously and felt their way through the complete darkness of the vestibule. Drawing the portieres, they entered the moonlit court. Oni called. There was no answer. "I will go and make a light," he said. Abram returned into the vestibule and barred the street door.

Then he walked into the courtyard and looked up at the canopy of heaven. The planet Nebo, seeming to rival the moon in brilliance, shone down on him. "Can it really be an omen?" he thought. "Did I really hear a voice when I sacrificed in this house to the God of my fathers? Did it tell me that our people must find a new country and that I must find the true God?

"Who am I to lead a people? A fugitive without a following, a breaker of idols, not a builder. Perhaps my father did better than I! He made idols, many idols. He even thought they came alive when he had finished working on them. But what good have they done him, or any man?"

The picture of Nannar plunging down the ziggurat came to his mind and he laughed aloud.

Just then Oni returned with two lighted lamps. He looked at Abram anxiously and, giving him a lamp, told him to get the clothing that he might need for himself in the swamps while he, Oni, went back to the kitchens for supplies.

But Abram did not seem to hear what he said. He continued to stand with lamp in hand, his eyes fixed upon the open doorway that showed the interior of the idol market. He walked to the doorway and stood looking in at the line of images.

"My father made them and I break them." He set the lamp down and continued to stare into the room.

The flickering flame cast wavering, beckoning lights and shadows over the rows of images with their bulging eyes and fat bellies. He looked away as though he had seen something unbelievable and then looked back again. It still seemed to him that he saw the gods beginning to dance, one after another. Then the whole troupe of them, with upraised arms and open mouths, came swarming toward him.

He gave a shout and rushed into the market. He hurled one image to the floor and then another and another and another. "Come on Marduk, Shamash, Enki, Enlil! Ha, ha, ha! and down goes Ishtar! Curse you, curse you, curse you!"

Attracted by the noise, Oni came running to the doorway, his arms full of provisions. "Abram," he cried, "by all the gods, Abram! Stop! Are you mad?"

But Abram did not stop. He did not hear him. Oni dropped his burden and leaping over a fallen idol threw his arms about Abram and held him still in his powerful embrace. "Be quiet Abram. Be quiet. You will have the guard on us. We must get ready to leave Ur quickly. We must find Sarai."

Oni led him back into the court. Abram seemed bewildered. He looked back at the idol market and passed his hand across his forehead. But now he saw only broken clay and stone and lapis lazuli littering the floor.

"Why did I do that?" he said. "I thought — I thought I saw them come to life. I'm all right now. Yes, what are we to do about Sarai?"

Abram shook himself and the two men stood in the court debating what their next move should be. Presently they heard a quiet rapping at the door. "There she is," said Abram and ran to the door.

"Hold on," cried Oni, "it may be someone else," but he was too late. Abram had pulled back the bolt and the door was open.

Instead of Sarai, a frightened-looking camel boy staggered panting into the room. He looked from one man to the other and no one spoke. Then he exclaimed: "Don't you know me?"

And he pulled off his desert headdress. Auburn hair came tumbling down to his shoulders and Abram and Oni exclaimed with one voice: "Sarai!"

It was indeed Sarai. She stood there panting while her eyes filled with tears. "Oh, oh, I've found you at last. I ran all the way from the palace." Then she sank in a forlorn heap on the floor but continued to talk between sobs.

"I discovered that you had gone out on the river and then I hoped you would come back here for me. But I was afraid you would not wait. Afraid I would come too late. Oh, the crowds, the crowds! I knew you might be up there on the ziggurat with your princess. Then something happened and there was such a panic. Men knocked me down and walked on me." She put her head on her knees and sobbed.

Abram stooped and tried to lift her in his arms, saying as he did so: "Sarai, you never should have come back. This is no place for a woman." But she struggled away from him and got to her feet.

"Take your hands off me. Keep that for your Shub-Kudur." She was not sobbing now. Her eyes blazed with anger. "Of course I came back. I don't run away with the concubines and I'm not a child any longer. And please forget that I'm your half sister."

She pushed back her hair and stood facing Abram, defiant though disheveled and covered with dirt from the streets. "Don't think I came back just because I wanted to see you. Someone had to lay a plan for your escape. You're stupid about such things. Nasir has a net around the city and you'd have been caught in it.

"I've had a message this afternoon that Magog has his camels ready in the desert, on the shore of the great swamp. I do not intend to go with you except at the beginning. I shall return to Drehem, to my grandfather Salah. Oni will take me through the swamp to Magog and his camels."

She turned her back on Abram and held out her foot to Oni. "Take off my sandals . . . please."

Oni dropped to his knees and removed the sandals, saying as he did so: "We must hurry. We must get away from here."

Abram had listened to Sarai's outburst with amazement, mixed with admiration. He walked around now to stand in front of her. "But how did you discover that Oni and I had gone out on the river?"

"I went to the apartment of your friend Shub," she replied. "I knew Oni had gone there and I hoped to find him. They would not let me in until I told them I was your sister and took off my turban. Then I saw the princess, alone, in her chamber. When she found I had news of importance to you, she talked and I learned a good deal from what she said — and more from what she did not say. She is beautiful . . ." Sarai stopped and looked down at her clothing. "Please let me change into a woman's clothing."

"Go to your room," Oni said. "Be quick, run. Get your warmest cape. We are nearly ready to leave and we must hurry, hurry."

Sarai lighted a taper and ran up the stairs and along the gallery to her room. Abram stooped and picked up her headdress from the floor where she had dropped it. He folded the kaffiyeh carefully and placed it inside his jerkin.

Oni returning said: "Quick, Abram, help me carry these things to the boat."

The two men hurried down to the landing and wakened Kerkha, who was asleep in the *machouf*. Then they came back to get Sarai, leaving the street door open. She was still in her room, and as they entered she called to Oni to come up to help her with something. He bounded up the stairs, while Abram picked up the great mace of Rim-Sin, which he had left lying in the court.

He swung it. "Beautifully balanced," he said aloud, "but Ur-Nammu must have been a strong man as well as a wise ruler." He swung the mace round and round. Suddenly he was startled by a laugh and a heavy voice.

"Are you enjoying yourself?"

Abram whirled about. The voice was the voice of Nasir and there in the doorway he stood. Behind him was a soldier, spear in hand.

Nasir walked slowly toward Abram, drawing his sword as he

came. "Don't stop your pleasant little exercise. A madman should be allowed to enjoy himself before he dies."

The two men faced each other, the flickering light of the little oil lamp on the floor between them causing the shadow of each to leap up and down over the walls and gallery of the court, as though they were two giants.

Nasir sneered. "You seem to have grown tired of the bed-chamber of Princess Shub very quickly. Don't worry, I will take your place, you dog."

Abram laughed. "Tonight, I am invincible. I warn you that I hold here the mace of Ur-Nammu, the mace of Rim-Sin, and the God of my fathers has given me strength. I warn you."

"Look," cried the soldier. "It is the mace of Rim-Sin. Better leave him alone."

"No," said Nasir, "it is not, and no man can fight with a thing like that. Stand close to us with your spear while I kill him."

As he spoke Nasir lunged suddenly with his sword. Abram grunted as he leaped aside, and swung his mace, but Nasir dodged beneath it.

"I struck you that time, priest," Nasir shouted.

The two men circled and dodged about the little lamp, their huge shadows dancing around the court. It was the final struggle between Sumerian and Semite.

Nasir was strong and an experienced fighter. But Abram had greater strength, and added to this he had great agility. Again and again only his quickness saved him. Soon Nasir realized that his task was not so easy as he had supposed, and he called to the soldier to close in on their prey. Abram backed off toward the stairway that led to the gallery.

But at that moment there was a piercing scream from above. Sarai had discovered what was happening, and almost simultaneously Oni jumped from the gallery and came hurtling down upon the soldier, who crumpled under him on the floor. Oni raised a dagger and struck the prostrate form, then leaped away to come to the assistance of Abram.

But that was not necessary. The scream had distracted Nasir for an instant, and in that instant the mace had found its target. There was a sharp cracking sound. Nasir whirled about and toppled to the floor, limp and motionless.

Sarai came running down the stairs and sudden silence fell on the courtyard. The soldier stiffened convulsively and then lay still. Abram, still panting heavily, picked up the lamp and bent over to look at Nasir closely. Then he set the lamp down beside his head and laid the mace across his body. A trickle of red ran down the temple of the fallen man and a pool was forming on the floor.

Oni wiped off his dagger and replaced it in its sheath. "Come," he said. "Be quick."

The three pulled back the portieres, passed through the vestibule and entered the street. At a little distance up the street was a group of men and women with a torch.

"It is only our neighbors returning home," Abram whispered.

They turned into the lane and ran to the canal's edge. All was quiet below. They climbed over the wall to the stairway, and ran down to the landing stage.

The little *machouf* moved out swiftly through the shadows of the canal and turned into the river, heading downstream. Its occupants were silent for a long time. The boatman Kerkha sat in the stern and paddled, facing forward, while Abram and Oni faced backward, each pulling on a spoon-shaped oar. Sarai, in the bottom of the boat between Abram and Kerkha, sat rigidly erect, clutching the gunwales and trembling with emotion.

Gradually she relaxed, and after a time exclaimed in exasperation: "I wish I had been born a man. I could have done so much. They almost killed you, Abram."

"You saved my life with your scream, Sarai," Abram replied,

"and you also, Oni, with that magnificent leap. I am very grateful. But my life is not worth all these risks. I thought I was saying good-by to life up there on the ziggurat. But here I am — still living. What is more, I'm free. Why was life given back to me? Only that I might become a fugitive? A wanderer looking for a new country?"

He was silent for a time and then he continued, as though talking to himself: "That is not enough. Instead of being cursed for breaking idols, I have been protected as though by a power from without. Can this be the arm of the God of my fathers? What does He want of me, I wonder?"

After that there was silence in the little *machouf* until Oni, with a great sigh, said: "I think we are reasonably safe now, but that was a narrow escape. I never expected to see an old-fashioned mace used that way! Neither did Nasir, I suppose." Oni chuckled to himself, and then went on:

"Now, Kerkha, we are coming to the place where the sluiceway that leads out to the swamps runs alongside the river. We want to carry this *machouf* over the river embankment and down to the sluiceway. But we want to do it where no one will see us. Is that possible?"

"Yes," said Kerkha. "I tell you when we reach the place."

There were other boats on the river, all moving away from the city, and from time to time one of them would land and discharge passengers to country houses.

"Ur very full of people," said Kerkha. "Why you no stay tomorrow and see Nannar leave temple. They carry him on their shoulders through country. He makes the seeds grow in Sumer every year and everybody eats and drinks very much. Good date wine for me!" Kerkha laughed.

"Don't talk quite so loud, Kerkha," Oni said. "Nannar is feeling ill tonight. He won't be able to take his little journey tomorrow, and he won't bless the crops for a long, long time. You find the sluiceway for us that will lead us through the great date palms and out into the open swamp, far away from Ur. We will pay you well enough so you can have good date wine every day if you like." Again Kerkha cackled his high-pitched laugh.

Sarai, looking back along the river, could see Ur now receding into the distance, a pale phantom of a city in the light of the setting moon. "I am sad to leave Ur," she said. "It was our home. Will you be sorry to leave it behind, Abram?"

"I don't know," he replied.

"What about Shub?" she continued. "Are you content to leave her behind?"

"Shub?" Abram held his oar suspended. "Princess Shub is like a beautiful blue-rock pigeon. Her nest is empty, but she will strut out her life on the temple parapet, I suppose. Enannatum will give birth to a new monster, a new Nannar, who will serve the purposes of the king." He began to row again. "She will try to help her father, but Rim-Sin is old. He is not the warrior he was once and the Sumerians are weak. Ur may well be conquered, and that very soon. Then she will die in the ruins of the temple, or become a fugitive like us. Ur is doomed."

"How awful!" Sarai said. "But I hope Hammurabi will not treat Ur as Rim-Sin did Isin." She lay down in the boat and pulled her cloak about her, shivering with the cold. She looked up at Nebo sparkling overhead and listened to the *plosh-swish, plosh-swish, plosh-swish* of the three paddles that propelled them onward into the night.

A path of silver rippled back over the dark surface of the great river toward Ur of the Chaldees, as one of the most fateful adventures in history began.

CHAPTER XIV

The Marsh

Dawn found the little boat well out in the great marsh and threading its way through a maze of water channels. These channels could be followed for hundreds of miles through a wide zone of swampland that bordered the head of the great gulf. In these swamps the sweet waters of the great river and the rivers Idiigna and Karun mingled with the bitter waters of the sea. Here the silt from Akkad, Sumer, and Elam was deposited to form a rich and ever widening delta.

The three men had paddled or poled their craft all through the night, and Abram had not spoken. Sarai slept in the bottom of the boat, covered by her cloak. With the rising of the sun she awoke and opened her eyes to the beauty of a strange world. The marsh reeds growing on either side rose gracefully to a height of ten or twelve feet; for a little time, she lay still, watching the walls of waving green slip by and gazing up at the deep blue of the sky beyond.

At last she sat up with an exclamation and looked about her. Down in the clear water at the side of the *machouf* she could see fish swimming over the gray mud floor among the reed stems. The marsh reeds were gold in color at the bottom as they emerged from the mud, but changed to yellow, and finally green, as they passed through the mirrored surface of the water into the air. From time to time side channels and bayous opened up new vistas to either side of them and she discovered the teeming bird life of the marsh.

Flamingos and royal egrets stalked off in sober awkwardness through the shallow water. Ducks quacked excitedly as the *machouf* passed, and led their little broods away to safety. Other birds splashed into the air and took wing at their approach, beautiful mallards, widgeons, pintails and even wild geese and swans. She heard the plaintive cry of the yellowshanks, and watched them fly away dangling their legs behind them. Terns poised on rapid wings above them and from time to time dived into the water with a great splash and came up carrying fish.

She felt thirsty, so she dipped her fingers into the water and put them to her mouth. To her surprise she found it salty. She looked at the three men swaying back and forth with each paddle stroke. Their faces were gray and haggard with fatigue.

"Oni," she said, "Have you had nothing to drink? Is there fresh water in the boat?"

"No," he replied. "It was left behind in our haste, but Kerkha thinks we are not far from the pasture land where we expect to find Magog."

"Kerkha," Oni continued, "you were born in the swamp, weren't you?"

Kerkha looked up and showed his white teeth in a delighted smile. He was a muscular little man with a round face and slanting skull.

"Yes," he replied. "I was born in the village of Suga, but my father went to Sumer and I learned to speak good Sumerian, like you see. I got wife and children in Suga, four girls." He smiled again. "But the chief, he send me with fish and dates to market in Ur. He pay me good, but I like to live in the swamp."

He would have continued gladly, for he loved to talk, but Oni interrupted him. "You understand, we must hide, and we can pay you very well."

"You pay well?" The little man laughed. "Maybe I never leave swamp again."

"But when we reach the highland," Oni continued, "will there be any people there?"

"No, probably not now. The flocks all gone in the springtime, just as soon as the water begins to go down — sheep, goats, water buffalo, shepherds, all leave. My people lead them around on dry land to summer pasture near Suga, and when they get there they have beautiful festival. You want I tell you about the festival?"

"No, not now," Oni said. "You take us to this highland as fast as you can. Will we find drinking water on the land?"

Kerkha laughed again. "We come to open water pretty soon, away out in the big lagoon. There the water is good to drink. We fill our water pots soon."

Sarai looked over the gunwale again. This time she saw her own tousled head reflected in the water. She sat upright and groaned as she did so, for she was very stiff. She then produced a comb and metal mirror from somewhere inside her cape and ran the comb through her hair. It curled softly around her face and she tied it up in a beguiling knot behind her head. At least Oni thought it looked beguiling. Abram only stared at the bottom of the boat. Oni also observed that the level rays of the sun turned her hair to gold when the *machouf* passed out of the shadows.

She examined her own reflection in the mirror and made a little face as she discovered an unsuspected scratch on her forehead. Then she put the comb and mirror away with a shrug and settled herself again in the bottom of the boat. She watched Abram reflectively.

He was paddling, stripped to the waist, and seeming oblivious of his surroundings. His jaw was set and there was a vertical furrow in his forehead. His eyes seemed to see nothing. Yes, he was handsome. His face was strong and at the same time sensitive, and a little sad, she thought.

She watched the play of his muscles. Now she noticed that there was dried blood on one arm. It must have run down from his neck. She leaned forward and pointed to it inquiringly. Abram glanced at it and grunted impatiently. "It is nothing." Still he did not look at her.

This strange half brother fascinated Sarai. To have him ignore her was intriguing in itself, and to some extent it was a new experience. She had met men of many types in her short life, for she had been her grandfather's constant companion and had traveled with him on numerous occasions. Young men had declared their love for her, and she had accepted this as a natural occurrence.

But Abram was clearly not like other men. She recalled the night of their walk in Ur when they stood together in the moonlight. She had thought she understood him then, and had wanted to comfort him as though he were a rebellious little boy. After that she had laughed with him in Terah's house and he had teased her as though they were children together.

Then she had seen him stand before the Habiru leaders in his father's house on the night when he himself had made the decision for voluntary exile. As he stood and talked that night he was a stranger, not like other men. He was certain of himself and had seemed to have a knowledge and power which set him apart.

When she met Princess Shub-Kudur and heard her speak of Abram, she had a sense of resentment. Nevertheless, it did not occur to her that she was jealous, nor that she might actually fall in love with her half brother, in spite of the fact that Terah had hinted at such a possibility. A woman could not marry her full brother, of course, but her half brother — that was another matter.

Her mind turned to her other half brother Nahor. He was a

man, she thought, whose heart was easy to read — clever, vain, avaricious, secretly suspicious, but likable when all was going well.

Melchizedek — now, there was a man! . . . Her reverie was interrupted by Abram's voice, and she was startled to find that he was looking at her intently.

"Tell me again," he said, "what was the death blessing that you brought to me from my grandfather Nahor?"

"Oh!" she exclaimed. "Is that where your thoughts were?" She leaned back and closed her eyes as though to help her memory.

> " *'The God of your fathers shall help you,*
> *The Unseen shall bless you with blessings of heaven above,*
> *Blessings of the deep that lieth under,*
> *Blessings of the breasts and of the womb.'* "

She opened her eyes and discovered that Abram was staring at her again with a strange expression.

They had come to an open lagoon where they found a strong wind blowing across the water. The sky had turned gray and the sun was pale. They stopped long enough to fill Kerkha's water bottles and to quench their thirst with the slightly brackish water. On the far side of the lagoon there were trees, and as they approached they could see reed huts on the shore, but the huts seemed to be deserted and there was no smoke to be seen.

Kerkha guided the boat toward a clump of tamarisk trees. The feathery green branches tossed as though to welcome them and they glided silently into a landing ditch in the shadow of the trees. When they stepped out on dry land they saw fresh prints of sandals and of bare feet in the soft earth.

"My people gone to summer pasture," Kerkha said, "but someone else is here."

They heard a shout and saw someone hurrying toward them through the trees. It was Magog.

"God of our fathers be praised," the old man cried, out of

breath. "I came as soon as I could be sure it was you. There are strange people about. Yesterday at sunset we saw camels in the distance. I don't know whose they are, but I thought the police of Ur might have hired them. This morning, luckily, there is a dust storm and we cannot see them any more. If we leave at once, they will not see us and we can escape in the dust easily."

Sarai ran to the old camel driver and embraced him. "You see, Magog, I did get word to Abram after all. You thought I was too young, too much a woman. I was afraid you might not be here according to plan. Is Naamah with you?" Magog nodded. But she continued before he could speak. "We saw the sun grow gray and I was afraid of a dust storm. Dust in your eyes and hair and mouth. But I am going with you, back to Father Salah."

"Sarai is going with you," Oni said. "But Abram is not coming, and I shall remain here with him until he finds a safe place of hiding. You are to take Sarai north to the farms of Drehem and then return here for me."

Magog turned in surprise to Abram, who nodded his agreement.

The wind was making a rushing, soughing sound through the needles of the tamarisk overhead. The sound came and went, rising and falling in pitch. Abram looked at Sarai soberly for a moment. "You must go at once. Magog will bring you through safely.

"There are many things in my heart that I want to say to you — but that must wait. I know that I am confused. You will understand when no one else does. You will know why I must seek the truth alone. Tell Salah that you brought me the Habiru leader's death blessing. Tell him that this leader does not know where to lead; that he waits here, hoping to see the Unseen."

Abram turned abruptly and walked back toward the boat. Sarai hesitated, then ran after him.

"Wait," she said sharply.

He turned back toward her while she tore a strip of cloth from her inner tunic. This she dipped in one of the water pots and washed the caked blood from his arm. She found that Nasir's sword had made a flesh wound in his neck. She made him stoop down. Then she washed the wound well, pouring water over it. As she did this she sang an incantation that she had heard from childhood:

> *"Ea has made, Ea has loosened.*
> *Remove the evil, ease the pain.*
> *Undo the evil knot, Ea be with thee . . .*

"That must have hurt you last night," she said. He shook his head. "Do you object to my using the incantation of the water god Ea to help you? After all, he is a good god. His waters bring healing and he is the god of wisdom too. Perhaps he will help you in other ways."

She was tearing long strips of cloth now from the wide hem of her tunic. With these strips she bandaged his neck and shoulder carefully.

When she had finished, she raised her eyes to his for a moment. She seemed to see something unexpected there, for she dropped her eyes quickly and when she spoke again she faltered: "I . . . we . . . all of us need you. We are like sheep. Come back, even though you should not find . . . whatever it is that you are seeking."

She turned away from him as he replied: "A blind shepherd is useless to sheep. And you must remember that anyone who is found with me now will be in great danger. Every man who worships Nannar will search for me throughout the world and try to kill me."

Oni had listened and watched in silence. Sarai turned to him now.

"Oni, you are strong. I don't know what we would do without you. Don't let anything happen to Abram."

Oni shifted his weight from one leg to the other but found no words for reply. Suddenly she threw her arms about him and kissed him. Then she walked away quickly through the trees with Magog.

Abram looked at Oni in silence, while Oni turned his head to hide the hot flush that he could feel rising in his face and neck.

The three men stayed on the shore a little while. They washed themselves and rested, eating the dates and cheese which Oni produced.

"From here to Suga," Kerkha said, "is two days in a boat, but we go very fast." He reached up admiringly and felt the swelling muscle of Oni's arm.

"It would not be safe for us to rest yet," Oni said. "We must push on farther." He looked at the *machouf* as it floated in the landing ditch. The little boat matched the earth in color, and its high prow resembled the arching neck of a black swan. "It looks as though our *machouf* had come back to its home," Oni said, as he motioned Abram to his place.

Abram obeyed but did not reply. He paddled in silence through the afternoon until Kerkha finally guided them in to shore. They chose a sheltered spot where they could hide, and slept the sleep of utter exhaustion.

When the first gray light of dawn appeared on the following day, it found Abram sitting with his head in his hands, while Oni and Kerkha slept.

Presently Kerkha roused. He spoke to Abram but received no answer. He then took the short spear which every swamp native kept by his side, and a small net, and slipped off through the reeds at the water's edge in search of game.

Silence followed his departure, broken only by the heavy

breathing of Oni. Abram, without raising his head, spoke aloud: "No! the world is not all bad. Children are beautiful, nature is lovely, men serve their families. They even sacrifice their lives for friendship. If all gods are false, where did this good come from? Who made us what we are? What drives me to find the answer? Is it a god, or a devil, or am I mad? My mind is numb; my head feels as though it would burst; my shoulder aches. I wish I could sleep — or die."

He raised his head and saw that Oni was looking at him with startled eyes. Neither spoke, and at that moment Kerkha reappeared triumphant. Over one shoulder he carried his spear, and, transfixed upon it, a fish. With his other hand he dragged an enormous water fowl which flopped and struggled helplessly. He deposited the fish upon the ground, and with an air of excited importance lifted the beautiful white bird with both hands. The wings had a span as great as the height of Abram. Oni exclaimed in amazement and admiration. The boatman explained that he had knocked it down with his sling and that his people would make a great feast from such a drake. They were very rare, he said, and this was the biggest one he had ever seen.

After a breakfast of dates and fish, Kerkha placed the bird, which he had tied carefully to prevent its struggling, in the boat, smoothing out its feathers. Then as the sun rose, they pushed off and continued their voyage through the waterways of the swamp. Abram still paddled in silence, though his shoulder was paining.

Toward evening, Kerkha exclaimed with excitement: "There is Suga!"

Looking down a broad water channel they could see, at a considerable distance, reed huts with arching doorways, beneath lofty date palms.

"Here," Kerkha said, "if my people let you stay, you will be safe. No Sumerian ever comes here. But," Kerkha hesitated, "I hope our chief likes you. Maybe you give him present?"

Abram ignored this question, but he turned to Oni and said: "Let us talk. It is better that these people should have the opportunity of watching us for a little time. I intend to remain here if they will have me. How long a time I do not know."

"Why will you not come with me into Elam and find Father Terah?" Oni asked.

"Because," Abram replied, "I must stay here alone until I can find my people's God."

Oni laughed and looked about him at the palms and thickets. "Not a very likely place to find an old god, and not many materials with which to make a new one!"

Abram was silent for a time. Then he said: "How can I explain it? For years, in the temples of Ur, I have watched men come and go, praying to various gods. Why do they come to the temple, and for what do they ask?" After a pause he continued: "Most often they come because of fear, fear that some god will harm them, and they make offerings to buy his good will. But they pray also for success, for favors and, sometimes, for guidance in times of difficult decision.

"Since time began, all people have made images in order to worship them. And when these peoples were conquered, they sometimes were forced to accept the gods of the conqueror; but more often the gods seemed to be so strong in the land that the conqueror forgot his own gods and came to worship the gods of the people he had conquered.

"My studies of the records show me that the Semitic peoples from the north, of whom we are a branch, have conquered many lands here in Sumer, and Akkad, and also even in Egypt. But the Semites always seem to have adopted the gods of the conquered country."

Oni was listening now, puzzled and surprised at this outburst from his friend, who up to this moment had scarcely uttered a word since leaving Ur.

"I do not say," continued Abram, "that by worshiping these many different gods men have not been helped sometimes. Perhaps they have even had guidance and protection. But if so, the guidance and the protection have not come from the idol, nor from the priest. The burnt offering has not been smelled by the image. No! Help, when it comes at all, must come from a greater god, not made of stone, whose name is not Nannar, nor Osiris, nor Anu."

At this point Oni interrupted. "It seems to me," he said, "that if this greater god were hiding around our temples to help people out, we would have seen him. Where is he kept?"

"Yes," said Abram, "that is one of the questions I cannot answer. Where is he?" He was silent for a little while and trailed his fingers in the water. Then he said, "And who is he, and what is his name? Idol worship is blind, senseless, and degrading. There must be a way of securing the help of a mighty god without all this. These are the questions I must learn to answer before I leave the wilderness."

Oni shook his head in despair. "I can't see who is going to answer these questions for you in this swamp." He looked at the boatman sitting in the stern of the boat and chuckled. "Kerkha doesn't look as though he or his kind had the answer."

Kerkha, having welcomed the respite from paddling, was eating dates and gazing toward Suga. On hearing his name spoken, he showed his white teeth and offered Oni some dates.

Abram, however, continued as though there had been no interruption: "I shall remain here alone until I find some answer. If there is a great god who can be worshiped, as we worship our family god, without images, then I must find him. I must walk with him. If I fail, I cannot lead my people and I shall never be happy to return to them."

He turned toward Kerkha. "Paddle slowly toward the village and let us see their reaction to us. They have doubtless been watching us while we waited here. How many wives has the chief?"

"Only one wife," said Kerkha. "He have concubines too, but he like his wife very much."

"Good," replied Abram. "Have you anything we could give her, Oni?"

"Yes," Oni replied. "I visited the idol market to better purpose than you did and I have ornaments that would please anyone, man or woman."

The village seemed to be a large one. Clean-looking huts of lemon-yellow reeds could be seen scattered among the trunks of the lofty date palms. The water's edge was already lined with natives, and others could be seen running down to the shore.

"We wait here," said Kerkha. "Don't come too near until chief say yes. My people can throw spears long way. Never miss." His white teeth flashed in a proud smile.

Abram examined the natives carefully. They were a swarthy little people. The men had black beards and sparse mustaches. Their faces were round, like Kerkha's, their heads long and made to look longer by the hair which was fastened in a bun at the back. They were for the most part clothed in a single garment of sheepskin. The men stood in front and some of them carried short spears. Behind them stood the women, giggling and craning their necks. Most of them were naked, their skin elaborately tattooed. Some wore ornaments of rock crystal hanging from ear lobe or nostril.

Kerkha called out in his own tongue. When he had finished speaking, Oni asked Abram what he had said.

Abram replied: "The dialect is a little difficult, but the speech is that of the sailors and boatmen on the waterfront of Ur. Father Terah saw to it that I learned it as a boy. It is useful to merchants. Kerkha asked that the chief give permission for us to land. He said also that they should tell the chief we were bringing presents. I am glad you thought of such things, Oni. One of the men is evidently going off now to interview the chief."

More little people gathered on the shore. Suddenly there was a commotion in front of one of the nearby huts and a slender girl came running like a frightened deer down to the water's edge. She was pursued by two old women as far as the shore, but the girl ran on into the water, making straight for the boat. She cried out to Kerkha as she came. Kerkha shouted back to her in great excitement, paddling toward her. When she reached the edge of the boat, he put his arms about her and drew her in. The two talked excitedly, deaf to all else.

Finally Abram got the boatman's attention and asked for an explanation. Kerkha then exclaimed: "This is my oldest daughter, my Nana. She says they want to burn her on the altar of the god. The fever has come. The priest says swamp god wants virgin to stop water sickness."

"Keep her quiet," said Abram. He looked at the trembling child for a moment. Water dripped from her black hair and smooth brown skin. She sobbed aloud and her face was contorted with fear.

"Tell her we will try to help. Perhaps we may save her somehow." Abram looked down at the great water bird lying beside her in the bottom of the boat. Then he turned and studied the situation on the shore.

Presently a man appeared bearing a large spear, and the natives drew back to let him pass. He bowed, and made a speech of considerable length.

When he had done, Kerkha said: "The chief send word that we may land."

"Tell the messenger," replied Abram, "that we wish to go directly to the chief so that we may bring him presents. You yourself must stay close to us, and bring with you your daughter and the great white bird."

As they landed, the women who had evidently been the girl's captors tried to carry her off, but Oni picked her up and carried her as though she were a baby.

A curious procession wound its way along the path that led into the village. Abram, preceding the others, had removed his headdress, displaying his shaven head which declared him priest, and as he strode along with beetling brow and sharp-cut profile he made a strange contrast with the bearded little men. He was followed closely by Oni, carrying with one brawny arm the daughter of Kerkha, and with the other a shawl and sparkling jewelry. Close behind him came the diminutive Kerkha bearing the great white bird, while the swamp men ran before and after.

They entered a large clearing ringed by palms. Oni allowed Kerkha's daughter to slip to the ground, but she followed him closely, clinging to his mantle.

On one side of the clearing was a curtain made of reeds, and before the curtain hung a large metal shield on which strange figures were painted. On the opposite side of the clearing was a long reed hut made in several sections. The entrance was formed by a graceful arch, and just back of the arch within the house was a rectangular screen, high enough to provide privacy to inmates but low enough so that they could see out.

On a heavy mat under the arch the chieftain sat, and on either side of him stood a half-dozen young men fully armed. He was a paunchy, quick-moving little man whose earrings jingled as he spoke or nodded.

Abram came and stood before him. The chief rotated forward over his rotund abdomen so that the bun on the top of his head touched the mat upon which he was sitting. Abram and Oni bowed elaborately, then Abram spoke slowly, using the tongue of the little people to the best of his ability:

"I bring you gifts," he said, and motioned to Oni, who placed the shawl on the ground and spread out upon it the ornaments which he had taken from the idol market. Then Abram continued: "I seek permission to live here in the great marsh that you rule. I want to be alone, quite alone. I beg to be allowed to remain here."

The chief was delighted with the gifts and it was readily agreed that Abram should occupy a vacant reed hut some distance from the village.

When this had been arranged the chief rose and said to Abram: "You come here just as we are prepared for a burnt offering. The fire is ready for the sacrifice. The water fever has come upon us as it did years ago. The great swamp god is angry once again. We have made whole burnt offerings, and great fires, but the fever is still with us and the god has turned his face from us.

"His priest says we must make a more precious offering. He says that when the god smells the burning flesh of a virgin he will turn his face back to us and the fever spirit will leave our homes and the people will no longer sicken and die." The chief turned to a sinister-looking little man with a long iron-gray beard who had stood in silence by his side throughout the talk. "Let the sacrifice begin."

When he heard these words a fire of excitement came into the sunken eyes of the priest and he produced a cruel-looking knife that glistened in the sunlight.

The clearing was now ringed round by all the people of the village, who listened and watched in silence. The priest crossed the clearing and stood in front of the reed screen, which, Abram observed, was suspended by loops to a horizontal bamboo pole.

The priest raised the long knife and struck with it three times upon the metal shield which hung before the curtain. A deep-toned sound went ringing out through the aisles of arching palms, and the people threw themselves, as though in terror, upon the ground.

The priest removed his sheepskin garment and putting out his hand he drew the curtain back. Abram made a quick gesture to Oni, and Oni dropped to the ground, while Kerkha's daughter clutched him in terror. Abram remained standing, and pulled out the shoulder pin which held his own cloak in place. He then removed his kilt and sandals and tossed them on the ground. Thus Abram and the swamp priest alone remained erect.

When the curtain was pulled back a hideous idol was disclosed. Before the idol a fire was burning fiercely. Kerkha's daughter screamed, and buried her face in Oni's mantle. Kerkha raised his voice in a shout of protest.

"Be still!" Abram cried in a loud voice, and there was silence.

The marsh priest turned and looked at Abram in astonishment, seeing him naked and erect before the god. "Are you also a priest of the great marsh god?" he asked.

"No," replied Abram, "but I have served the moon god Nannar in his temple at Ur," and then he continued before the marsh priest could speak again: "Tell me, what says the marsh god that you serve? I see a fire upon his altar."

"The marsh god is angry," replied the priest. "We have made him burnt offerings of kids, and of goats, and of birds. But his heart remains hard. He demands something far more precious. This fire was kindled that we might burn the daughter of Kerkha."

Abram observed now that although the natives had remained prone, each had lifted his head and was listening and watching intently. He therefore raised his voice in order to reach a larger audience and continued: "In the distant land of Canaan the people worship a god named Baal, and in order to please him they sometimes sacrifice a first-born child upon his altar, but the child must be given freely by the father. Otherwise the god may become more angry than ever. You have heard the ancient proverb

— A gift is sweet in the nostrils of God, but a stolen sacrifice is without savor."

The marsh priest tried to reply but Abram held up his hand and raised his voice still higher, speaking the native dialect slowly and distinctly:

"Kerkha has returned to his people. Does he give this child willingly to the flame? Or can he give the god a richer, sweeter sacrifice?" Then turning to Kerkha he cried: "Stand up, Kerkha."

The frightened boatman stumbled, trembling, to his feet, still holding the giant white bird by the legs. "Do you wish to give your child to these flames?" said Abram.

Kerkha, unable to speak, shook his head and set up a dismal wail.

"Then," said Abram, somewhat impatiently, "I see that you have in your hand a gift that you have brought to lay before your god. Hold it up before the people, and give it to the priest, that he may see how rare it is."

Kerkha dragged the bird forward, and as he did so the ties came loose and it flapped its enormous wings, beating up a fine dust, as though it recognized its fate.

The face of the marsh priest was livid with anger, but he did not reply. Instead he turned around and put back the screen, whereupon the people got to their feet, and the chief seated himself again upon his rug. Abram replaced his clothing quickly and approached the chief. Kerkha came and stood close to him with his arm around his daughter.

The marsh priest crossed the clearing and stood, the long knife of sacrifice still in his hand, staring at the shrinking child. She was graceful and delicate — a bud just bursting into the bloom of maturity. Abram, watching the priest narrowly, saw an expression of cruel lust sweep over his face before he turned and slunk back to the side of the chief, to whom he spoke in a low tone.

But Abram made an exclamation of anger and stepped forward.

"I demand the ear of the chief. Presents of silver and gold lie before you, but one more present I bring. It is a charm of greatest power. It comes from distant Egypt."

He then drew from about his own neck the charm which Terah had given him. He held it aloft and, as it turned about on its chain, the sunlight fell upon it and made it glow like an eye in the dark. An exclamation of admiration came from the screen behind the chief and Abram saw the head of a woman appear. She said something which he could not understand.

"This," he said, "is the *utchat* of the god Horus. It is used by the great healers of Egypt to keep away all diseases. Let the chief wear this."

Abram stepped forward and placed the chain about the ruler's neck. The chief smiled vainly and watched the amulet slide down and sparkle upon his rotund belly. Then he held it up so his wife behind the screen could see it.

Abram spoke again. "Let the chief open his eyes and see the priest of the marsh god. This man is telling a lie when he says that the idol has asked him to make a sacrifice of virgins. The idol has never told him anything. Other men love women to marry them, but this man" — he turned and pointed to the priest, who was shaking with anger — "this man loves women to kill them."

With a gesture of disgust, Abram turned to walk away. As he did so, Oni, who had understood little but who had watched every move from the beginning, suddenly jerked Abram off his feet. The priest's knife went hurtling through the air, missing Abram by a hand's breadth. The knife winged its way over the heads of the people to sink into a palm trunk and quiver there.

A great hubbub followed. The chief could be heard screaming orders, and the natives rushed into the clearing. But Abram paid no attention. He got to his feet slowly and looked at the knife for a moment. Then he said to Oni: "That marsh devil would have made a sacrifice of me if you had not been so quick. Perhaps it would have been just as well." He walked off toward the water's edge as though he had forgotten the whole incident.

Oni remained behind long enough to see that they were binding the arms and legs of the marsh priest. Later in the afternoon he made practical arrangements for Abram's stay, using Kerkha as interpreter.

That evening the two friends sat before the reed house that was to be Abram's home. Oni asked curiously what his master intended to do.

Abram shook his head. *"He who seeks water from an empty vessel may choke on its dust.* I am an empty vessel, empty, empty."

Oni persisted with his questions, hoping to dispel Abram's depression by inducing him to talk.

At last Abram did talk, unwillingly and slowly at first. "You were born a slave in my father's house. I am your master. You have served me well, very well. When you took me to the palace of Rim-Sin that night of the audience, I wanted to let you go free. But you refused. I remember your words now. You said to me: 'Your dangers are my dangers; your enemies are mine. Your projects are my projects and your god is mine.' "

Something in Abram's voice suggested that he was not far from tears. He cleared his throat. Oni shifted his position and looked up at the tamarisk which spread its branches over the little house. The feathery green needles made a lacy screen through which he could see the colors of the evening sky.

Abram broke the silence again. "We never talk of these things, you and I, but I love you as a friend. If you were to ask, I would give you goods and advice. You would not need to buy them, nor to sacrifice for them.

"Surely a good god would do no less than that. If there is such a god, perhaps he will be a friend to me. If I could find him I should fear him and serve him."

Oni shook his head and got to his feet. As he did so he saw

a face cautiously protruding itself from behind a tree trunk. "Kerkha!" he cried. White teeth appeared as the face smiled. "Kerkha, come out here."

It was Kerkha, but he was not alone. As he emerged, he was followed in single file by his wife and by four daughters of diminishing sizes, each carrying upon her head an earthen vessel of a size proportionate to the bearer. One after another they placed their vessels on the ground before Abram. For a moment they stood in a silent row before him, and Abram saw that they had brought him, in their gaily painted vessels, barley, dates and fish. The mother's body was tattooed, all but her pendular breasts, with figures resembling those on the jars. The eldest daughter was the child that had been saved from the flames earlier in the day. As Abram looked at her she threw herself upon the ground and kissed his feet. Kerkha then gave a word of command and waved his family away.

Kerkha was obviously a man of authority at home. "You gave me my daughter Nana. I give you my food. The old priest is dead," and he made eloquent gestures to indicate how it was that his head had been cut off and had rolled over the ground. "The young priest took his place, and he burned my bird before the swamp god."

A few days later, with grave misgivings, Oni prepared to leave Suga. Kerkha brought food and water and placed them in the *machouf*. Abram stood at the water's edge to send him on his journey, while the villagers formed a ring about them at a respectful distance.

"It seems to me," Abram said, "that it would be best for my father Terah to remain in hiding for at least a year. Then it may be safe for him to travel back through Sumer and Akkad to the home of our people in Haran. During the winter months the desert, for a very great distance, will be flooded, and this village will be no more than a small island lost in the marsh.

"When you find Father Terah in the highlands of Elam, tell him that if I should not return, it is my wish that the death blessing of Habiru leadership should pass to Lot.

"Embrace my father for me. Tell him that I remember how he said to me: 'You must build up something for yourself. It is not enough to overthrow the work of others.' Tell him the idol breaker hopes to build — but not with his hands."

CHAPTER XV

Drehem

IT WAS with a heavy heart that Sarai left Abram and Oni at the water's edge on the border of the marsh. She followed the old camelman Magog up through the trees without turning or waving good-by, although she suspected that Abram was watching her as she disappeared.

As she and Magog approached the palm thicket where the camels were hidden, Naamah came running to meet her, and took her in her arms and held her there. Then Naamah began to scold and praise her all in one breath, bringing her water and food as well as a desert cape and kaffiyeh.

But Magog would tolerate no needless delay. They left one camelman behind with three camels to await Oni's return.

As they set out from their hiding place the palms were tossing and slapping their branches together as though the wind had driven them into a panic. They headed out into driving wind and dust, four camels trotting in single file, their heads thrusting back and forth and bodies moving swiftly, smoothly forward.

There was a curious silvery light on the desert. Sarai discovered that she could look directly at the sun without discomfort, for it was pale and white like the moon. The dust made her eyes burn. Visibility was cut down so much that she could scarcely see Magog ahead of her on the lead camel. She drew her cape and hood close about her to keep out the choking, sifting sand.

Her mind slipped back over the panorama of her days in Ur. Could it be no more than fifteen days since she and Oni had left their camels behind and crossed the great river? How exciting to see Ur as they had approached it at sunset — a city of dreams and of stirring expectations! Now it was a city of memories, strange, unbelievable memories, and again a city of dreams. She was sad, lonely, anxious. The house of Terah was broken and scattered, the future dark with danger and insecurity.

All morning the wind blew and fine dust penetrated every crevice of their clothing. Magog kept his general direction by the sun, but twice they discovered that they had come to the water's edge and had to retrace their steps to get back on higher ground.

By evening, however, the wind had dropped, the air cleared and they found themselves well north of the great swamp. They halted here for the night. They were now in the desert that lay east of the irrigated zone bordering the great river and west of the river Idiigna. From here they knew they could journey northward to Drehem without passing through any settled land.

It was good to step off their camels and feel solid ground underfoot again. Magog and the camel boy worked quickly at a well-known routine. In a short time the camels were hobbled and a black tent was pitched. The tent had four central poles set in a square and was staked down to the ground securely. Inside was a curtain that divided it into two compartments. Before the tent, a cloth was spread and on it were set out barley cakes, dates, cheese and water.

Sarai looked off across the level plain carpeted now with spring flowers. The sun was setting and the western sky glowed yellow and orange along the desert's rim.

How peaceful, she thought, how far away from the turmoil of Ur and from the little *machouf* threading its way through the channels of the great swamp.

For five days they traveled northward, and at length they left the desert and slipped into a well-beaten road that led them through the meadows of the Drehem farms. Before long, the road wound up the side of a hill, and at the top the little camel train slipped quietly across a great open square and halted before the house of Salah.

The square was deserted. Its mud-brick surface reflected the dazzling light and the heat of the noonday sun, except where a giant palm tree cast its shadow before the house.

Salah's house ran along the whole side of the square opposite to them. Its cream-colored wall was unbroken except by the large wooden door in which was cut a smaller door. But both were closed. A little cloud of pigeons wheeled across the square, and circling, came to perch on a giant dovecote located at the far right where the barns were built. Sarai could see the birds entering their nests through the little holes in its side, and the drone of cooing came to her ears. How familiar it all seemed and how good was the smell from the stables.

She called, but no one appeared. It was the time for Salah's afternoon sleep, she thought, so she gave her camel the signal *Husssh, husssh, husssh!* and he rocked downward, first onto his front knees, then onto his back knees, and finally flattened down on the ground with a rumbling grunt. She stepped off the saddle, groaning a little herself with stiffness.

Then there came a shout from the roof of the house, and before long Prince Salah himself appeared through the little doorway and came running toward her. He seemed as spry as ever, his hair and beard pure white and his weather-beaten face ruddy.

"Back, Sarai, my girl! What brings you back so soon?" he cried. "And coming as though you were running away from a storm or maybe a league of demons." They embraced in silence. Then he greeted the others. "May the God of our fathers bless you, Naamah and Magog. Your camels are tired out."

Returning to Sarai he put his arm about her and led her into the shadow beneath the palm tree. "Well! In the name of Nannar, what has happened?"

"A storm," Sarai said. "Yes, you might call it that. Terah, Abram, Nahor, Lot, servants and slaves — all fugitives."

"So!" He wagged his head. "It has come at last. I told Terah he was much too successful."

"Perhaps," Sarai said, "I should have gone with Father Terah, but I wanted to come back here to you. You seem to me as much my father as he does."

He took her tired face between his hands and peered at her. "Don't talk any more now. I don't see as well as I did, but it seems to me there is enough dust on your cheek to make it a good clay tablet to record our gains on. All right, all right — whatever has happened to bring you back, I am going to be the gainer for it. Go to your apartment now, and after you have slept and washed and eaten, I shall be waiting for you."

When the cool of the evening had come, Sarai found him waiting for her on the roof. Soft rugs had been spread for her. The old man and the young woman sat together and she told him everything that had happened from beginning to end. It grew dark and the night was silent, except for the barking of dogs in the distance.

"Fifty years ago," Salah said, "your father, at about your age, thought that he could become a Sumerian. I believe he could have, if he had been content with moderate success, content to marry one of their women. But his allegiance was only to himself and to his own family. He took wealth from the people of Ur, within the law of course, but he could not become one of them. I dare say he has a goodly fortune laid away somewhere, in Haran no doubt. In spite of success, Terah was never satisfied. It is the way of our people. We are wanderers, shepherds, herdsmen, always looking toward better pasture, never content with life.

"And now it is Abram's turn to dream a new dream — the land of Canaan and the true God! I wish he were here now, I should like to talk with him. If I were younger it might have caught my imagination, but not now.

"Let them go, Sarai. You and I will remain here. The little gods of the pastures and the wadis will welcome you, as they did after your mother was killed. Since she died here, you have been more a daughter than a granddaughter to me. If Terah does not object, I will be your father and find you a husband. I can give you a substantial dowry, you know."

He stood up and walked to the edge of the roof and pointed to the barns, whose roofs could be seen in the lingering twilight one after another along the commanding height of land on which the house stood. Then he pointed out over the pastures that sloped down from the house to the pens where thousands of animals were shut into their folds for the night. The sound of distant lowing and bleating came to their ears. "Half of all this stock belongs to me. The other half to the god Enlil. Your husband might manage these great farms after me.

"There is a distant kinsman of ours, Sarai. He is young and handsome and he understands the care of flocks and herds. He has come to me to ask your hand in marriage. If you will let me arrange this for you, you will be happy here and have sons and daughters. Why should anyone want to go to the land of Canaan?"

Sarai got to her feet and walked to the parapet beside him. She looked up at the myriad stars now appearing above her. "There is peace and quiet here and the air smells good," she said. "I am content to be here — and yet I like to wander also. Do you suppose that the heavens could be as beautiful as this in Canaan? And I have always dreamt that some day someone would take me to the land of the Nile. Perhaps that is because Naamah talks to me so much about her memories of it.

"No, Father Salah, do not ask me to be married, not now. Let me live here with you and tend a flock of sheep by day as I used to do sometimes when I was a little girl."

"What is this?" cried the old man. "Have you met a man in Ur who has taken your fancy?"

"I met many men," she replied. "But my fancy is my own."

"Tell me about Abram," he said.

"Abram," she replied, "seems to have found the king's daughter beautiful. Certainly she found him attractive. Abram is a man not easy to explain. He is in a cloud. He told me to tell you that he must find the truth before he will be worthy of leadership."

Silence fell between them. Then Salah said: "No ordinary man would be able to change our scattered people, nor to induce them to follow him."

"Abram is not an ordinary man," she said. "Make no decisions for me now, Father Salah. Let me tend your flocks. I shall enjoy being alone with you for a time."

The old man smiled. "Have it your own way for the present. My flocks must be tended, and why should I refuse employment to such a lovely shepherdess? But I warn you that Cush may not let you rest. Perhaps when you see him you will find him captivating."

"Perhaps." She shrugged.

A few days later Sarai went to work at the break of day. *Clickety, clickety, clickety* — she galloped across the pavement of the square. Her little donkey was followed at a distance by Jabal on a second ass that refused to gallop, regardless of the whip. Jabal was a herdsman, a responsible retainer in Salah's employ. He had been instructed to initiate the new shepherdess and to keep an eye on her from a distance, making sure that she was not molested.

About a mile down the road they came to the well where cattle and sheep were watered. As they approached, they could hear the wailing squeak of the water treadmill. A donkey harnessed to a long wooden arm was walking slowly round and round with drooping head and ears, while a succession of wooden buckets came up on an endless belt from the cool, deep water of the well and splashed their contents into a trough. From there the water ran out into large clay tubs where the animals could drink.

At a little distance there were folds for sheep and goats and pens for cattle. There they had spent the night, safe from wild animals. Jabal and Sarai opened the door to one of the folds and entered. Inside there was a deafening chorus — *baa, baa, me-heh-heh, me-heh-heh*. There were many big brown sheep, and a sprinkling of black and white ones. With them were a few goats with black curling hair as well as many lambs and kids. Each animal had been marked on the rump with a splash of red dye so that the flock could be kept together.

After Sarai had walked among them, Jabal opened the door and Sarai stood to count them as they bolted out, one hundred in all, including the lambs. Then the two walked ahead, calling as they went, and the flock followed. Sarai had often practiced the sheep call during her girlhood, a long-drawn treble tone followed by a deep tremolo, not unlike a human imitation of the bleat of an old sheep.

They led them to water and then out over the rolling meadow to pasture. After a time Jabal left her, but before going he warned her to keep well away from cattle, particularly when there were bulls about. Then he said with a little hesitation: "I was present when your mother was killed. I saw the bull start for her, attracted by her red cloak. You were a little girl then and I carried you home in my arms. I have never forgotten it."

"I remember too, Jabal. It is like an evil dream that I can never forget."

And so Sarai tended her flock by day and led them back safe

to the fold at sunset. She watched them as they cropped the lush grass and rescued them from briers and pitfalls. She explored the wadis where bulrushes told the tale of the streams that had gurgled through them a few months earlier. She lay in the meadows among the wild flowers or sought the shadow of a tree at noonday. For her this was a welcome period for reflection and for dreaming dreams.

One evening as she led her flock to water, she discovered a strange man waiting for her. From a distance she could see that he held himself erect. His gray kaffiyeh dotted with black and fastened in place by a colored headband showed that he was a herdsman from some other district. On closer inspection she could see that his black pointed beard was carefully trimmed and that he had black eyes and a fresh, youthful, even handsome face.

"Let me help you," he said.

She did not object. He obviously knew how to handle sheep, but his speech was slow and halting. When the flock had been counted and the door of the fold closed, he said, "I am Cush, a distant kinsman of yours. Once in Nippur I saw you with Prince Salah, and since then I have kept you in my memory. Stay a little while and talk to me."

She smiled at him and they talked for a time. But she was not to be delayed, and trotted off home with a gay good-by to him and the other shepherds.

After that he appeared often. She was always friendly but gave him little encouragement.

One night after the evening meal she found Cush talking to her grandfather. Salah asked her to sit with them and they talked of the weather and the condition of the crops, the wheat, the barley, the onions. The men compared the prices that cattle and sheep brought in Ur, Nippur and Babylon.

"When I have cattle to sell," Cush said, "I take them to the market in Nippur and get payment directly. I give my tithe to the god Enlil in good sheep. I don't like the temple scribes and their clay tablets. I can read the figures they put on them, at least the amounts, but I'd rather not be bothered and I don't like the smell of a city." He stroked his pointed beard with a big work-stained hand. "I like to have the wind off the meadows blow through my tent. I like to live my life where no one touches me unless he is my equal or my own servant."

Salah closed his gnarled fingers over Sarai's delicate little hand and she responded by placing her soft cheek against his arm. Then she straightened up to hear what she had already guessed.

"Our kinsman," Salah said, "has brought me a marriage gift, a surprisingly large one. He is a very good herdsman and has flocks of his own. You have seen him in the fields and I want him now to say to you what he has just said to me."

Sarai smiled at the young man and tossed her head, but said nothing. He flushed, and then got to his feet and swallowed. "It was easier to talk to you, Prince Salah." He cleared his throat. "I am a countryman, a herdsman." As he said this, he drew himself up proudly. "I understand animals and my flocks multiply and grow fat. If you will come to my tent, Sarai, I will take good care of you. I can give you slaves. In the dry season we will follow our sheep from one good pasture to another. In the winter we will live in the house of my father. You will not be hungry."

He paused, and when she did not reply he said: "You enjoy a shepherd's life and our children will multiply and prosper with the flocks. We shall be honored in the sight of all men. I want you, I want you to be my wife." He extended a hairy hand toward her, the sweat standing out on his forehead.

Sarai rose. She did not smile now. "This is a question which Prince Salah will have to decide for me, but not until my father comes. It is true that I love the flocks and herds and I like to wander, but there are many pastures." She hesitated and color surged into her face. "And there may be other shepherds. I must have time to consider." She bowed. "Good night."

When she had gone, Salah shrugged his shoulders and thrust out his hands. "You must keep your marriage portion until you can see Terah. Unless she asks me to accept you, I will do nothing without his permission."

One afternoon some months later Sarai had taken her flock across the fields, now turning brown, to a considerable distance from the fold, in search of better pasture, and Jabal, who usually managed to keep her in sight, had wandered even farther off with his flock. The sheep had lost their heavy coats to the shearers and the lambs were half grown. The spring flowers had vanished and the grass was brown, for autumn was here.

Sarai sat in the shade of a clump of laurels. A hot breeze stirred the dark green screen of leaves about her head. She could see that the flock, which had drifted away from her, was still in view, except for the few inevitable stragglers. From trees and meadow the ringing tone of the cicadas waxed and waned in a never ending cycle of sound.

She leaned back against the great gnarled trunk. Life had settled down to a routine, yes, a tedious routine, she thought. Nothing had been heard from Terah, and no word at all from Abram, although winter was approaching.

The rams had finished jumping her sheep and the he-goats were quiet again. All the things that grew in nature seemed to be preparing for sleep. It crossed her mind that this was the time of year when the god Dumuzi would begin his wandering. He was impotent now and would descend into the underworld.

It was time for Nin-Anna to begin her winter wailing, time for the women of the world to join in the chorus, waiting for love and springtime, for the resurrection of Dumuzi.

She wondered what Abram would say about such folklore now.

People only half believed it all, of course, but they loved the mystery, the poetry, the music. She reached for her pipes and began to play. . . . It was a haunting melody, the wailing of Nin-Anna.

Presently she heard a heavy panting sound and she started up and reached for her shepherd's staff. Fear clutched at her heart and she peered through the foliage expecting to see an animal, perhaps a bear!

But instead she saw a strange little man toiling up the incline toward her. He had a big body but his thighs were amazingly short and his legs were so bowed that it seemed at first that he had no legs at all as he came toward her through the grass. His upper arms were short also, but his head was large, unusually large, and his forehead bulged and seemed to push his eyes downward in his face.

She had seen this dwarf before, she thought. Then it all came back. This was the servant of Unzie son of Gudea.

She stepped out into the open and the little man stood before her. He bowed and paused to catch his breath. "I have found you at last," he said. "I've been over the hills and I've fallen into the wadis. Why in the name of Enlil should you hide your beauty here under a tree with nothing but goats to gaze at you? Why should you wear the rough homespun of a simple shepherdess and eat black bread and cheese?" He pointed to her lunch, which lay untouched on an open shawl beside her. "Don't you know that you could wear the finest linen and grow fat on the food that is served to the wife of a patrician among the amelu?"

Sarai looked at him with a mingled feeling of anger and dismay. She knew this meant that her presence in Drehem was no longer a secret, at least not to those in Nippur.

"Go away," she said. "I did not ask you to come scrambling over the pastures and I do not want to listen to your insults. Who sent you here?"

"I came here today only to bring you a message from my master, and I humbly crave pardon if I have offended the beautiful shepherdess." The little man now bowed so low that it looked as though he might pass right through his bowed legs and come out on the other side.

"My master Unzie," he said, regaining an erect position, "plans some day soon to call upon Prince Salah to ask your hand in marriage. He will bring with him princely gifts and a message from the patesi of Nippur. You know that the patesi has power of life and death over Salah. My master is his close kinsman."

Sarai made an exclamation of disgust. "Your master! I'm told he is married already."

"Oh, no," the servant expostulated, "at least not for long. He is getting a divorce from his wife now. I myself collected complete evidence that she had committed adultery during his absence from Nippur." The dwarf chuckled to himself. "The villain who was finally discovered in her bed was a friend of mine. He enjoyed himself thoroughly and when her case was tried he admitted his guilt before the judge. Then he escaped from prison. He does not like living in Nippur anyway." The little man gave vent to a raucous laugh.

"Oh, how dreadful! She could be killed by drowning. But I don't want to hear anything more." Sarai stooped to pick up her mantle and her lunch. "Tell your master that my father — " she hesitated, wondering what she should say about him — "that my father is not here and I cannot marry without his permission. Anyway, your master is a drunkard and I would rather die than marry him."

Sarai started off toward her sheep and called over her shoulder: "You can tell your master that I do not like his servant either."

The little man trotted after her, ignoring the reference to himself. "My master drinks only enough heavy wine every day to keep him in a pleasant and jovial mood. He has always done that. He loves you profoundly. He would prefer you to his wine. But it is bad for him to go without it. You will like him better when he drinks. He instructed me to tell you of his love. I would like to describe the jewels and the fine garments and slaves. They will all be yours when you marry him."

The servant was falling behind and was quite out of breath. But he followed manfully. "Your father and your brother Abram — they are wanted — in Ur — big reward — but the patesi could protect them in Nippur."

At last he gave up the chase and with his bowed legs wide apart and his hands on his hips he shouted after her in his heavy rasping voice: "Remember, you will have to marry Unzie some day. Prince Salah can never say no to the patesi."

Sarai gave no sign that she had heard, but the servant's words came to her again and again through the long afternoon.

At last she led her sheep to water and folded them for the night. She was unhappy and had a feeling of foreboding. The period of peace and protection had come to an end. It did not seem to her that she had reached any conclusions about life nor about the gods. She had hoped to think things out. She wondered if Abram had done better.

Her little ass, walking with leaden feet, carried her along the dusty road toward home.

Though the sun was setting, rippling heat still rose from the plain like a million tiny tongues of colorless flame flickering and waving in a breeze. The surface of the road ahead of her shimmered as though she were seeing it through troubled water.

Looking upward toward Salah's house on the top of the hill she saw it and the barns beyond it — floating high in air, as it seemed. Below was a lake that stretched far into the distance; in its mirrored surface the house and the barns were reflected upside down, floating, fantastic.

This was not the first mirage she had seen. But this one seemed ominous, and her mind slipped off into a daydream. She seemed to see Drehem vanishing forever, and the words of the dwarf came back to her: "Prince Salah can never say no to the patesi." She would run away rather than marry Unzie, far away. In her fantasy, she and her grandfather were walking together out across the desert, while Drehem was no more than an insubstantial dream of the past, and Terah was lost and Abram had forgotten them.

The little ass began to gallop, and soon his little feet went *clickety, clickety, clickety* over the hard surface of the square. He was nearing the barns and his supper. Sarai looked up and saw that Salah was coming out to meet her.

"We have an important visitor," he said. "The son of the king of Salem is here and he has asked especially to see you."

"Melchizedek!" she exclaimed. "What a pleasant surprise! I am delighted."

"When you have eaten," Salah said, "come to us, and don't be long about it. Don't linger over that mirror of yours. You can't improve on what I see." Salah laughed. "Here, let me take your ass and I'll turn him over to Jabal." The animal had begun to bray dolefully, and Jabal appeared from the barns.

Sarai had forgotten Unzie and his servant now. She kissed her grandfather and ran off, calling over her shoulder: "I won't be long."

But she was long. When she looked in the mirror the words of the hateful dwarf about homespun came back to her. For that reason, or for some other reason, her toilet took a considerable length of time. But when she left her room, followed by Naamah, it was quite apparent that the time had been well spent. At all events, the simple shepherdess had vanished.

They passed along the gallery, she and Naamah, and down the stairway which reached the court at the side of the outer door. From here they walked across to Salah's great reception room which opened widely on the court. He had had the hanging lamps lit and the finest rugs were spread on the floor and out into the court.

Sarai had not remembered that Melchizedek was so tall and distinguished in appearance. But then, she reflected, he had stood beside Abram, who made other men seem small.

She greeted him now: "What good fortune brings you to Drehem?"

Melchizedek looked at her with admiration before he replied. She was tanned by the sun, which seemed to increase the brilliance of her smile as well as the beauty of her eyes beneath their long lashes.

After they were seated he said: "I suppose you are surprised to see me here. It was part of my original plan of travel to visit all of the great temples of Akkad and Sumer. When I came to Nippur to the temple of the god Enlil, I heard a great deal about the god's farms at Drehem and about the hereditary overseer, Prince Salah.

"But I may as well admit to you both that there is an additional reason for this visit. I have a message for Abram and I hoped that here I might — see him." As he said this he shot a questioning glance at Salah, but the old man ignored it.

"It is months since we saw you in Ur," Sarai said. "What news do you bring us?"

"If you have not heard from Ur," Melchizedek replied, "I have a great deal of news to give you. Abram's defense of the Habiru before the king seems to have had a good effect, for the persecution that was planned was not carried out. It is said that the Princess Shub has also influenced the king toward leniency. I have no doubt that what might be called Nasir's accident had a good deal to do with the failure of the plan to kill the Habiru in the city."

At this Sarai interrupted him. "You speak as though Nasir

were living, but surely I thought — " She checked herself just in time, as it flashed through her mind that perhaps no one knew what had happened in her father's house, and that she must not betray Abram's part in that affair. She saw again, in her mind's eye, Nasir's prostrate body while Abram stood over him. She saw the trickle of blood running down from Nasir's temple, and Abram placing the lamp on the floor beside his body.

Melchizedek smiled, as though he surmised her thoughts. "No," he said, "Nasir did not die. He is recovering now. You might be interested in the rumors that have spread through Ur as to what happened to him. It is known that after Princess Shub climbed the ziggurat for her marriage with Nannar, Nasir took a corporal of the royal guard with him and went to the prison cell where the corporal had last seen Abram. When they found him gone, they set out for your father's house.

"Other soldiers found the two lying in the court of the house. The corporal was dead from a stab wound. Nasir, however, was lying unconscious from a powerful blow that had made a depression in his skull, and across his body lay the enormous mace which King Ur-Nammu presented to Nannar, the mace that Rim-Sin carries as a symbol of his authority. Actually, as you saw at the betrothal, he has someone else carry it now, for it is too heavy for him in his old age.

"For many days Nasir continued to be unconscious, and then he began to recover; but he is still afflicted by a strange disability. His sword arm is paralyzed and he cannot speak, though he obviously understands.

"Some say that the king himself struck down Nasir, since the mace is kept in his chamber and no one has access to it except Rim-Sin or his chamberlain. Those who believe in that explanation tell strange stories of how the king came to Terah's house.

"More thoughtful individuals about the court know that there are few men living who could use that mace as a weapon. The king at his present age is not one. They say that Abram could have done it, or Abram's giant slave.

"Many say that this is all the work of the mighty god that Abram worships. This is the explanation that almost everyone in Ur believes and it is supported by the strange type of curse that seems to have fallen on Nasir, and by the surprising fact that the idols in Terah's own market were found to have been broken to pieces.

"These are strange happenings, you will admit." Melchizedek looked quizzically at Sarai, and then continued, "Did you know that the great image of Nannar rolled down the ziggurat?"

"Yes," she replied. "I saw it happen."

"Well," he continued, "that also is accepted as the work of Abram's God. There are those who claim that Abram himself was with the princess and Enannatum at the top of the ziggurat and they saw him carried away into the sky after the idol was overthrown.

"Of course, Enannatum has since explained that he had had the god moved to the top of the steps so the people could see him during the ceremony and that the scaffolding under the idol gave way spontaneously. He had the workmen who moved the god publicly executed.

"Nannar has since been remade and he sits on his throne in even greater splendor than before. The jewels that were given to the god by Rim-Sin as the Princess Shub's dowry now sparkle in his crown."

Melchizedek chuckled. "That high priest has a genius for creating spectacles, but this one seemed to go wrong! I too was standing in the audience, and I thought I recognized one of the actors in the little show at the top of the ziggurat. It was the figure that stood on the scaffolding with upraised arms as the god came plunging down the steps toward us."

Melchizedek brought his hands together with a thwack. "What a thing to have seen! The people said they saw the demons dancing all up and down the ziggurat after the fall of Nannar and after the altar fire was out. I fancied that I saw them too, and the people went wild as though the same demons had entered their hearts."

"That was when I was knocked down by the crowd," Sarai said. "They trampled on me and I had black and blue spots all over me. There is still one here on my shoulder, I think. — No, it seems to have disappeared." Melchizedek examined her gracefully curving neck and shoulders with apparent sympathy.

"And what is said as to the whereabouts of Terah and his family?" Salah asked.

"Some say they are dead. But Rim-Sin has let it be known that Terah will not be harmed if he returns to Ur. He has set a great price, a king's ransom, for the safe return of Abram.

"It is generally believed that Abram left a curse upon the city. He was heard to warn the king that vultures were gathering in the sky above Ur, and that jackals would soon find food in its temples.

"This brings me to the message that I have promised to try to deliver to Abram. The high priest, Enannatum, instructed me to tell Abram he would not be harmed if he returned to Ur."

"And what about Shub? Is there no message from her?" Sarai asked.

"The Princess Shub-Kudur has been seen rarely since she became entum. But I saw her. She was standing beside Enannatum in the temple of Ningal while he gave me the message for Abram. After Enannatum had left us, we talked together privately. She has changed in appearance since the day of the betrothal. She is beautiful still, but — how shall I express it — more like a widow than a bride."

"What did you talk about?" queried Sarai.

"She asked me to explain Abram. I found that difficult, but we did discuss the most high God who is worshiped in my father's little kingdom."

Then Salah broke in: "Would you yourself advise Abram to return to Ur?"

"For my own part," replied Melchizedek, "I would advise him to stay away from Ur. If he wants to worship the one God, let him go into a new country. But I have delivered Enannatum's message to him as it was given to me." Melchizedek made a gesture as though to indicate that he had finished.

Salah looked at him shrewdly, then said: "We know that Abram escaped from Ur. We have had no news of him since that time. If he is still alive, and if the God of our fathers brings him here, I will give him this message as you have delivered it."

Salah rose and paced the floor. He was short, but broad-shouldered, confident, and quick in his movements. His white hair and short white beard seemed to form a frame about the large Habiru nose and the bright black eyes.

He clapped his hands to summon a servant, and asked that a certain rare wine be brought for their guest. He was never serious for very long at a time, and could not tolerate protracted discussion unless it had to do with land, or with the beasts of the field.

He stopped in his walking now and, stroking his beard, looked down at Melchizedek. The myriad wrinkles about his mouth suggested a smile and his eyes twinkled.

"I think we might learn something from sheep and cattle; they don't worry about the gods, at least not in this country. But it may be that in the land of Canaan they are reflecting upon the most high God when they stand and chew their cuds and look at the green hills far away." He laughed merrily at the figment of his own imagination.

"No doubt you are right," Melchizedek answered. "But here

I've heard it said that although there are four hundred and ninety-nine gods in Sumer, only the camel knows the name of the five hundredth. When you look at a camel, it is clear that he is smiling to himself about some dark secret. Probably it is he alone in all Sumer who knows the name of the most high God."

Perceiving that Melchizedek was a kindred spirit, Salah poured out the wine with gusto and they talked of many things. When the visitor turned the conversation to the history of Drehem, Salah needed little urging to launch forth on this subject.

"About two hundred years ago," Salah said, "the cities of Sumer and Akkad were ruled each by its own patesi. The patesi was the high priest of the principal god of each city and also the civil ruler of it. Ur-Nammu, who was patesi of the moon god and governor of Ur, conquered the other cities, and established himself as supreme ruler of all these lands and called himself king of Sumer and Akkad. He forced the other cities to pay him tribute and began to appoint their patesis."

As the old man talked the others listened with deference. But Melchizedek allowed his eyes to wander more than once toward Sarai, as she sat on the rug beside him — erect and poised like a bird, he thought, about to take flight. The soft light from the lamps made her fine hair glow and he noted the girlish grace of her arms, the pleasing curve of cheek and breast.

"In Ur and the country round," Salah continued, "the people feared Nannar and paid their taxes there willingly. But elsewhere throughout his great kingdom Enlil, the father of Nannar, was much more feared by the people; so Ur-Nammu, in his wisdom, forced all the other cities to pay their tribute to Enlil in his temple at Nippur. The patesi of Enlil in turn forwarded a very large share to Ur. Some of the tribute was in the form of grain and fruit, but most of it was cattle, sheep, goats and fowl of different sorts.

"Thus the temple of Nippur could not contain all the beasts

that were sent to Enlil, so the patesi created these farms at Drehem. City dwellers have never understood the care of animals." Melchizedek corroborated this statement with a nod, and the old man smiled. "Consequently, from the beginning Semitic herdsmen were put in charge.

"The descendants of Ur-Nammu who sat on the throne of Ur and who were named Dungi, Bur-Sin, Gimil-Sin, and Ibi-Sin, continued this practice, and with the proceeds of taxation they beautified the temples of Nannar and of Enlil. Then came the armies of foreign Semites from the north and the Elamites swept down from the mountains to the east and destroyed Ur and carried off the divine Ibi-Sin."

"Yes," said Melchizedek, "I have seen the lament on the great tablet in the temple of Nippur. It goes something like this:

"Whereunto, O Sumer! Did they change thee?
When Enlil gave command to end thy peace
And, o'er thy land, storm spirit of Anu hastened,

All gone thy city, temple, sacred dynasty.
And Enlil, turning gaze to distant land,
Beheld, borne off to Elam, Ibi-Sin divine."

"Excellent," cried Sarai. "What a good memory you have! I like the sound of the words *o'er thy land, storm spirit of Anu hastened.*"

"After the time of Ibi-Sin," Salah continued, "the tribute paid to Enlil in Nippur was greatly reduced, and consequently fresh animals were no longer sent out to the farms. But the farms were now being run by the Habiru and so they continued to prosper by themselves and to pay back income to the god.

"My father was overseer of these farms before me. I succeeded him as a young man, and the farms prospered so greatly that the patesi of Nippur was pleased, and he raised me to the amelu class, changing my name from Karnebo to Prince Salah.

"Now my granddaughter whom you see sitting here beside me is my only descendant. That is how she came to be called Sarai, Little Princess. She will inherit my share here, and she or her husband could become the hereditary overseer. That is why I want Sarai to marry a man of our blood and remain here."

During Salah's discourse Sarai had been biding her time, and now she said to Melchizedek. "Abram said that he would not return to us until he had found the truth. He said that I would understand, when no one else did, why he must be alone. But I'm not sure that I do understand."

Melchizedek did not reply and so she continued: "I know he learned to hate all idols and did not want people to worship them, but what does he hope to find to take their place? You have talked with Abram and you and your people do not worship idols. Can you help me?"

Melchizedek had been studying her as she talked. "You have a thoughtful mind," he said, "as well as a woman's quick perception. You will understand most of what I say before I say it.

"Your people worship your family God without making images of Him. And yet, because you have no faith in His power, you also pay tribute to the gods of other people and take part in strange rites before their idols. Your people use charms and incantations to frighten away evil spirits, just the same as all the idol worshipers.

"In the land of Salem, the God of my people is called the most high God. He has all the good qualities which other people have attributed to all idols, and yet he has none of the bad qualities. He protects the mother, the child, and the aged. He gives fertility to the land and to the flocks, and grants success to the warrior, but He must be worshiped as the sole God.

"Abram has studied all the gods of Sumer and Akkad and he

has rejected them. Back of them he is searching for the truth. That is, he is searching for the true God. In a sense this is the problem that every man must face for himself."

At that Salah interjected: "I don't see how you get along with just one god in Salem. In this country one god seems to do one thing well and another something else. You don't ask Marduk for rain, you ask Enlil, and you don't ask Enki that your wife may conceive and bear a son, you go to Ishtar about that.

"The God of our fathers is all very well in his place. He may look after the spirits of our dead and may bring us little blessings, but he has no temple, and seems to have no power." Salah shook his head dubiously and then continued:

"Then there is another practical advantage to our present system. People pay taxes to an idol, the priests organize things, spend the money and govern the land, with protection from a king or patesi. It seems to me the only practical way of doing things in a large country."

Sarai replied to Melchizedek, as though she had not heard her grandfather: "You believe, then, that Abram is learning to worship the one God, the God who created all things and who has the power in Himself, and the understanding, that men have thought could be found only in many gods. You believe that every man should be able to worship the God who has no image."

She hesitated and then continued slowly: "I'm not quite sure what you mean by worship . . . but I think Abram hopes to talk with someone, face to face."

Melchizedek smiled. "You have a way," he said, "of sifting out the wheat of truth and letting the chaff of conversation blow away."

Sarai laughed gaily. "I only took the broken harvest as I found it on the threshing floor under the feet of the ox. I threw it hopefully into the air, and you blew the chaff away like the wind off the meadow — a wind from a far country.

"And then," she continued with exaggerated respect, "you, Prince Salah, sift out our grain and you tell us that we have harvested wild tares instead of wheat!"

Again her manner changed swiftly and she was serious. "Grandfather, is it true that you can never say no to a command from the patesi of Nippur?"

"Yes," Salah replied, "I suppose it is. He is our ruler."

"Oh, oh!" Sarai exclaimed. "Perhaps it would have been better if I had gone into hiding with Father Terah." Then, in response to Salah's expression of astonishment, she added: "The servant of Unzie son of Gudea found me in the meadow today. He says the patesi will force you to give me to his master to wife!"

Salah was silent until Melchizedek said to him: "Is not the patesi kinsman to Gudea?"

"Yes," he replied abruptly, "brother." Then he got to his feet slowly and when he stood as erect as his old joints would permit, he said, "I fear that we may have wearied our noble guest." It was clear that he was not prepared to discuss Sarai's announcement. But as she was about to leave he put his arm about her shoulder and quoted an old saying: "*Men ponder through the night, but understanding waits the dawn and wisdom the break of day.* We will talk again tomorrow."

When Sarai and Naamah had disappeared, Melchizedek said: "Prince Salah, may I ask you whether Sarai has had many suitors?"

"Many!" Salah exclaimed, and threw out his hands as though in despair.

"Is Abram a suitor?"

"Not as far as I know," Salah replied, looking at him searchingly.

"If I could be sure of that, I would accept your kind invitation to remain here for a longer time. But . . . as it is, I shall return to Nippur in the morning. Sarai shows a remarkable interest in Abram, more than might be expected of a sister.

"It was not my plan to return to Salem for some months yet, and I will give you an address in Nippur where I could be reached if you or Abram should wish to send a messenger to me.

"I am not married. My wife died just before I began this journey through Akkad and Sumer. If I were to remain here I might well come to desire your granddaughter for my wife. I have never seen such beauty, never known such spirit, and I believe my father would welcome her as the future queen of Salem.

"I hope that Abram is safe, that he finds the truth, and that he returns here before it is too late. Blessings of the most high God on him, and on you and Sarai."

The two men looked at each other with understanding and said good night.

Next morning when the little shepherdess rode her donkey across the square and started down the road that led to the meadow, Melchizedek was waiting for her.

"Oh!" she cried, and jumped off the ass. "You are dressed as though for a journey. Surely you will not leave us. We have many things to show you, and I was counting on more evenings of pleasant talk."

She looked up at him, wondering whether it might be his princely bearing and his fine, waving brown hair that made him seem so distinguished. She noted that the expression in his eyes was kind, as it had been the night before, but now he seemed sad.

"Why are you sad?" she asked.

"I am sad," he replied, "because I see someone who is lovely beyond compare, a bud about to bloom in another man's garden, and that other man is my friend."

He turned as though to go, but she said: "Don't go. I don't understand what you are saying."

He hesitated and then turned back. Sarai observed now that there were gray hairs in his carefully trimmed beard, and lines in his forehead and about his eyes that she had not noticed before. He spoke to her gently:

"Forgive me if I ask a blunt question. Do you love Abram?"

She realized that evasion was impossible with this compelling man.

"No," she said, "at least, I don't think so. I don't know."

"Would you be willing to marry someone else before Abram came back, or before you knew that he was . . . not coming back?"

She blushed deeply, but replied: "No . . . I would rather wait."

He smiled at her. "Your grandfather knows where I shall be in Nippur, if you should ever want to see me again.

"Good-by," he said.

She gave him her hand, and he kissed it. She watched him as he walked to the square, to disappear without turning to look back.

CHAPTER XVI

Spring

A SECOND SPRING came to the great marsh, and for the second time Oni approached the village of Suga. He was paddling alone in a light *machouf* that he had brought to the water's edge on camelback.

Many things might have happened, he thought. Would he find Abram alive? Would he be greatly changed, or would he be sunk in doubt and despair, as he had seemed when he left him almost a year ago?

On arriving at the village Oni found they were expecting him, for the marsh shepherds had sent word of the approach of camels. He was conducted with shouts to the chief, who welcomed him warmly. Even the chief's wife came out of her reed hut to greet him, smiling broadly and wearing the jewelry which they had given her.

Kerkha was summoned and told to conduct Oni to Abram's new house. It was obvious at once that Kerkha had become a man of some standing among his people. Together they left the village, and, as they went, Kerkha pointed to the changes that had been brought about by Abram.

They passed a smoldering fire and Kerkha explained that the refuse from the reed huts was no longer dumped into the water channels. Instead it was brought here, and every seventh day it was burned to drive the swamp fever demon away. The natives, he explained, thought it was a sacrifice to Abram's god. Then his round face broke into a smile. "No fever this year, Suga happy."

They followed a winding path through the date palms and came at last to a clearing in which there stood a splendid reed hut. "I build Abram new house," said Kerkha, "here on high ground."

Oni called, but there was no answer, so he passed under the arch that formed the entrance of the house and stepped around the reed screen that served as a door. The hut was empty. Abram's cloak hung on the wall. It was tattered and soiled but Oni recognized it and was happy. There was a long rug on the floor and at the far end was a bed of rushes. Just behind the screen was a small circular fireplace; a wisp of smoke showed that coals were alive beneath the ash. On a stool were fish and dates and beside the stool a clay vessel of water. In one corner there was a supply of clay and a pile of completed tablets on which there was writing. Several bamboo styluses showed that someone had been writing there.

Oni stepped out of the hut into the sunshine and hallooed. There was no answer, but Kerkha, who had been waiting for him, pointed with pride to the construction of the new hut. The skeleton of the house was formed by a series of arches placed one after the other. Each arch was formed of a great bundle of reeds bound round and round with other reeds. On the top of these arches long bamboo poles had been laid horizontally and lashed securely to hold the arches in place. Waterproof reed matting had been placed over this structure and was held down by more bamboo rods at top and sides. Kerkha wished to point out the excellence of the weaving of the reed sides, but Oni was not to be distracted. He shouted again, but there was silence except for the deep-toned melody of a distant bulbul.

Kerkha pointed to another path and said: "The Sumerian priest spends his days under big tree."

So Oni placed the pack he had been carrying on the ground before the house and followed Kerkha along the well-beaten path through the palm thickets. Soon they reached higher ground that rose abruptly, and here the palms stopped at an open clearing. In the center of the clearing there was an enormous terebinth tree. The small oval leaves were quivering as though there were unseen life there.

In the shade of the tree and next to its rough gray trunk there was an altar, built of dried mud, upon which a fire smoldered. He must have been here recently, Oni thought to himself, but something kept him from calling again. Instead he advanced and stood quietly before the altar. He saw that the earth under his feet was worn smooth. This, he thought, is where Abram must have stood day after day. Is it possible, after all, that he has gone mad? The silence was complete except for the recurring throaty scream of a vulture high above him, wheeling in great circles over the marsh, each scream ending in a long-drawn high-toned tremolo.

A wind stirred, and the tree began to whisper mysteriously. Oni's mind was filled with vague apprehension and he felt a tingling sensation that passed up over the skin of his back and neck. He looked around for the marsh native and discovered that Kerkha had remained at the edge of the clearing and that he lay prostrate as though in the presence of a god. Oni then stooped and removed his own sandals, not quite knowing why he did so.

He returned to Kerkha, who got up and said: "God of Abram there, but I never see him."

Then they heard a voice calling in the distance. Oni put on his sandals and ran back along the pathway. He answered the call and finally burst headlong into the clearing before the reed hut. There he saw Abram standing before the doorway.

But this was a different Abram. He would hardly have known him, had it not been for his voice. He was dressed in a sheepskin coat, his hair was long and his face covered by a black curling beard.

"Oni," cried Abram, leaping forward and throwing his arms about him. "I thought this pack must be yours. I've been waiting for you to come back. Welcome, welcome, welcome!" He thumped his friend, and talked and laughed. "We'll have a feast here in my swamp palace. I shall prepare such a meal for you! But if you've anything good to eat in that pack of yours we might do better!"

The two friends laughed and chatted, and after they had eaten settled down to talk.

As boys these two men had been inseparable, and now, although one had become a scholar-priest and the other a herdsman, the strength of their mutual affection had not lessened. Oni was faithful, practical, dogged. Abram was brilliant and changeable. When Oni had left him, Abram had seemed slow, preoccupied, depressed. Oni returned to find a changed man — alert, vivacious, full of drive.

Abram poured out some date wine. Oni, watching him with a smile, said: "Well, Abram, many people are waiting for you. Tell me what has happened."

Abram leaned back against the wall of the hut and looked up at the palm tops, just now breaking into beautiful bloom. He did not reply. So Oni asked again: "Did you find the answers to your questions?"

"Yes," said Abram, "I think so. I am now at peace. But this has been a long struggle, a strange experience, and it is difficult to explain it."

Oni, looking at him closely now, realized that he was thin. New lines had appeared in his face, lines that he had not noticed at first because of the beard and his own excitement.

"For some time after you left me, I was in the depths of despair. I could not sleep at night and I found it difficult to think by day. The wound that I had from Nasir-Sin healed very slowly. In the end I must have had the fever for there were days that I do not remember. Kerkha and his wife and daughter must have cared for me, for as I began to recover they were here every day, and I discovered that the chief had sent back the talisman that Terah gave me, the *utchat* of the god Horus. You see it still hangs about my neck.

"As my strength returned I could contemplate our lives quietly. I reviewed again the history of the gods that I had prepared for Enannatum and which he sent to Hammurabi with the king lists. I even summarized it all, as well as I could remember it, on clay tablets.

"Then I began to see the world of today, as though from a great distance. It seemed to me that I stood on a high mountain and could actually see the people of Ur and the people of Babylon fearing different gods, gods which their leaders, past and present, have made. I saw them preparing for the greatest of all wars, the one nation and its allies against the other, a war that both peoples would gladly escape.

"These peoples, on both sides, I saw were impelled by fear, fear without understanding — fear of gods that are false, fear of an enemy that bears no grudge, fear of imminent destruction that may well prove to be real.

"I saw the Habiru in Ur and those in Babylon as well, bowing down to gods that are not their own. I saw them retaining their pride of race that has forever separated us from all others. Wherever we go each of us retains his nomad heart, even within the walls of cities.

"The past and the present I could see. The future was dark. Then I built an altar but I made no idol. I called upon God but all was silence. For months I was desperate as I argued within myself.

The swamp natives began to shun me, or they eyed me strangely, as though they thought me mad.

"Finally a change came over me. How shall I explain?"

Abram got up abruptly and told Oni to follow him. He led the way to the border of a water channel that wound between grassy banks. They sat down and Oni observed that a well-beaten path followed the edge of the wandering channel as far as he could see.

"You see," Abram began again, "I turned from the past to the present and I began to look at the things around me. There," he exclaimed pointing, "do you see that small movement on the tree? It is a caterpillar. He spun himself a house to sleep the winter months through. Now he is about to emerge from it. See him moving his arms?

"Soon he will spread them out and float away, flying on gossamer wings. It is the first time he has ever done this and yet, strange to say, he knows how it is done. Once up in the air he will seek out the flowers that his mother preferred — the mother who laid his egg, the mother he never saw. More than that, he will seek out his mate, who will look exactly like his mother, and together they will dance out their little lives in the summer sunshine. Who taught him to do these things? No one. The memory of his race was in the egg from which he came.

"Who taught that bird up in the tree there to build its nest and feed its young? No one. Who warned the duck swimming yonder that our presence may mean danger to her eggs? How is it that she is disturbed? Who taught the ant in the grass to seek out his food and carry it to the anthill?

"Each of these creatures may learn something new in his lifetime. I do not know about that; but each has, within himself, the memory of his race. Somehow he remembers what was good and what was bad for his ancestors. He does not have to ask about it. The wisdom of a thousand thousand years of life is in the body of this ant and it will be handed on forever and ever.

"These creatures have been my companions and they have taught me much.

"But man is different. He cannot remember the experience of his ancestors. He gets no knowledge in his mother's womb, nor does wisdom come to him in his mother's milk. He must be taught by words and example, and in this teaching there is both wisdom and folly, right and wrong. Alas for man, he must choose.

"You and I can sit here and consider what we will do. Decisions do not come to us in our bodies. The arrival of spring does not force us into this or that change. It is true that it may bring longings and impulses that we share with the animals. Yet we can control them. There is, in each of us, a body — but it is blind and dumb.

"There is something else within us, a spirit. And the spirit may well do this or that.

"Men say that the spirit is in the heart and that we think there. But wherever and however we do it, it is obvious that we do learn and store up knowledge each in his own life. We seek wisdom and guidance from other men.

"In our hearts we can ponder and plan. We take council with ourselves and with other men. It is given to us to understand the world and to perceive that there is a spirit also.

"God is the great spirit of the world. He is not made of mud or stone, or gold or silver. Perhaps He is in all things, as my spirit is in me. Somehow, I thought, I must take council with Him.

"Thus, I tried to comprehend Him not knowing whether I should expect to see Him, or to hear Him or perceive Him in my heart. All men, I thought, since time began, have sought God. When they failed to see Him and hear Him someone made an idol. The others, seeing the idol, no longer tried to understand.

"I considered the heavens, the sun and the moon and the stars, which move in their regular courses; the land, the waters, the rainfall and the multitude of living things large and small. Considering the ordered movement of all things I knew that there could be but one God behind it all, not many striving spirits. I knew also that He must be wise and just. Among living things only man is able to have knowledge of these things and so I understood that my mind must be somehow like the mind of God.

"I stood long hours before the little altar that you saw. I built a fire there. I listened. At last He seemed to speak within me. He revealed Himself to me and gave me counsel. I have walked with God. I know now that there is one God. To fear Him is understanding. To obey Him is the beginning of wisdom."

Abram stopped talking and there was silence. Oni scratched his great hairy arms. He wrinkled up his swarthy forehead, moving as he did so his shock of curly black hair. He pursed his lips and looked at Abram with eyes which expressed admiration. But he found no words. He cleared his throat with a deep guttural growl.

Finally he said: "Does this mean that you are ready to return with me?"

"Yes," Abram replied, "ready and full of plans for the future. Ready — and longing to get back. For weeks I have been waiting. I knew you would come. I've visited the natives in their huts, helped the chief to make wise rules for them and paced back and forth through these paths. I thought you would come when the water receded, but it has been very long.

"I have been thinking about other things too. This morning as I sat on the bank here two ducks came gliding across the water. They came so close that I could have touched them, a sleek brown bird followed closely by a handsome drake. The morning light glowed on the blue-green of his head and neck, and his red legs moved beneath him with power. I watched her feeding with her head deep below the surface of the water and her tail in the air. All the while he circled proudly about her. The will to protect her was evident in every movement he made.

"I would have talked with him if I could, for I felt welling up inside of me impulses that I shared with him, desires the fulfillment of which brings happiness and satisfaction to man and beast and bird alike. But I felt much more. Things he could not share with me.

"You see these creatures have been my companions. I have had to talk with them. Don't laugh at that. But I cannot share things of the spirit with them. Yes, I'm ready, ready for the work and strife and joys of common living . . . ready to woo the woman I love, if it is not too late."

He reached into the leather purse that hung at his belt and drew out a long strip of rough brown linen. He held it up. "Do you recognize it?"

"Well," Oni replied, "it looks like a turban, and not one of very good quality I should say."

"This is what Sarai wore bound about her hair when disguised as a camel boy." Abram was folding it carefully. "The perfume of her hair seemed to cling to it for a long time. I talk to it as though Sarai were here. . . . Did you see Sarai before coming here?"

"Yes," Oni replied. "I went to Drehem some months ago."

Then Abram asked: "Is there anything, anything important between you two?"

Oni smiled and shook his head, a little sadly perhaps. "You are thinking of the kiss she gave me when she left us in the swamp? That kiss was not meant for me. Possibly she meant it for Kerkha, or you." Oni chuckled at Abram's obvious anxiety. "No, no, she is not for me. I have seen no one that I cannot forget — except —" Oni seemed embarrassed — "except the handmaid of

Princess Shub. Do you remember Berri? I suppose I shall never return to Ur. . . .

"But you, Abram, might have a chance to win Sarai, if you do not wait here too long with your feet in swamp water and your hair and beard looking like a thicket. She was still free when I saw her last, but suitors are buzzing about Drehem like hornets about honey."

Abram ran his hand through his hair and began to pace up and down. "Did Sarai send no message to me?"

"Yes," replied Oni with a smile.

"Well, why don't you give it to me then? Speak, man!" Abram was shaking Oni by the shoulder now in his exasperation.

Oni laughed. "She said: 'Tell Abram to search for Dumuzi in the marsh,' and when I asked again, she only repeated it."

Abram looked at Oni in surprise and then threw his head back and laughed.

They heard an exclamation, and turning in the direction of the sound saw that Kerkha was watching them. When he found that he was discovered he said: "First time I hear him laugh like that." Then seeing the two friends still smiling, his round face broke into a brilliant smile and he began giggling uncontrollably. Eventually he drew himself up with great dignity and said: "My chief invite you both to banquet tonight."

"The great chief does us honor," Abram said. "We will come to his feast with hunger, happy to sit at the feet of the great chief. We shall say farewell."

Kerkha bowed and disappeared, and Abram said to Oni with a smile: "You see I have learned marsh etiquette. These are proud little men. We shall visit Kerkha's house and you will see that his daughter, whom you carried under your arm so easily, has flowered into full womanhood. She has the beauty of a marsh lily now. You may meet her betrothed also."

Abram walked into the sunshine, drew himself up to his towering height and held out his arms so that his muscles rippled under bronzed skin. He threw back his great shaggy head and stood for a moment in exultation.

"Tomorrow we leave at dawn, and I shall lead the life of a man among his own kind again. First, a council to lay plans for my people. Then the meadows of Drehem, and God grant that Sarai will be there, still free. After that, we will turn our eyes toward a country of our own — and the one great God will go with us."

◀◖

CHAPTER XVII

Karnebo

T HE NEXT DAY when the first light was appearing along the eastern horizon, Abram and Oni stepped into their little *machouf* which was floating in the narrow trench that served as its harbor. There were hundreds of such trenches along the waterfront of Suga and each contained a larger or a smaller boat, for the rising and the falling of the tide was never greater than the width of a man's hand, and sometimes there seemed to be no tide at all.

They pushed off and glided out on the glassy surface of the still water. Abram looked back for the last time at the village, the reed huts with their yellow arched doorways beneath the lofty ceiling of palm branches, wisps of white smoke rising in the still air between the clean boles of the palm trees.

Every man, woman and child had come to bid good-by to this strange priest whom they had made a member of the village and who had done so much for them during the past year.

The men stood at the front, along the water's edge. For once, there were no brilliant smiles. There seemed to be a common sense of sorrow, and the small black beards accentuated the sadness in each round face. Even the chatter and laughter of the naked women and children behind them was silenced for the moment.

Kerkha was there, weeping openly, and the chief, who was wearing the Egyptian charm that Abram had returned to him.

In the silence, the chief raised his hand and said a few words of farewell.

Abram shifted a garland of lilies that Kerkha's daughter had placed on the bow of their skiff. Then the two men dipped their spoon-shaped paddles into the water and the *machouf*, with lilies trailing, sped across the open space in front of the village. Just before it disappeared in the reeds Abram turned and raised his paddle. This was answered by a great shout from many throats. And so their boat slipped out of sight and passed silently down an aisle of arching reeds.

"How different this was from our arrival a year ago!" Abram said. "Every man held a spear then. They have changed a little and I — I have changed much."

In the half-light of the morning, ducks quacked and swam excitedly to either side of them and the yellowshanks as usual cried plaintively, spreading their wings and making off into the air.

For a time they paddled in silence. Then Abram said: "I remember your words, Oni, as we were approaching Suga: 'This is not a very likely place to find an old god and there are not many materials for making a new one!'

"In solitude there was new light. Old knowledge changed into new understanding. I see in part now. Other men who come after me will see God's face more clearly than I. From knowledge — understanding, and after understanding — wisdom.

"When I was a boy Sarai's mother Amtelai once said to Father Terah and to me that understanding has its first birth in a woman's heart. I wonder what Sarai has been thinking? If I could talk with her she might help me to understand the meaning of many things."

After several hours they emerged from the reeds into open water. On the far side were trees and a beach along the shore line. Oni guided the *machouf* toward the beach while a flock of scarlet flamingos shook their great beaks in disapproval and left their fishing, stalking in ungainly haste out of the water and onto the shore. It was a brilliant procession that seemed to welcome Abram back to land as they set up a harsh chorus of cries and beat the air with their wings.

A bracing wind was blowing and Abram exulted in his return. The graceful tamarisk trees seemed to bow and dance before him as the wind soughed softly through their needled limbs. Even the palms, it seemed to him, rejoiced as he passed, clapping and clattering their branches together.

Old Magog was waiting with the camels. "Welcome, welcome, welcome!" he cried, and ran to embrace Abram.

They lost no time here but mounted their camels and set off over the marginal zone of the flat plain that was beginning to emerge from water. For several hours their camels plodded, *plop, plop, plop* over the soft soggy surface. Then at last they came to higher ground where flowers grew in great profusion, and the earth was firm and dry in the hot sun.

Magog pointed ahead of them. There in the distance Abram could see a tent. He urged his camel on, leaving the others behind. Soon he perceived that it was a large tent, the black cloth supported by many poles. And now he could see a white-haired man pacing up and down before the tent. While Abram was still far off, the man began to hurry toward him. Then he stood still with his feet planted wide apart, shading his eyes, and Abram knew that it must be Prince Salah.

"At last!" Salah shouted. "Ha, Abram! You are not dead! May the God of our fathers be praised!"

On reaching him Abram halted his camel and smiled down at the old man. He had changed little, it seemed, in the last few years; the broad shoulders, the air of quiet strength and dignity, the leathery weather-beaten face with its myriad wrinkles that seemed to make his white hair and short white beard whiter.

He leaped to the ground and the two men embraced. Then Salah backed away to look at his young kinsman.

"Sound in body?" he queried. "Older certainly, and rougher, since I saw you last — and wiser too, I suppose. Your grandfather Nahor predicted that you would leave the temple and return to your people. Many decisions are waiting for you."

As the two men reached the tent together they heard a shout and Lot came running across the plain to throw himself into Abram's arms. He was taller than a year ago, a handsome young man now of seventeen years.

A rug had been placed before the tent door. Here Oni joined them and they seated themselves, cross-legged, while camel's milk was brought to quench their thirst.

"You have many men with you, and a big tent and provisions," Abram said, looking about in surprise.

"Yes," replied Salah. "We were determined to remain here and search for you until you were found, dead or alive. But we were not the only ones looking for you. King Rim-Sin has promised an enormous reward for your return to Ur, if they can find you alive. I am told that the people of Ur believe a curse has been laid upon the city by a god they call the God of Abram."

Abram smiled. "I am more interested," he said, "in the news from Drehem. Tell me about Sarai."

"Sarai," Salah said, "is living the life of a shepherdess at Drehem. She has tended my sheep and we have had much talk together about many things."

"Is she — " Abram asked, and stopped. Then he began again. "Has she been promised in marriage?"

Salah shrugged. "No, not exactly. There is a distant kinsman of mine, a fine young herdsman named Cush, who gives me no peace, nor her either. He has his marriage gift, a substantial one, in readiness. I would gladly see her marry him but she asks me to wait until her father Terah comes, and I hesitate to force her into this. Then there is Melchizedek, the shepherd-prince from the land of Salem. He would woo her, I think, if you gave him leave."

"I!" exclaimed Abram.

"Yes, you. He is a real friend. Perhaps he knows more about you than we do, or even you yourself." Prince Salah looked at him with a twinkle in his eyes, but continued: "He knows a great deal about many people and many things. In any case he speaks as though you had priority in regard to your half sister.

"There are others. But the most troublesome of all is Unzie, for he is a close kinsman of the patesi of Nippur."

"Unzie!" exclaimed Abram. "I remember him, a drunkard!"

"Yes, yes," Salah continued. "But you must bear in mind that the patesi of Nippur owns the farms of Drehem and I am his overseer there. I don't like Unzie either. I've managed to postpone the decision but I do not know how much longer I can continue to do so."

He shook his head and shrugged his shoulders.

"She really should marry Cush at once. That would settle the matter, and then they could both remain with me at Drehem. The patesi would not permit his kinsman to carry off a married woman, I am sure. If she does not do that then she may have to run away and hide with her father Terah.

"You know," he went on, "beauty like Sarai's can be a curse. She has lived with me most of her life, and I love her more than anyone, but she might have a happier life if she were plain-looking. Confidentially too — " he shrugged and smiled — "she might well prove to be a doubtful blessing to a weak man. There will always be competition. The man who marries her must be strong for many reasons. She has a will of her own, and a temper that sometimes blows as hot as a fire of rushes."

Salah chuckled. "I had to send one of my shepherds away because of trouble between his wife and Sarai. The wife was jealous, for no good cause. But when the woman was insolent to Sarai, my granddaughter behaved like a lioness coming out of a ravine. But the fire burns away quickly. She gave the woman a sheepskin rug to cover herself and her husband when they left!" Salah chuckled again.

"Naamah has had a very good influence over Sarai. She came from a gentle family and is intelligent and patient, even if Sarai does find her tiresome at times."

Abram had risen and was pacing up and down now. He realized that Salah was willing to talk on about his granddaughter indefinitely. This was a subject that interested him too, but plans were seething in his mind, so he interrupted him now.

"Tell me about my father. Is he well, and is he ready to travel?"

Salah's reply was to make a gesture toward Lot. Up to this time Lot had said nothing. Instead he had remained sitting with his chin in his hands and his elbows on his knees, watching every move that Abram made, fascinated by the changes that he saw in his uncle — the black hair that had grown down almost to Abram's shoulders, the unruly mustache and beard that made his long face seem almost round. Lot observed too that his twenty-six-year-old uncle was thin now, very thin, but that he stood erect and his muscles were hard, his movements quick. There were new expressions too, new lines which he had never before seen in his face; and there was a new light in his eyes.

Lot laughed before he spoke. "Do you know," he said to Abram, "you look more like a desert chief who has never been inside the walls of a city than you do Abram the scholar-priest who rarely lived outside city walls. I've been wondering whether you really are the same man." The tense expression disappeared from Abram's heavy features and a smile lit his dark, sunburned face. But before he could reply Lot continued:

"You have asked about your father Terah. He is neither well nor ill. His tents are favorably placed in a lonely portion of the hills of Elam. He has bought a herd and it has good pasture. Indeed, I have been his chief herdsman, except when I could slip away to Susa for a little amusement."

He tossed his handsome head and smiled. Then he became serious again. "Father Terah has grown older. He has mourned over the death of Haran. He has mourned for you as though you were dead, and we all thought you must be. He has mourned because Nahor deserted him and because his possessions in Ur are lost. He fears he may be captured and taken back to Ur. He walks back and forth on the hilltop, looking toward the west and talking about you and hoping that you will come back to him.

"But once when I was in Susa sitting on a terrace where good food was served and where there were dancing girls from high Elam, a soldier sat down beside me. He talked openly, and said he knew that Terah, the idol merchant of Ur, was hidden away in the hills and that he was being watched there so that his son Abram might be caught if he were still alive and should return. He told me also that he had a friend in Ur who saw it with his own eyes when your god threw Nannar down the ziggurat and then carried you off into heaven." Lot laughed again.

"If Oni had not found you," Lot continued, looking up at Abram, "we had planned to search the swamps for you by boat while Prince Salah followed along the bordering desert. I'm so glad," the boy added impulsively, reaching out his hand to Abram, "I'm so glad you are alive and that we have you back. No one would ever recognize you as the priest of the moon god, no one except those who have known you and loved you as I have. But you must be very careful not to be discovered."

Abram smiled at the lad. He had always been fond of him and felt toward him as an older brother might.

"Now," Salah broke in, "it is my turn. I want to know whether you were all of you escaping from the just wrath of the Sumerians because of the treachery of your brother Nahor? Or did you leave to lead the Habiru back to the hills of Haran? Or are you really setting out in search of a new country?"

Abram nodded his head and sat down. "Those are fair questions and I think I can answer for my father and for myself.

"This departure was of our own choosing. We could have remained in Ur if we had been willing to cast in our lot with that of the Sumerians for better or worse. When it came to the time of decision, I turned to the God of our family and I heard a voice within me that said: 'Go into a new country and build there a new nation.'

"But on leaving Ur I was angry and confused. I did not know where the truth lay. I had broken the idols that I had known since childhood. I went into the wilderness, half fearing that a curse would still fall on me for the breaking of those idols. But no curse came. Instead, God walked with me there.

"I know now that the voice I heard in Ur was the voice of the one God. There is no other. I know now that it is His will that we go into the land of Canaan, and He will guide us and protect us if we worship Him and Him only.

"I must discover how many among the Habiru will follow me, for we must go in strength, not in weakness."

"Hah!" Salah cried and held up both arms. "At last I have heard the voice of a leader. I too have believed in the future of our people, but blindly. Now I have met a man who sees the way. When our people have their own God, their own country and their own cities they will become a great nation.

"We have been wanderers since time began. When we enter the gates of others to fatten on their wealth, they hate us. Better for us to continue to be herdsmen until we can fold away our tents and build our own cities."

Abram and Salah looked at each other with understanding. But Salah was rarely serious for very long, and now the wrinkles

of his face formed themselves into a sly smile and he gestured
with shoulders and hands like a merchant.

"And who will breed the sacred cattle in Canaan?"

"You, Prince Salah!" Abram cried. "Come with us, for you are
young in heart."

"No," Salah replied sadly. "No, I shall go with you in spirit
but not in body."

After the evening meal the cloth was removed and Abram
called a council of responsible men: Prince Salah, Lot, Oni,
Magog, and Jabal.

"I am sorry," Abram said, "that my father is not here to help
us, but we must lay a plan of action. If we would hope to find
and hold a new country," he said, "we must not leave this land
as fugitives. On the contrary, we must organize our forces for
conquest. Our strength lies in the speed of our camels and in
our knowledge of tent life.

"I must have a company of young herdsmen mounted on the
swiftest camels. They should be well armed and trained for a new
type of combat. When wisely led, they will be able to strike and
be gone before a heavy army moving on foot and with asses could
be ready to resist. Our strength depends on speed and surprise.

"I shall myself remain in the uninhabited land, leaving it to
visit the chosen Habiru herdsmen of Sumer and Elam. Lot and
Oni will go with me. We will bring them the good news that the
Habiru people have their own God who will lead them and protect them. We will select this company of fighting men and will
train them. I will promise to make them my herdsmen in Haran
and also in the land that we shall find after we leave Haran. Thus
they will inherit it with us.

"The camels with which Grandfather Nahor came south are
at pasture in Drehem, I understand, about fifty swift animals.
There are hundreds of Father Terah's camels now available at
Drehem and elsewhere, since the camel traffic into Ur and other

large cities has nearly stopped. Magog, my father's camelman, will take charge of them all and of their drivers, as captain of the camelmen. He will establish camel centers at certain points in the desert outside the irrigated farming districts.

"We have the spring and the summer to prepare and train the young men who volunteer. Toward the end of the summer the borderlands of the great swamp will be dry and firm. Then we can move north along the margin of the great marsh lake to Drehem without passing any habitation.

"My plan is that all who are to go with us will reach Drehem at an appointed day. Then we will move quickly to the great river and cross it by barges in the night. From there we will continue west to the great desert where we may turn and move north toward Haran. Only in that way can we hope to pass Babylon in safety."

Abram was tense as he talked, and his eyes burned with excitement.

"Once we have gathered our people and armed them well, once we are on the move, no power in Sumer or Akkad can overtake us or capture us. But until the day of our departure we are vulnerable. There must be no concentration of our peoples, except the company of fighting men during their period of training.

"Since we must be able to travel fast, any families that would eventually join us must sell their property, their cattle and their sheep. They must carry money or treasure with them sufficient to buy stock from time to time. On arrival in Haran, we will all purchase herds and flocks. There we will rest and lay our plans for moving toward Canaan.

"There is room for us in the land of Canaan. The people there are herdsmen, and the life is like that on the hills of Haran. Canaan is near to the land of the Nile where a people live as rich as the Sumerians, but powerful and at peace. The Egyptians will doubtless buy all that we can sell them."

Salah had listened with keen interest while Abram outlined his plan. "Now," he said, "you have done a great deal of thinking while you were in the swamp, but what have you planned for me to do?"

Abram smiled. "I hoped you would ask that question, Prince Salah. You are to collect an adequate supply of weapons quietly without attracting attention. Magog will transport them from Drehem to my headquarters. But there is another, most important consideration, the plans for crossing the great river. At present you send your cattle for the market in Ur to a point south of Nippur. Is that so?"

Salah nodded.

"That is where we must cross. Could you assemble a large number of barges on the appointed night?"

Again Salah nodded and this time he chuckled.

"Now the plan is this: You, Prince Salah, return at once to your farms at Drehem. Magog will go with you to assemble camels and secure camelmen. My father will repay all costs, in time.

"Oni and Lot and I will go into Elam to get Father Terah and bring him as quickly as possible to Drehem, where it might be wise for him to hide a little way off. Oni will then enter Ur secretly, to organize the escape of those Habiru who are willing to sell their goods and come with us.

"I shall stop in Drehem only long enough to consult with you and to spend a few days with my half sister. I hope she may continue as a shepherdess . . . unmolested until I arrive."

Salah smiled. "Old Nahor prophesied before he died that a leader would return to the Habiru. That prophecy has come true.

"But let me warn you, Abram. This people of ours are stiff-necked and stubborn, not easy to lead. They are of all kinds, some wise, others foolish, avaricious. There are murderers and thieves among them. When you go into Elam beware of the

bandits in the hills. You three men are too few to protect your-
selves. Most of these robbers, alas, belong to our people, and
I am told that a kinsman of mine, Karnebo by name, is a notori-
ous chief among them. Karnebo was my name, as you know,
when I was a young man, and this kinsman was once a brave
soldier. But that is a long story. . . .

"I will give you a tablet to say that you are the heir to Nahor
of Haran. I'll put my seal on it. Some of them might know the
seal and believe your story, if you should be so unlucky as to
fall into their hands. I will give you money, good camels, water
and food.

"Be careful that you yourself are not taken. You have much
to learn yet about the ways of nomad life. Lot is quick-witted
but young. Rely on Oni. He has experience."

Abram, Oni and Lot were off early next morning. They traveled rapidly toward the east during the next few days, crossing
the river Idiigna by barge at a little-frequented point near its
entrance into the great swamp. Then they turned their camels
northward and eastward through the foothills of Elam. Thus
they came into a pleasant plain where there were trees and grass
and lowing cattle. But farther into the hills the country became
rough and wild. From time to time gazelles went bounding away
in startled herds, and coveys of sand grouse rose from their feeding grounds and whirred into the air.

They came to the highroad that led to Susa and moved along
it until they knew they were near to the tents of Father Terah.
Then Lot left the other two and went on ahead, since his re-
appearance there would not attract attention.

"Go to Terah," Abram said to Lot, "and tell him that his son
has returned never to leave him again. Beg my father to make a
pretext of a short journey. Let him fold and bring the tents that
he may need for the journey to Drehem and bring only the

members of his immediate household. He must leave behind his cattle, sheep and extra camels and all new servants.

"Bring Father Terah along the highroad here at sundown tomorrow and turn aside into yonder ravine. Oni and I will be waiting for you there. Then we will travel far into the night to escape from anyone who may follow us."

After Lot had gone, Abram and Oni led their camels a considerable distance up the ravine, which was in fact a dried river channel. Before long they came to a small, level opening surrounded by cedar trees.

"A very good place to spend the night," Oni said, "and we have enough water for ourselves. The camels will be all right until we find water tomorrow."

As Oni hobbled the camels and set up a small tent, Abram walked through the cedars, his thoughts turning idly toward Drehem. Sarai must be leading her sheep back to the fold now, for the sun was setting. No doubt Cush might come in time to help her. Perhaps, as Salah had said, it was hard for a woman to be beautiful. But there was no way in which he would have her different. Her face, her figure, her hair, her smile; no, nothing should be altered. Shub had been beautiful too, but somehow the thought of her did not seem to be exciting now.

As he came back to the tent where Oni was preparing supper he realized that he was following a path. "Someone uses this ravine," he said to Oni, "for there is a pathway here."

"Yes," Oni said. "I saw it. I think we would be wise to move away before nightfall."

Abram made an impatient gesture. "No, we are safe enough here." So they remained where they were.

Next morning before it was light Oni wakened. Had he heard something? Or was it only that he smelled the dawn. He listened. Yes, someone or something was moving outside. He heard it on one side, then on the other. Certainly it was not the camels. He laid one hand on Abram's shoulder and placed his other hand over Abram's mouth so he would not speak.

Abram sat up and the two men listened. Again there was a noise, this time unmistakable. Oni drew on his belt and felt for his knife. Abram did the same. Then Oni lifted the tent door flap and stepped out quickly, followed by Abram.

As they emerged a voice cried: "Stand still or I'll run you through."

And Oni felt the point of a spear against his chest. In the first pale glow of dawn they could see an enormous fellow confronting Oni and other men with spears behind.

"Don't fight, Oni," Abram said. "Hold still." Then he demanded: "What do you want? Who are you?"

"Never mind who we are. Give me your knives." They did as they were told. The big man, who seemed to be the leader, gave orders to the others to saddle the camels and to load on the tent and saddlebags. This was done quickly and Abram observed that the men seemed to be familiar with camels.

Their hands were then tied behind them and they were blindfolded. Abram felt a man come to either side of him and grip him by the arm. He was then propelled forward and upward over a pathway, the same, he thought, that he had walked on the evening before. Finally they came to level ground and walked for a half hour or more.

A hundred questions, regrets, and exasperations raced through his mind. These were the agents of Rim-Sin, he thought, who would return him to Ur and receive the reward. What then would happen to his plans for his people? What would happen to Sarai? He pulled at the cords that bound his wrists, but they were strong and he could not break them. He heard Oni stumbling along in front of him. No, it was obvious that they could not escape, not now at any rate.

He must be wise, he must outwit these men if he could. He

listened to them talking and his quick ear caught several accents, but certainly most of these men must be Habiru. One or two might be Elamites.

Suddenly he collided with someone and he heard Oni's voice say: "What's to be done?"

He replied quickly: "Nothing. Wait."

He realized that Oni had thrown himself backward against him so as to ask the question, probably carrying both his captors with him, for there was a great deal of cursing going on.

He heard the voice of the leader say: "Here, I'll lead that big fellow. He looks strong but he's soft and I'll knock him over the head if he doesn't come along easily."

These men, Abram thought, might be the robbers that Prince Salah spoke of — but if so why do they bother with us, why not rob us and let us go free, or kill us? Stories of the cruelty of the hill brigands ran through his mind.

At last they seemed to meet other men and the bandages were taken from their eyes. Abram looked about quickly. They were in a small clearing in a forest. It was broad daylight now. The burly leader of the men who had captured them was reporting to someone else, obviously his chief.

He heard the burly fellow say: "They spent the night in the ravine and we watched them according to your command. Now I have both of them and all their goods. I don't know who they are."

Be careful, Abram thought to himself. Be careful now. If they don't know who I am they mustn't learn. If they knew they might still take me to the king for the reward.

The chief, a powerful bearded man with a scar on his forehead, strode across the clearing and stood in front of them. He addressed Oni:

"Who are you?"

Oni was dumb.

"Answer me," the man bellowed and slapped him across the face.

"I'm — I'm his slave," Oni said and glowered furiously.

The chief addressed him to Abram: "Who are you and what are you doing here?"

Abram was silent, groping in his mind for the right reply.

The chief came close to him and sneered. "I'll tell you who you are. You're a spy sent out from Susa by Rim-Sin. You might as well know that you are going to die. We kill spies who come into these hills. You're not the first ones."

I have it, Abram thought. This man is an outlaw; I must tell him the truth. After all, we are both outlaws.

"Well," shouted the man, "will you speak or shall we kill you?"

The men of the company were standing now in a circle with Abram and Oni at the center. Several drew their knives. The big fellow tossed his knife whirling into the air and caught it dexterously by the handle. He looked around at his comrades and grinned.

Yes, Abram thought, the truth is best. This might well be Karnebo himself. Aloud he said:

"I am Abram, son of Terah, son of Nahor. I belong to the Habiru, like most of your men. I am looking for — but I would rather talk with you alone."

There was a startling change in the man. He flushed so that the scar showed like a white streak across his forehead. Then the color drained from his face and he stepped back.

"Abram, son of Terah, son of Nahor," he muttered as though to himself.

"I want to talk with you alone," Abram repeated and walked across the ring, his hands still tied behind him. The men fell back and the chief followed him. When they were beyond hearing the chief spoke suddenly.

"Stop. How do I know that you are telling the truth? Many

lies have been told me here." He turned and called to his men. "Bring me those saddlebags."

He looked Abram over carefully. "You're not shaven like a priest. Your hair and beard are not even trimmed." The men dropped the saddlebags in front of him. He nodded and they withdrew. Then he untied Abram's hands.

"Which saddlebag is yours?" Abram pointed. The chief shook the contents out on the ground. "Which is your cloak?" Abram pointed again. "And the pin here. Is this yours?" he asked, drawing from the cloth a long pin of the roughest type, made of bamboo. Abram nodded.

"This, the pin of Abram without a seal! Ha, ha! You were lying to me. And yet —" He shook his head.

Abram was silent but he pointed now to a tablet which lay on the ground where it had fallen.

The chief picked up the tablet. "Can you read?" Abram asked.

"I went to a temple school, years ago," the man replied. He turned the tablet over and made an exclamation. "The seal of Karnebo! Prince Salah! It is his seal. I know it."

"And you are Karnebo also," Abram said quietly.

The man nodded. "Yes, I am Karnebo." He drew his knife and with its handle tapped the tablet. The clay envelope fell in pieces to the ground. Then Karnebo held up the tablet and read:

"*I am giving this tablet to Abram son of Terah. I was present when Nahor of Haran died. He sent his death blessing to Abram. He is now hereditary chief of the Habiru. — The seal of Prince Salah.*"

Abram had studied Karnebo's face as he read. He had a big head covered with curly black hair streaked with gray, and his eyebrows were prominent. His eyes were deep set, his nose large, his lips thick. Yet it was a sensitive face with rapidly changing expression.

"Well," Karnebo said, "what do you want of me?"

"A great deal," Abram replied. "I left Ur a year ago —"

"Yes, I know about that," Karnebo interjected.

"Since then I have been alone in the great marsh. I have found the one God who will be our God, the God of the Habiru. He bids us leave the countries that belong to others and journey into a land that he will give us for our own. Now we must prepare to defend ourselves."

"I see," Karnebo said as though dazed and still incredulous. "And I suppose you have come here to take your father Terah away. His tents are not far off." After a silence, he spoke, as though ruminating. "Our own God! And a land of our own, where a man might find fair treatment!" He hesitated and looked at Abram keenly through his bushy eyebrows, his face thoughtful. "I wonder if you could use a man like me?"

Then with sudden excitement he exclaimed:

"Let me tell you my story. Once I was captain of the temple guard in the sacred city of Nippur. But I fought with a rich noble. His name was Gudea, and he was a kinsman of the patesi. He gave me this scar." He pointed, and his face, all except the scar, flushed with anger as he spoke. "The patesi banished me from the city without a trial. My wife and children were drowned in the great river when they were leaving the city. I know Gudea must have been responsible for that. My concubines were sold as slaves.

"Some day, if the gods would only bring Gudea along this highroad!" He threw back his lionlike head and Abram observed that his lips were trembling. "I live for that day. I curse him by every god." Karnebo looked off through the boles of the trees for a time and held up his huge clawlike hands, as though expecting a signal that Gudea was approaching.

Then he turned and said: "Your grandfather Nahor sent word urging us to rejoin our own people in the hills of Haran. But

I could not be content to lead a flock by day and stand on guard at night, at least not then." He made a gesture of impatience and began to pad up and down.

"I am an exile from Nippur. A reward is offered for my head by King Rim-Sin. Will you take me with you to this new land? I can fight. I might forget Gudea. I might even worship God again. I don't know." Abram looked at him gravely and did not reply.

"You know," Karnebo began again, "that Prince Salah is my kinsman, my uncle. His name was once Karnebo also. But after I became an outlaw and an enemy of Nippur, the patesi changed his name to Salah and made him a prince. He is famous, that little man, and a good overseer and herdsman."

Deep within the forest a cliff rose sheer, towering upward into a rocky pinnacle from which a sentinel might see a great distance. From this height even the highroad was visible at times as it wound its way through the hills. Not far off, a mountain brook went tumbling and rushing across the floor of the forest, and between the brook and the base of the cliffs was a line of tents.

This was the headquarters of the bandit Karnebo, well known and much feared throughout that part of the world. Few men had seen this headquarters and lived to tell the tale. There were stories of cruel murder, but there were stories, too, of acts of kindness by this legendary outlaw; stories of what were called good deeds to the poor.

The midday meal was served to a strange company, for Abram and Oni sat down with these robbers as honored guests. A sheep had been roasted and strong wine brought from caves in the face of the cliff. A few women appeared who cooked and carried and watched in silence.

When the meal was over Karnebo sent off men to relieve the

sentries of the morning. The rest indulged in games, boisterous, rough games, for they were rough men and some had drunk deeply. There were contests of strength and of speed. In the former the big fellow called Ham, who had led in their capture that morning, was more than a match for the others.

Abram and Karnebo were in deep discussion and Oni was watching quietly when Ham presented himself to Karnebo. He waited with deference until his chief looked up. Then he pointed at Oni and said: "A challenge of strength. No wrestler has ever beaten me at the line game." As Ham was completely stripped except for a loincloth, he proceeded to bulge out his enormous chest and swell the muscles of his arms. Then he grinned at Oni. "Some of the men say this stranger can beat me."

The men had gathered behind Ham and were urging him on.

Karnebo laughed and looked at Abram, who nodded and said: "Yes, if he wants to do it."

Oni said nothing, but his face lighted up with ill-concealed joy. He removed his mantle, jerkin and sandals. Then he ran back and forth across the clearing swinging his arms to loosen up his muscles, after the manner of athletes. There were exclamations of admiration from the men, and the women laughed and drew nearer to watch.

Karnebo himself, with obvious anticipation, drew the line across the smooth, hard surface of the earth. Oni was no stranger to the line game, in which the two contestants stood on either side of a line and, gripping their right hands together, each attempted to pull the other across to his side of the line. Only when both of one contestant's feet were pulled across the line was the struggle decided. Indeed, since he had gone to Drehem Oni had often been challenged because of his mighty muscles, but none of the herdsmen had ever beaten him in this test of strength.

There was shouting and keen excitement as the two men faced

each other. Ham was considerably heavier and probably ten years older. But Oni had a superb musculature from neck to arms, chest and trunk, and he moved with the grace of a panther. No wrestler who had entered the popular public wrestling spectacles of Ur had had a more beautiful body than Oni, though many were heavier.

The two men clasped their right hands. Karnebo gave the word and set himself to act as umpire.

The tussle was on, and the clasped right hands went down to the ground, up above their heads or to either side, as one man or the other jerked and heaved and tried to throw his opponent.

Oni realized that here was strength such as he had never felt before, and Ham pushed the contest hard, hoping for a quick victory.

Oni recalled the indignity of their capture by this man and wondered if Abram would be ashamed if he should lose. He wished that Berri, Princess Shub's handmaid, were here. She had said she loved to see wrestling. She wanted to see him use his strength sometime; so she said as they watched the ziggurat the night that Abram overthrew Nannar.

Ham jerked and lifted suddenly so that Oni was pulled across the line but with one foot only. Then he did it again, and each time the onlookers shouted. Each time, however, Oni pulled the clasped hands down, making a queer high sound in his throat, then slowly pulled himself back.

Sweat poured from their bodies as they grunted and heaved. Oni shifted his footing constantly, while Ham remained with his feet planted in one place and worked with great skill. But Ham had failed to score the immediate victory for which he had worked so hard. Now he was panting for breath.

Oni could feel sweat in his own eyes. It stung and he could hardly see. It ran into his mouth and he noted how salty it tasted.

He heard Abram's voice behind him. "You are tiring him out, Oni. Wait for your chance. Remember this morning."

Oni took the initiative now. Back and forth he moved his opponent's hand, forcing him to shift his footing backward, backward parallel to the line. Suddenly he put forth every ounce of strength at his command. The clasped hands went up; then down and crossed back of Ham's foot with such power that he lost his balance, toppled, and was pulled backward. Oni went with him, shifting on his feet like a tiger. In a flash he had dragged him down on his back on the line. Then he towed him across the line as though he had been a fallen ox.

There was a din of shouting, cursing and laughter from the onlookers. But Oni was oblivious of this. He walked, staggering a little, back to where Abram was standing. His chest was heaving and sweat ran down, glistening, over his magnificent body. As he passed Abram he glanced sidewise at him and gave him one of his rare smiles.

And Abram said: "Well done, old friend."

Oni started to pick up his clothes, but turning about he found that the men had followed him and Ham was with them. So he stepped forward quickly and held out both hands to Ham. "The strongest man I have ever faced," he said. Then the two of them went down to bathe and cool themselves in the rushing stream.

As the sun neared the western horizon, Abram and Karnebo walked downward through the ravine in order to meet Terah on the highroad at the appointed hour of sundown. Ham and Oni walked ahead of them, discussing the public exhibitions of wrestling that each had seen. Guards followed in the rear leading their camels.

"I am guarded wherever I go," Karnebo said. "We have sentinels always on watch. They saw you two enter the ravine yesterday and watched you through the night."

Karnebo seemed anxious to talk. He was wearing a copper helmet, heavy leather jerkin, kilt and short cape. He carried a short spear of the type used for in-fighting. A dagger and a small scimitar hung at his belt. The guards who followed were armed with bow and arrow. One or two carried shields and had long spears which could be thrown.

"I learned to handle soldiers," Karnebo said, "when I was captain of the guard. Now that I am a chief among thieves the problems are little changed. After all, the life of the highway robber differs little from the life of the soldier in wartime. But we are always at war, and our war is against the rich. Peace will come only when we are captured. Then I suppose we will find peace in prison or in death." Karnebo laughed cynically, while Abram watched him. The two men walked on in silence for a time.

"Contests and games such as you saw today," Karnebo continued, "are important among thieves and soldiers alike. It keeps them from knifing each other. Wonderful wrestling today! What a man your Oni is!" He chuckled.

"Ham wants to go with you, although he does not understand where you are going. He is really no more than a friendly boy with a big body, except when he is fighting. Then he is a demon. He would like to go back to his father's farm, but there is always the penalty he would have to pay, the thing he ran away from.

"We have all run away from something. That is what a thief is. A man who has run away from laws and rules and hard work. But we have established new rules, new laws and we work hard in order to take away what belongs to others. Hah! We run away from authority and set up a little nation, and a discipline of our own. The difference is that here I am the chief, but in Nippur someone else is."

"Are you satisfied with this life?" Abram asked.

"No. The truth is that we are always afraid. Fear never leaves us here. Of course we miss the things men have always wanted. We have no home, no children, no god. I wish I could start over."

They had come now to the level spot where Abram and Oni had spent the night.

"Here we leave you," Abram said. "It seems strange that of all the ravines in Elam, Oni and I should have chosen the one that leads to your headquarters. Strange also that good has come of it and not evil. Perhaps that is the way the one God guides us when we seek to serve Him."

The two men looked at each other. Abram saw, in the heavily armed robber chief who stood before him a rugged, forceful, cruel man; but a man who longed secretly and in a wistful sort of way for a better life — longed for love and friendship and justice.

Karnebo, looking at Abram, did not see simply the tall, broad-shouldered, dynamic young man with straggling black hair and beard. In Abram's searching gaze he thought he saw a mysterious insight. He felt that he stood in the presence of a great prophet, the anointed leader of his people, and there welled up within him the longing that is part of the heritage of the Habiru, a longing for spiritual understanding. But Karnebo would have been the last to put such a feeling into words.

Abram said: "You asked to go with us when we travel to Haran and on into Canaan." Karnebo nodded his great head eagerly. "My answer is yes, and you may bring Ham with you.

"You know where my father Terah's camels graze. Bring all the camels that he leaves behind and cross the river Idiigna by means of a barge that you will find near the point at which the river enters the great swamp. Tell those who keep the barge that Abram son of Terah has sent for you. Then remain near the drying land that borders the swamp, until my messenger finds you.

"I must train a company of young men, some hundreds of them, and they will be armed and mounted on swift camels. You are an experienced soldier and your knowledge will be of great value to me.

"When you join our company it will be forgotten that you were once a thief and an outlaw. During our journey you will obey my command. When we reach our destination you will live the life of a shepherd and a herdsman.

"Each man who comes with us, whether he has been shepherd, merchant, priest, farmer or thief, must give the best that is in him to create this new nation. All alike must learn to worship the one God who has promised that He will guide and protect us."

Karnebo took off his copper helmet and tossed it on the ground before Abram. Then he raised his right arm, as a salute and as a promise.

Abram smiled. "May the God of our fathers be with you."

CHAPTER XVIII

Dumuzi Comes

Spring had come to Drehem also, and Sarai stood gazing across the meadow while her sheep cropped the grass and bleated about her. Wild flowers made a starlike pattern on the carpet of green. A newborn lamb which had arrived long after his fellows tottered near her on spindle shanks. She imagined to herself that he looked about him with astonishment at the meadow, the flowers, and especially at his own feet that patted the ground so unexpectedly. Did lambs think about these things, she wondered, or was it just the warm sun and the bracing air that caused them to kick up their heels and twitch their tails in awkward exuberance?

The rains were past. She could hear the interminable cooing of the turtledoves in the distance. She recalled how the unending song of the turtles had seemed to make a curtain of sound along the riverfront as she stood with her father on the battlements of Ur. Then it was that she had heard the eerie scream of the vulture above her and a shadow of foreboding had passed over her — a year ago, only one year.

Life was pleasant enough, here with her flock, but rather dull. Little seemed to be demanded of her at present.

Cush had been coming to see her often, and Naamah thought him very handsome. She said that if Sarai decided to marry him their sons and daughters would be beautiful to behold. Of course, Naamah was like most handmaids, she talked too much. But she had said that Cush was so much in love with her that he would never want to add concubines to the household. She would hate to have concubines about.

Well, mused Sarai, it might be nice to do things for Cush. But could I really be content to look after him and listen to his continual conversation about sheep and cattle and pasture? Perhaps I would get used to it. He must be a very good herdsman. Grandfather Salah seems to think he would be a good husband. He should know. Of course, if I did marry him then I could remain here. These farms would be my own dowry and Cush could run them for me until my sons . . .

But the other evening when I said that the Pharaoh's new pyramid in the land of the Nile was supposed to be higher even than the ziggurat of Babylon, Cush asked silly questions. Even a herdsman ought to know that the pyramids were nothing but tombs for the Pharaohs . . .

Melchizedek has been in Egypt. I should like to ask him more about it. I wish he would return . . .

And then she slipped off into one of her daydreams. She was entering the Pharaoh's court and there were handsome men and languid women sitting on lion skins and tall black slaves stood to fan them with fans of feathers. When she entered the members of the court rose and spoke to her with courteous admiration, the way Melchizedek had spoken when he met her in Ur. . . . Abram would probably go to the land of the Nile some day and those people would admire him as everyone always did. . . .

Abram was always worrying about the God of his people. She wondered how important that was after all. What the Habiru needed most was to be fruitful and to have many sons and daughters, sons who should be tall and broad-shouldered like Abram. In that way they would outnumber the other people some day and take new lands for themselves.

Where was Abram? Probably he had gone back to Ur. Melchizedek said they wanted him back there. Probably he would want to return to see Princess Shub. Did he really love Shub? She was beautiful, although some of her beauty was put on in the morning and taken off at night. That was something Abram wouldn't understand.

He had gone into the swamps to think and she had done a great deal of thinking too, following her sheep. What were her conclusions? She couldn't seem to remember now. Abram would find her older, and changed, when he returned.

Perhaps it would be better for her to marry Cush at once, and then when Abram came back he would see how lovely she was. She would be wearing her blue robe and her jeweled headdress. How sad he would feel when he discovered how beautiful his little half sister was — too late.

No, she thought, rousing from her reverie, the best way was to keep Abram out of her mind altogether and think of other things as she had been doing. She looked about her. The sheep were bleating and pressing toward her, as though they were disturbed by something. She looked up and saw, coming across the meadow, a strange man. He wore a rough goatskin kilt and a tattered cloak, quite a different kind of cloak from that worn by shepherds. He was about as big as Abram — but there she was again, allowing him to creep back into her thoughts! This man had hair that hung down over his ears, and a ragged beard, a very ragged beard.

The stranger continued directly toward her, and she wondered why he made no gesture of salutation. She began to feel a little frightened, so she held up her own hand, and said: "Greetings, stranger."

But still he advanced until he stood before her. Then he said: "Sarai, don't you know me?"

Her heart seemed to stop when she heard that familiar voice speaking her name, and she cried: "Abram!" Then she threw her arms about him and he held her, but only for a moment, for she drew back and looked up at him, laughing. "How you've changed!"

Then after a pause: "You have long hair and a lovely short black beard! I was a little girl when you first shaved your head and I never thought of the fact that you could grow a beard." She put her head on one side. "From shaven priest to hairy goat! Well, I think I like you as a goat better," and she laughed again, "but you look as though the pasture had been very poor." Her manner changed then with a suddenness that was characteristic of her. "You are thin. Have you not been well? You are covered with dust. Did you see Grandfather Salah? Did he not take you in and give you food? And where have you been?"

Sarai stopped, out of breath, and Abram put back his head and laughed aloud like a boy. "Where can I begin to answer your questions? You give a man no chance at all. But first, Sarai," he looked into her eyes, "first let me tell you something you have not asked me about. All the way across Sumer I have been planning how to say this and I must do it quickly before — before I lose courage. I wanted to tell you how beautiful you are. But you are more beautiful than I remembered, more lovely than anyone in the world, and I — "

She held up her hand to stop him, saying: "You haven't answered my questions and I must know what has happened."

"All right, all right!" he replied. "Here is my story. I have been alone a very long time, ever since you left us, alone in the wilderness. I was ill for a time, but the swamp natives cared for me and I recovered.

"Now I am well again, very well. The period of revolt, of anger, of questioning is past. I have peace of mind and a plan of action. I know that the one God will guide me and I think I have become a different man.

"As this change took place you began to come into my

thoughts more and more often. I feared something might have happened to you, and I thought the water would never recede and that Oni would never come for me. I have longed to see you again. No one else seems to matter.

"You see, I am no longer a city man, no longer a priest, no longer a fugitive. I must learn to live a new life, far away from temples and libraries and courts. I must become a herdsman, a wanderer. I must find a shepherdess for a wife."

"Oh," she interrupted, "there are many shepherdesses at Drehem. I shall have them march in a line before you so that you may choose one to your liking."

Abram ignored this observation and continued: "After I left the marsh, Oni and Lot and I went into Elam to find Father Terah and bring him here. But as we came nearer to Drehem I could not wait for the others. They should arrive this evening. I pushed ahead with the swiftest camel riding on into the night and my heart seemed to sing."

"You must be very tired," exclaimed Sarai, and she sat down on the grass. He sat beside her and they talked together while the sheep drifted away, cropping the grass unobserved.

Finally Sarai said: "Now that they want you in Ur and Enannatum promises that you will not be harmed, I suppose you will return to see Princess Shub."

"No," he replied, "that part of my life is over."

"Perhaps," she said, "but I think you will change your mind. You will not be satisfied with a nomadic life. It is not exciting here, though it is beautiful." They looked out over the meadow.

After a pause, she continued: "Salah is now in place of my father and he wants me to marry Cush. He says Cush is a born herdsman. And then, you remember Unzie, the kinsman of the patesi of Nippur who came to Ur with the messengers from Hammurabi? He would like me to be his wife, or perhaps he means one of his wives.

"I think Salah wants me to marry a herdsman who would live with me here at Drehem. I had hoped to find a more interesting one than Cush. If I were married that might keep Unzie away. Perhaps he might come and kill my husband! I think it would be dangerous for anyone to marry me."

Abram laughed and said: "There may be some truth in that but I would be willing to — "

She did not let him finish, but looking up at the sun sprang to her feet and said: "It is growing late, and look at my sheep! They have started back to the well all by themselves. It is time for us to water them."

They walked across the plain after the flock. Soon they came to an irrigation channel and beside it a great oak. Sarai paused under it. "Here," she said, "I have spent a great deal of time. I call this my oak."

She drew out her pipes from the bag that hung at her belt and her eyes danced as she looked up at him. "The sheep seem to like this air," she said, and pursed her lips and blew into the instrument, playing a melody that shepherds had known from time immemorial. "I have not had many listeners here, but sometimes the wild hares that go hopping by will stop when I play and sit up with their great ears tipped toward me.

"But now that spring has come and the flowers bloom in the desert again, I should play the song of Nin-Anna. Do you remember how the people were singing it in their boats on the great river at Ur, a year ago now? You sing with me!"

She put her lips to the pipes and presently he joined in:

> *"Nin-Anna wailed the winter long,*
> *Dumuzi dead, Dumuzi dead.*
> *Nin-Anna wailed the cold night through.*
> *Dumuzi comes, Dumuzi comes,*
> *Nin-Anna naked, undefiled,*
> *Dumuzi comes, Dumuzi comes."*

She put down the pipes. "It seemed to me, during the winter, that you had gone into the underworld. I put you out of my mind as much as I could; I almost forgot you. . . . Listen to the rustling in the leaves overhead. Sometimes, Abram, this oak has seemed to talk to me about you." She looked up into the spreading branches above her. "I told the whispering leaves that you had forgotten us, but they seemed to go on talking about you just the same."

Abram looked up into the branches above them. "In the great marsh," he said, "I stood under a terebinth tree very often. It was there I built an altar. The tree seemed to speak of many things."

They stood quiet for a moment, listening to the whispering above them and aware of a strange bond of understanding. He reached for her hand, but she pulled it away and was off across the meadow, running like a gazelle, her hair flying behind her. He pursued, and caught up with her only as she reached the well.

Naamah was waiting there. She looked forbidding as she stood with her arms folded over her ample breast. She bowed in great surprise when she saw Abram, but she turned and spoke to Sarai. "Prince Salah bids you to come to him early this evening. Cush was with him this morning and there are other arrivals from Nippur. You said you would come back early, but now it is already late."

"That is enough, Naamah," Sarai said, interrupting her sharply. "You may return now, and I will follow." Naamah rode off, shaking her head in disapproval.

While the sheep were drinking their fill, Sarai walked a little way over the field with Abram. "I think it might be best for you to return ahead of me," she said. "I can fold the sheep alone and the shepherds will help."

Abram looked down at her for a moment. "During these

months of solitude," he said, "I have thought of you, remembered every gesture and glance, have stood in fancy again with you in the moonlight looking from the walls of the city out over the great river. Every time I have passed a flowering shrub I have recalled that you said you loved its perfume. I have felt again your hand upon my arm as on that night in Ur. You know, Sarai, that all this must mean something."

Their eyes met and she turned away. But he came a step nearer and continued: "You know what it means, and I know. It means that I love you and can never be happy without you."

"But," she interjected, "you also carried with you memories of Princess Shub when you went into the marshes, and how can I tell what tender thoughts went with them."

Abram drew from his wallet the turban. "Look," he said, "a brave little camel boy lost this the night we left Ur. I have carried it with me constantly. I have no other keepsakes from anyone. Strange that this piece of homespun should have such a magic power over me."

Sarai looked at the rough brown turban. Then color surged into her face and neck. She looked into his eyes again, but only for a moment, for she saw there something new. This vibrant, forceful man frightened her a little. She placed her hand on his arm and pushed him away gently. "Go now," she said. "I will see you later perhaps, but you must talk to Salah first. Cush is there, it seems, and there may be others."

Then she added with a little smile: "Abram, I'm glad you're back and I like the man who comes now from the wilderness better than the man who went there." She watched him walk away, but before he was out of earshot she called: "Abram, don't let anyone cut off your beard. I like it, but you might let Salah's barber trim it and your hair too. I wouldn't want to have to search for my half brother among the goats!" She laughed and waved.

Abram walked directly across the fields toward the hill crowned by the house and barns of Salah. At other times he had taken delight in recalling that this grass-covered hill must hide the ruins of a city that had been forgotten even before the building of Babylon; but today his mind turned to other matters.

He was aware of a sense of strange excitement. There was a pressure in the lower part of his chest that seemed to make it difficult to draw a long breath, and yet he longed to make use of the muscles of his arms and legs. He looked down at them, hairy and bronzed and hard. How different they had seemed when he was a priest in the temple.

After all, he thought, I'm young. I seemed to be growing old during the last few years, old and unhappy — but I'm only twenty-six and I feel young again.

He felt the muscles of his upper arms and looked out over the fields.

Which of those flowers, he wondered, would look best in her hair, or in her arms held to her breast. Her laughter still echoed in his ears. What did it remind him of? Perhaps it was the calling of the sand grouse as he used to hear it when the flock passed over the ziggurat at dawn.

When Sarai reached the square before the house, Naamah was waiting for her.

"What now?" Sarai said, and the tone of her voice made Naamah aware that her mistress had resented her attitude at the well. Naamah had learned long ago that Sarai was capable of flashing anger, and she replied now with caution.

"Prince Salah wishes to see you before you go to your apartment."

Sarai obeyed her grandfather's summons, although a little unwillingly, and climbed to the roof top. Here she found the stocky little prince pacing up and down impatiently while Cush and Abram stood facing each other.

Sarai took in the situation at a glance. She noticed with satisfaction that Salah's barber had done his work skillfully and that Abram looked well groomed and handsome. She saw also that Cush made a good appearance. The spotted white kaffiyeh fell in folds from his head and partly covered a black cloak, and his pointed black beard was tilted proudly upward.

However, she appeared to ignore the two young men and went directly to her grandfather and stood before him. He stopped his pacing and peered at her closely. She was windblown but her color was high. Her gray-brown eyes shone with repressed excitement and her hair fell over her slender shoulders like a cascade of copper light.

"By the father of the gods," he exclaimed, "you do look like your grandmother." He turned then to the two young men, and said, "When I first saw her grandmother she was tending flocks on a mountainside and the wind was blowing her hair. It was of this same burning color, and she came and stood before me like this."

Then he spoke to Sarai gently. "You are all the family that is left to me. My sun has set. The friends of my youth have departed. But life is sweet and in this twilight I need you with me. I would miss your laughter if you left me.

"This morning I was ready to promise your hand to someone because I can no longer protect you from that drunken noble Unzie in any other way. Cush has brought me an excellent money gift. But now Abram has come and he demands the hand of his half sister for himself! I thought it best to let you know this."

The old man held out his arms in a gesture of despair and began to pace up and down.

For the first time Sarai raised her eyes to Abram, but she did not smile. Instead she seemed to look through him. Her expression and attitude might have suggested that she was listening to music.

Finally, Salah resumed: "Terah has also arrived with his grandson Lot, Oni, and a caravan of camels bringing servants and women and goods. Even Nahor has suddenly decided to honor us with a visit!" The old man chuckled.

"We shall entertain in our best manner tonight. But after dinner Terah and I will take council. We will decide, Sarai, perhaps with your help. We will decide what is best for your happiness and for the future of our families. I only hope that the patesi of Nippur and his kinsman do not interfere."

◀◖◗◖◗◖◖

CHAPTER XIX

The Star Over Canaan

THAT EVENING there was great activity in the kitchens of Salah. A lamb and an antelope were roasted on a great spit over red-hot coals and various birds were turned on smaller spits. Onions were stewed and cakes of many kinds were baked. Savory odors reached the nostrils of the men who were to be guests, as they left their rooms on the second floor and walked around the gallery to descend the stair to the central court.

This court was open to the sky, but as the evening light failed, lamps which hung beneath the gallery were lit, and Salah's lofty reception room opening on the court blazed with light.

Abram and Lot came down the stairs laughing and talking. They were dressed like herdsmen but wore Sumerian cloaks held in place over the right shoulder by the traditional long pin to which, in the case of Lot, a cylinder seal was attached. Abram had given his seal to his friend Dudu before leaving Ur. They were followed by Cush, who walked in silence dressed in his black cape. He had no seal attached to his shoulder pin, being a herdsman. Magog, the old captain of all the camelmen, came last.

They were welcomed by Salah in the reception room. Lot, slender, quick, and boyish with a short silky black growth of hair on lip and chin, was describing his experiences in the city of Susa with great enthusiasm.

"Father Terah," he was saying, "had pitched his tents on the slopes of the mountains of Elam. It was two days' journey for me by camel to reach Susa. But it was well worth the journey just to see the young women of Elam. They carry pitchers of water on their heads and pass up and down the streets with grace and beauty such as you never saw in Ur, and they turn and smile as they pass!" He illustrated his meaning in pantomime. "Then also there were eating places where the wine came from the east, and the food — " His account was cut short by the appearance of Terah on the stair.

Salah went forward to meet him, and the others followed with respect. Terah had grown older during the past year. His hair and beard were now snowy white and Abram observed that his face was thin and his hands trembled. Salah escorted him into the reception room and seated him in the place of honor on a rug at his right hand.

Then the small door in the great gate opened and Nahor stepped through. His appearance seemed to be a signal for silence. No one had seen him since he fled from Ur. But he approached the others with elaborate composure.

Terah rose and ran to embrace him, crying: "My son! My son!"

When the greetings were over, Nahor said: "I was sorry to leave Ur in the middle of the night without taking proper leave of you, Father Terah. But it seemed best for me to hurry away to Nippur with Unzie son of Gudea. As a result of the time spent in Nippur, I am now in a position to offer protection to my kinsmen."

At this, Lot laughed and clapped his hands. "Do you include Abram?" he cried. "And who is to receive the reward that has been offered for his capture?"

Nahor ignored this question. He did not appear to be at all embarrassed by the coolness of his reception. His black hair, which was cut just below his ears, was sleek. He wore a more luxurious mantle than was usual in the country, and his beard had been freshly trimmed in what might have been called the Babylonian style. Furthermore, this short curling beard of his must have been recently sprayed with a potent perfume, for when he talked the aroma was wafted to his hearers.

Prince Salah gave Nahor a curt welcome. Then he turned back to the others and asked if all the guests were present. Terah then said:

"There is to be another guest tonight. With your permission I have invited Oni to join us. Abram and I have made Oni a free man. He has served us well and Abram has no better friend."

Salah was about to send a servant for him, but Abram stopped him. "Let me go," he said, and went quickly up the stairs and along the gallery in the direction of Oni's room.

But on the way he encountered Sarai unexpectedly as she was stepping out of the women's dining room. She looked up into his eyes for only an instant and then passed on to disappear without a word into her own apartment. Abram stood quite still looking after her, while his heart pounded. Then he walked slowly along the gallery, forgetting his errand and passing the door of Oni's room.

He heard Oni's voice behind him. "Where are you going, Abram? Did she take your wits away?"

Abram turned. "Oh! I came for you, Oni. Prince Salah invites you to join us at the evening meal."

As they entered the reception room, Oni, who had been born the son of a slave in Terah's household, became suddenly shy and awkward, but Terah embraced him. "Abram has told me how you saved his life. May the God of our fathers bless you for it."

At that moment, the small door in the great outer gate opened again and a herdsman entered and announced to Salah that a man had arrived who said he was a priest of the moon god in Ur. He had come here, he said, "in search of Oni, the giant slave of Abram son of Terah." All present showed their astonishment.

"It would be very dangerous," Salah said, "if it were learned in Ur that Abram is here. The reward for his capture is very large."

Then Abram said to the servant: "Is the priest alone?"

"Yes," the servant replied. "He and a camel boy, who was once in the employ of Terah son of Nahor, arrived alone on two camels."

Abram approached the servant eagerly. "Describe the priest," he said.

The servant hesitated. Then he replied: "The priest would be a heavy load, I think, for an ordinary camel. But," he added with a faint smile, "a strong carrying camel would do it easily."

Abram laughed. "I think I know who it is. Ask him what he brings. If he says he has a purse for Oni, let him in." Salah hesitated, but finally gave his consent and the servant disappeared.

Before long the door opened again and a large man stepped in. He had a round face and no beard. As he crossed the court, he took off his turban as though he were hot, showing a shining bald head.

"Dudu!" Abram exclaimed and ran to welcome him. It was indeed Dudu, the physician-priest. But when Dudu saw Abram, he stood still and his mouth dropped open.

Finally he said: "But — Abram — but we thought we knew that you were dead! A messenger brought this word to Ur and received a reward for the information."

Abram sent for a basin of water and, removing Dudu's dust-covered outer cloak, led him back to the curtained vestibule. Here he knelt down and removed Dudu's sandals, washed his feet, dried them and put on the red slippers which the servant had brought.

As Abram did this, Dudu expostulated; but presently he peered down over his ample abdomen at his friend and said: "Perhaps it is just as well. My feet and I are practically strangers now."

The two friends talked for a little while, and then Abram brought Dudu to Salah. "This is my friend Dudu, the priest and physician in the temple of Nannar. I am sure we can trust him to keep our secrets."

Dudu bowed stiffly and said: "Prince Salah and Terah son of Nahor: Forgive this intrusion; you might well look on my presence here as a sign of danger, so I will explain.

"The hiding place of Terah in Elam was discovered quite early. King Rim-Sin and his daughter are Elamites, as you know, and it was expected that Abram, if he was alive, would eventually come to meet his father there. If he had done so he would certainly have been taken. Now, if you would like your secret kept from those in Ur, I suggest that you prevent me from returning, forcibly."

Dudu permitted himself a deep-toned chuckle, and sniffed. "But if what I smell is what I think it is, I warn you now that you may yet pay dearly for keeping me captive." He sniffed and chuckled again.

Then he continued: "We learned that Oni had reached Elam alone and so we were eventually forced to conclude that Abram must be dead."

But now the servants were issuing from the kitchens in single file, the chief cook at their head. Across the court they came with smoking meats, savory vegetables, browned flat slabs of bread, crisp cakes, fruits, sweetmeats, nuts, and wine. The lamb and the antelope were placed partly carved on their platters in the center of the long cloth, and other delicacies on stools within easy reach.

So Prince Salah sat down cross-legged at the top of the cloth and welcomed the guests, motioning Terah and Abram to places on either side of him. Dudu took his place, rubbing his hands with glee. Even Nahor smiled (but thought he should be sitting in a higher position), while Lot laughed and talked as always. Oni, the freeman, watched it all in silence, his mind slipping back to Ur and the apartment of the Princess Shub.

Sarai and Naamah were busy meanwhile. Naamah bustled about their private apartment and cast occasional admiring glances at her mistress as she sat before her mirror.

Finally Naamah said: "I have never seen you take so much care in your dressing for Cush before. You are planning to marry him, aren't you?"

Sarai looked up at her with a startled expression. "Oh, surely not. Perhaps I did say I would marry him some day, but he must know that that was just to please Father Salah and to keep him still. You don't suppose he believed me, do you?"

"Well, it is not for me to say, but he brought his marriage gift to Prince Salah this morning! Yesterday you remember you told me you took no interest in Abram any more. Then this afternoon I thought you were quite interested in him and had forgotten Cush completely. I saw Abram looking at you the way Melchizedek did before he left Drehem. I liked him. I wonder why he went so unexpectedly. Then I really ought to tell you that when Nahor arrived today he told me that Prince Salah would have to give you in marriage to someone in Nippur whether he liked it or not.

"Of course," Naamah chattered on, "you and I know that you can influence the decisions of your grandfather, and your father too. Women always have to make up men's minds for them. But I sometimes wonder if you really know what is going on in your own heart." She sat down on the couch beside Sarai and shook her head, adding, "I can't help thinking that something is going to happen very soon. I wonder what it is."

Sarai put down her comb. "Yes," she said, "I wonder too."

Then after a pause she jumped up and left the room. Passing quickly down the gallery, she ran up the stairs to the roof. The roof was deserted now but Naamah came puffing after her with some anxiety, for her mistress had just finished her bath and wore nothing but a light gown. Sarai walked to the parapet and looked out toward the sunset. The rim of the plain was bright with the sunset afterglow, beginning at the horizon with orange and shading upward into yellow, green, blue and finally the violet of the desert's night sky.

The planet Ishtar had begun to burn above the sunset zone, and a few stars made pale points of light in the vault of heaven. She had been hot, but now the evening breeze blew cool on her neck. She opened the gown and let it blow out behind her. The coolness flowed down over her swelling breasts and shapely white body.

She began to sing softly. It was an old, old song of springtime:

> *"Rise up my love and come away;*
> *The time of the singing of birds is come,*
> *And cooing of turtles is heard in the land."*

She wrapped her gown about her again and, turning to Naamah, said to her seriously: "Do you think it is a good omen that Ishtar the goddess of love has set her lamp tonight across the great desert to the west? It must be over Canaan."

Naamah put her arm over her shoulder and laughed a little. "Does Abram still look toward Canaan? Let your heart speak, my little Sarai. There are many omens. Men trust them blindly, but a wise woman selects her omen with great care. I remember a proverb that my father used to quote:

> *"Three things that I cannot fathom,*
> *Yes, four remain obscure:*
> *The birth of the dew on the meadow,*

The eagle soaring on high,
The secret thoughts of the camel,
And the way of a maid with a man."

They returned down the stairs to Sarai's room and after a time a woman servant spoke outside the curtained doorway. "Prince Salah is asking for you in the reception court."

Sarai hurried back to her mirror and rearranged the pendants of spiral gold that hung trembling in her hair; she adjusted her shoulder pin and seal, picked up her reticule and left the room. Naamah stopped for a shawl and came hurrying along the gallery after her mistress, scolding and clucking like a squat hen.

As Sarai came down the stairs and crossed the court, silence fell on the men in the reception room. She walked with dignity and without evidence of embarrassment, while a faint jingling of unseen ankle rings came to their ears. She was wearing her blue robe that did not altogether hide the lovely curves of her body. Her hair seemed to be gold now in the lamplight. Another woman, if there had been one present, might have realized that her long lashes were slightly darker in shade than usual and she might have suggested that that was what made her eyes so lovely and so exciting.

She smiled at each of the guests in turn, and greeted Nahor. All of the men had risen as if each intended to escort her, but Terah took her to the place between himself and Prince Salah.

Salah put his arm around her shoulders and kissed her, saying with a chuckle: "I am the oldest here and must have privileges." Then he added to Sarai, "You see a stranger sitting here with us tonight. It is Dudu, a friend of Abram's. He is a physician-priest from the temple of the moon god."

Dudu rose and again made his stiff little bow, which consisted largely in flexion of the neck, first to Salah, then Terah and finally to Sarai. He spoke in cultured, mellow tones, using the polished phrases in which he took delight:

"Now that we have taken from your generous hand food of such savor and drink of such flavor that it might have been more fittingly placed before the gods, may I present the messages which until a few hours ago I had thought to bring you from a man who was dead. Now I rejoice to discover him alive." He made his little bow to Abram.

"On the fateful night of Nannar's downfall, when Abram had no doubt decided what he would do, he told me about his beautiful half sister. During the days and nights that he spent in prison he said he had seen her in his dreams, 'always beautiful and gay.'

" 'I should be sorry,' he said, 'never to see her again. . . . You may tell her that, if you should ever see her.' " Again he bowed to Sarai.

"But there was more. 'If I should die before morning,' he said, 'find my slave Oni. Tell him that Abram was no more than a breaker of idols, that now he will never light a fire before the true God . . . give him my purse. In it will be . . . a tablet . . . which will make him a free man.'

"I thought to give this purse to Oni or to leave it for him with you, Prince Salah, who are Abram's kinsman. Now, since Abram is still alive, I return it to him."

Dudu removed a leather purse from his belt and handed it to Abram, who rose and, opening it, drew out a clay tablet. "Come here, Oni."

Oni came and stood before him.

"This is your contract of freedom. It was my last writing before what I thought would be my death." Then he drew out a shining gold stiletto, about six inches in length. On the lapis lazuli of its bulbous butt a bull was carved. He removed the seal which was fastened to it by means of a hole in the stem. "I want to give you my own shoulder pin. In the years that lie ahead you will be the captain of my fighting men."

Oni took the tablet and the pin without a word. He stood beside Abram, and removing his short slave pin, tossed it away; his cloak slipped from his shoulders, exposing the mighty muscles of his neck and trunk. He held up the beautiful gold pin, and then, picking up his cloak, passed it through the soft wool material to hold it securely in place over his shoulder.

He looked down at the head of the stiletto. It shone blue and gold in the lamplight. He turned proudly to Terah, who was watching him. But as usual in times of emotion words seemed to fail him. "I will . . ." he stammered, "I will follow Abram always. I will . . . serve him and his God."

"There is yet one more duty I must discharge," Dudu said. "Before I left the temple, the bride of Nannar, Princess Shub-Kudur, sent word that I should come to her and bring with me this purse. When I stood before her she asked me to open it, which I did for the first time. She removed a pendant from her own ear and put it in the purse. Finally she rose quickly, as though to leave the room, but she turned in the doorway.

" 'I can send no message to the dead,' she said. 'But his slave Oni loved him too. Tell him the ornament is his. It is heavy gold. Let him have it melted and made into two gold earrings. My handmaid Berri has not forgotten him. Perhaps he may return to her some day.' "

A hush fell on the company, and Abram, turning to look at Sarai, saw that she was weeping. He removed the beautiful ornament from the purse and handed it to Oni. It was shaped like a pair of twin boats side by side. The high curving prows and sterns continued into a delicately wrought rope of gold which fitted over the top of the ear.

Then Nahor spoke up. "I have matters of importance to bring to the attention of my father Terah."

But Salah cut him off quickly with: "Your turn will come, young man," and addressed himself to Terah.

"I have told Abram that my heart goes with him, but it is useless for me to drag my old bones into this promised land. What is your decision?"

Terah shook his white head. "No, I also am too old. The Sumerians killed my eldest son Haran, a good merchant. Two remained to me, Nahor, a merchant, and Abram, a priest of Nannar. There is something of me that went into all my sons. There is something of each son that I find in my own heart.

"Abram has left the moon god. He has seen a vision and my young men will follow him. It may be that a new faith will be given to a new generation; but it is not for me. The things for which I worked have vanished. My images are broken; my goods lost. My journey will end where it began, in Haran.

"There is a strange spirit in my people, a flame that nothing can quench. Whether they build their own temples, or whether they wander over the face of the earth, they will go on through prosperity and adversity. Prophets who dream dreams will rise up from time to time to lead them."

Sarai slipped her hand, unobserved, into her father's, while Lot cried out: "Grandfather Terah, it is as you have said. I speak for the young men. When Abram calls, they will come and follow where he leads."

"Well spoken, my boy!" Salah said. "And now, Nahor, it is your turn. Are you prepared to follow Abram into Canaan?"

Nahor scowled. "I prefer to remain where I can make a good living," he said. "If I am smart enough I have a right to fatten where I like. One god is as good as another. My brother stayed too long in the swamps. This talk of a new god sounds to me like madness.

"Now let us face the facts like practical men of affairs. I tell you that war is coming. Ur will probably be destroyed and we are lucky to have escaped in time. Let others do the fighting. It is better for us to seek wealth and safety in the country that has the largest army."

Prince Salah interrupted him. "These are the words I should expect from a nomad born in the city's market place!"

But Nahor ignored the interruption. "I have had interviews with important men in Babylon," he continued with an air of importance, "and I may tell you that the great Hammurabi needs the camels and camelmen and he has asked me to secure the Habiru as his allies. This is our great opportunity, Father Terah!"

Nahor then turned to Salah with condescension. "I know that at your age, Prince Salah, you take little interest in military matters. But I feel it would be wise to stop your river traffic to Ur. Hold your sheep and cattle until the Babylonian armies arrive in Nippur and then — what a profit will be ours! I will gladly act as your agent."

"I see," Salah replied, trembling in his effort to control himself, "and may I ask what plans you have made for Sarai — you who have such influence, such wisdom?"

"Yes, of course," Nahor replied. "The patesi is ready to protect her and to protect Father Terah in Nippur. He would be very pleased to have her marry his brother's son Unzie. After that, our position would be quite secure."

Salah was walking up and down now in an effort to control himself. "Are you willing," he said, "to have Sarai marry that man?"

Nahor shrugged and spoke now with the air of a man of the world. "Of course Unzie drinks a little. But nevertheless Sarai would be very fortunate to become his wife. I may tell you that Unzie will call on you in person tomorrow. There is no better household than his in the whole of Nippur. In that way, Sarai could protect her father and improve your standing as well.

"The patesi knows that you are doing the best you can, at

your age, to run these great farms. He regrets that you have no son to appoint as your successor. I suggested that . . ."

A servant had begun to follow Salah as he strode back and forth in his fury, and at last Salah stopped to listen to his message. At the same time the whole company became aware of shouting from the square outside the great gate. Jabal, Salah's herdsman, was evidently bolting the small door to keep someone out.

Jabal then ran across the court in great excitement and told Salah that Unzie son of Gudea had arrived at Drehem earlier in the evening with many asses. But Unzie's servant had stated that his master was not well and that he must sleep. "And so," Jabal said, "I took him into my own house for the night. He lay down in my own bed. But he says there are crawling things in it, and he demands to see you at once."

As Jabal spoke, there was a pounding on the gate.

"If that is Unzie at the gate," cried Salah, "let him come in at once."

The company rose to go, but Salah said: "Wait, there is no reason for you to leave. Let the man plead his suit now, before us all. I have tried to prevent this for a long time. Now it can no longer be avoided."

Jabal shook his head anxiously and hurried back to the door. With the servant's help he swung the great gate wide open. There stood Unzie and his bow-legged little servant silhouetted against the darkness. The servant seemed to be trying to pull his master away, but Unzie threw off his hold and walked unsteadily across the court, passing Sarai as though he did not see her.

"Prince Salah," he cried, "I must talk to you. Your herdsman's house is filled with lizards, thousand-legged lizards. They are everywhere." Unzie's face was pale and he trembled. He put his hands before his eyes for a moment and then dropping them he peered at Salah closely.

"Yes," he said, "that's right, you're Prince Salah." He drew himself up in an attitude of dignity. "I've come here with many asses. They are loaded with presents for you, my marriage gift. I am going to marry the most beautiful woman in Sumer. The patesi has given his permission and you are going to give me yours. I have a big house and — and — what?"

The servant had been pulling at his sleeve and now stood on a stool and spoke in his master's ear, pointing at Sarai.

Slowly an expression of recognition appeared on the master's face. "Sarai!" he exclaimed, "daughter of Terah, beauty from the desert! I had to leave you in Ur. But here I am. I've come for you. I am a free man, a Sumerian noble. I will have you for my first wife. I have been divorced just for your sake."

Salah stepped between them and said: "I do not give my consent. Not now. I will talk this matter over with the patesi. Pray sit down now and be quiet."

"Ha, you old jackal!" Unzie cried. "You can't stop me. The patesi has decided he would like a younger overseer here anyway and you have no son. Maybe Nahor son of Terah would do. Ha, ha! What would you think of that? Don't worry, I will give your granddaughter clothes, jewels, slaves, houses, wine."

He turned back to Sarai. "We will live in Nippur. I'll protect you and your father and even your brother Abram, if you can find him. We'll invite old Salah to visit us. Ha, ha, ha!" He started toward Sarai. "We'll have banquets and wine, wine, rivers of wine!"

Abram seized Unzie roughly by the shoulder, but as he did so Unzie seemed to change, to shrivel and subside. His eyes were fastened on the wall above Sarai's head with a look of abject horror, and he sank to the floor slowly. All present turned to follow his gaze, but there was nothing they could see there.

They brought their attention back to Unzie. His eyes were

bulging now and he pointed as though he were following something up the wall and across the ceiling.

"Look, look!" he cried. "It is going to fall on me! Sacred Ishtar, save me!" He leaped to his feet and rushed across the court and out the gate into the night, his servant scuttling out after him.

The company stood still in amazement. But Dudu snorted. "Wine, wine, wine. Yes, that is it. This man Unzie has wine-drinker's delirium! Do you remember, Abram, one of our own priests had a similar attack after he returned from the drunken orgies of Ishtar?"

Salah nodded and sat down suddenly as though he felt weak. Dudu continued: "It usually comes on when a heavy drinker stops his drink too suddenly."

Lot laughed as though to express his relief. "I've searched," he cried, "through Ur and Susa for entertainment, but I never saw a show like that. What a clown this fellow is. His first show was when I found him on his knees trying to run Abram through with his sword." Lot demonstrated the action in pantomime. "I took him home that time and put him to bed. Then, when Sarai wanted to see him, I found him in a brothel and drew him away by promising him Sarai's smile. He played the patronizing noble that time. Then that very night he fled from Ur with Nahor on Father Terah's best camels. I shall follow him now and tell you the next event."

"Wait, Lot," Abram said. "Take Dudu along with you. This man needs care, and we have a physician with us now."

Dudu made his stiff little bow and said: "I will go. We have a sovereign remedy for this condition. But he must be some days under my control."

"Do whatever seems best," Salah said. "He is yours until cured. But send him away from here as soon as possible."

So Lot and Dudu walked off arm in arm to follow Unzie,

while their laughter echoed across the square. Nahor vanished abruptly and without ceremony. The others followed, leaving the two elders with Abram and Sarai.

Sarai came and sat down close to Prince Salah. "How awful it was," she said. "It frightened me."

"There is an old proverb," Salah said, "that runs something like this:

> *"Look not upon the wine when it is red,*
> *When it goeth down smoothly:*
> *At the last it biteth like a serpent,*
> *And stingeth like an adder.*
> *Thine eyes shall behold strange creatures,*
> *And thine heart shall utter perverse things."*

The old man shook himself and then clapped his hands. When a servant appeared, he said: "Bring us wine of pomegranate." Then he added, "It will refresh us. The man who knows how to restrain himself may use all things to his purpose, eh, Terah?"

Terah nodded his head and picked up his daughter's reticule. "What do you carry in this? Paint? Pigment? Strange powders? I know the women of the court carry them, but you have no need of such things. It would be wrong to change anything about your face. Your lips are red. No one would want to change the color of your hair, and the color of your cheeks comes and goes. Look at it now!"

Sarai had cast a quick glance at Abram. She was blushing, and her father laughed.

"My grandfather," she said, "bought this reticule for me in Babylon."

Prince Salah broke in. "Yes, I bought it, but you saw it in a bazaar and carefully called my attention to it!"

"Well, Sarai," Terah said, "we are avoiding an important matter. I have not been able to choose a husband for you, as I intended to do in Ur. I suppose we have seen one suitor eliminate himself tonight, although he may make trouble for us yet. It is evident that you do not care for Unzie, and I think it would be wise for you and me to live in tents not far from Drehem until Abram returns. Otherwise this man might return with soldiers and capture you. I would not be willing to have you marry him, in spite of his wealth. Our people have always married among themselves. It is not good to bring Sumerian blood into the inheritance.

"I don't know what is in your heart, Sarai. You know Cush. I give you my permission to marry him and stay here, according to your grandfather's wish, if you desire. On the other hand, you may wait until we reach Haran, where I can select a suitable husband for you from among the young men who are our kinsmen. Abram will speak for himself."

There followed a period of awkward silence, so Terah resumed: "It was about eighteen years ago that I came here with a wedding gift to ask Salah for your mother Amtelai. I remember that she carried something that looked like this reticule, but it was smaller."

"My mother had no grandfather to buy her a larger one," Sarai laughed.

"I do not think," Abram said, "that women have changed very much. A box of elaborate cosmetics has been found in the grave of a very early queen. It was buried with her as one of her most precious possessions."

"Enough of this," Sarai said. "You men have talked too much about things that you do not understand! Perhaps you would like to have me leave you so that you may speak with undisputed authority on these matters!"

"She is her mother's daughter," Terah laughed, turning to Salah. "She does not look nor act like those on my side of the family."

"I know her better than you do," Salah interrupted. "She may not be a scholar like Abram, but she has no need of great knowledge. She has understanding without it. I have learned to rely on her. She has unaccountable insight into the character of those who come here to trade with me in Drehem. Her mother had the same sort of wit, and her grandmother before her. You are right, Terah, she is like them."

Abram had remained standing all this time, shifting his weight from one foot to the other with increasing uneasiness. But as he did not speak, Salah continued:

"Women are different from men anyway. Their understanding does not need to be based on reason. It is a gift. It comes to them in their mother's milk. Wise men," he said, turning to Abram, "learn to depend upon it. Leaders must hope to find it in the wives they choose."

Salah and Terah were silent now. Sarai gazed at the floor. Abram cleared his throat. The assurance with which he had spoken earlier seemed to have disappeared. His voice was husky and low when he began:

"I came here to ask for Sarai as my wife. I don't know what I can say except that I love her. When I was in prison in Ur, she seemed to be with me, waking and sleeping. When I climbed the ziggurat, my heart was heavy with the thought that I would never see her again. In the wilderness my mind turned back to her. Now at last I am free, Sarai." His voice rang out. "I bring you no wedding gift, unless you will accept the precious things that are in my heart. I cannot offer you riches, ease, peace

"With me you will be a wanderer. There will come times of danger and privation. I shall often need your help and understanding. Our future and our happiness will be bound up with the fate of our people.

"But in the land of Canaan there is beauty and wealth. Streams run down from high mountains into green and pleasant valleys. We should be free there and happy — you and I."

Sarai raised her eyes to Abram for a moment, but she did not answer. Instead she stood up and went to Terah and kissed him, then to Salah and whispered something in his ear. He nodded.

She turned and walked toward Abram, her eyes like two stars. "It is enough," she said, "to have your love. I want no wedding gifts. I understand what is in your heart, and I sense what it is you hope to do. I will go with you and remain with you wherever you may go, even to the edge of the world. I have always loved you."

He took her in his arms, and as he bent toward her, she said: "My sons will build a great nation for you."

Clear thought is difficult during or after love's first kiss. But Sarai, turning away, started to speak. Then she exclaimed: "They have gone!"

The reception room was empty.

Abram and Sarai crossed the court and, opening the little door, passed through into the moonlight.

❖❘❘❖

CHAPTER XX

Dawn

THREE MONTHS LATER, on the night of the full moon, the meadows of Drehem were almost as light as day. Along the slopes of the hill below the houses of Prince Salah there was a strange commotion of men and camels and there were new arrivals all through the night until the hour before dawn, when all was quiet and it grew dark.

In this darkness Magog, who had been camelman to Nahor, to Nahor's son Terah and now to Terah's son Abram, made his way up the hill. As he climbed, the old man turned his memory back to that dawn so many years ago when he had set out, with his master Terah, to go from Haran to Ur.

Terah was a black-haired boy then, he thought; I can see him now sitting on his white camel, with all the idols he had made hidden in the saddlebag. More than once he took out one of the little images and talked to it as though it were a man. Sometimes he would speak to me of how he meant to make greater images for the temples, and then a strange light came into his eyes. I think it was a little like the fire that comes into Abram's eyes now when he talks about his God.

Very strange it will be, to have no idols at all — just a god that no one can see. But Abram says it must be that way.

The old man paused in his climb, telling himself that he could think better if he rested. But perhaps he stopped also because his heart was pounding and his breath was coming quickly. He shook his head. Then he stroked his long beard and began to speak out loud as was his custom on camelback in the desert.

"When I am alone I have my doubts about all this. But when I stand in the presence of Abram a new spirit fills me. It brings me pleasure and excitement. I rejoice that I shall see the dawn of this great day; the dawn of the day of Abram — the priest, the dreamer, the herdsman of his people."

Magog looked up. The brow of the hill made dark outline against the canopy of stars that sparkled overhead. He climbed to the top and saw the moving outline of a man.

"Who are you?" he called.

"Jabal, chief herdsman to Prince Salah," came the reply.

"Good, is this the meeting ground?"

"Yes, who are you?"

"I am Magog, Abram's captain of camelmen. I brought in the caravan of camels carrying those who escaped from Ur. We did not arrive here, as you know, until after midnight. Some of them had lived all their lives in Ur, and they did not know one end of a camel from the other, so we had many delays."

The two men stamped and swung their arms to warm themselves. Then Magog continued with a chuckle:

"There was a Sumerian woman who joined us, dressed as though she were going to a reception in Rim-Sin's palace. She said she was Oni's wife. I didn't know he had one! But I let her come along."

"It was lucky," Jabal said, "that last night was the night of the full moon."

"No luck about it," Magog answered. "If you knew Abram as I do, you'd know he planned it that way. He thinks of everything. Are the others all here?"

"Yes," Jabal replied.

The two men pulled their sheepskin capes about them and walked back and forth. A line of light began to show along the eastern horizon, and on the slopes below them small fires were appearing here and there. The glow from each fire outlined a small black tent faintly, and dark figures moved back and forth.

"That is the encampment of the household of Terah," Jabal said, "over there to the north. They came in yesterday afternoon and pitched their tents at sunset. Off to the south are your fugitives from Ur, and beside them the Habiru herdsmen. This is the tent of Abram just below us here, and beyond that are the tents of his fighting men.

"These men were all here yesterday. Some of them had been wounded in the battle, and that fat Sumerian priest has been dressing their wounds all day. Look there, someone is coming now, two men I think, and one has a white robe. Yes, it must be the priest Dudu himself."

From out of the darkness at that moment came the voice of Lot. "Hello, Dudu, I can see your white gown in the dark. I think we have come to the appointed place in front of Abram's tent."

"Yes," Dudu growled panting, "but my aim in life has been to avoid hills. When I became a physician, I thought I was through with climbing. I no longer had to get myself up that cursed ziggurat. Yesterday Abram kept me busy all day climbing up and down, climbing up and down to take care of his fighting men. Nothing very serious, however; a few bad bruises and flesh wounds, but no broken bones.

"Then I had to write out the marriage contract for Abram and Sarai yesterday and roll their seals on it."

"Yes," Lot said. Then he added, after a pause: "Sarai had a strange look of happiness. I've never seen her quite like that before. The jewels Abram brought for his wedding gift had belonged to her mother Amtelai. What a man is Abram! Any member of our camel company would die for him gladly, if he were to ask it."

Dudu shivered. "This little sheepskin doesn't cover my white cloak. Perhaps, after all, there is a little too much of me inside it." He swung his arms and paced up and down to warm himself. Then he stopped in front of Lot.

"You and Abram have accomplished a great deal in three months, haven't you? And now you have won a battle!"

Lot laughed and nodded. "It's all Abram, of course. You should have heard him talk to the Habiru herdsmen in their tents. Some families decided to come now. Others will follow. But many of the young unmarried men volunteered for the camel company at once and he promised to make them his herdsmen in the new land.

"Old Magog sent us hundreds of camels and he sent the weapons, beautiful weapons, that Salah had collected for each man." Lot allowed the small arms that hung at his belt to clank, proudly.

"When Abram had enough men, he and Karnebo trained them for fighting on foot and they learned to move swiftly, as a unit, with their camels."

The two men began to walk back and forth in the gray of the dawn. "In Ur," Lot continued, "they laughed at us and despised us for being camelmen. Now, as Abram says, we can conquer because of them and we are very proud to be camelmen."

Dudu chuckled. "What do you think the high priest, Enannatum, would say if he could see me setting off for the wilderness on one of those beasts — priest of the moon god, physician and master of every spell and incantation, now become a camelman! But I wish Magog could arrange to draw me behind you in a chariot. I am better off near the earth and I fear that no one beast can carry me all the way to Canaan.

"Now, if I were only someone else, and not myself, I should prescribe for that someone else a long period of starvation. After all, perhaps I am like a camel myself. I shall dine on Dudu as we cross the desert. Ugh!"

Lot laughed, and slapping his companion on the back interrupted him: "Let me tell you about the battle! Our company moved north along the border of the great swamp lake that lies east and south of Drehem. As we went we kept in touch with the fugitives from Ur and the others. We knew that all was well with them.

"But the Babylonians apparently learned our plans from someone." He paused and then went on: "Yes, they knew our plans to the very day. I don't suppose it could have been my uncle Nahor who told them. I hope not . . .

"In any case, they saw the opportunity of capturing the camels, and the camelmen as well, that they need to help their armies. So they sent a small army marching toward Drehem on exactly the right day. It was made up of Babylonians with a goodly addition of soldiers from Nippur. But our spies were watching for this. It was the very thing Abram feared.

"The spies brought us word just in time and we moved with great speed. When we had passed around Drehem we soon saw, on the horizon, the dust of marching men to the northwest. That was the day before yesterday. And they were in a position then from which they could have reached Drehem in a short day's journey.

"Abram divided his men. He took half of them to the south and Karnebo led the other half to the north. I went with Karnebo.

"We watched until the Babylonians made camp. Then we came near and hobbled our camels. In the darkness we moved in on foot until we were very close to them and the camp dogs began to bark. Then we waited."

In the half-light, Lot stooped and drew a plan of battle with his finger in the dust. There was excitement in his voice as he continued:

"About three hours after dark, we heard a great shouting on the other side of the camp. We knew that Abram and his men had begun the attack. So we took up the shout 'Haloo Habiru! Mighty is the God of Abram!' We rushed into the camp with our spears while Abram's men came in from the other side.

"Ha! The Babylonians ran in all directions and most of them made no resistance at all. Abram had given orders that there must be no unnecessary bloodshed and the battle was over in a very short time.

"But alas! Karnebo ran wild through the army asking the prisoners whether his old enemy Gudea of Nippur was among them. Somehow he learned that Unzie, the son of his old enemy, was one of their leaders. He found him, and Unzie must have fought like a man, for we found Karnebo dead and Unzie also slain not far away. That giant fellow Ham who came with Karnebo knows something about it but he won't talk.

"We took the prisoners' arms and left a few men to guard them until we shall have crossed the great river, which we intend to do before tomorrow morning. Then the guards will join us."

"A great victory," Dudu said. "During that battle the future of a people hung in the balance.

"But I am sorry to hear of Unzie's death," Dudu continued. "He was the suitor who came here to carry off Sarai and ended with wine-drinker's delirium, was he not? He must have followed my prescription after all! I am amazed."

"How did you treat his delirium?" Lot asked.

"I gave him small amounts of wine until he recovered his senses. Then I frightened him and told him to stop drinking. But very few have determination enough to resist red wine. I didn't expect him to do it. Perhaps he hoped to capture Sarai after all."

The rim of light in the east was broadening now, and the breeze that precedes the dawn blew upon them.

"Jabal, Jabal!" called a hearty voice. It was Prince Salah. "Jabal, you may go down to the tents and tell the leaders of each group to climb up here as the sun comes over the horizon."

"Yes, Prince Salah," Jabal replied. "But will they go to the shrine of Pa-Sag to sacrifice, as we always do before starting on a journey?"

Salah turned and looked at Lot inquiringly. Lot shook his head in the negative.

Salah then turned back to his herdsman and said with some emphasis: "No, Jabal, certainly not. The God of Abram will lead us and protect us. You see, Jabal, I am not too old to learn."

"Did you say lead *us?*" the herdsman Jabal exclaimed. "But are you going too?"

"No, Jabal. But I shall go with them in spirit. Now carry out my orders."

Salah turned to Dudu. "I had not realized that a priest of the moon god could be so useful outside the city and the temple. We thank you for writing out the marriage tablet yesterday. Did you set down all the things there for the protection of Sarai according to the law of Sumer?"

"As well as I could recall such things," Dudu replied. "I had to get Abram's help. Neither of us had taken much interest in the work of the scribes. But I wrote in the principal things — the penalties for infidelity, the conditions of divorce, the owner-ship by the woman of betrothal gifts and dowry, the ownership of her slaves and the right to bequeath such things to her chil-dren.

"That protects Sarai," Dudu continued, "but it may be my old friend Abram who needs protection!"

"How is that?" Salah asked.

"Sarai has a peculiar sort of beauty. When Abram meets the kings of Canaan, they may want her. He will have to keep her in his tent! Her beauty is more a thing of the spirit than it is of the body. No man appreciates her beauty until he has talked with her. But then — " Dudu made a gesture.

"Here they come," Salah said. "They have eaten in my house for the last time."

None of them spoke as Abram and Sarai came to the brow of the hill and passed them to enter Abram's tent. They were talking as they walked and seemed oblivious of others. Following came Father Terah and Naamah.

The tent doors closed behind Abram and Sarai and the tent began to glow as Sarai, inside, applied a taper to the lamp.

Outside, Prince Salah went to meet Terah, and the two old men stood face to face.

"This is our last farewell," Salah said. "All that is best in me has been passed on to Sarai. It goes with her now toward Canaan. I am older than you, you know, and you're old enough! I shall remain behind to watch my herds, to talk with the little spirits that live in the pastures, and to see the shadows of life lengthen on the meadow."

The two men embraced each other in silence.

Then Salah continued: "On the other hand, the Sumerian priest here will go with you on this journey."

"Sumerian, yes, but priest, no," Dudu interrupted. "I go with you as physician and to be one of you. Abram tells me that I am no longer permitted to use the incantations of the gods of Sumer. For years I have disliked the worship of the moon god, but, unlike Abram, I did nothing about it. I had neither time nor inclination to break idols. I kept myself busy in the temple clinic. A physician can forget the need of fearing the gods when he is busy serving men.

"Abram's revolt against Nannar amused me at first. Finally, it interested me. Now I should like to discover if others can worship his God as well as he. He tells me that his God is the God of all the earth.

"There comes Melchizedek now," Dudu continued. "He is not one of your people and yet he seems to be able to worship the one invisible God."

As Melchizedek reached the edge of the hill, the door of Abram's tent opened and Abram stepped out, followed by Sarai. Seeing Melchizedek they greeted him warmly.

"I have received word by messenger," Melchizedek said, "that my father is dead. With your permission I shall travel north with you as far as Haran. From there I must hurry back to my kingdom — alone. When you have arrived in Canaan, I shall be the king of Salem . . ." Then he added, "A lonely king," and his eyes met Sarai's for an instant. "But I will be a friend to you in a strange country."

Abram smiled and the two men faced each other. They towered above Sarai in the pale light of the dawn. Both were dressed in long dark cloaks that fell from shoulder to foot. Their kaffiyehs were held in place upon their heads by circular bands so that they seemed to be wearing crowns. Melchizedek was obviously older, his well-trimmed beard was longer, his eyes a little sad, reflective; his expression kindly but quizzical. His head, Sarai thought, was the head of a seer, a prophet.

Abram's face radiated vitality, energy. His long nose and heavy lips were sharply, delicately cut and the short black beard seemed to add strength to his profile. His eyes were a little prominent, and they shone with a light that no one could ignore, and none forgot.

"Melchizedek," Abram said, and there was emotion in his deep voice, "Melchizedek, you have shown that the heart is greater than the loins, the spirit than the body. Wisdom dwells with prudence in the heart of the king of Salem. To know your friendship has made me understand what the one God may yet do for me and for my people. When we come to Canaan I shall kneel before you."

There was a commotion below them on the hillside and a woman, who was hurrying upward, called out to Abram.

When Magog saw her coming, he stepped forward and said to Abram: "It was late last night when I arrived here with the fugitives from Ur, and I have had no opportunity to tell you that this woman who is coming toward you joined us as we were about to leave. We brought her along because she insisted that she was Oni's wife. But Oni had left Ur some days before."

Abram looked at the woman in surprise as she reached the top of the hill. She was quite small, obviously a Sumerian, and not dressed for the desert. In fact, her clothing, which seemed to be of the finest, was very much bedraggled and soiled, and she wore a makeshift kaffiyeh on her head.

"Where, oh, where is Oni?" she cried and began to sob.

"Oni will be here soon," Abram said. "Who are you?"

Between her sobs, she looked up and said: "Abram, don't you know me? — Abram! I am Berri, handmaid to Princess Shub-Kudur — she wanted me to be hap-hap-happy."

Just then Oni himself appeared. He hurried forward and cried in great excitement: "Berri, Berri!" Whereupon that young woman threw herself into his great arms.

After several unsuccessful attempts to get Oni's attention, Abram cried out sternly: "Oni, is Berri your wife?"

Oni looked up. His face flushed red and he stammered. "N-no. I could not find — I could not find — the words to ask her and then I had to leave Ur in a great hurry to join you and anyway I thought — I thought it would not be right to take her out into this kind of life. But," he stopped and looked down at her, "I'd like to have her. Will you marry me now?"

Abram laughed, and there was laughter and applause as he went to Oni and put his arms around them both.

Abram turned back and said to Dudu: "Here is another marriage contract tablet for you to write."

Dudu replied with his stiff little bow.

The hillside sloped downward toward the east, and on the eastern horizon a focus of fire appeared. It widened, running out like molten metal in both directions. The sun rose and seemed to lie like a great red orange on the distant rim of that vast level plain. Those who stood at the top of the hill saw their own shadows projected in prophetic hugeness across the level hilltop to the house and barns of Prince Salah, while the people on the slopes below, looking upward, saw Abram and those with him transformed to gold, high above the dark meadows.

A small group of men, the leaders of divisions in the caravan, came up the hill, fine-looking Habiru herdsmen they were, with short pointed beards. Each wore a kaffiyeh that fell from the top of his head to shoulder and a desert robe from shoulder to ankle. Abram's trained company of fighting men followed, proud, gay young nomads in blue kaffiyehs who talked and laughed among themselves as they came. And men and women could be seen coming from the tents far down the green slope and climbing as high as they could, hoping to hear what the leaders would say.

Terah stepped forward now to the brow of the hill and looked at the people waiting below him. He spoke in a thin, high-pitched voice.

"My children: We have folded the tents that we pitched for a time in the gates of strangers. Again we are nomads, wanderers, habiru. Again we mount our camels and listen to the wind.

"My son Abram has my blessing. He has the blessing of our fathers. Follow him."

Then Terah's voice quavered, so that only those standing near him could hear his closing words.

"As for me, my day is done; I was rich, powerful — now I am a fugitive. Each man has his little day. He comes out from the womb of his mother. He grows and prospers till the setting of the sun. Then he slips like a shadow into the darkness of the night. But new flowers will bloom and dance through the sunlight and shadow to the end of another day. This is your day, Abram."

Sarai had been standing with Naamah as Terah spoke. Now she observed that there was a small pile of stones on the crest of the hill, and that wood was heaped upon it, with pitch and dried tamarisk needles ready to be lit.

Then she heard Abram's voice booming out over the meadows and turned back to see that he was standing where Terah had stood.

"We cannot go on this journey," he was saying, "without the blessing of Salah, prince of herdsmen."

The old man came forward briskly. "I shall not go with you," he cried in a high, clear voice. "What good are old legs for this journey and crooked hands for the building of cities? It is for you who have youth in your limbs and laughter in your hearts to go out and find the new country, found a new nation. Live there in your own cities. But I warn you that you must not look back to the ease of Ur nor return to the gods of Babylon.

"Listen to your leader Abram. Write his words upon the tablets of your hearts and bind his name upon your foreheads.

"I give you my blessing: May you find pleasant pastures, peace and length of days and, in the end, wisdom and understanding."

Abram stepped forward again and holding up his hand to the people he cried: "*Habiru!*" This was followed by silence.

Then Lot sent back the answering shout: "*Habiru haloo!*" The young men of Abram's trained company repeated it and the others echoed the cry on down the slope. "*Habiru haloo! Habiru haloo!*" It was the cry that Abram had taught them, the rallying cry of a new nation.

When at last they were silent, Abram spoke to them in a voice that was resonant with power:

"From here we travel with all speed to the great river; after crossing it we turn north toward the place of our origin in the hills of Haran. After that, those who have the strength and the courage will follow me westward into Canaan.

"You know now that there is a God above the gods of every nation in the earth, and that He has spoken to me, your leader. This God will go with us through wilderness and danger to guide and to protect us. He is invisible. He will have no image made of Him. But to every man who puts wrong thinking out of his heart, He will speak, as He has spoken to me. He will speak within you, and He will hear you when you need His help, whether you are alone in the stillness of the pasture or in the din and furor of the city.

"He is not like other gods that you have known. Wisdom and might and understanding are His. For us — there shall be no other gods from this day forward."

Sarai turned to Naamah and spoke aside. "Naamah! Last night I bore upon my body a man who has walked with God. His seed is in my womb. Today a new day dawns."

A flame leaped up on the altar of stone before which Abram stood, and a column of smoke rose far upward into the blue dome of heaven.

Background Notes

It is recorded in Genesis that "Terah took Abram his son, and Lot . . . and Sarai his daughter in law . . . and they went forth with them from Ur of the Chaldees, to go into the land of Canaan." This is all the direct information the Bible gives of the early history of Abram and Sarai during the time in which this story is cast.

This was the only historical reference to Ur, the forgotten city, until it was stumbled upon by excavators one hundred years ago. Since that time, discoveries of the greatest importance have been made at Ur, and at the sites of many other cities in Mesopotamia. Thus the information is now available from which to draw a picture of the everyday life of the people who lived there so long ago.

No reference to Abram has as yet been discovered by archeologists, and so there is no extra-Biblical evidence of exactly when it was that Terah and his son Abram lived in Ur.

The Biblical account states that, after leaving Ur, Terah died in Haran and Abram traveled on, taking "Sarai his wife, and Lot his brother's son . . . and they went forth to go into the land of Canaan."

But later in the record (Genesis 14) there is a statement that "in the days of Amraphel king of Shinar" a battle was won in Canaan by "Abram the Hebrew." Abram, it seems, with his three hundred and eighteen trained servants, overtook and defeated the army of four petty kings, thus liberating his nephew Lot. After this victory it is said that he was blessed by Melchizedek king of Salem, who "was the priest of the most high God."

It was long assumed that the Biblical Amraphel king of Shinar, mentioned above, was the same as archeology's Hammurabi, the mighty king of Babylon. If this could be substantiated it would relate the two men in time with certainty. Reckoning time by Biblical evidence placed Abram about 1900 B.C., and consequently Hammurabi was given the same approximate date.

Recent archeological evidence suggests that the date for Hammurabi is somewhat later. Further study of the evidence from both sides will be required to establish finally the exact inter-relationship between the Biblical story and archeological research.

In any case, Hammurabi king of Babylon was the great rival of Rim-Sin, the king of Ur. He finally overthrew Rim-Sin and sub-jugated Ur. The story of this novel opens in Ur when Rim-Sin was still king of that city.

It would be absurd for the writer of this book to pose as an au-thority on archeological or Biblical research. Most of the sources of his information are listed in the Bibliography, which follows these notes. The author has also made use of his own familiarity with the objects to be found in the principal archeological muse-ums, as well as his personal discussions with Sir Leonard Woolley and Dr. Francis Steele.

But there are other sources. Four thousand years have not changed the birds, the animals, the blue of the sky, the scent from the desert, the beauty of the night and the colors of sunrise. Some-how, during my travels in Mesopotamia the actors who speak in this book became real in my mind.

Once as I stood on the ziggurat of Ur looking down on the de-serted waste below me, two strangely beautiful birds poised them-selves on rapid wings above my head — "bee catchers," Group Captain O'Neil called them. Their long breasts shone, iridescent gold in the sunlight, until they drifted away side by side toward the Euphrates, like two spirits high above the world. And in my fancy I saw Abram and Sarai at my side — young, eager, with un-suspected destiny before them.

That Terah was an idol maker and his son Abram an idol breaker is legendary among Hebrews and Arabs alike. And there are other stories about Abraham that pass from mouth to mouth in Mesopotamia and Turkey today. Some of these tales of Ibrahim, as the Arabs call him, are even collected, in the *Turkish Dictionary of Arts* (*Kamus ul Alam*, Vol. 1, p. 528), as pointed out to me by my friend Dr. Ibrahim Tükel of Istanbul.

In the making of historical novels such as this one, the writer has before him three tasks. He must learn to see the background of tradition, custom and belief on the one hand, and on the other, the figures he has chosen for portrayal as they are outlined in the pages of history or the Bible. When this is accomplished, the third task remains, to trace the evolution of these historical characters from their childhood environment and inheritance to adult achievement. This is what should form the substance of his novel.

Men call his writing fiction, yet the novelist who has learned to look into the hearts of men and women with sympathy and understanding may come to know the unchanging patterns of human behavior, and this knowledge constitutes in itself a basic science. It is the science that explains how men grow, the stupid man and the genius, the common man and the seer.

Thus the novelist, in writing fiction, may strive to chronicle truth with as much assurance of success as the physician and the scientist in their fields of endeavor.

In this book an inquiry is made into the religious thought of Abram's time and the nature of the revolt in his mind. He was the greatest iconoclast of all time, the founder of monotheism as we know it today, acknowledged as the first great prophet in the Hebrew, Christian and Mohammedan religions.

The historical objectives of this book will have been achieved if the author has succeeded in presenting a true picture of the times; if he has described the intellectual and spiritual problem that Abram faced; and if this story constitutes a valid commentary on the character of the Hebrew race.

Explanatory notes on miscellaneous subjects are given below.

Golden Leaf

On the dust jacket of this book is a golden beech leaf. It was drawn from a lovely necklace found in a burial pit in Ur. On the jacket it is a falling leaf, suggesting the end of the glory of the great civilization of Sumer.

Abram and Abraham

Abram led his followers into the land of Canaan, and some time later, the Bible states, his name was changed to Abraham, to signify that he was "a father of many nations." His wife Sarai's name was changed to Sarah.

Habiru

The followers of Abraham living in Canaan came to be called Habiru, as shown by archeological evidence. It seems likely that the word Hebrew is the present equivalent of that word. There is no archeological evidence that the word Habiru was applied to a particular race group before the migration into Canaan, as has been pointed out to me by Dr. Francis Steele.

Nevertheless, since Genesis refers to "Abram the Hebrew" I have chosen to apply the term to the large family or tribal group from which Abram was sprung. They were the men of Haran, herdsmen and wanderers, who penetrated far into the southland.

With this interpretation, the Habiru form one subdivision of the Amorites, who occupied the great country of the north known as Amurru, covering territory now included in northern Iraq and Syria and southern Turkey.

Haran

Haran was a city and a district in Amurru which formed the headquarters, as well as the place of origin, of the Habiru. It is well known to all who read the Bible that, in his old age, Abraham sent his servant back from Canaan to Haran to fetch Rebekah (whose father was Abraham's brother Nahor and whose mother was his niece Milcah), to be the wife of his only son, Isaac. Isaac's son Jacob likewise returned to Haran to seek a wife. Jacob was forced to work for fourteen years by his crafty father-in-law, but he managed to return eventually with two wives, Leah and Rachel.

Akkad and Sumer

Haran was located in what is now southern Turkey. From here it is a short journey to the mountains of Kurdistan, where melting snows give rise to the Tigris and to the Euphrates. These great rivers, on their way to the Persian Gulf, water the plain where civilization seems to have begun. Here man learned to write in clay and to cultivate wheat. Here he established just laws. Here Hebrew tradition placed the garden of Eden. In this great plain also "the waters of the flood were upon the earth," and it is said that it was the tower or ziggurat of Babylon to which the story of the tower of Babel referred. It is to Sumer and later Akkad that we must turn to see the very dawn of history.

Civilization

In the time of Abram the civilized peoples of the world occupied a large area shaped like a saddle, straddling the great Arabian desert. The seat of the saddle lay in Amurru, north of the "great desert." On the east it extended down the Mesopotamian plain to Akkad, where Babylon had become the great capital, and to Sumer, of which Ur had been the center for several thousand years. West of the desert the area extended downward through what is now called the Holy Land to the valley of the Nile, where the Pharaohs were then building their pyramids.

Camels

It is a curious fact that archeology provides no evidence of the existence of these animals in the time of Abram. An almost unlimited number of bills of sale are available written on the clay tablets. They refer to asses, cattle, sheep, birds and all the usual subjects of merchandise, but none mentions the camel. And yet Abram and his people seem to have come riding into the "promised land" on camels, and the earliest reference to these animals is found in Genesis.

It has been assumed in this story that camels were owned then, as later, only by wanderers like the Habiru, and never by the city folk who dealt with written agreements. The city dweller may well have looked upon camelmen with contempt. Three thousand years later the Crusaders expressed their zealous scorn of Mohammed by calling him a camel driver!

Shub-Kudur

She is the fictional daughter of Rim-Sin. Her name is a hybrid combination, Shub being Sumerian and Kudur Babylonian. In her collection of libation urns she may be compared with the Princess Bel-Shalti-Nannar, daughter of King Nabonidus and sister of Belshazzar of Biblical fame, who became high priestess at Ur, as has been proved by the excavations of Sir Leonard Woolley. Bel-Shalti-Nannar was also a keen archeologist and actually assembled an extensive archeological collection in her house adjacent to the temple. (See Woolley, 20, p. 139 *et seq.*)

Sumerians and Marsh Natives

The Sumerians, or black-headed people, are said to have come from the east somewhere between the Indus and the Tigris rivers (see Lloyd, 11, 12). Some think they came overland, but others suggest that they came in boats, because their oldest city, Erech, was also the southernmost. However that may be, the Sumerians eventually built cities, draining the land and irrigating it.

But the natives, displaced by the more cultured Sumerians, lived on in the marshes (like their descendants of today, the marsh Arabs), little affected by the progress around them. Two thousand years before Christ, these natives doubtless represented a culture some thousands of years older than that of Sumer.

The descriptions of the "great marsh," the bird life there, the huts and the way of living, are drawn from a visit which Mrs. Penfield and I were able to pay to the marsh natives.

Proverbs, and Quotations from the Bible

It may be observed that certain sayings have been taken from the Bible, which was actually written much later than the time of Abraham. This was done on the assumption that the Book of

Proverbs, for example, which was written about 1000 B.C., was to some extent a collection of sayings that had been current among the Hebrew people for a very long time.

In Chapter XIX, when Sarai looked to the west and saw Ishtar (the star of the goddess of love, which was later called Venus), she sang a song that is reminiscent of the singing of the rose of Sharon, in the Song of Solomon.

Verses that begin like those in Chapter XIX, "Three things I cannot fathom, Yes, four remain obscure . . . ," take the form of verses that appear in the Old Testament and at least once in the New Testament. This form, however, is encountered not infrequently in other ancient writings brought to light by archeologists.

The words of Nahor's death blessing for his grandson Abram (Chapter XVI) are taken from the words of Jacob's blessing of Joseph when Jacob lay on his deathbed. (See Genesis 49:25.)

The Flood

The recitation by the "fat boy" in Chapter V is taken from *Babylonia,* by Delaporte (cited by Woolley, 19, p. 207). The similarity of the story of the good man Uta-Napishtim to that of Noah is evident at once.

Hymn to the Moon God

The chanting in praise of Nannar in Chapter VII, "Who in heaven is high exalted . . . ," which is echoed in later chapters, is extracted from the liturgical hymn to the moon god, according to a tablet in the British Museum. (See Tomkins, 18, p. 21.)

High Priest's Cabinet

In Chapter VII, Abram was offered the post of minister of commerce under the high priest, Enannatum. Woolley (21) has pointed out that the god Nannar had also his minister of finance, his ministers of war and of agriculture, and his master of the harem, transport officers, archive keepers, and treasury staff.

Machouf

The escape to the swamps in Chapter XI was made in a light wooden canoe with gracefully curved prow and stern.

Such things change little. A toy silver boat with silver paddles was found in the grave of Queen Shub-Ad (Woolley, 22), who died well over a thousand years before Abram was born in Ur. It was identical with the boat described here and with the boat, called a *machouf*, used by the Arabs today in the lower Euphrates and the Shattel-Arab.

Gouffa

The *gouffa* is a circular boat made of reeds cemented together with bitumen. From earliest times these little saucer-shaped boats were used to carry heavy cargo on the Tigris and Euphrates rivers. In Sumerian mythology, the moon was sometimes referred to as "Nannar's *gouffa*," in which the moon god was thought to ride across the heavens bringing light to a dark "lapis-lazuli sky." (See Kramer, 8.)

Arabic Names

The author must confess that he has been somewhat inconsistent in his use of names and terms employed in Mesopotamia today intermixed with ancient Babylonian and Sumerian names and terms.

The sacred cattle farms of the god Enlil were described as being situated at Drehem, whereas I am informed by Dr. Francis Steele that the town of Drehem was known in the days of Hammurabi as Puzrish-Dagan! The only excuse for such inconsistencies is that Drehem is more familiar and lends itself more kindly to the modern tongue.

The moon god, patron deity of Ur and of Haran, should perhaps be called Nanna, but Nannar, again, is more familiar.

Bibliography

1. CHIERA, EDWARD. *They Wrote on Clay*. Chicago: University of Chicago Press, 1938.
2. COUTENAU, GEORGES. *La Vie Quotidienne à Babylone*. Paris: Librairie Hatchette, 1950.
3. DANIEL-ROPS. *Israel and the Ancient World*. London: Eyre and Spottiswoode, 1949.
4. FISH, T. *The City of Ur and Its God Nannar in the Third Dynasty of Ur*. London: Manchester University Press, 1928.
5. GELB, IGNACE. *Hurrians and Subarians*. Chicago: University of Chicago Press, 1944.
6. GRANT, CHRISTINA. *The Syrian Desert*. New York: Macmillan, 1937.
7. HITTI, PHILIP K. *The Arabs*. Princeton: Princeton University Press, 1943.
8. KRAMER, S. N. *Sumerian Mythology*. Philadelphia: The American Philosophical Society, 1944.
9. ———. *Schooldays*. Philadelphia: The University Museum, 1949.
10. LEGRAIN, LEON. *The Babylonian Collection of the University Museum*. Philadelphia: The University Museum, 1944.
11. LLOYD, SETON. *Mesopotamia*. London: Lovat Dickson and Thompson, Ltd., 1936.
12. ———. *Ruined Cities of Iraq*. London: Oxford University Press, 1943.
13. MALLOWAN, M. E. L. "New Light on Ancient Ur," *National Geographic Magazine*, January, 1930.
14. PRITCHARD, JAMES. *Ancient Near Eastern Texts*. Princeton: Princeton University Press, 1950.

15. PENFIELD, WILDER. "Ur of the Chaldees and the Influence of Abraham on the History of Medicine," *Bulletin of the History of Medicine*, Vol. 19, 1946.

16. RADAU, HUGO. *Nin-Ib. The Determiner of Fates*, Vol. V of *The Babylonian Expedition of the University of Pennsylvania*, Series D., Philadelphia, 1910.

17. STEELE, FRANCIS. *The Code of Lipit Ishtar*. Philadelphia: The University Museum, 1948.

18. TOMKINS, H. G. *Abraham and His Age*. London: Eyre and Spottiswoode, 1897.

19. WOOLLEY, LEONARD. *The Sumerians*. Oxford: The Clarendon Press, 1928.

20. ———. *Ur of the Chaldees*. Baltimore: Penguin Books, Ltd., 1929.

21. ———. *Abraham*. New York: Charles Scribner's Sons, 1936.

22. ———. *Ur of the Chaldees*. London: Pelican Books, Ltd., 1938.

Acknowledgments

THERE ARE MANY to whom the author owes a debt of gratitude. From the point of view of archaeology, much help was received from Sir Leonard Woolley, Director of the joint expedition sent by the British Museum and the Museum of the University of Pennsylvania to Mesopotamia, Dr. Francis Steele, Director of the Babylonian Collection of the University of Pennsylvania, and Dr. Nazi Al-Asil, Director-General of Antiquities for the Government of Iraq. But full responsibility for any inaccuracies or misinterpretations of historical evidence belongs to the author.

Group Captain C. T. O'Neil, Principal Medical Officer for the Royal Air Force in Iraq and Iran, came with me as guide and companion on my first visit to Ur. Six years later, Colonel Johnson, Director of the Port of Basrah, made it possible for my wife and me to pay a friendly visit to the marsh Arabs, a rare experience for anyone from the East or the West.

Mrs. Christina Grant Harris, then Associate Professor of History in Bryn Mawr College, and Mr. Leonard Bacon, poet, read and criticized constructively the first draft in 1946.

Finally, I must express my gratitude to Mr. Wilder Penfield, Jr., and Mr. Crosby Lewis for their constructive criticisms, and to Mrs. Clarence Bonynge, who suggested the title, *No Other Gods*. I am especially indebted to Mr. Stanley Salmen of Little, Brown and Company, who gave me wise editorial counsel and showed me how to recast the manuscript in its final form.

The writing of this book, like many other things in life, would never have been possible, in the midst of a busy professional career, if it had not been for the encouragement of my wife and her unerring appraisal of the good and the bad in this literary labor.